Spoils of War

I0562841

Tereska Karran

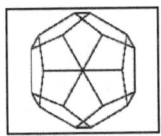

STREET PUBLISHING

1

Published by STREET PUBLISHING 2018

Disclaimer

STREET PUBLISHING

Streetpublishing.co.uk

I would like to thank Laura and Jack for their encouragement during the writing of this book. Without them it may never have seen the light of the internet.

Dedication:

For all victims of conflict including women and children.

Contents

Introduction:

There are lots of stories about war heroes and the glory of war. This is not one of them.

In war, the people not directly involved in the conflicts ignore atrocities too horrible to describe.

Those involved in conflict are average folk. In peacetime, most of them would go entirely unnoticed.

Yet someone has to perpetuate the war crimes, and not just one or two individuals.

They need not be monsters to start with...

Prologue.

Petrograd September 1917:

Sofia's last memory of Petrograd was of tea time, an hour which she spent with mama daily. The afternoon tea was always served in the small salon, a luxurious and opulent room with several rare Dutch paintings on the walls, as well as a couple of major Italian masters.

The rest of the apartment was a mess of packing cases. They had been getting ready to move for the last six months, wrapping and boxing up Renaissance art, jewelled Russian trinkets, French furniture, Chinese jade and Faberge knick-knacks. Still, her mother insisted on maintaining the sitting room for the reception of friends.

She stared out of the window at the pouring September rain. A man lurked in the shadow of the gated courtyard. She had seen him before and wondered if he could see her peeking through the heavy lace curtains. He was tall, bearded, and she could see deep lines etched on his face. He wore a military coat, ragged and stained with huge brown smudges. Their armed guard, a young boy of about 16 (only six years older than Sofia), stood to attention at the other side of the magnificent portico. He was avoiding the skulker.

'What are you staring at Sofia?' asked Rebecca. 'Drat the girl. She cannot be still for one moment.'

Sofia's mother was a modern woman. She had undergone the latest psychiatric treatments and had been indoctrinated with the newest theories. Thus she knew that her feelings were innately hysterical and that her frustration was motivated by insane jealousy of men. She accepted her decorative role in life and inhabited a tiny frozen world surrounded by beautiful and well-chosen things.

'It's that soldier, mama,' Sofia replied. 'The one you said was a deserter. He looks cold and wet.'

Yesterday she had given the man delicate pastries from their tea. As a daughter of the house she could do pretty much as she liked so long as she behaved like a lady and stayed out of busy folk's way. She crept out of the huge mansion and gave him money stolen from the giant urn, fashioned from Lapis Lazuli and finished in gilt ormolu, which was packed full of paper roubles to give to the coachman as tips

'No one cares about him,' she thought and her eyes filled with tears. She planned to redistribute even more tiny pastries from the tea table tonight.

Rebecca got up impatiently. She twitched the heavy lace curtain and looked through the window as the ex-soldier was joined by another, limping over a crutch.

They were deserters, from the hopeless conflict at the Eastern Front. The limping bedraggled man was trying to light a sodden cigarette. It was soaked through.

'Oh whatever can we do?' twittered Rebecca. 'Deserters all over this god-forsaken city! We shall be murdered in our beds.'

'They don't look like robbers, mama,' said Sofia gently. 'They're merely sheltering from the rain.'

She twitched at one of the many silent servants in the room.

'Call Mr Braun. See if he can come!'

The servant left, noiseless in the thick Persian carpets.

*

Women in Europe were obtaining some freedom, but not in the Braun household.

Mr Braun, the head of the house, considered women an inferior version of men, unable to contain their instincts, slightly higher than animals. They were a necessary to perpetuate his dynasty.

After 10 minutes or so, Izaak Braun entered. He sighed patiently and kissed his distraught wife on the forehead.

'What is it my dear?' he said.

His beautiful spouse attempted to contain her hysteria.

'Izaak! There are starving men outside our house day and night she wept. They are desperados! What are we to do?'

Sofia's father sat by his wife and stroked her hand, disengaged and cool-headed.

'The servants have been instructed to send them to the back of the house for alms,' he explained.

Sofia ran to the window. A servant under a huge umbrella barked an order to the guard, who approached the two ex-soldiers with dragging steps.

He called to them. They answered warily, then walked off, presumably to collect their alms.

Sofia noticed other ex-soldiers standing nearby.

The guard politely asked them to keep their distance.

They stood back a few steps, giving an overall impression of watchfulness.

*

Izaak sat with his women a few minutes.

He was a tall aquiline featured dignified man with a dominating presence, if slightly corpulent. He looked a little predatory in the nicest possible way, like an eagle at rest.

Despite sympathising with Kerensky, he had decided to abandon Russia. He claimed that he had always known that anarchy was inevitable, from the moment that the bedraggled Russian army entered the Great War.

He was right. The country was disintegrating. His factory had a huge order for uniforms but no workers, as they had been conscripted.

Petrograd was filling with soldiers who had fled the front, peasants really. They told tales of men being asked to pick up the guns of their fallen brethren, marching without boots. Officers whipped and shot them if they did not storm machine gun nests unarmed.

Rebecca paced the ornate sitting room.

'The poor Tsar. Whatever must he think of how this war is mismanaged? You will see that they will beg for him to return and save us all.'

She identified with the doomed Romanovs and dreamt of a return to the stuffy days when society moved in tight proscribed cycles. She wanted to remain in Russia. Her friends were convinced it was quite safe.

Izaak felt no connection to Russia and had little affection for it.

He loved being Jewish. He was proud of his faith, although he did not practice it. If pressed he would explain that Jews had heard the word of god first. They were a source of unorthodoxy and independence since their expulsion from Judea by the Romans. They were in the forefront of political and industrial progress.

'Jews have been part of every advance in Europe,' he often repeated. 'We are innovators.'

His articles of faith sanctified the paternalistic male and the rule of science. With properties in Warsaw, Lviv and a small estate in Poland, the family spoke excellent accent-less Polish, French with a Polish accent, Russian, German and Yiddish. They were used to travel.

Unlike his wife, he had Socialist leanings. He belonged to a Fabian Socialist group. He attended seminars investigating such topics as:

'Is socialism synonymous with progress?'
'Industrial organisation of the workforce. Is it correct to build factory cottages?'
'Women in the workforce. Can a mother work?'

Yes, he believed in paternalist socialism. However, discussing such topics theoretically was a different matter from the threatening atmosphere on the streets. There was even talk of taking over successful businesses. He had made light of the soldiers outside their door, though he knew that it boded badly for the future of his factories.

There was a knock on the door.

'That must be Ivanka,' said Rebecca, brightening at the thought of a long gossip.

Izaak hurried out, making his excuses. Rebecca turned to her daughter.

'Sofia darling, it's time for you to go upstairs.'

Sofia was escorted to her room at her mother's behest.

'Take care of my baby,' she wailed, as new visitors arrived to discuss their impending departure. 'She held a scented handkerchief to her eyes, dabbing them carefully.

'Ivanka! We are leaving. Have you heard?'

The next day they left the country forever, almost, but not quite, fleeing the chaos of impending revolution.

11

Part 1.

Ghosts

The height and breadth of a civilisation depend on the freedom of its people.

When women and children are treated like chattels, men rule by force.

Inevitably, they will consider force as the solution to any argument.

In such circumstances, peace is ephemeral. In fact, it doesn't actually exist.

1.

Izaak Braun

Izaak Braun was a grand patriarch whose faith centred on science and industry. He foresaw a world in which man did not need to work hard because most the work would be performed my machines. He loved the hum of industry and was a brilliant employer. He saw himself as part of a great enterprise to bring progress.

After leaving doomed Russia he had settled in Warsaw.

From this centre of operations, he and his sons realised an enormous fortune in East Germany, Hungary and the newly created state of Poland, building factories from burnt out shells. They bought up bankrupt clothing factories and set up a production line. They were benevolent sweat shop affairs, using Singer machines for mass production of fine linen shirts.

Izaak constantly worked on improving both the production line and the working conditions, which he believed to be linked. They employed the latest machinery to cut costs rather than wages.

A handmade tucked and frilled linen shirt was prohibitively expensive. But any of Mr Braun's factories could produce shirts of the same quality at a twentieth of the cost. His business was expanding and profitable. In order to maintain the quality, Izaak Braun's seamstresses were trained and experienced in hand-work and finishing. His workers were highly-paid and he allowed no compromise on quality, believing his reputation was the source of growth.

He supplied several top stores in the capital and enjoyed an enviable reputation among store owners. Indeed, he had a lucrative contract for producing Polish officers' dress-uniforms. He had only touched the tip of the iceberg of success.

'My workers know me,' he had boasted. 'They know me by name and trust that I will provide for them. We work together to create the finest clothes in Eastern Europe.'

He gave speeches to his employees over lavish Christmas dinners, when his staff would get bonuses, and a band would play.

'The day will come when anyone, peasant proletariat or

bourgeois, will be proud to wear our clothing.'

He beamed at his workers to loud cheers.

His drive to keep production costs down ensured continuing expansion and his ambitions went far beyond Poland. He trusted in the industrialisation of the clothing industry and improvement of the workers lot. His long term dream was to produce high quality designer clothes for ordinary people, as well as profit sharing for his workers.

'Best quality, lowest price!' He encouraged his workers. 'Be proud that you are part of this successful enterprise. We are making the world a better place.'

He was one of the forward-thinkers who recognised the importance of mass markets. He ensured his foremen knew the strengths and weaknesses of each worker and there were fixed benefits and holidays for his staff. He recognised the need of a committed workforce and instituted a humanitarian programme in the work place.

*

Despite his free-thinking attitudes to industrial progress, the atmosphere at home was frigid and authoritarian. The workers in Braun factories had more independence than his wife and daughter.

Izaak's view of the world was entirely male-centric, and it never occurred to him that women had any need of independence. They were to be provided for.

Rebecca, who was an intelligent and highly educated woman, channelled her thwarted energy into her daughter, Sofia, who calmed her mother's hysterical outbursts and joined her in retreats to expensive sanatoria where they were pampered into silence.

At 17, Sofia had her mother's fine looks, coupled with the tall dignity and aristocratic appearance of her father. She had black hair and blue eyes, with a clear skin, and startling, white, even teeth.

Rebecca was proud of her daughter. She entertained hopes of an alliance among the wealthiest families in Europe and planned a complex campaign to marry her daughter.

They headed for Society, a battlefield where warring parties, headed by cliques of older women, won status by dint of social bloodshed. These harridans skirmished with vast politeness, deploying the achievements of children and grandchildren. The balance of power was managed through strategic marriage unions.

Whole mornings were wasted consulting the social diary and referring to a book which noted clothes and jewellery displayed on previous occasions. Maids were on hand to fold away discarded clothes and bring out new ones.

Sofia's opinions were irrelevant.

'Sofia I do hope you are not going to slouch!' her mother complained. 'Keep your head up and, yes, smile like that! Turn around, and now curtsey. Yes, charming. Maybe we should try another hat? And corsage?'

Sofia was sullen. Like her mother, she felt utterly trapped.

All pleasure drained away by the second change of clothes. And by the third she was hoping to fall under a tram. She heartily resented the promenades, constant changes of outfits, and formal visits where conversation was strictly confined to trivial topics. She took exception to the family wealth in the face of the great poverty of the post war era.

They often clashed.

At such times Rebecca called on Izaak to apply his oppressive authority. After all, she had to learn that in resisting her father, she was taking on god.

'Take care, Sofia!' he pronounced, 'you do not want to fall into the sin of your biblical sister, Eve.'

*

Rebecca planned her daughter's debut with military precision.

She took a respite from her collections of beautiful artefacts and long health cures to find a suitable alliance.

There was a dearth of men and hordes of giggling and simpering beauties to choose from, but Sofia had a luminous beauty that her mother felt sure would win out.

*

Sofia was presented at a musical evening in the Baroness Rothschild's salon.

'Sofia! Come here.'

Sofia curtsied with exaggerated modesty.

'Yes, Rebecca she is charming,' from a vicious old lady sparkling with diamonds. 'Come here, Sofia. Tell me about your music. I hear you play well. Maybe you can play us some Mozart?'

Sofia waited in silence for music to be placed before her.

'No! Chopin! Let her play Chopin.'

New music appeared.

She was directed where to sit, and which succession of ladies to impress. Tiny pinches indicated those who were particularly important. Her playing was disregarded unless she made an error, when the viragos immediately gripped their ears and groaned.

She was introduced to Daniel, a distant cousin from the Ashkenazy tribe, a blond Jewish boy with a sulky expression, clearly as uncomfortable as she was. He was padding around the drawing room stealthily, as careful as Sofia not to annoy the phalanx of grannies.

'Sofia did you like my Daniel? Is he not handsome?'

A handsome young man, no doubt he was under orders from his own brigade of crones.

The two stood together awkwardly.

'Look! The girl is blushing. She has fine skin and complexion. Come and talk to my son.'

Sofia and Daniel muttered a few words and then cold-shouldered each other, trapped in the basilisk glares of the watching generals.

*

Sofia left that gathering in a state of anxiety mixed with resentment.

She was a pet poodle! Her mother complained, no matter what. She was pushed, pinched, stood up, sat down and always criticised!

'Why did you talk to Daniel? He's a hopeless wastrel. Of course Lady ----- wants to get rid of him. Don't do it again. You were blushing! It was so forward.'

'How was I to know whether to talk to him or not? I hate it all. Why do I have to go? I don't want to do this. Can't I sit at home and read?'

*

A week later, as a maid stuck sharp pins into her hair in the name of beauty and decency, she heard that Daniel caused a scandal.

Rebecca was gossiping on the telephone.

'Imagine! He has run off with a 'hussy' and became a 'communist'... yes, Lady ----- has been forced to retreat from society in shame. She has gone to visit friends in America...'

So there was an escape?

Sofia had no luck though.

She had no idea how to access communists and anyway communism was something Satanic. She only saw their graffiti being scrubbed away and occasionally found a few pamphlets in gutters. She knew from them that she was rich and that her wealth was responsible for the troubles of the poor.

She felt trapped, and planned her own escape endlessly.

She was determined to reject worldliness. The worship of all things iron and gold had taken the heart out of her life.

Poverty and simplicity would give her the peace that she craved.

2.

Sofia Braun

Every week, the debutantes visited a nearby convent, where they learnt to sing with virginal purity, as their maids and footmen chatted in a nearby cafe.

The poverty, compassion and perfection embraced by the nuns appealed to the teenager's spirit of defiance. They were pious and naive, and promulgated an idealised view of Catholicism. She secretly read the New Testament, and discovered that she did not have to obey her parents if they were wrong.

*

After only one month, the triumphant Rebecca managed a fine alliance.

It was true that he was an older man, perhaps a little grey, but wealthy, kind and charming and with a title too!

Sofia had scarcely noticed him. But she was horrified at the thought. One of her father's chums, and so old! She envisaged a relationship like that of her parents and determined to get away.

Matters came to a head when her parents sat her down and broached the engagement to someone she saw as a tobacco stained uncle!

Sofia spouted idealistic cant she had heard from the nuns.

'Father,' she said, 'I do not *love* him. I am *free* to do as I feel is right. I should be allowed to choose my own husband. We should be *in love*. *Love* is all that matters. Jesus allowed women to be free, and all that his chosen needed is *love*.'

Every word was an attack on all that her father believed in.

'You cannot compel me to do what is wrong father. You cannot use your wealth to control others. Blessed are the poor, they will reach the kingdom of heaven.'

Izaak's face grew purple at such female disobedience.

Love! A sign of the lechery and degeneration! He was horrified.

'Go to your room Sofia! I do not need to hear this nonsense. Do not leave until I hear an apology! Your mother knows what is best for you.'

Sofia ran out and locked herself into her room.

Later that night, she packed her bag and headed straight through the servants quarters to the convent.

She took a cab with money from the old green urn and arrived late in the evening.

She informed the shocked nuns that she had been forced to run away from a tyrannical father who was forcing her to marry a man she hated.

The nuns were alarmed.

They cooed over her beauty, her softness and her jewels and almost sent a message to the Braun household. When they heard about the nightmarish oppression of the 16-year-old beauty in a Jewish household, they thought better of returning the girl and took her in for the night.

*

Rebecca learned of her daughter's defection the next morning. She burst into hysterics and the doctor was called.

Sofia's act of insurgence was a masterstroke. It struck a fatal blow to her mother's delicately laid plans and destroyed her status in the social rat pack. She had been shamed by her daughter!

The next morning the nuns related the tale to the horrified priest, who had a far better idea of the world than they.

The priest made subtle efforts to return the child. Unfortunately, the girl was adamant. She had moved in, and refused to leave.

She had attached her rebellion to the division of faiths by asking to embrace Catholicism.

The Brauns made every effort to extract their daughter, but she asserted that her conversion was a matter of free choice.

There was a polite, fierce stand-off between religious leaders.

Finally, both sides accepted the situation.

Izaak was prepared to wait. Life at the convent was far more confined than home, and he expected her to return after a while. He paid for her study, and ensured that she was cared for.

Rebecca had a hidden fury at life which she now expended on her daughter. She was enraged at her humiliation and persisted in a state of dramatic nervous collapse for a month.

*

Providentially, Rebecca's life was easier after her daughter's departure.

Izaak sullenly accepted that women had feelings, which ought to be considered. He was an extreme authoritarian, but not a tyrant. He finally recognised that the role of women was evolving and it was necessary to keep up with the times.

As Rebecca recovered in the care of innumerable psychiatrists and doctors, he grudgingly allowed her rights to an opinion.

'I realise that your lifestyle is rather confined,' he opined magnanimously. He spoke in the manner of a man talking to an animal, or patting a dog.

'There must be something you want to do, Rebecca,' he added, while looking out of the window and thinking wistfully about his new factory in Germany.

Rebecca did not notice. She gabbled for hours about her interest in archaeology and the places she wanted to see.

Izaak yawned, but bore it all very well. He agreed that she should travel, visiting Egypt to recuperate from her loss. He needed domestic peace at a critical time in the growth of his empire.

*

Rebecca sprang into life and action.

Within two months she had reorganised the running of the home, calling in countless relatives to supervise the various tasks which made the houses run like clockwork.

She left for Egypt with an eminent professor, among a ponderous collection of trunks which even contained furs in case it grew cold at night.

In the next three months she supported and participated in several excavations in the Valley of Kings.

As a funder for a fair proportion of each expedition she was allowed to take part in minor discoveries. She brought back numerous finds, and boxes of Middle Eastern knick-knacks. She purchased many books on Egyptology for their library, including several which contained daguerreotypes of her standing before important excavation in full evening dress.

She redecorated their Berlin apartments in an Egyptian style and started a minor fashion in Egyptian style jewellery.

She grew more confident and planned to excavate in Greece, following in the footsteps of Madame Schliemann. Unbeknownst to her husband, she wore makeup.

When she finally returned from her adventures abroad, home life was far less oppressive. Izaak spent time talking to her. He listened to the stories of ancient civilisations, demonstrating his liberal approach and yawning profusely. The Brauns were recognised and invited almost everywhere and no one ever mentioned Sofia. As a result, she completely forgot about her recalcitrant daughter.

*

Unlike his wife, Izaak thought about Sofia often, and finally, it was agreed that she should visit with a view to reconciliation.

It was a momentous occasion involving chaperones from both religions. There were careful negotiations over complex spiritual matters which no one but religious leaders understood.

The meeting was not a success.

Sofia's resentments had hardened in the anti-Semitic sentiments she had learnt at the convent, nevertheless, she still craved love and attention from her mother. She would certainly have returned if Rebecca had shown any affection.

Distressingly, Rebecca had been psychoanalysed into perfect detachment; and did not care to revisit the wounds that her daughter had inflicted. After all – it was just female hysteria.

Thus pride and hurt hardened on both sides. Sofia stubbornly resolved make her own choices without 'respecting' the wishes of her elders and rejected wealth and ostentation.

*

Her restoration to the convent caused Catholic rejoicing and over the next three months she blossomed in the nuns' naïve affirmation, becoming their favourite. The naive girl became entrenched in the ideals of self-sacrifice love and forgiveness.

She relished structured days based around high-minded matters, interspersed with periods of gossip and fun when she was petted and adored.

However, she was a clever child, with the strength of her mother and the shrewdness of her father. She was beginning to see a narrow future. She had exchanged one prison for another.

3.

Janek Maslow Sr

Jan Maslow was a 55-year-old managing director of the railway network from Warsaw to Kiev, a fat and whiskery old plutocrat. He was a rich old man who owned majority shares in the South-Western railway network from Warsaw to Kiev.

He was widower with a daughter, Irma, 22 years old, five years older than Sofia.

Irma was of a highly liberated disposition. She had annoyed him by being totally uninterested in his welfare and refusing to marry any of his capitalist friends. She was mixing with Socialist students at the University of Warsaw, and studying medicine, a most unfeminine subject.

His wife had died a mere 6 months ago and he rather fancied another wife over whom he could exert total power. As a benefactor of the convent of St Agnes he had a special relationship with the simple nuns. He swanned around on open days, leering at the young school girls and presuming that their pious prayers would ensure his place in heaven.

Sofia was pointed out to him on several occasions. The defection of rich old Izaak's daughter had rocked the convent, where nothing much happened from year to year.

Now that was his idea of a proper female! She had a crystal, clean purity as well as beauty. Above all, she was both alluring and absolutely friendless.

He determined to take the child as his second wife.

He concocted a careful campaign to entrap her. He extracted every detail of her life from the naïve mother superior. He had been careful to seem absolutely uninterested, merely surveying education at the school with a view to opening a new classroom.

The first introduction was given quite openly and he took care to ignore her.

Their next 'chance' meeting was the result of weeks of planning.

The encounter occurred as his prey was walking 5 of her charges to the local park for a walk in the spring sun.

The location, close to an expensive and luxurious ice-cream parlour in Warsaw, had been a matter of careful artifice and meticulous preparation.

'My goodness,' he blustered, blocking their path entirely, 'I recognise the uniform of the convent. Is this Miss Braun? I met you at the open day. Are these your charges?'

Sofia was obliged to stop and reply politely as she vaguely recognised the man. She had lived a sheltered life, and the convent was even more cloistered than home.

She avoided his gaze.

He blusteringly and good naturedly invited her charges to partake of the ice-cream, a treat she could not deny the excited pupils.

The two chatted as the young girls tucked into whopping sundaes with biscotti. She was modest and retiring. He was a careful and experienced predator, unwaveringly seeking to win her to wife.

To the gullible Sophia, their meeting seemed heaven sent.

He shared her religious fervour and extreme idealism!

They discussed the Catholic concept of love and she spouted her idealistic views.

*

After this chance meeting she begged that Janek took the girls out again.

It was true love! They agreed in all matters, particularly the freedom of women, and had similar tastes! He was perfect, if a little old and fat.

The nuns were delighted at the romance, and the priest was keen to get rid of her.

The Brauns made little objection, relieved that she had married relatively well.

Janek had gained his object with the minimum of opposition.

23

4.

Sofia Maslow

They were married at the convent. The groom's family consisted of a few of Maslow's friends and his daughter, Irma.

The bride was given away by the resident priest, and the nuns were allowed to attend.

Sofia's brothers attended the modest reception; they were cool and withdrawn. Her parents did not arrive, although Sofia checked many times just in case. Nor did the widow's parents attend. They were shocked at the young hussy and dragged their grand-daughter away from the house of sin.

Sofia felt sure that her act of rebellion made a statement for women.

*

She had not, in fact, escaped her fate.

Like many neglected children, she thought she had made a stand and escaped, while choosing exactly the same situation all over again.

Sofia was intent on building a new world. She adored her Victorian husband and impressed his friends by her genuine piety and modesty. She wanted everything to be perfect, so much better than the arid relations between her mother and father.

However, Janek had chosen and young and naïve wife for a reason. He was autocratic, controlling and dictatorial. She soon learnt that he agreed with the *principal* of women's emancipation, but not the *practice*, relegating it to an ideal future.

In fact, his attitudes were identical to Izaak's, and the two men, once introduced, regarded each other with a distant deference. Faith was a serious barrier; however, Maslow was exactly the kind of man Izaak had had in mind for his daughter - a man with no idea of women's rights, or feelings.

'Sofia!' said Maslow, when discussing their future domestic arrangements. He always barked her name as if she were a corporal in the army. (She once heard the captain and sergeant's strangled yells during a parade and was curiously reminded of her husband.) 'Sofia!'

24

She almost stood to attention.

'The concept of female emancipation is useful - in principal - and I completely agree with it, as I always told you.'

He paused, almost twirling a baton as he marshalled his tiny troop of one.

'It is not the same here in this house. This is the real world.'

He marched to and from across the dark Victorian drawing room.

'Please do not question anything I have settled, you would be giving a frightful example to your daughter!' (He was referring to Irma, who was older than Sofia, and already studying medicine.)

*

On their return from honeymoon, the servants were ranged in a row to meet the new bride.

The young girl was already cowering before their boor of a master - they felt little sympathy.

He stopped at the flower arrangements in the hall. Before even removing his coat, he knocked a vase containing what he deemed 'common' blooms, smashing it and spilling water over the floor.

Servants came scurrying over and cleared the mess in absolute silence.

'Sofia!' he shouted.

Silence from the assembled servants.

'My poor child! We do not appreciate this vulgarity.'

She knew they were all thinking 'Jew!'

'Chrysanthemums are overblown and ostentatious,' he declared. 'We do not keep them in our home. You need to study good taste.'

'Why don't you tell the housekeeper which blooms are acceptable, Jan?' she asked. 'I do not buy flowers myself.'

'Well you should! My dear girl! That is women's work. Flower arranging is your feminine duty. That is the kind of housework a proper, decent woman does. I am amazed at the laxity of your upbringing. You are quite spoiled. Please arrange the flowers daily.'

She heard the servants whispering about her poor taste and relating it to her 'background'.

It puzzled her.

Her mother and father had protected her from anything of that kind as a child. She was slowly becoming aware of a powerful current of anti-Semitism around her.

She had first encountered ill-feeling towards her kind at the convent. It was related to Christ being a Jew in some way.

Slowly, she absorbed the guilt of her people, on top of the guilt of all womankind, for the evils of this world.

*

Janek berated her and continually cast aspersions on her background.

'It is different here,' he said, subtly suggesting that Jewish households were run on inferior lines.

Sofia could not understand it.

His home was arranged with a stuffy gentility which was indubitably far less pleasant than the easy, open luxury which she had come from.

Sofia was resilient. She regarded it as poverty and enjoyed it. She luxuriated in the quiet and the lack of intrusive relatives and parents.

Her low status as second bride did not concern her. After all, this was the type of humility which Christians espoused. She escaped into her new religion and felt free.

She viewed the growing tide of anti-Semitism around her with a kind of horror and despair.

5.

Rebecca

Rebecca, who had tasted a modicum of freedom, watched her daughter's mistreatment with growing rage, recognising that she was trapped in a marriage like her own.

She visited often when Janek was out of the house, and invited Sofia to tea whenever she was in the country.

Sofia was sinking under a weight of guilt.

He made her feel responsible for every wrong in the household and berated her for every error she made as a new housewife. He did not forget them either, and would list them carefully whenever he felt like making his child-wife miserable.

Rebecca listened to the tale of her daughter's perceived incompetence and lack of education with disgust. But Sofia would hear no ill of her husband, taking the bible's words of obedience strictly to heart. She bore with Jan meekly and blamed herself for his behaviour.

It was not long before she accepted Jan's opinions and agreed with them implicitly.

*

There was never any question of her leaving the house to go on what Janek called 'frivolous jaunts' with her mother. She accepted her limited world. She accepted her intrinsic wrongness as a birthright and strove to correct it at all times.

His acts of petty tyranny and his endless criticism did not affect her other than to make her strive to be better. They drove her deeper into her new religion.

However, since she placed no dependence on her reputation as a housewife, she was not troubled by her failures and learnt his lessons without complaint. She did not clash with the servants when they arranged the house with a frigid gentility. She arranged flowers, chose meals with the advice of the cook, supervised the housemaids and checked the laundry, tasks which she had never done before.

*

Jan Maslow was a spiteful and vindictive man, who had been

27

given far too much power over his workers and his home. His petty demands and criticisms had harassed his previous wife into an early grave. Unfortunately, because Sofia had her mother's support, he never broke her spirit.

First, he turned his attention to his wife's appearance.

Sofia had brought a magnificent and lavish trousseau from her mother, prepared over years by a collector with a brilliant good taste.

He got rid of her expensive fashionable clothes and made sure her garb was simple and modest in the extreme; her hair long, plaited, uncurled and her jewellery minimal.

If he expected rebellion, he did not achieve it.

Sofia agreed with him entirely.

'You are right, Jan,' she said. 'All this changing of clothes is tiresome and fills up the day with pointless activity. I am happy to wear the clothes you recommend. It is precisely what I want.'

*

Rebecca would never dare to stand up to Izaak. Maslow was another matter entirely. If he wanted plain, she could arrange that. She collected together the finest materials and couturiers. They prepared a new trousseau in black and charcoal grey.

Sofia was surprisingly grateful and hugged her mother.

'It is just exactly what I wanted! Janek says I look' she paused and her eyes filled with tears, 'ostentatious and vulgar otherwise.'

Rebecca almost snarled at this mistreatment of her daughter's beauty. She took it as a challenge and always ensured that Sofia always looked elegant and refined.

Her daughter, dressed by the finest couturiers, looked like a film star dressed as a Quaker. She walked elegantly and was always at ease, because she preferred simple clothing to the lavish ostentation she had worn before.

*

As soon as his young wife was pregnant, he began a campaign of extreme intimidation. He regarded female emotions, other than frigid calm, as signs of mental illness. Even wet eyes were signs of instability.

He treated morning sickness as weakness and insisted she attend every gargantuan breakfast and partake of fatty foods, for the sake of the child.

When she raised her eyes to her husband in argument, he threatened a short stay in a sanatorium where he knew the doctors.

He failed to intimidate her with this formidable threat.

Sofia completely agreed with him.

*

Janek had always been suspicious of women in groups of more than one.

With Rebecca his worst fears were confirmed. He loathed his mother in law (who was younger than him) and often reflected that if he'd met her before, he would never have married Sofia.

Rebecca recommended the latest treatments at a highly fashionable spa. It was beyond his price range.

'Don't worry Mr Maslow, she offered, 'my husband will pay. I will go with her. She needs rest and quiet. I know just the right place…'

He was out manoeuvred, yet did not give up.

He knew a doctor and treatment which had proved excellent for his previous wife's constitution, he warned, at a less fashionable location. The specialist knew that women were 'delicate' and hysterical.

Rebecca blinded him with articles which she insisted he read, and knew all the doctors.

He sensed that she had money to overwhelm the most exacting specialist and relented.

*

Sofia had her first child in comfort and luxury at an expensive spa. And from her next three pregnancies, one after another were spent in the comfort of resorts in various parts of Europe, under the care of her mother.

Her first child, Janek, was born almost exactly 9 months after they were wed. Shortly thereafter, she had Katya. Just a year later she had another son, Casimir. Her youngest, Anya, was born two years later.

*

From the moment of their birth Sofia devoted every drop of thwarted hopes and ambition on her brood.

Her children pleased everyone and she treated them like little gods. She droopingly accepted that they were far better than her.

6.

The young Maslows

The children grew up believing that their mother was somehow inferior to them, and often treated their parent with haughty disdain.

They inhabited two almost diametrically opposing worlds, one of easy comfort and the other of repressed frigidity.

They enjoyed Rebecca's light and airy mansions and life of jollifications: skiing, staying at their dacha every summer and pony trekking through the lowlands of the Carpathian Mountains. They admired Rebecca – guiltily - papa hinted that there was something very wrong with her.

'We are not like that,' he said to the children when they reported the wonderful things they had seen at grandmother's. He subtly suggested that Jewish households were run on inferior lines.

They grew to believe that luxury, comfort and even learning of their maternal grandparents were somehow suspect.

Their father established his authority over them from the very beginning and after his death the one thing they clearly remembered of him was his canings. They did not recognise the heavy beatings he meted out as abusive, not knowing anything else.

If he was angry with Sofia (and he often was), his favourite revenge was to hit the children. He had a large stick for this purpose and beat them soundly for Sofia's tiniest transgressions.

Whenever this happened, which was often, his young wife locked herself in her room to muffle her sobs.

As a result the children respected him a great deal more than mama, who they quite unreasonably blamed for their punishment.

*

They did not admire their beautiful mother and learnt to disregard beauty. Their father took anyone's interest in her appearance as a personal affront.

'Sofia, dearest, a woman is not a painted puppet.' He complained. 'Do not dress up like scarlet woman. You are representing me and the family. You do not need you to change your clothes for dinner and we do not attend balls. A simple outfit in a neutral colour will

31

suffice. You will be sufficiently elegant.'

The children were always silent when he told her off for looking 'too fine'. Were they to be beaten for it?

In his repressed imagination, any beautiful woman was hanging out for a man, like a flower trying to attract bees. He subscribed to the view that women were innately wicked, and was averse to feminine frippery. It was indecorous. When men stared at his wife with admiration, he accused her of flirting.

After a while the children grew ashamed by their mother's beauty and their grandmother's stunning, perfumed wealth and elegance.

*

Sofia grew increasingly downtrodden. She accepted Jan's repressive views and passed them on to her children without questioning. She admitted her intrinsic wrongness and strove to correct it at all times.

She prayed endlessly and read Lamentations carefully, sighing for the fate of her fellow Jews, long before the holocaust began.

In truth it did not take too much vision to foresee a hard future. They were already blamed for the boom and bust economy. The business skill of the rich and successful like Izaak was legendry. Their success caused serious resentment among the beleaguered old guard.

*

Perhaps Sofia would have sunk under the unkind regime she lived under. Perhaps the children would have realised that he was an abusive brute. But their father died when they were still quite young.

Jan was a fat old man who smoked a pipe, indulged in fatty food and drank wine with every meal. Unsurprisingly, he had a heart attack and died at the age of 61.

The first attack, 1926, caused his immediate retirement from the presidency of the railway.

Every doctor in Warsaw was consulted to no effect and Rebecca arranged a visit to a spa which dealt with his particular symptoms.

He faded too fast to correct the damage down to his heart, and died within a year. He was buried with full honours. A plaque commemorating his leadership of the railway was erected at Warsaw central station, with his half bust in an oval recess.

Sofia was left a young widow with four children and a large pension. Her children all had the Braun's excellent complexion and straight white teeth, with their father's light brown hair, large heavy jaw and thin lips. They had the slightly dried up appearance of children who spent too much time indoors.

Rebecca tried to keep the censure about their plain appearance from her voice.

*

Izaak still hoped that their daughter would return to the family fold; perhaps marry a charming Jewish widower.

Sofia might still have obeyed her father if her mother had appreciated her. Still, Rebecca made it clear that no heretic could contemplate a full return to the fold. She would accept no less than a full recantation. After all, she had been shamed in front of her social clan and hadn't forgotten it.

Sofia remained aloof. She had a large pension and an apartment in central Warsaw. Like most abused women, she saw her life entirely through the eyes of her children and guessed that they would be looked down on by the Brauns.

In any case, she was better off without a husband!

Janek had been controlling, manipulative and denigrating. Without him, she could sleep in peace. She did not need to worry about his capricious tempers. Her husband had suffered greatly with bronchitis and his weight. She was secretly disgusted by his whiskers, his stink of tobacco and his obvious ill health. He snored and touched her up possessively. She was forced to lie over his sweaty body to keep him warm. He liked her to stroke him to sleep. It had been vile.

33

7.

Lvov 1929

Unfortunately, within a couple of years, their pension was rendered worthless by rampant inflation.

The hardship of the Great Depression divided the republic of Poland. It had been a patchwork of politically and religiously divided peoples, who lived in an uneasy harmony. Now they were falling into tight racial groups. Instead of uniting in hardship, the communities split into hostile factions.

The children were able to choose their allegiance and stuck with their Maslow connection. It had more status.

The boys grew increasingly ashamed their Jewish connection. They became aggressively nationalist and not a little right wing.

They warned Sofia to keep quiet about her Jewish roots, and for the most part she did.

*

Sofia's pension became increasingly valueless, and she was increasingly dependent on her parents. She was forced to ask her mother for help with the children's education.

When Janek's apartment lease came up, they moved into one of the Brauns many apartments in Warsaw.

'This is father's apartment,' she explained to her new neighbours.

Her eldest son, who was only just hitting his teens, interrupted.

'No mama, we are *renting* from the Brauns. They are kind, very kind, *acquaintances.*'

The look on her children's faces shut Sofia up, although she complained afterwards.

'Papa Braun is a good man. You should be proud of him. He has done so much for you. You would have nothing without him. And this is *his* apartment.'

The luxury apartment in the centre of Warsaw was surrounded by squares and the beautiful tree lined avenues constructed on a grand scale.

The huge houses were increasingly being let out to the rising bourgeoisie, who understood the power of the markets. Those in work did well in the chaos; everyone else was in financial trouble.

From their huge glass windows on the first floor, they were able to observe the growing misery and political instability.

Every day the streets filled with men looking for work, beggars and war veterans.

Even so, the communists made little headway among the dispossessed. Political power remained in the hands of the wealthy few.

All around the central area, Warsaw ethnic groups lived and fed and cared for each other in ethnic quarters.

Ukrainians, Slovaks and Poles accused each other of hoarding supplies. Fighting often broke out among young unemployed men from different backgrounds, and riots were common. Religion and race, was dividing people once again.

*

The Braun's who lived among the rich and privileged, scarcely noticed the tensions.

Rebecca spent time with educated people and knew practically nothing of it the anti-Jewish extremism rampaging through the poorer community. As to the rumblings of hatred, surely people around them were civilised and educated? The future was rosy and progressive.

Weren't these anti-Semitic rants just potty conspiracy theorists? Communism was a failure, struggling to feed its own people, who flooded the streets as beggars fleeing from a terrorist regime. Catholicism was a sad religion, obsessed with death and mourning.

She was slightly baffled by her daughter's religious fervour, treating her own Judaism as a clan membership rather than a faith.

'Why do you pray every day Sofia?' she complained. 'It's not natural. It will make you ill. And why go to this church all the time? Surely the teacher (she insisted on calling the priest a teacher) needs some time to himself? Why not leave him alone? Oh dear, pray, pray, pray. That's all you do.'

Sophia was riven with guilt.

She was glad that her husband was dead! How could she be so pleased? Surely she was a bad person.

She attended church every day to pray for his soul.

*

The streets in the centre were still relatively safe though, and the boys walked home from school alone unless it was dark, when a servant came to collect them.

They steered around pathetic bundles of cloth covering poor wretches who had slept outside in the blighting winter. They ignored barefoot children and their starving parents and complained that their mother gave stuff away when *they* were suffering the effects of poverty. Like a lot of people at the time, they were sure beggars hoarded millions and lived in luxury.

*

On the contrary, Sofia felt a deep sympathy for the suffering around her. She often accompanied the boys on the way to school, stopping at the church on the way back.

She had great sympathy for the oppressed.

Every day, as she walked her boys to school, she carried small coins, bits of food and prayer cards for the destitute wretches who hovered nearby.

As soon as her boys disappeared within the school gates, she was mobbed by ragged young children and mothers with babes in arms.

'Bless you,' they cried.

Their thanks were balsam to Sofia's wounded soul.

Once day, her eldest son once ran out to get something he had forgotten from her. He was shocked by the beggarly hubbub around her, outside his school too!

Had she no shame? In future, he warned her, she was to keep her disgraceful behaviour out of sight.

She did too, though she wept for her selfish son and made many excuses before god.

'The other boys laughed at him,' she explained to her Lord. 'It was nothing to do with the poor. He loves and cares for them just as he should'.

8.

Poland 1929

At the beginning of the depression, the sclerotic government was controlled by a predominantly White Russian and Polish aristocracy. The depression ate into their liquid wealth alarmingly.

These 'Houses' held themselves as the natural leaders of the disparate groups, and harked backwards to an agricultural society.

The concept of a Polish nation was mainly geographical and incorporated several different racial minorities. The government managed to retain control of the area, despite the attempts by 'terrorist' minorities such as the Ukrainian nationalists to gain independence.

The aristocracy managed to hold on to a great deal of wealth despite the depression. Their ancestors had been awarded care of the land (including its inhabitants) for defending the population from foreign incursions. No one knew who precisely had awarded it – although divine agency was considered to have played a part. All of the Braun's spectacular wealth could not compete with their huge castles, power and glory. They imitated the German Nazis and strode about like higher beings.

Their contribution to the widespread suffering was to blame others. They made excuses for themselves. It had to be a communist plot, supported by profiteers and Jews. Many of the conservative landowners did not invest in industrial growth. However, they were aware of the suffering of the horrific winter and dished out alms while their wives ran soup kitchens.

They strode about importantly, representing superior standards of courage, morality, and education. They created sanitisation corps, designed to weed out the moral ills of society. It was a futile gesture, since on the contrary, they were mostly venal, selfish and narrow-minded.

This was excusable; a fall from grace was natural, the *standards* were there.

*

The forward thinkers in the government saw the importance of industry, and were encouraging to Jewish investors in industry.

Luckily for the Maslows Izaak Braun was one of these investors. He opened new factories in Poland, Hungary and East Germany.

He still nurtured socialist sentiments. He ensured his workers were secure, and had many savings schemes to ensure that they could weather economic pressures. He moved them from factory to factory at every whiff of market change. His was a rare response to the hardships faced by workers.

Unluckily for the Brauns, the disenfranchised and disaffected had a found their voice; and it was focussed on finding a scapegoat for all their woes.

9.

Janek Jr

Rebecca visited her daughter regularly. She took an interest in her grandchildren and rather liked the eldest Maslow boy, who was handsome and tall.

'Janek is the image of Izaak.'

Janek Jr was not a clever pupil. And he did not approve of the Brauns. He saw himself as one of the elite.

He attended a good Gymnasium, but showed little aptitude. His reports stated he was lazy.

He was spending a lot of time on politics. He had joined the right wing party, which mirrored many of the opinions of the Nazis. He joined their political rallies and screamed slogans with the rest of the disaffected youth of his country. He marched about attempted to restore the nation to it moral health.

His grandmother was concerned to see one of the nasty nationalist newssheets on his desk. She warned him not to get involved in street politics and demonstrations. He needed to work harder, or she would no longer fund his schooling.

Janek Jr was not cowed. He made veiled threats, suggesting that somehow, Rebecca was at fault for the state of the nation.

Sofia tried to intervene and her son turned on her.

'Mama, everyone knows you are dotty, why are you telling us what to do?' he shouted, 'I am a high level student. Did you ever finish proper gymnasium?'

Rebecca tried to show him that disrespect of this kind was fatal to his future. To no avail.

Sofia's cowering humility had done immense damage to his sense of self and he thought he really was rather a superior creature.

There was a passionate row for nearly an hour, where Janek's comments grew increasingly racist.

Eventually, the women, used to being shouted down by men, backed down and the argument blew over.

Rebecca did not mind and forgave him. She was devoted to her family.

'He is a bit of a hothead, he'll grow out of it.'

Rebecca believed in education. She was sure that a wider knowledge would leech the extremism out of the boy.

She paid for the best tutors for the two youngest Maslows, Casimir and Anya. They shared a series of tutors with their cousins whenever they visited Warsaw.

They were witty, carefree teenagers, and the social upheaval gave them exciting new freedoms. They revelled in their new life and totally ignored their praying mother.

Ania rarely got down to study. She laughed at her mother's piety and ran off to visit their friends on every occasion.

'Mama,' she stated, 'god knows where I am going. Tell him to find us!' at such times Sofia sent their one servant to keep an eye on them and did her chores for herself.

10.

Katya

Katya, Sofia's second child and first daughter, favoured her father most.

She had brown hair and a thin, slightly crooked mouth. Her heavy eyebrows which she refused to pluck, gave her a frowning expression. These disadvantages were offset by a clear complexion and nice figure. She was not plain, but the tiniest hint of envy made her face unattractive.

She together with all educated elite Poles, hated religion. She was mortified at their mother's simple black clothing and everyday attendance at the local church alongside peasants and common people. She loathed her endless processions behind gilded statues.

She met with her wealthy cousins regularly, and coveted their expensive toys. Her mother's platitudes 'blessed are the poor for they shall inherit the earth' were just annoying moralising.

Katya remembered little of her father. Her brother Jan told her that Sofia was hysterical, and she assumed it was true. Her earliest memory was of Rebecca hugging her weeping daughter after she had been beaten for some minor transgression.

*

When the question of Katya's schooling came under discussion it became clear that Rebecca had not entirely given up her social aspirations.

'Katya is clever,' she conceded (suppressing her opinion of the 'Ghastly Maslow' as she called him) 'although she favours the Maslows. Let us see if she can get into Tseder.'

This was high ambition!

Tseder was a school for the most aristocratic and talented girls in Poland. It was difficult for a commoner from a racial minority to get a place.

She had tried for her granddaughter Ruth and failed (the Brauns were too well known in Warsaw and anti-Semitism was running high).

This time she was determined to succeed.

Katya was a studious child who worked very hard. She was always aware that she was intended to go to Tseder, one of the oldest gymnasia offering education and deportment to young ladies. She was brilliant at maths and science, encouraged by both mother and grandmother.

'Who says women cannot study sciences?' said Rebecca. Sofia beamed at her mother's approbation.

Grandmother was delighted when her granddaughter won a scholarship to that illustrious institution.

She offered to pay the fees for her younger sister Anya if she studied hard.

*

There was a little tea party for the children on the night before Katya started at her new school.

Katya sat among her rich cousins, pointed out as an exemplary child who would go far.

11.

Tseder 1935

Katya arrived on her first day bolstered by a tide of hope. The school had permitted her to join in the spring term because of the brilliance of her test results. She was to take advanced maths and the sciences, and would be almost the only girl in the class studying physics. A specialist professor had been called in for higher level physics; no expense had been spared. Tseder's headmistress foresaw kudos from getting a girl into engineering.

She had been dressed and pressed by an ambitious grandmother and doting mother. She was neat and clean and plain.

'There,' said Grandmother. 'She is entirely suitable for a schoolgirl. There is absolutely nothing wrong with her appearance.'

*

She stepped through the palatial frontage of the ancient institution, with its ornate porticos, carrying heavy family expectations.

It was a shock.

The place was dark and dingy and smelled of cabbage. The furniture in the classrooms was rickety and the parquet floors were scratched and unpolished. The porter smelled of vodka.

Most of all, she was astounded by the girls.

Coiffured and powdered young ladies drifted past her, greeting each other like old acquaintances. They assumed that they were gorgeous and addressed each other by their titles, even in the classroom. They smelled of perfume, and their uniforms were laced with silks and satins!

If they dropped or spilt something they walked off expecting someone to sort it, without looking back. The most modest occasionally gave gracious thanks for an unusual service. She later learnt that they did not even keep themselves clean – even that was arranged for them.

When she introduced herself as a scholarship student, one brass faced long nosed girl openly stated that she deplored what the world was coming to. How come scholarship pupils were allowed to attend an exclusive college?

*

Her first class was French.

French was the language of the salon, and the girls were naturally fairly fluent. Katya had spent time among the best tutors and was appalled by the way that the girls spouted ghastly grammatical errors, confident that anything they said was word-perfect. They chatted while their teacher tried to explain the subjunctive and handed in appallingly sloppy essays.

Their dejected Parisian teacher brightened considerably when she heard Katya master the intricacies of the subjunctive, and saw the young girl take notes.

The next class was German.

The girls were slightly more fluent, though nothing like as good as they thought.

Katya was keen to show off her excellent knowledge of the language and interspersed it with several Yiddish words.

At first, it caused a roar of hilarity.

'*Where* did you learn your German darling?' they giggled. 'That is not a German word. It is *Jewish*!'

Then Katya noticed how the blond teacher looked really angry too, as if she had sworn out loud or something. He looked at her harshly, and said, with a repressed rage, that the words she had used were an abominable travesty of the pure German tongue.

'I pick up languages easily,' Katya muttered, shamefaced. 'I probably heard that word in the market.'

'Never repeat them,' snarled the teacher.

'The *market*!'

'Whatever were you doing there? It's for *servants*.'

'Maybe in the kitchen then?'

The girls were astonished.

They clearly had no experience of kitchens and markets.

It was her first experience of such breath-taking self-importance and deep rooted racism.

*

On that first day she faced sneering enquiries about her name, which lacked crucial nobility and history. They were baffled at her

44

presence and unimpressed that her father was an industrialist. She felt small and insignificant.

The dug deeper, questioning every relationship in her family. Who was her paternal grandfather? *Who* was her maternal grandfather?

They thrilled at the Braun name, which surprised her.

'Millionaires darling,' they whispered amongst each other.

So money did count then, as well as breeding!

The girls wandered off to classes, trailing a scent of powder and stale makeup.

Lucia Orloska remained.

She had been asked to show the new girl the ropes and had already heard the news.

'Rich darling, really oodles of coin,' it was rumoured.

Katya resented her commiserating glances and kind looks.

'We are going to the patisserie, Katya. *Do* say you would like to come.'

Her voice was upper class, insincere.

Had she deliberately chosen the most expensive shop in Warsaw?

'Sorry Lucy,' Katya replied, in what was meant as a subtle Socialist comment, 'I have to do some *work*. *Some* of us have *commitments*.'

Lucia smiled graciously and wandered off. She had done her duty and suggested the expensive patisserie because she assumed that Katya was wealthy. She couldn't afford it either.

She forgot the new girl almost immediately. She was caught up in the social whirl of Warsaw high society, and did not share classes or subjects with Katya anyway.

12.

The Aristocracy

Katya had been taught that education was a key to success. She was therefore utterly astonished that the girls believed too much knowledge was harmful. She was told that it might make a pretty woman's head explode, or turn her into a trouser-wearing lesbian.

These high aristocrats regarded learning as part of talking sensibly about the arts and making small talk with politicians. Their highest ambition at university was to meet suitable men.

Apparently, Warsaw University had a special women's college which did not lean on their pupils too hard.

Katya fitted in somehow, not as far out as the Cossack girls and the dark, sloe-eyed Ukrainians, yet obviously not quite the right sort.

Oddly, her status was improved by her relationship to Izaak. The girls often asked about his sons, if they were married and so on.

As a possible *connection*, she was occasionally invited to their immense Warsaw mansions (she lived in an apartment) and bore with their well-meaning insults and intrinsic racism.

*

Her grandmother Rebecca was fascinated by every detail of the girls and knew most of them by name.

She cross-questioned her great-niece about every detail of visits to noble houses and rubbed her hands with glee at her progress.

Rebecca had been locked out of Izaak's world but her main interests still lay in society and the arts. She had hopes that Katya would marry into the aristocracy.

*

Only Katya knew how unlikely that was. She was extremely clever, even calculating, and saw how the racial minorities at the school were treated. There little chance of an alliance unless a huge fortune was involved.

None of them would have turned down the heir to Braun wealth, even though they firmly believed that there was a Jewish conspiracy to eradicate their wealth. The country was falling apart, but they never once conceded that their rulers might be incompetent.

Katya listened blank-faced while her heart seethed with animosity at the unfairness of the caste system.

*

There were many different views of the worsening economic and political situation. She listened to Janek's rants without enthusiasm and her mother's pacifist prayers with still less.

She heard even more from the girls and drew her own conclusions. The girls' parents were heavily involved in governing the new republic. The rearmament of Germany was viewed with great dismay. They regretted that Hitler was not a Pole.

*

Flattery helped her socialise.

'Oh what a divine dress!' she addressed the vapid beauties who she secretly despised, 'you *are* a true princess.'

Mostly her status rose because the girls needed help with homework.

A smattering of knowledge about important subjects was necessary in order to pass the secondary school exams.

The girls always crowded round her before class.

'What's the answer to problem 6?' they fawned.

They scribbled the answers and corrected their untidy sums just before class, not really caring for explanations; they really didn't *need* subjects like maths.

Her easy nature and plain looks ensured invitations to balls and soirees. She was no competition.

Each invite was taken extremely seriously by Rebecca. She planned every party dress carefully. She wanted to know what every girl was going to wear. She perused fashion journals and ensured her granddaughter wore the very latest styles. She dressed her granddaughter in the highest fashion and in colours which made the best of her sallow complexion.

Katya enjoyed herself a lot. As an outsider she did not belong to any cliques, heard all of the gossip and listened to their private dreams.

*

She found a friend soon enough.

Angela was dyslexic, which was not a recognised disorder in

those days. She found written work almost impossible and was redoing her year for the second time when Katya started at school.

Teachers accused her of misspelling things on purpose and she required help for every bit of work. The two clung together, trying to understand the mystifying complexity of school life.

Angela's grateful mother invited Katya on a formal visit to the family mansion in Warsaw.

It was the first time Katya had ever received a formal invitation from the highest tier of blue blooded Polish aristocracy - even the Brauns did not move in such high circles.

On the day, Katya was scrubbed extra clean and her school uniform pressed. Everything was double checked by grandmama's personal maid and she bore an exquisite, tasteful gift of high value.

*

Immediately after school, the girls were whisked off in an old Bentley, even though Angela did not live far away (walking distance really).

It stopped in front of a palatial residence dominating one of the main squares in Warsaw. From the armed footmen outside, Katya at first assumed that it was a bank.

She was escorted past a phalanx of tall, elegant footmen in white gloves and ushered into a hall which looked like an over furnished glittering art gallery entrance with giant chandeliers.

From there she was herded into a smaller room the size of her whole apartment.

She curtsied before the old countess, who was already seated in glory, and presented her offering, which was passed unopened to a maid.

They were served tea by armies of servants in black and white uniforms.

The food was more lavish than that served at the Brauns, and there was more of it, yet it was not so tasty and well-chosen. It seemed to be placed in colossal pyramids for the purposes of display and some of it was stale.

It was like being at the theatre, on public display.

Mother and daughter lounged around biting on this and that and leaving most of the food.

48

The bevies of silent standing maids were treated as completely invisible.

'Angela is a bit special,' her mother stated, ignoring a maid standing almost behind her, ready to frisk away her teacup or anticipate any sudden desire for food, 'I am *so* glad you are helping her through school. We tried home tutors, they got nowhere. We're hoping that she might get her diploma. *Where* are *you* going to college? Maybe with my daughter?'

Katya was disconcerted to discuss such personal matters in front of a large silent audience.

She changed the subject, pointing to a fine Rembrandt, a rotund lady bathing. Jan would not allow such a painting in the house, but she knew grandmamma Rebecca would love it.

'Oh that,' Angela pronounced 'isn't it Elizabeth 1 of England!'

The original Rembrandt in no way resembled the Tudor style, Katya pointed out.

'Of course, Rembrandt, the French king, or was he cardinal?' Angela replied.

'I do so admire Rembrandt,' said Katya, hastily changing the subject.

The countess smiled pityingly.

'It has been in the family a long time. Look around if you like.'

Her arm swept broadly over the extensive mansion.

She did not notice or regard the treasures around them. Paintings hung askew, and the great master was slightly damaged by damp.

*

The Grand Countess Liana of the House of Dobrowski had an arrogant drawl and talked with authority about matters of which she had the most ephemeral knowledge.

When she heard that Katya had been taken to the Louvre as part of her art education she discussed the contents of that museum with the ineptitude of true ignorance.

At some level she must have been aware of the critical looks of her guest, because she changed the subject. She began to speak of her innate connection to the land; money just appeared. Aristocracy were defenders of culture and people; an example of 'nobility', the meaning of which was never crystal clear.

49

*

Looking at the countess, Katya could not help respecting her grandmother a great deal more.

Rebecca Braun was a tall elegant and beautiful woman who only ever spoke with authority on subjects she knew. She was lively and beautiful and always polite. She treated her servants with respect, and expected excellent service in return.

And yet she was considered an inferior creature, a Jew. If the two ever met the countess could easily have been mistaken for a money lenders wife, with her huge hooked nose and intrusive manners… while Rebecca looked every inch the aristocrat.

'As the youngest girl,' droned the old lady, 'little is expected of Angela. She is clumsy and graceless, lacking the perfect confidence needed for the true ruling class.'

Angela squirmed at having her faults discussed so openly. She was just another possession, a work of art.

Even faulty Angela was a treasure, continued her mother, 'she has great *sympathy* and makes friends with *anyone*' (she glanced at Katya speculatively) 'she is a kind child, with great understanding. Despite being one of the highest in the land, she has the *common* touch.'

She questioned Katya about her family and her grandparents.

Of course she had *heard* of Maslow, and industrialist, she said portentously; she understood that industry was a necessary evil and sighed deeply.

'Our *people* need to reach out to the *world*.' Every word she spoke was heavily emphasised, as if just by saying it she had added extra meaning.

She talked of her sons; *geniuses* and *leaders*.

Katya was to meet these paragons. The countess hoped that Izaak would *do* something for them.

The young men turned up late.

They were typical arrogant aristocratic males, who sauntered along the boulevards of Warsaw and completely ignored Katya at balls.

The eldest arrived at the little tea party, dressed for the street in the latest fashions with a twirling moustache.

He put his feet on the exquisite chair before him. Servants scurried about as he stuffed several sandwiches into his thatched face.

He asked his mother for a huge sum of money. They argued loudly and he took a lesser sum and hurried off.

He had completely ignored her visitor, rightly considering her a bourgeois nonentity.

The younger brother Leszek arrived shortly after. Was he going to ask for money too?

He was a good-looking, vacuous young man; he stared at Katya appreciatively, bowed to her and drawled,

'Charming, Angela, bring more friends home, darling. Do.' He winked at the young girl, who blushed fiery red.

Katya had never been addressed as charming before. She was secretly highly flattered, and fantasized that he wanted to meet her again.

13.

Tseder 1935

Rebecca was waiting at the Maslow residence when Katya returned. By dint of close questioning she managed to extract every piece of information about that illustrious tea time.

Rebecca was delighted at the friendship between Angela and Katya. She was hoping to gain an entrée to that exclusive enclave. The Dobrowkis were among the few houses in the land that owed their titles to the Hapsburgs. Between them, those five or six families owned most of Poland.

'So,' she muttered, 'Angela is to go to the same university?'

She took this in and agreed to consider it.

Katya could see she was making plans.

As to the 'genius boys', Rebecca huffed sharply.

'Poor Izaak!' she complained. 'Every week some useless fellow approaches him and offers to act as director of his many enterprises. Beggars the lot of them - and useless! Izaak would happily take them on if they did any work!'

She smiled triumphantly. It was a great start to her re-born social ambitions. Even the countesses needed her.

She was satisfied with her first social skirmish, conducted through third parties as it was.

'What is the countess like? Is she beautiful? Elegant?' she demanded.

Katya thought of the disdainful countess, who moved among hundreds of servants, drawn from family estates. She did not even bother to learn about the treasures which littered her residence.

'Not really,' replied Katya. 'She is not as beautiful, well-dressed, or even as nice as you.'

Rebecca smirked in a self-satisfied way. This time Katya was not flattering her grandmother. Rebecca really was cleverer, and far more intelligent.

*

Several weeks later Angela rushed into the school to tell his tale.

'Listen everybody, guess what?'

Nobody much heard.

'Oh come on,' she spoke more loudly. 'I have some news!'

She acquired an audience of a few girls and huddled close to them.

'Leszek killed himself last weekend; He broke up with his girlfriend two weeks ago. He threw stones at her window pane in the night, and when she opened it, he blew his brains out in front of her.'

A few girls came closer, and for the next couple of breaks the on-going discussion centred on stories of cousins, uncles and even brothers who had committed suicide for no good reason.

There was usually a highly romantic tale: love lost, or money gambled away.

The wealthy aristocrats had sustained extensive losses during the depression.

White Russians princesses reported huge fortunes and land mismanaged and lost.

They had all grown up with tragedy. Suicides, accidental death and shootings of brothers and cousins, were debated with an insouciance which made Katya certain that wealth healed everything.

'My brother committed suicide at 16,' confessed a young beauty. 'He had got one of the servant girls pregnant. Mama and papa declared she was a wicked tart - so he hanged himself.'

Katya was mesmerised. It sounded futile and nihilistic.

That night, she wept over Leszek, her lost-almost-love. It seemed that here suicide was a spiffing romantic tale.

'The duke's son has just committed suicide,' they gossiped. 'He had unpaid gambling debts and so drove his Bugatti off the bridge on the family estate. His papa was furious because the car hadn't been paid for!'

They laughed at his shameful death, and treated it as heroic.

Katya was shocked and jealous.

She enjoyed a lifestyle which most would accept as wealthy and easy, though her large Warsaw apartment was run with only two resident servants (the shame), and the children had to share skis and tennis rackets.

Mother would sometimes iron the boy's uniform before school.

On the servant's day off they secretly cooked their own evening meal.

The crass superiority of the schoolgirls around her made her increasingly covetous.

She saw, at first hand, the hierarchy which blocked movement between castes and stifled change.

She hated the aristocracy, and the stuffy formal rigour of daily life at Tseder. She loathed the Catholics, who yearly made her pray for the Jews. She felt every injustice to minority peoples, and sympathised with the Soviets across the borders, who declared religion to be the opium of the masses.

She flourished away from home.

*

She was soon the school's star pupil. The Brauns encouraged her to study engineering and work for their factories. She was guaranteed a university scholarship.

Izaak adored all his large diverse family and saw himself as producing a great dynasty.

He even helped Irma, Sofia's step-daughter, by contributing to a new medical school. He paid for tutors and music lessons. He funded their holidays in the mountains. Rebecca coached them and watched over them. They occasionally attended synagogue with him and attended their cousins' lavish bar mitzvah parties.

Life was looking up.

14.

Lucia Orloska

Katya observed Lucia Orloska with growing envy. She never seemed to work or study and gained praise for her neat work.

Katya's writing was spidery. Lucia's was rounded and beautiful, and much admired, even though her spelling was not so good.

Lucia was one of the elite at the school, titled and of pure blood.

She was a true Orloska, daughter of the great, impoverished House Orloski, one of the six great families.

She looked Eastern European and had her mother's high Tartar cheekbones and her father's blond colouring. She had mousy coloured hair which had clearly been bleached to blond since the roots showed through regularly.

Katya's colouring could best be described as drab.

Lucia was charming. She was invited everywhere, and was always at the centre of fun.

Younger girls crowded round her and asked her stupid stuff like how she did her hair.

She was likely to be the next head girl, an honour she laughingly despised, although it was something which would have made the entire Braun family almost burst with pride.

Everyone had heard of the Orloski palace Louvinka and its huge estates (except Katya, but she wasn't *anyone*.).

The immense Orloski estate was populated by Ukrainian peasants, Protestant Germans (who had lived there for centuries), Jews, and a few Poles.

They had been a great family, with and illustrious military history, but the Depression hit the family hard and her father struggled to find a dowry for his only daughter.

*

That summer Lucia returned to Louvinka to find the whole family languishing in an unusual heat wave. The huge windows of the palace heated the place up unbearably.

The place still looked wonderful all the same, although the army barracks were getting a little dilapidated.

The Orloskis of long ago had one had their own standing army, though now the huge barracks were used as servants' quarters and storerooms for ancient furniture.

The main palace, which had been constructed on the labour of legions of serfs, was still in excellent repair, furnished with antique Oriental and Eurasian artefacts pillaged from retreating armies in ancient battles.

The family still owned the local town and villages which had been entirely reconstructed in the 18th century to match the main palace.

Lucia sat next to her mother, Princess Maria Kamienska-Orloska.

The two looked very alike.

*

Maria was the same age as Sofia. But the two did not look at all similar. Sofia's forehead was lined with worry; while Maria's easy life meant her face was smooth and held on to its youthful calm.

The princess was tall and elegant with thick blond hair. Beside her, her dumpy husband looked like a country bumpkin.

Princess Maria had brought substantial wealth into the Orloski family, in the form of jewels and gold pillaged from Lithuania when her family abandoned the country during the revolution. Her parents owned a small palacio in Italy where they hoarded what remained of their vast wealth before the revolution.

Twenty years ago Maria had fallen for handsome Peter Orloski on his grand tour. He was ancient nobility (looters and rapists to the last man).

Like most women with spirit, she was hoping to achieve something in the world and saw herself as Brunhilde[1], a warrior heroine who would save her country and her people.

Peter Orloski spouted a lot of nationalist nonsense about ruling the land. He claimed to be bonded with the earth by blood and would fight for it with every drop of his own.

Maria was seduced by his fighting talk, and his stolid self-belief. She saw a great future, a return to her Russian heritage on a white charger, a saviour of her family.

*

---

[1] In German myth Brunhilde was a female warrior, one of the Valkyrie

The marriage was not a success.

Count Peter Orloski was boor-like and almost preternaturally stupid. He had very few ideas which he repeated endlessly, mostly about his right to rule.

What had Maria seen in him? He had seemed so strong to her in her Italian haven and going back to Eastern Europe seemed so romantic! It wasn't long before she realised that his tutors had dinned a few simple concepts into his thick head and then given up.

He loved his country home and was amazed that his wife was bored. He had heard about Hitler's eugenics programme, and believed his family to be pure-blooded Aryans. He molested his peasants' pretty daughters, regarding his seed as a gift to the populace.

*

In those days, divorce was out of the question. Maria had made the best of her marriage.

Unlike Sofia, she had enough of her own money to be independent of her husband. She and count Peter lived in separate apartments in the echoing halls of the cavernous castle.

Like Sofia, she devoted herself to her offspring. She dreamed that her children would achieve the fame and the kudos which she craved. Her daughter would be a great heroine, and her sons would be young Tolstoys.

However, she had other interests: her horses and her estate. With a large part of her fortune, she had converted the slightly dingy castle into a glittering Romanov extravagance.

Horses were her chief hobby. She venerated horses, and kept several breeds on her stud, including Przewalski ponies[2]. She wore fashionable riding habits of military cut, and occasionally made society pages in foreign newspapers as 'White Russian Princess Kamienska-Orloska'.

Every year, horses from her stables entered important race meetings as far away as East Germany. The princess had refined the state's breeding stock, breeding racing horses in a model stud farm,

---

[2] A miniature horse native to the steppes and an endangered species in the wild.

which she maintained from her own income. There was a large picture of a startled racing horse on the wall of their drawing room. It had come second in a major race.

She often travelled with her horses and always kept in touch with their trainers. If she could afford to go to the racing meets she strode around the paddocks, smoking like a chimney (a sign of suffragette tendencies).

*

Sadly, she rarely travelled lately. The children were extremely expensive and she and Count Peter had wasted most of her huge fortune on poorly planned projects.

She had dreams of being a great reformer, just to show those Bolsheviks what an aristocrat could achieve. She had goaded her rather dim and irascible spouse to create a modern infrastructure for the town of Louvinka.

The locals wanted gas, trains, buses, roads, and modern items like public telephones and she could deliver.

She was the driving force behind several grand modernisation projects, basing her knowledge on light reading of the newspapers, and visits to Germany.

*

Neither she nor count Orloski had any idea what to do, but they had the arrogance to attempt titanic projects without bothering to understand them.

'Just do it!' Peter ordered the engineers. 'I will pay.'

He dealt with the problems by blustering at his subordinates.

'Make it work. How hard can it be?' he bluffed.

He had no administrative skills, yet insisted on directing. He refused the advice of clever 'new' men and wasted huge fortunes on projects which went bankrupt.

Electrification was one.

His architect designed a generator for the centre of town.

'It must look like this!' insisted the count. 'It must have the family crest and is to be called the Orloski Generator, an example of progress for future generations.'

The architect had no real idea of the buildings' purpose, and did not care anyway.

The structure proved too small for the generators and there was no route for the cables to leave the station.

The company went bankrupt.

Then German and Jewish businessmen bought the heaped materials for a song.

They built a generator on wasteland near the river which Peter sold cheaply. The new company realised lavish profits.

Count Peter saw it as conspiracy, and was antagonistic to every innovation. He complained of telegraph poles across his land, objected to reservoirs, and charged rent for cabling. He refused to release land for freight, and overcharged on timber.

Generally, he impeded rather than promoted change.

*

The central building had stood empty, a massive waste of money and time for several years before finally it was purchased, for a song, and used as a head office for the electricity board.

Jurek, the eldest boy had just been offered board membership on the Electricity Company. He was needed to act as facilitator in disputes between their Count and the new bourgeoisie.

He had agreed to the sinecure, in the face of opposition from Count Peter, who threw him out of the room when he first heard of it. It was a drama which starred their mother, who calmed things down with promises of money and gifts.

She had scrimped and saved for her daughter to go to Tseder and planned her education right through to university.

Peter, who had never been to university himself, was astonished. 'Why? There's nothing useful to learn there.'

'How will she marry if she doesn't go to Warsaw University?' remonstrated Maria. 'Who is to see her here? And I cannot afford to go to Warsaw myself to supervise her debut,' she shuddered. 'I would have to meet countess Dobrowska,' (her rival in rank and status and therefore a sworn enemy) 'and I don't have a *thing* to wear!'

Peter was silent. None of the seven platitudes he relied on precisely fitted as an answer to this rhetorical question.

'And *where* could we stay? The damned woman owns half of Warsaw Square. And *we* have *rented* out our house.'

She looked at Peter significantly. It was his fault that they had so little money….

Peter had a bright idea.

He started to say, 'the countryside.'

'Yes dear, yes, yes,' interrupted his wife, 'just as entertaining as the town.'

She ignored this irrelevance.

'Much worse,' she continued, 'our palace there is *smaller*! Who cares what we have here? Our palace in Warsaw is *tiny*.'

She shivered at the potential for losing her status.

She kissed Peter on the forehead. He was miles away.

'Hmm dear?' he mumbled. He was thinking about visiting one of his peasants, old Borlow, who, he heard, had a pretty young daughter.

'I'll look through my finances again. Lucia will stay with her aunt in Warsaw next summer and she'll study history of art at Warsaw University School of Art.'

Peter opened his mouth to speak.

'My mind is made up.'

His wife swished off to her beautiful Austrian desk.

Shortly after, Peter whistled for his dogs and set off for the village.

*

Summer was a great time for Maria, when Lucia was at home and her beloved sons came to visit.

At Tseder her illustrious parentage gained her admiration. Unfortunately she had to stay with an aunt in Warsaw while at school to save money.

She had been invited to stay with friends in Berlin over the summer, but her mother was at her wits end as to how to keep her daughter decently attired. She returned to the palace to save money.

Maria listened avidly to her daughter's tales of what the girls wore.

'How do they afford it?' she wailed.

The same story was being repeated in every home that summer; the girls instinctively knew how competitive their mothers were, and always exaggerated.

*

The boys were at the palace too, if only for a couple of weeks. They had run out of money and come home for more.

The pair were on the Italian leg of their grand tour with their mother's relations. They had brought back poorly-chosen *objets d'art* for their darling mother.

The spent the visit pacing the huge salons and describing Fascist Nationalism in heroic terms.

Maria was suitably impressed.

'Jurek,' Maria advised her oldest son, kissing him lightly on the cheek. 'Write down those grand ideas you have.'

'I don't have time mother.'

'You will, I have been saving up some money and there is same arable land we've put by. You must build a model farm here, I will pay for it.'

Her son twitched his collar arrogantly.

Of course, he *could* do that, he preferred to stalk about Italy with the Facsisti[3].

'Yes, mama, I will do it in time.'

(Tolstoy sounded like a boring old fool, who did not know how much fun there was to be had flirting in drawing rooms and talking political matters.)

*

The family sat in the large tea room with the huge windows open.

The huge park was totally deserted. The gardeners had all finished work on the parterres early in the morning so as not to disturb the family.

The crystals in the gigantic chandeliers twinkled rainbow colours on the damasked walls.

*

Later that day, Maria took her daughter round their great estate. She had to learn how to manage a palace and its environs.

Part of the training involved visiting the peasants. Maria complained that her daughter, like her brothers, was always short of

---

[3] A right wing group led by Mussolini who believed Italy to be the resurgent Roman Empire

money.

'Mama,' Lucia grumbled. 'You give all your money to Jurek. I couldn't even go to the pastry shop last week of term. I have only ever been there once. And the cakes are *delicious*.'

She spent the rest of the day describing them to explain how she was being deprived.

Maria sighed.

They were being driven to the village.

'Angela has a Bentley,' Lucia whined. 'And we are still using this old thing.'

The 'old thing' was a fairy tale carriage, emblazoned and crested and upholstered in pale blue velvet.

'The Bentley has a *fan*.'

Maria changed the subject. 'Old Bogdan was asking after you'.

She sighed. They *all* wanted more money.

'You know I wish you could take some wisdom from our people,' she suggested. 'They live hard lives, yet suffer none of our existential angst. They respond to seasons and weather, and their spare time is occupied by procreation and festivals to mark the seasons. They live and die without question.'

The princess occupied the long boring days of summer by listening to their stories and judging their disputes. Their stoic suffering never ceased to impress.

Old ladies did not linger; Maria always told strangers with admiration.

'If they are no longer fit for work they just walk out into the snow.'

Maria told her daughter about old Etta who died last winter. Did Lucia remember her?

She didn't.

Maria had brought some of her best herbal medicine to the sick old lady, only to find the cottage, more like a barn, was being emptied and cleared. Where was old Etta?

'Dead,' Etta's son informed her 'She lost her husband and youngest son last winter. It was for the best.'

She had dragged out her chair and was found seated in it knotting a fringe, frozen to death. At 44, she looked 70.

Part 2.

Occupation

No psychopathic leader ever claimed to represent evil

They use religion or political creed to excuse their actions.

Superficially, they act in the name of good, for the good of the people.

They cannot lead without followers. A large portion of the population has to agree with them.
Large numbers of people are needed to carry out their policies.
They succeed because they have myriad followers.

1.

Warsaw 1939:

Izaak worried about the anti-Semitic content of Germany's words, and advised emigration.

The Germans were confiscating Jewish property and rounding up German Jews His German factories had been impounded.

'We left Russia, Sofia,' he warned his daughter. 'This is the same, only worse, because *we* are the enemy, not the aristocracy,' he advised.

He held out a newspaper, admittedly a rag for the working classes, barely literate.

'Jewish man rapes young girls,' howled the headlines.

According to the lurid tale, a Jew was purposely attempting to dilute pure Aryan blood.

It was complete rubbish. No one could credit such nonsense.

Sofia wouldn't hear of departure. She had been 10 when they fled Russia and the trauma of that period was still with her.

She would not impose exile on her family like Izaak had done. She asked her children what they wanted to do.

Janek was doing so well too.

At 20, Izaak had obtained her eldest child Janek an excellent post as assistant post master in the Warsaw post office.

Janek was a nationalist and did not think of departure. Casimir, the younger of the two, had already joined the army.

*

By June 1939, many of the heroic Polish aristocrats, who had been talking so bravely of resistance, started slipping away to France.

Izaak organised the dispersal of the whole family. He had transferred large sums to banks all over Europe and had a large Swiss bank account. He had gold, jewels, and paintings stored in every country and apartment.

His oldest son Izaak Jr. was in Austria, managing vast factories which provided army uniforms and accoutrements. His second son, David, promised to look after their business interests in Poland and

Austria from Hungary.

Izaak persuaded Sofia that staying in Warsaw to face the threatened German invasion was foolhardy.

'If you *have* to stay Sofia...'

Jan looked at his mother and interrupted.

'She does, she really does. Think of Katya and Anya, still at school. What will happen to their education if they start gadding about Europe?'

He had taken to puffing a pipe and blew clouds of white smoke everywhere. He sat authoritatively in a large armchair and puffed again.

'We will be quite safe,' he said wisely, 'I will look after mama and the girls.'

He was not going to give up his superior post and all that he had achieved. Post masters were safe!

'Then,' sighed Izaak, thinking how like his father the boy was, 'I have arranged a transfer to Lvov, I have a large apartment there as you know Sofia. You can use it until we return. And I can arrange a transfer to the Lvov Post Office too.'

Jan bridled up. He was a highly self-important young man and had a strong sense of dignity like his papa.

Izaak had planned for this. 'It is a slightly junior post but *better paid*,' he added. '*And* it is the central post office for the whole of Lviv, not a sub post office as you are working here.'

Rebecca knew the weaknesses of her grandson too. 'The apartment is far *grander* than this one,' she chimed in sweetly, knowing that it would make no difference to her daughter but a huge difference to her prideful grandson.

'It is frightfully grand.'

Jan allowed himself to be persuaded.

*

Izaak spent a further two weeks arranging his affairs. Just before Sofia left for Lviv with her children, he and Rebecca took off for Paris with a huge wardrobe, several servants and three large limousines.

People spat on the entourage as they left.

'Cowards!' they yelled. Although it was mostly envy.

There was a quiet panic among the populace and offices in Warsaw were closing because so many workers disappeared.

*

Janek moved into the cosmopolitan, luxurious apartment and strutted into his new post.

As a key worker, he had not been conscripted. He was needed to maintain the country's infrastructure.

His mother trusted in god to keep the family safe and spent increasing amounts of time in church.

*

By mid-August, it was difficult to leave officially.

Resourceful people were still creeping away at night, using expensive underground networks run by gypsies who knew the border routes.

Two weeks before the invasion Sofia's nationalistic younger son Casimir deserted the army and joined Izaak in France.

He left his uniform in his mess and crossed the border dressed as a peasant. There were thousands of such peasants with him, many of whom wore business suits lightly covered by sheepskin coats and carried briefcases full of money bonds, and gold.

*

It was the first week of term at Tseder, and the girls knew that war was coming. Germany had already occupied Slovakia and Austria. Poland was next.

By this time most Poles were aware that they faced occupation and partition by both Russia and Germany.

The girls sat in school classrooms chatting in lugubrious tones, casting tragic poses and sighing deeply. They had little idea of war even though they had been trained as brave warriors' wives.

It was quite obvious that the struggle would be both bloody and hopeless. The girls ranted of war to the death, of women taking up arms to defend their lands. All of their plans were suicidal and harebrained.

'We can drive tractors at the tanks, all of us,' they mused.

Katya listened and made ironic comments.

'Where would you find tractors in Warsaw?'

They were unfazed.

'Or taxis, or even horses and carts.'

They looked down on Katya. They disapproved. Her sarcastic comments were regarded as anti-nationalistic. She was suspected of being a fifth columnist.

Why was she a coward when even the Lithuanians and Ukrainians were prepared to fight! She was far too intelligent.

'We can never be defeated!'

'Death before dishonour!'

*

The tiny Polish army prepared for the worst. They paraded through the squares with the few horse drawn anti-aircraft guns.

The cavalry followed in their brightly polished armour and cuirasses looking very fine.

They were greeted with cheers.

*

In the event, that September in 1939, the depleted Polish Army, backed by volunteers and firemen, fought both Germans and Russian invaders in Warsaw.

It was a tragic massacre.

The German army was powerful, clean and highly disciplined. Massive tanks drove up narrow streets opening up the ground floor of Warsaw houses like tins of sardines.

Bombs rained down on civilians and soldiers alike.

There was hand to hand fighting in the streets.

*

Colonial rule was imposed on Western Poland. The German tongue was to be used in schools and offices.

The Eastern half of Poland was occupied by the Soviet army in a war to liberate the oppressed proletariat.

Those in Lvov trembled; they feared the worst.

The two dictators circled each other warily, waiting the moment for a final showdown.

Hitler offered the notion of superiority to the Aryan masses.

The soviets offered the proletariat revenge.

2.

Lvov November 1939

The Soviet army arrived in Lvov to free their half of the spoils for revolution.

They were less disciplined, definitely less clean, yet just as overpowering as the Germans.

Escape from the pincers of the two dictatorships was increasingly dangerous, and Poles skittered about at night in silence, moving valuables around the country, choosing which side would be safer.

The decision was complex and could be made on religious, ethnic and political lines.

Poland's large Socialist contingent had flown to Lviv, with high hopes of the new regime. The wary nationalists approved of the Soviet concept, so their resistance was not committed.

Most assumed that the army would not stay for long.

*

Janek was inexperienced and his office in Warsaw had been a bit of a sinecure.

However, as soon as the Soviets arrived, they removed all the senior staff form their posts as traitors to the revolution. He was the highest rank in the post office and felt seriously exposed. Now he was the acting head of the central post office in Lviv.

It was not easy to manage the post office. The staff looked to him for decisions. He blustered and shouted without having the slightest clue what to do.

'What should we do about these letters Mr Maslow?' asked a timid clerk.

'Do? Do what you always do!' he shouted. 'Am I to tell you everything?'

They soon learnt to ignore him.

A Soviet overseer was employed as Janek's junior. He was a friendly chap who asked a lot of questions. Janek rather liked him.

Had he but known it his crass inefficiency saved him from certain arrest.

*

For six months or so the residents managed well under their communist liberators.

The post office was busy and the staff were overworked. Everyone wanted to contact friends and family in various places and there were new stamps and new protocols to implement.

The invaders moved into an already overcrowded city. It had filled up with refugees encouraged by the notion of social justice as well as Jews fleeing German occupation. They had positive expectations of the Russian.

The soldiers were tall, good looking and highly disciplined. Their wives were desperately poor and uneducated. The men were clearly dumbfounded at the wealth around them. They looted, but for necessities.

The families of high ranking Russian soldiers moved into the best houses, claiming that they had been stolen from the people by the bourgeois. Within a week, the inhabitants of the large houses in Central Square had all been evicted.

Sofia and Janek spent a tense couple of weeks wondering if they were next. Fortunately there were plenty of huge aristocratic mansions far more desirable than their apartment block.

The Russian officers marched around in heavily decorated uniforms. They ogled at the humblest shops with awe, and picked over the simplest goods as if they were the finest money could buy at home.

Underwear was extremely popular as it was comfortable, fitted properly, and could be worn under the uniform. At one point, not a pair of long johns could be found in Lviv, until the clothing factories adapted to deal with the new demand.

Together with their great leader, they shared a love of opera. The first night at the reopened Lviv opera, four weeks after the invasion was an extraordinary sight. People with tickets of the expensive seats were turned away. The royal circle and boxes were occupied by elite army officers and their wives.

Officers' wives wore fancy nightdresses in the street matched with evening hats and mittens, and their husbands wore leather gloves indoors, just to show that they owned some. Officers proudly sported leather gloves and riding whips, or canes. Their wives were dressed in a collection of nightdresses, negligees and lace petticoats. They looked attractive enough.

Everyone in the cheap seats cooed with horror, they were in underwear!

The front page of the local newspaper proudly displayed a photograph of a general and his wife coming to the opera; she was wearing a negligee.

Reporters had a field day.

'Our Cultured Soviet brothers!' screamed the headlines.

Newspaper sales went through the roof.

'We always attend the Moscow opera,' the general informed the reporter, beaming at the camera. 'The Soviet people have the highest culture.'

Far less noticeable than the bluff peasant officers were the SSR[4] officials, civilian social engineers who were to arrange the revolution.

These were mostly tiny teenagers in ill-fitting suits; grey skinned and unhealthy from a life spent indoors. To them, the people were raw material for a utopian society which would take over the world.

These terrifying NKVD[5] officials aimed to revolutionise and reorganise the government structure rather than to steal.

Like all cults, they promised a good life, provided resistance was crushed. Communism would bring peace and happiness.

There were new passports, now protocols and massive corruption. The reorganisation of business had an equally pervasive effect.

The removal of food, shipped to Russia in prodigious quantities, soon had an impact on daily life.

The Soviet Revolution was a revolution on paper only. Revolution and idealism had long ago been replaced by a lust for power and control.

---

4 Soviet Socialist Republic

5 The NKVD (People's Commissariat for Internal Affairs) was a government department in the Soviet Union. It was the law enforcement agency which did the will of the All Union Communist Party. They mostly operated in secret and were greatly feared

Lenin's reformed party reneged on equality and justice, but remained ruthless oppressors for the cause.

They acted in the name of materialism and science, and were deeply suspicious of nature, beauty and happiness, suspecting them of counterrevolutionary tendencies.

Anyone with bourgeois jobs was at high risk of arrest and subsequent disappearance.

Fortunately, the Maslows status was defined by Janek, who was not an owner of means of production.

Simmering hatred between minorities was exploited to the full, presumably to divide the city and make it easier to control. It was already a hotbed of ancient vendettas, which were expressed in trivial matters such as hedges, and bins, unkind words about unruly children, as well as racial tensions and other disputes.

These arguments, simmering quietly behind net curtain and shutters, were now appeased in violence.

Mad and crackpot neighbours, who had been ignored for years, shot to stardom as street representatives. They strutted around, causing misery to those who had laughed at them.

Neighbours often scarcely understood each other's tongues.

For example, Old Mikhail lived on the ground floor of Sofia's apartments. He was an ancient Ukrainian policeman, and had the apartment on a low rent in exchange for cleaning duties and dealing with rubbish.

He spoke a heavy peasant Russki [6]which was difficult to understand.

He was grizzled and grey, dyed his hair an absurd black and sported a gigantic orange moustache. He was often drunk, and invasive of everyone's privacy.

He had long been obsessed that he owned the staircase to the apartments and that everyone needed to pay him rent for it.

He Janek had a row when they first arrived.

Janek had called him 'mental' to the sniggers of the neighbours eavesdropping from their doors.

---

[6] Russki was the language of the Ukraine.

Mikhail visited the Party Raikom [7] and was declared 'representative' of the block.

He knocked on doors at odd hours, and demanded that rubbish only be brought downstairs between the hours of 10.00 and 11.00 am.

No one was to tread on a large door mat he had placed outside his apartment, and he sent many notes about directives which did little other than cause intense inconvenience.

He was particularly spiteful to Janek, and frequently reprimanded him for spurious and invented transgressions.

One morning, they found a heap of potato peelings and stinking rubbish outside their door, which Mikhail claimed had been placed in the bins outside the proper hours.

'Mr Post Office Under-Master!' he declared, 'you are not above the law. These rules are for everyone's convenience. If this goes on, you will have to sit before a little tribunal we have devised here. It is for the good of all of us.' he smirked to himself, in a haze of authority.

He shuffled off, muttering darkly. 'We will reorganise this place in no time.'

The elite soon inspired terror in the populace. Resistance was properly categorised:

If it mentioned the past, it was counterrevolutionary

If it was intelligently argued, it was class enemies

If it came from the proletariat, it was a sign of insanity. Punishments were arranged accordingly: Class enemies to be re-educated; counter-revolutionaries to be utilised in projects to rebuild the country; insanity could be cured, if need be, in mental institutions.

*

Newspapers reported that a Ukrainian Soviet had been established by the will of the people.

No one had *voted* and there were no visible signs of a proletarian revolution, although senior officials had disappeared.

---

[7] District level representatives. They were apparently elected, but from within the party. Membership of the party was not automatic.

Over the next weeks there were carefully engineered signs of revolution, with some factories taken over by workers.

The papers showed photographs of workers in the grand boardrooms.

'Profits to go to the people,' trumpeted the banner headlines.

Newspapers showed cartoons of fat plutocrats stamping on the proletariat.

'Living of the fat of the land!' Was the caption

Such a seductive message was difficult and dangerous to counter.

*

Everywhere, denouncers were rewarded.

Malicious rumours were always acted on. There were summary executions for anti-revolutionary activity and people became wary of neighbours.

On top of all this, the economy was also seriously disrupted.

Wealthy citizens had to give up their businesses.

Gold and valuables were to be handed in to the party members at NKVD headquarters established in the Town Hall.

Silence spread to the streets, packed with refugees from Warsaw, the majority of them Jewish and socialist.

Greetings between friends and acquaintances were muted - anyone could be an informer. No one was sure what would be made of the most innocent conversation.

Cowering submission became the accepted stance close to any known secret police officer, and, indeed, any unknown individual.

Yet there was an effective bush telegraph, centred on the black market in the Lviv market square.

Stalls required permission from officials; and certificates were ostentatiously pinned to the barrows. These were carefully checked by patrolling soldiers at specific times.

Outside those times, there was a vibrant market selling all goods - for a price.

The black marketers, many of them gypsies, could disappear magically within minutes.

Gypsies had become the carriers of information and news. They were outside the system and mostly ignored.

'The mayor is dead,' they reported. 'Shot by firing squad.'

A gypsy ran his hand across his throat theatrically, 'in the river he went, yesterday 4.00 o'clock.'

The news echoed around the whole city within the hour.

The Polish officers had disappeared, apparently for re-education somewhere in Russia.

'Our officers have all been arrested and marched off,' whispered the bush telegraph.

How did they know?

Sofia crossed herself and thanked god that Casimir had gone with the Brauns.

'Watch out for the Town Hall. It is the new detention centre,' whispered mysterious voices. 'People are disappearing.'

It was common knowledge, almost as soon as it had been organised.

Individuals were spirited away for questioning, usually by night, in a storming visit which often woke everyone nearby. The home of the detainee would be sealed by the NKVD, cordoned off as 'under investigation'.

Fear of the invisible grew.

A family under investigation were living dead, and could not rely on support. Everyone avoided them, lest they fall under the shadow of the 'people's representatives'.

After a few days of social ostracism, a limousine would call for the 'enemies of the people' disappeared for re-education or on a Russian 'holiday' to Siberia.

How did this mysterious voice know so much?

'If they're not shot, they're being deported. Thousands are leaving for Siberia,' it reported.

No one believed it - at first.

Soon after, dead bodies floated down the Poltava River, horribly disfigured by torture.

The corpses achieved their aim, inspiring fear and establishing control.

Ukrainian SSR officials sped around the city in stolen limousines, confiscating entire buildings for official use.

People attempting escape were shot.

More apartments were requisitioned as the occupation took hold, the current occupants permitted to pack one suitcase each; under supervision in case valuables were removed. Many kept a suitcase packed in readiness, since those who left were given 15 minutes to depart.

Women no longer walked around wearing high fashion clothes, and teetering on high heels. This was prostitution.

They took to wearing black clothes and peasant kerchiefs covering their hair. They showed no anger at being roughly questioned or pushed aside, just hunched up like a peasant women.

'Comrade show some respect!' they whined in Russki, 'Show respect.'

*

Katya's education had been disrupted by the bombing of Warsaw.

Despite skipping the last year of schooling, she was well ahead of many girls, and started her first term at university at the age of sixteen. The university had closed for a while. A lot of its students had disappeared and it was glad of any new students.

Several professors had disappeared. Lectures were supervised and censors sat in the back of lectures and interrupted and corrected the teachers.

Katya sat in on her first engineering lecture which was on diesel engines.

The lecture began.

We will start by considering the Wankel engine,' the lecturer began, 'designed in Germany in...'

'I think you will find that the diesel engine was first discovered in St Petersburg,' the startled engineering lecturer was informed, 'it was stolen and renamed by German thieves.'

'Quite right!' the professor mumbled. He wasn't discussing the diesel. This was something he was not prepared to even mention... He went very red and the lecture petered out.

He shuffled his notes nervously. Most of his classes were about German engineering processes, and he had trained in Germany. He had no idea how to proceed.

There was a silence. He cogitated.

'I suggest we research the matter,' he declared at long last. 'I direct you to find references on the process in the library.' (He sincerely hoped that the books were still there, the collection of engineering texts at Lviv was second to none.) 'Long live the revolution!'

Lecturers self-edited their work at night. Students edited their answers.

Course works were checked and monitored.

The history department closed; its eminent professors disappeared.

Political education lectures were promised in the near future, attendance compulsory.

*

Despite the disruption and the misinformation, Katya enjoyed the first term at Warsaw University.

She had some happy notoriety as the youngest and cleverest girl in engineering.

She dutifully copied out everything, and rather enjoyed seeing the aristocratic girls humiliated.

As 'bourgeoisie', their work automatically failed. They were obliged to rewrite everything, with corrections dictated by a patient NKVD officer.

'You have been taught a lot of bourgeois pseudoscience and must unlearn it – fast.'

Whole subjects disappeared from the curriculum, and lecturers strove to catch up with the correct knowledge.

'Do you understand?' party officials asked them as they corrected their work. 'Is it clear now?'

They nodded miserably, knowing that they would be tested on it.

Most landowners had already been shipped out for re-education. Their families followed on later, exported for apprenticeship into peasant families in order to learn revolution.

The remaining aristocratic girls at university laboured under fear and grief. They bore their suffering with dignity and pride.

Only the bravest stayed on at college, living alone or with servants, or adopted by their house servants to evade deportation.

They assumed peasant names and affected common speech. They did not answer to words in French and avoided each other.

Katya would have informed on them. But she knew that informers were frequently 'asked' to report wider conspiracies.

They were provided with lists of suspects and what they said.

'I heard you say that comrade Stalin was mistaken', was a favourite.

'You denounced the glorious liberation as an invasion,' was another.

Everyone had to be circumspect.

Creative language, like 'Stalin is a pig', or 'Communists are retarded', was a death sentence for the informant, and resisting hints to incriminate innocent people risked deportation.

The most vindictive flourished, assisting at violent interrogations, and providing evidence of outrageous traitorous statements.

Katya was attracted to the ideology and impressed with the party officials, who commanded reverence and held so much power.

She would have scraped by through the war, but for Janek's betrayal.

3.

Lvov 1939

Janek had been head of the family since his father's death. He had a senior post at a very young age, albeit it was something of a sinecure. His role as under-assistant post master in Lviv kept the family safe.

The new government passports and protocols engendered massive work at the post office as well as corruption.

Janek had no idea what was happening, having been allowed to laze around in the larger Warsaw office. He had little experience and was too arrogant to ask for assistance. Nevertheless, he wore his civil service uniform with pride, with a slight tendency to strut.

He concentrated on his social life. He had a large number of connections, since he lacked deep-felt beliefs and agreed with everything. Deep beneath the bonhomie and friendliness, Janek suffered from a strong sense of injustice. He had obtained a relatively senior post by dint of his grandfather's influence and felt his workers lack of respect keenly.

Unknown to his doting mother, Janek had joined the Party as soon as the invaders had settled in. He foresaw a great future as a leader among the peasant folk.

His ambition had previously been hemmed in by his paltry talents, now it had few boundaries. He foresaw a high status in the occupation, playing an important role in the new regime.

His friendliness and easy going camaraderie reaped dividends with the commissars[8] and the staff treated him with fear and deference. As a progressive forward-thinker he agreed with all new orders, attended meetings and made enthusiastic noises for plans to censor and control opposition to revolution.

He was confident that a future proletarian revolution would bring peace and happiness to all. He agreed that the good life was round the corner, provided resistance to ideology was crushed.   SSR

---

[8] A commissar was a party official responsible for political education and organisation

officials were social engineers, and their methods justified by science. The people were raw material for a utopian society which would take over the world.

Janek supported all anti-individualist initiatives and agreed that it was necessary to root out the weeds in order to grow a better harvest. He was persuaded by the allure of universal tolerance, free love, and complete equality, never once considering how it culled those who were too clever of too stupid to fit into the norm. Above all, he believed that he had met his mother's high-minded aims. He felt he could tangibly change the world for the better.

However, within months, there was a change in the atmosphere at the Post Office. Janek's job, which he had done badly and with little faith, was now a sinister series of meetings with commissars who expected him to rubber stamp changes which were morally abhorrent and frightening.

Secret police were openly aggressive and intrusive.

Mail was opened and read, denunciations and arrests were common.

A visit to the post office was openly observed by secret police, who would ask what the visitor was doing, and sometimes open mail as it passed across the counter.

All post office savings accounts were closed; then reopened with strictly limited withdrawals, accounts were capped and savings simply melted away. Anyone who started questioning what had happened to their money was taken to a small office and questioned about its origins as a class traitor.

Janek would wring his hands greasily, as he invented new lies to improve his status, hiding the bitter compromises which he made daily.

'Times are changing, you know,' he explained unctuously, 'we need to move forward with to a glorious future.'

Every day he returned home and had a long bath, feeling that befouled by the decisions he had apparently made.

*

'Comrade, we need to open all letter to seek out class enemies. Please sign this directive.'

Or

'Comrade, you must fire comrade Liskaya, she has refused to give us the keys to the safe.'

Or

'Comrade, we must burn these empty parcels, they did not contain anything.'

The commissars were threatening and intrusive, and only his innate arrogance pulled him through day by day.

His strutting increased. He was part of an ethical revolution, and boasted that those who had oppressed the people should feel justifiably afraid. Membership of the party allowed Janek to feel superior to his mother. He deceived himself that tyrannical and oppressive measures were the key building blocks for a new society.

His mother prayed at him, to his intense annoyance, and he started to shout at his sisters, who merely made faces behind his back.

*

The looting of food, shipped to Russia in prodigious quantities, soon had an impact on daily life.

The spacious apartment, abandoned by Izaak, was full of antiques and well-chosen collector's items, jade, crystal, old masters and Faberge pieces.

Sofia forbade him to touch anything - it was not his. Yet, as the city returned to a barter economy, Janek removed small pieces and sold them at the black market in the fine old square.

Whenever he took something he would address his mother with deep hypocrisy.

'Mama, we do not need this vulgar gem studded cigarette case. What is it doing here? I am selling it. We need to eat!'

'Darling Janek,' she implored. 'You cannot take these things, they are not ours.'

He blustered, while his mother gently mentioned that selling it was theft. Yet she always made excuses for him. She had no control over her son, a legacy of old Jan's constant denigration.

*

The inhabitants of Lviv had been ordered to hand in gold, bonds and valuables to the NKVD.

Most had; a few used their hoards to escape. Those caught were

80

hung outside NKVD headquarters as a warning.

The Brauns had left money and bonds in a safe, hidden behind under a fake Rembrandt painting.

Sofia was adamant that the safe was not theirs to open, or to use. Only she knew the combination and she was confident that it would remain until her parents returned.

Janek viewed the unopened safe with annoyance. It was his emergency fund and he boasted that it contained a vast hoard.

*

The Party faithful did not care for individuals and would have been ashamed to feel kindness for Janek. People were buildings blocks to revolution. They took him out for vodka and blinis. They picked the drunken sot's brains for every word of gossip picked up at social gatherings. Their mark told them all about his mother, sisters and the safe.

More seriously, he described the growing resistance, letters being sent in code via the post office, and the escape of Jews. He was a mine of information, and they guessed the rest, based on his lists of attendees at each gathering, his contacts among the socialists the national socialists, and the names of key Jewish fundamentalists in Lviv.

Thus it was that, seven months into the occupation, the family fortunes changed irrevocably. The commissars had known about the safe from the first drunken session, when he confessed his resentment of his mother's stupid religious conscience.

'Grandfather is immensely wealthy,' he blithered. 'He left a fortune in the safe. Mama won't let us touch it. She has scruples. It belongs to us – and if you break into it we will donate some to the state of course.'

He had to be carried home.

They squeezed out the last morsel of information before pouncing.

The next day after work, he was arrested sober at the bar, before drop of vodka passed his lips. They needed him clear-headed. That awful night, Janek did not return. His mother stayed up, resolving to approach the NKVD for news in the morning.

He returned early in the morning, brushing off concerns. He was

81

moving into a new apartment with his Russian fiancée, daughter of an officer in the Russian forces.

He packed his case in a hurry, refusing all assistance, to the bemusement of his mother, who had not met his bride to be

4.

Paris December 1939

Izaak was embittered at his reception in Paris, the cultural capital of Europe.

He had been a man of immense power, and the future seemed to be under his complete control.

Unbelievably, everything had disintegrated almost overnight.

The Brauns had once been recognised and invited everywhere, now everything changed.

Izaak spoke excellent accent-less Polish, French with a Polish accent, Russian, German and Yiddish. He regarded himself as European and employed anyone who was qualified and never discriminated.

He and Rebecca were a handsome pair, dark haired and grey eyed. Their two good-looking sons had partner businesses in Hungary, Austria, Ukraine, and Germany. Only Sofia was a disappointment. They enjoyed the multiracial nature of Eastern Europe, which *was* multiracial. They were always ready to move, or change, believing in the myth of the wandering Jew.

Izaak had been thinking of retiring and writing a book on the Jewish contribution to banking in the Middle-Ages.

If pressed over his faith he would explain that he believed that Jews were slightly superior to the rest, having heard the word of god first. He suspected that Jews basked in god's favour and were natural leaders of civilisation. He was tolerant of different styles of worship - until Sofia had adopted Catholicism, when he realised that such broad-mindedness had strict limits.

*

The change had been imperceptible. Krystalnacht had given him pause.

His oldest son still lived in Austria but had clung on. He had a thriving factory and would not let it go.

By 1939 they had heard nothing of him. He had sent one alarming letter in code.

'Do not return.'

Izaak made great efforts to get him out of Austria, without success so far.

Izaak had moved large sums of money in bonds, diamonds and gold. His investment in paintings and antiques were also part of his hedge fund. Each of his apartments had a safe containing cash, diamonds and gold in case of emergencies.

They resided in Paris, expecting their sons and daughter to join them if the situation degenerated any further.

It had.

From the apartment of the most expensive hotel in Paris, they incredulously observed the collapse of civilisation.

His younger son David had only just escaped Hungary and was on his way, disguised as a peasant.

Just before Poland fell, his Christian grandson passed through the hotel and, as an army officer, moved easily to join the allied forces regrouping in England.

Their meeting was cold and brief; Casimir did not want to draw attention to his Jewish ancestry.

'We will see you when this is all over,' he assured their grandparents, insincerely.

He did not contact them again; which was a sobering experience.

As this elegant and cultured couple moved around Paris, they became acutely aware of anti-Semitism. People looked at them askance.

'Waiter!' Arrogant rich young Germans would call, 'this place is not clean. I must move.'

5.

Louvinka November 1939

Taking over an entire country takes time. And intimidation.

Louvinka was deep into the countryside and it was not until November that the Russians arrived there.

Tseder had closed, and Lucia was staying with her parents when the invaders arrived in the village.

Her father attempted to raise a militia to fight an overpowering army of 20 or so well-armed soldiers without success.

The aristocracy had subjected the area to vendettas, massacres, and pogroms over the centuries and he had little positive support.

On the contrary, the peasants had great sympathy for the tenets of communism and did not believe the stories of famine and oppression in the new Soviets.

The local businessmen had heard the stories of large-scale industrial projects bringing Russia into the modern age and were enthusiastic.

Almost everyone was optimistic about the new regime.

As a result the old man attacked the army alone, using the sword his ancestors had used against heretics.

He was knocked out and slightly wounded by a gigantic soldier, then marched off to the tiny prison in the village for trial.

The Count had maintained his country's honour - but his arrest was popular among the populace.

*

The defeat of the irascible aristocrat caused chaos in the Louvinka.

His wife and servants expected to be raped and murdered by the second. Family and servants spent a terrifying night in the palace, making unrealistic plans to defend themselves, hide, or die in glory.

Princess Maria realised that she was going to be captured by the Soviets and relived the terrors of her childhood when the family fled the revolutionaries at their home in Lithuania.

She had been lonely and isolated in marriage, and had few emotional resources. The trauma of travelling through First World

War battlefields to reach a safe haven in Italy returned.

She locked herself in her closet with her jewellery and clothes.

The closet had a secret passage to the outside.

She was ready to die by poison, using arsenic hidden in a fine jewelled ring on her finger.

Her personal maid stayed by her, ready to lay out the countess in a glorious death.

The remaining servants turned to Lucia for direction.

The young girl, left to deal with the invaders, prepared to die gracefully, wearing her grandest ball dress, an antique tiara and her mother's lavish family diamonds.

The knock came early in the morning, before she was quite ready.

The servants did not answer the door.

Several had fled with money and bonds. The rest were locked away in their quarters, accompanied by ample supplies of food and spirits. They were alternately gossiping and sobbing in the great kitchens, as they got drunk and discussed which valuables were rightfully theirs.

Lucia had hidden a knife and pistol in her corsage, and they were already proving immensely uncomfortable. She intended to kill herself in the manner of an operatic heroine.

She struggled with the massive door which was embarrassing - she did not know how to open her own front door!

She finally wrenched it open. It was heavy and she was sweating slightly.

A pleasant young commissar stepped into the house. He was tall, good-looking and well spoken.

'Good day comrade,' hailed the young man. 'I will sit down if I may'

'And you can sit too.' He added politely.

Lucia was disarmed by his use of the polite forms and his gentle, non-aggressive manner.

'Are you the current occupier of this property?' he enquired.

Powerful soldiers stood to attention outside, completely obedient to a man not much older than her.

He sat down in the hall way, where it was normal for the servants to sit waiting for callers and to take their coats, and waited for her to speak.

He sat in silence.

After a short time, she broke.

'Perhaps you would like to come in?'

The young man gestured for the soldiers to sit in the hallway chairs and entered the reception area.

Lucia had never noticed how glittering it was. Her home was full of lavish Italianate ornamentation, glorious chandeliers. There were huge gilt mirrors everywhere, fine paintings and gorgeous trinkets on every available surface.

'May I ask to what reason we have the honour of this call from the Soviets?' she asked. 'This is a sovereign country.'

She hoped that her words sounded sufficiently brave and dignified. They emanated from an overdressed 16 year-old, who was aghast at the sight of heavily armed soldiers.

'Well, young comrade,' stated the man both smugly and sweetly.

He mixed the deferential forms used by the peasantry, with lordly imperatives. 'It is excessively kind of you to ask.'

He lolled in a comfy and magnificent armchair. 'I have to inform you that there has been a revolution,' he explained, hands in pockets. 'The people now rule this demesne. It is part of the Ukrainian Soviet.'

There was a pause.

He looked around distastefully at the brilliant and sparkling decor.

His attention was diverted by a tiny paper knife embellished with diamonds and rubies. Her mother used it to open invitations from neighbours in the presence of their maids.

He inspected it and pocketed it carefully.

Lucia tried to appear disapproving and dignified at this open theft.

She managed sulky.

'This house is requisitioned for the new Soviet,' he stated. 'As from now.'

He handed her a paper printed entirely in Cyrillic. Then he gestured to the soldiers outside and they marched into the room.

'Put up the notice outside,' he ordered. The soldiers stamped, saluted, and left.

'Please comrade.' He perused his notes, 'Orloska,' he read.

He smiled triumphantly. 'You will need to vacate these premises for the Soviet.'

He got up and waved across the room.

'All this now belongs to the People.'

Lucia looked through the expansive windows, and noticed with horror that the soldiers had brought a large wooden notice board covered in Cyrillic and Latin scripts.

She could not see it properly but imagined it stated something like 'Headquarters of the New Government'.

He faced the window and watched the men at work, digging up the magnificent parterre and completely ignoring Lucia.

Then he turned around, and slid her mother's ornate desk into the corner, moving some easy chairs around it.

He walked around the room whistling, picking up this and that, opening their visitors' book and reading the entries carefully.

He set what he wanted on his new desk. He sat down, got up, picked up the ormolu mantel clock and moved it to the desk to see if it improved the space.

He decided against it.

Lucia huffed like a spoilt child and tapped her foot angrily.

'This is *our* house,' she remonstrated. 'You can't just *take* things. It's theft.'

She tried for dignity. It did not come out as she had intended. She just sounded petulant.

The commissar wagged his finger at her like a child.

'I am afraid you are wrong, comrade Okinska.' She assumed he got her name wrong on purpose, 'It was never yours. You stole it from the people.'

He walked towards her; she immediately backed away, hampered by her sweeping crinoline skirts.

He loomed over her.

'Tell me,' he challenged, aggressively, 'did you make this clock? Or this knife?'

He pulled the knife out of his pocket. It clearly appealed to him a great deal.

'Tell me comrade, what is it that you *do*?'

Lucia stared at him, wind taken out of her sails.

'Do you manufacture this – decoration?' he looked around him and then down at her, and she was almost six feet tall.

'I am a student,' she stammered at last.

'And what do you study?'

'I am not yet at university. I intend to study history and art.' She replied in an imperious voice.

He contemplated her pityingly. '

Such subjects are nothing but lies. Thank goodness it is not going to happen.'

He turned his back on her, scrutinising a painting of her ancestor in boyar costume, wielding a sword, with dead heretics at his feet.

'You admire a dead past. This is rubbish! You are a fossil, a relic.'

He looked her up and down.

'What are these clothes? Could you go out into the field in those ridiculous clothes? Could you even cook something to eat wearing such a dress?'

Lucia could not think of an answer to his question.

She would never wear a ball gown anywhere except to a ball. On the other hand, she could not explain why she was wearing it. She was completely deflated.

'You are a waste of a good human being. You will need thorough re-education in the fields of workers. There you will learn the meaning of history and literature. Have you read Marx? Lenin? Stalin?'

Lucia shook her head. No one would contemplate such books at Tseder. Anyone reading such literature would be expelled.

'No?' he clucked with disapproval. 'You will learn. You will study; we will make a good comrade out of you. Never fear.'

Lucia had been prepared to die heroically.

Now she was scared stiff.

The idea of re-education was more alarming than torture; she could not imagine working in the field with the ignorant villagers. She realised that she despised their lifestyle and their coarse, red, weather-beaten faces.

She knew many of the villagers by name, and was always kind and friendly. She would occasionally visit the sick with medicines and provisions; she could not imagine talking to them as equals. They tended her horses and planted her flowers. They were inferior. She had been taught that they had no breeding, no sensitivity and few deep feelings.

She began to tremble and weep.

'Please, do not put me with the villagers,' she begged. Then she reconsidered, her face like an open book.

Maybe they liked her and would help her. Maybe they would remember that she had always been good to them.

Her head lifted and she stood up proudly.

'I accept. I will join my people.'

He stared at her in surprise.

'With your serfs?' He asked. 'You think we would let you batten down on the goodwill of the oppressed people here? No, my dear comrade, you will be joining real workers in a real collective, far into the soviet Republic. You will need to work for the first time in your feeble little life.'

'What about my mother and father?' She implored. 'Please do not make them go. They will die.'

'Your father, dear comrade, has been put down. He was justly exterminated this morning by the workers in this Revolutionary Ukrainian Soviet.'

Lucia was shocked.

No one had ever spoken so coarsely in front of her, and regarding such upsetting news, too.

She became hysterical. She noticed how her tears were ruining the fine pale-blue silk of her ball gown, she no longer cared.

'How? Murderer!' She cried. 'You killed him,' she screeched.

She erupted in blind indignation, attempting to remove the revolver which was now nearly in her underpants. As she struggled, the commissar called in a soldier, who slapped her out of her hysteria and held her arms until she calmed down.

The pistol fell to the floor, and it was picked up and handed to the commissar, who was trying not to laugh.

Everyone seemed to be amused.

'No hysterics, comrade,' smiled the boy.

The soldier held her down in a large armchair. He too was trying not to giggle.

She must have been quite ridiculous, with her heavy tiara and jewels awry and her stupid frilled petticoats all over the place. She had not tied them up properly and they had crept out from under her dress. Hilarious.

In time, she regained her dignity and everyone calmed down.

The commissar straightened his face.

'Your father was an oppressor and a criminal.' He explained kindly. 'He died at the hands of the revolutionaries here. It was for the best.'

He sounded like he was explaining the death of a dangerous dog, which she had mistakenly trusted.

'Your mother will join you in the new Soviets, far into the East. If you study, Comrade Stalin will judge you to be purified after a safe period of honest toil.'

This had not gone as planned.

She collapsed onto luxurious sofa, utterly defeated and trying not to cry for her esteemed father. She wanted to be brave and noble. She had no idea what to expect at the hands of the invaders.

She covered her face in her hands.

He called the soldiers in.

'Seal the rooms,' he commanded. 'Do not let these thieves remove anything which rightfully belongs to the workers.'

He turned to her.

'You will be joining other class enemies tomorrow afternoon for deportation. You are permitted three suitcases each. Only pack things which you will need for your new life out East.'

He came threateningly close.

'Do not steal anything which belongs to the people.'

He pocketed some sparkling crystal paperweights and left the room.

She heard him talking to his men. He was leaving to manage a rebellion elsewhere.

Two soldiers remained at the house.

'Tell your mother we will be coming back at 3.00 tomorrow to collect you. You will be searched before you board the train.'

He cast his eyes around the breath-taking luxury of the room and repeated, 'do not steal anything which is not yours.'

He laughed to himself.

'Don't forget to tell the Princess what has happened. I expect she is hiding somewhere; perhaps in a cupboard. Tell her not to bother with the secret passage. We have blocked it. '

6.

Maria Orloska

It was another three months before the princess and her daughter were deported.

Revolution moved forward slowly in the countryside. There were a great many country estates to take over and peasants to forcibly revolutionise.

Rebellions had to be properly controlled.

The commissar returned after three days.

He introduced himself as comrade Victor, and declared their home to be his headquarters, as it was the largest of the country estates and conveniently central.

Victor was tall and handsome - from a distance.

He was the son of a printer, and had shown talent as a wordsmith from an early age. He had believed in the tenets of revolution for so long that he could no longer remember why it had drawn him in the first place.

His faith had got lost in the drifts of power and alcohol. He had a great deal of intelligence, and seemed to have absorbed the principles of propaganda from the presses.

He enjoyed the power obtained by manipulating language. To him, truth was just raw material. He was uninterested in wealth; in point of fact, he had not seen any before he came to Louvinka.

As a young boy he had shown signs of being remarkably handsome, but heavy drinking had made his skin red and his face swollen; he was dirty and unkempt.

Close up, he was pimply and smelt bad. Nonetheless, he thought he really was rather gorgeous.

He had already acquired several house maids.

He quite fancied Lucia, though he considered her a complicated creature. After a few flirtatious overtures, he abandoned the attempt.

She completely ignored him.

*

Maria reluctantly emerged from her closet.

As she slowly calmed down, Lucia introduced her to Victor, who

93

immediately became fascinated by this graceful woman.

She was clean, elegant and neurotic in a thoroughly exotic way.

He wanted to dissect her and extinguish her, in the same way as he planned to do with the palace.

The introduction was one of Victor's 'scenes', a type of propaganda he specialised in.

It took place in front of a selected audience with a planned mise en scene.

Unfortunately, he was not the only one who had a command of the theatrical, and he ended up severely trounced.

He had heard that the Princess was weak and feeble-minded and brought her a bunch of flowers from the greenhouses at the bottom of the kitchen garden, thinking that the old lady would be flattered and perhaps even fall for him.

He was unctuous.

'Great princess,' he started.

Then he paused.

She looked so young!

At first he assumed it was Lucia, then he realised that the lady was actually quite old.

Immensely elegant, she moved forward like a queen.

Victor had a sense of drama, and he recognised a diva. She *owned* the stage.

His attempt at charm fell horribly flat.

She smiled at him as if he was a jester making a poor joke.

She took his flowers and dropped them to the table. She swept towards him and pecked him on both cheeks. The greeting was icy and disdainful.

The princess was accompanied by her maid, dressed in tragic black, who was carrying keys and papers.

She took them carefully, and handed them over - the tragic heroine in a war of words.

'This is the documentation for the land. As you see, some of the papers are medieval. They show the *rightful* ownership of the land.'

Her trustful glance towards the soldiers would have melted any heart.

'Read them please,' she said meekly. 'I must bow to *force-majeure.*'

At the key moment Victor was left with little to say.

Princess Maria Kamienska- Orloska dominated the room declaring he had arrived to *occupy* their lands.

Having taken the floor, she wondered if they might be related, picking on his name and tracing it through various unknown Lithuanian cousins she knew before the revolution.

He was cornered into the role of a dishonourable, *evil* relative who was taking over from the *rightful* ruler.

Victor was almost at a loss. Nevertheless, he chose to play along in order to gain time.

'Comrade,' he began.

She interrupted just as he was about to speak, raising her finger theatrically.

'Be careful!' she intoned. 'The land is delicate. It has been cared for and groomed by the *kindest* hands. It is in excellent heart.'

She looked him up and down.

He was silenced, feeling like a corsair who had looted and pillaged the town and surrounding countryside.

He took the papers.

'You will need to repair the *damage* that you have done.'

Victor was crushed.

'You will need to be *careful*,' she repeated in a sepulchral tone, which deeply annoyed him. 'The land will not *provide* for you if it is not *well* cared for.'

*

It was a minor triumph.

Despite the staggering odds against the Princess, Victor went along with the deception, to a minimal extent.

He accepted this minor setback and planned his next move.

He was not afraid of a woman. The forces of history were on his side.

He used his mastery of rumour to bring down her reputation. He declared her deranged.

The soldiers were ordered to stay away from the 'mad' Princess.

She lurked all day in her apartment grieving over the land, unaware of the gossip, while he isolated her as much as possible.

Victor resolved to act compassionate.

He had removed most of her jewels early on, though she was allowed to keep her pearls and her wedding ring.

She ignored everything, both bad and good. When she did go out, she looked magnificent and dignified, yet scandal repeated that she was extremely fragile, and her innately dramatic behaviour and tragic air told against her.

Despite this modicum of success, Victor was provoked that she did not beg for mercy.

He remained extremely polite and formal around his prey, observing her carefully. She was kind and deferential to him, yet her every action exuded power, and demanded respect.

He observed her closely and secretly imitated the way that she walked and addressed people.

It was statesmanlike.

When she was out, she was the focus of all attention.

She deferred to Victor at all times, treating him as the new master.

The servants obeyed her in this and addressed him as 'Master', or, when corrected, 'Master Comrade'.

When she was in the room, everyone waited for her opinion. Victor was aware of it, chagrined that he fell into the habit himself.

However, he was implacable in his determination to be her replacement, and was always searching for a way to reach that goal. He strove zealously to break her and distil this dignity. He debated raping Lucia, as an attempt to discredit the family.

Unfortunately, the girl was heavily protected. She was never without a servant. They appeared as if by magic if he was nearby.

Maria was softened by her sorrow, and her shame gave her a sensitivity to others which was communist perfection.

She truly cared about her people, and wanted them to be happy. She shared her possessions and gave away things which he would otherwise have burnt and smashed.

Beggars received crystal paperweights and Egyptian ashtrays, icons and inlaid cigarette boxes.

She had the common touch, and Victor tried to achieve that gratitude and care she engendered.

Whenever he attempted the same, even using identical language, he came over as a thief giving away 'hot' property.

People took his gifts, furtively, showing little awe and no gratitude.

Mother and daughter lived in the anxiety of occupation for two months, as soldiers piled through their rooms and removed personal things at random.

Rooms were cleared and turned into offices or dormitories. Paintings were burnt. Portraits were defaced.

They had time to bury the Count. They had scarcely any help with the laying out of her husband's badly beaten body and his coffin was laid in the family vault.

Old Orloski had enemies.

As his heartsick wife slowly accepted the reality of her pending homelessness, she realised that some of the peasants with pretty daughters were unhappy with this older man philandering among very young girls. Paedophiles generate a degree of anger.

Maria was under intolerable strain. She successfully hid her feelings, and collected together precious photographs endlessly, sorting them in order of importance.

She packed and repacked her cases with her favourite frocks, shoes and furs, pretending that they were leaving on a visit, and flitting in and out of different hopes and fantasies as she tried to come to terms with her loss.

On the surface, she was unchanged. If she broke down, it was only in the confines of her closet, which was now her tiny fortress.

Victor was aware that she spent a great deal of time alone, weeping quietly, burning personal papers and diaries and reliving her youth with her faithful maid.

He knew that he had won in every way, but was falling under the spell of romance exuded by aristocracy.

He worshipped power, and desired the same perfect understanding of how to effortlessly exert authority. He admired the princess's bravery and the impassive face with which she bore bad news.

He strove for the same high-minded stance and had to give it up. His troops kept asking if he was well.

The princess rarely approached Victor, and he avoided her.

He observed her walking and riding from his windows, intending to become a stylish oppressor like her.

In the end, his curiosity overcame him. He asked her outright how she managed the estates so well.

She glanced at him piercingly, as if she had seen him for the first time.

Victor became aware that he was dirty, and he hadn't shaved. He normally wore a slovenly appearance in order to look like a worker.

This morning, he rued it.

She seemed to scan his soul.

After several long moments she asked him, 'Where are you from?'

He answered that he was from Moscow.

'A good city,' she sighed, 'the capital of a great *Land*.' She articulated 'land' like it was a religious word, the same reverent way that people in the Soviets mentioned Lenin.

'What *is* it that you do?' She asked. As she looked at him intently, searching his face, he realised she had scarcely noticed him before. It rankled.

Victor went into a long explanation, trying to make it sound as grand as possible.

'Yes, yes,' she interrupted, 'lots of words, yet no *heart*.'

He was silent, his expression thunderous. He silently dwelt on the many options of disposing of her and stared at the door significantly, as if for his soldiers.

Most would have trembled. She just smiled and watched the vexation racking his body.

She waited for him to calm down, like a queen in audience with her vassal.

He was impressed. She must have been aware of the danger she was in. He was the invader, and her country had already surrendered. He was always armed, with soldiers on call. He had purposely made her aware that the rooms above her stables were used for 'interrogations'.

There was a pause until she judged him capable of listening. She repeated 'no heart,' tapping her foot regally.

She looked down at him kindly, as if he were a child, who had a lesson to learn. (He was a lot taller than her, how did she make him feel small?)

'You see, if you want to rule the land, you must love it, you must *become* it. You must *root* into it, like a plant.'

He glared at her uncomprehendingly, thinking it more of the mad mystical, nonsense which fuelled the aristocratic myth.

He attended politely, noting that she obviously did not care if he listened.

She seemed to just want to say her words. She turned her back on him and fixed her attention on the view out of the window, as if addressing the land itself.

'The land is a living thing. You need to love the earth and it will pay you back.'

There was a deep quiet in the room. Victor waited impatiently.

They both recognised that this was a battle of principles.

She mused in the silence.

'Even towns have a heart, you know. You need to listen to their heartbeat. It is the essence of good leadership.'

He grunted in a superior fashion, hoping she perceived how much he despised her primitivism.

'And this house, it is alive, of course.'

On cue, the furniture creaked, and a door slammed somewhere in the distance.

She got up and gathered her great full skirts to leave.

'It doesn't like you. *You* know that of course.'

She trailed out of the room like a prima donna, muttering something denigrating about science.

He noted that this grand behaviour seemed to be the essence of what was deemed as 'nobility'.

It irked him.

He sighed when she left.

'You have to admit it,' he said to himself, shrugging at a deaf portrait on the wall. 'She has a high sense of showmanship, and always acts as if she has a massive audience.'

Maria kept up her act, despite being secretly distraught about her own future. She would be exiled from the land she had identified with.

Neither she nor Lucia had any idea of what a collective was; they assumed it was a large country house, together with its adjoining farms.

They supposed it would be full of peasants and soldiers like their present home, and speculated that they would work as gardeners or secretaries; maybe they would have to sleep in one room. It would be hard, but they would have each other.

*

Maria was in deep mourning for her land. Without it she had little idea who she was.

She was a figurehead, not a person. As she could no longer play the character of great lady, she turned to her secondary maternal role.

Her remaining interests revolved around nepotism.

The ladies already knew that the Orloski boys had reached Poland; they had not arrived at Warsaw in time for the great battle.

They had surrendered to the Russians in dress uniform, alongside other officers, breaking their swords and acting honourably, as they had been taught.

There were dreadful rumours of what had happened to the surrendering Polish officers.

They had been marched off and disappeared.

Hearsay claimed that they had been massacred by Soviet soldiers and hastily buried in their shiny uniforms. Locals had apparently probed a giant mountain of corpses at Katyn[9].

The princess did not admit such a possibility and insisted that Katyn was a prison camp. She clung to her daughter and tried everything possible to assure her future safety in this turmoil.

Victor was close to Lucia in age, and he sometimes talked to her, mostly to ask about what all the fine trinkets and decorations in the house were to be used for.

He seemed ignorant of the purpose of many fine luxuries, exploring her home as if it were an alien landscape.

He picked up silver basins, sugar tongs, lace hankies, and laid out plates of different sizes, asking what the family ate on each.

He was unimpressed by the splendid trinkets he saw, and threw

---

[9] The location of a mass execution of Polish officers by NKVD

away anything which had no purpose, although Lucia noticed he sometimes did so with regret.

Lucia suspected that he was not serious over some of his questions. He regularly interrogated her in front of an audience of servants and soldiers, who watched his performance quietly and seriously, as if it were an act in a play.

On one occasion, he laid out every different size of plate knife and cutlery on the lengthy banqueting table. He collected his audience, sat her down in front of the plates. The settings were from a delicately painted Dresden banqueting service.

First, he asked her to lay the table setting. She was not sure how to do it, and had to ask the servants for help.

That was embarrassing.

Then he asked her what each of the different plates, tureens and cutlery were for, asking for details of every individual item.

'Why does one person need so many plates, spoons, knives and forks, comrade?' He asked.

She was sure he was being sarcastic.

'Does everyone in the village have one of these?'

She shook her head.

As instructed, she sat before the place setting laid out for a magnificent banquet.

The cook, servants, and soldiers who had been assembled to watch this pantomime, were silent. Lucia was deeply ashamed at being humiliated in front of her own servants.

'Why are these necessary?' He repeated.

She did not reply. He changed tack.

'What is this for?' he picked up a fork at random.

'It is for fish,' she replied.

'And this?'

'For meat.'

This went on for what seemed like hours. And then he questioned her again.

'Who cooks all this?' He asked.

'Who grows it?'

Lucia explained that her mother laid out the kitchen gardens every year and made sure that the food was properly prepared. She

101

consulted with cook and instructed...

There was an outraged gasp from the cook, and Lucia fell silent. 'And who eats it?'

Lucia left the scene in tears, and later heard that Victor and cook had made firm friends.

He had asked the cook to make him one of the lavish meals. He ate it alone, on the many plates, at his official new desk in their reception rooms.

She also heard that he was discussing the menus with the cook daily, like her mother had done. He was chatting up the stable-manager too, not quite so successfully.

*

Questioning sessions continued.

In every case the servant in charge of the service was present, and it transpired that the servants literally did every single thing.

Victor was cleverly teasing out their resentments. Whenever possible, he took over the role of estate owner and administrator.

*

It was easy to manipulate Lucia, a young girl of sixteen. On the other hand, Maria knew how to play this game.

She started to pass all matters of the estate to Victor. This was a problem because he preferred to watch her managing things first, and then wrest the power from her. Instead, she cleverly handed over some of the difficult decisions, waited for him to get into trouble.

She handed over matters of livestock breeding and what to do with the horses.

He was obliged to refer to her and she kindly explained to him how it should be done.

Victor loathed this, and took revenge in demolishing the things she held closest. He took time to discover her secret vanities.

Maria had been one of the racing elite, and had bred horses for most of her married life.

'Why do you have this painting of a horse here?' he asked Maria. It was the one horse of Maria's which had ever won a race.

The painting was very dear. It was rather a romanticised view of the beast, which seemed to be stepping over clouds.

She already knew that if she straightened an ornament, or admired a painting, it would vanish.

This was his first direct attack.

Maria blustered; she was not able to provide a cogent explanation.

The painting was removed, although not lost.

She discovered that the stable manager had it. It seemed that the man regarded the horse as his special success. He had deeply resented the way Maria went on about her 'work' in breeding this winner.

After distressing experiences like this, the abject women started to skitter about the house, hiding behind doors to avoid their servants.

She appeared vague and confused at times.

Victor watched her humiliation like a tiger; he reasoned that, as she lost control, power would devolve to him.

*

After a month, most of the obviously valuable things had been removed. Their home was been cleared and reorganised.

Victor had been methodically destructive.

The magnificent library was demolished, and its books consigned to the fire.

They were interrogated about the remaining possessions and tried hard to make sure to explain that each item had a practical use in case it were thrown away. Regrettably they had little luck in preventing the pillaging and obliteration of personal and valueless items.

It was odd how Victor was completely fascinated by the letter opener.

He carried it with him everywhere, certain that it had been used to torture money out of peasants.

He was certain that Lucia was trying to fool him that it was a letter opener; he pointed out the more useful pairs of jewelled embroidery scissors which he had located in her tatting box.

'Comrade Lucia,' he would say, shaking his head warningly, 'you are trying to hide your father's crimes. This will not go well.'

Lucia would flounce off in a sulk, while Viktor searched for dungeons and torture chambers.

*

This was not the only dispiriting aspect of their new life. Victor also attempted to re-educate the two vulnerable women.

He personally undertook this task.

He had memorised lengthy tranches of Lenin's speeches, and Lucia was almost sure he knew little outside the sayings of Lenin and Stalin.

He took a highly superior attitude, which agitated her, as it originated from a peasant.

He was amazed at her ignorance of the revolution. He spent time in explaining the nature of freedom to her, anticipating that she would become a good member of the Soviet in due course.

'Freedom means that every single member of society works. They *all* work Lucia.'

He would wag his finger at her as he related this, as if the extensive palace and stables ran themselves.

'Everyone gets their reward from honest toil.'

Every evening she would deride him to her mother in a loud whisper.

'Free to work! Mama that is nonsense! He never talks of leisure or hobbies. We work in order to rest. The communists want us to work all day and every day. This is not necessary. Why can people have no rest? Imagine mama! A world where everyone works, doing mindless tasks for no particular reason! They will have no time to make up their minds what they want and the state will be able to control their lives in every way. '

Her mother stroked her hair and quietened her down.

At such times she would call on their relationship to Victor, calling him our cousin and relative.

Lucia was never sure if she believed the fabricated family connection.

She was never fully persuaded by her mother. Perhaps she meant the relationship of one ruler to another?

'Men are peculiar creatures, Lucia.' Maria would say. 'The lot of women is to be passive and submit. He is one of us; we must let him do what he thinks is right.'

Lucia found it disturbing, but it silenced her complaints. Whatever she meant, it was vital to keep Victor on their side. He had control of their lives and they were effectively prisoners

When Victor cleared the nursery, Lucia wept for her children's books and her childhood drawings, which her proud mother had framed and hung in the empty babies' rooms.

'He has thrown our books away mama, even the children's stories.' She wailed, 'He only wants us to read his stupid Marx and Lenin.'

It felt as if they had died and were observing their descendants throwing everything away.

Maria had episodes of unreality, presuming she had become a ghost and was invisible. It was unnerving to the servants because, since she was dead, she stated exactly what was on her mind.

'Look at old Misha's nose,' she would say, 'He's like a snuffling badger. He *is*, isn't he? I never guessed he was *stealing* from us. You can tell that he drinks. He's drunk now, isn't he?' she would approach him, lightly touch his nose, and flutter off.

Lucia would have to keep an eye on her. If she had wandered off, she would run after her, apologising.

'She's not herself,' she would say, touching her forehead.

'Yes, young mistress,' the old retainers would say kindly, 'off wandering with the clouds as they say.'

She even dared to speak about Victor to his face.

*

Victor was sure that the time had come for the killing blow.

The unstable princess had assuredly been driven insane, and he would be her successor.

He was planning a touching final scene, having heard that they princess was 'better'. He came round to her apartment to check how she was. He had a great scene planned out to humiliate her.

Everything was ready.

He arrived. His soldiers were outside the room, and he had several of the senior servants in tow.

He asked her to sit at her personal escritoire, in her own boudoir, a magnificent room which was more like a small ballroom, with sofas.

The princess was ready for him.

She was far more experienced in the drama of rule. She watched him with vacant, glazed eyes.

She appeared to be possessed by one of her mad fits.

('Oh,' exulted Victor, 'this is perfect!')

She got up and floated towards him, she was wearing a most stunning dress, simple, satin and white (she and her seamstress had made it very recently; it was rather mediaeval in style). She had flowers in her loose long hair and looked fey and ethereal.

As he approached she started off in a theatrically dismal voice.

'He wants to be the new lord,' she declaimed, 'they all do. Their greedy hearts are hidden in the mask of hypocrisy. They want to cut out the beating heart of the land with the scalpels of science.'

She drifted towards him like Ophelia, and circled the room to ensure all eyes were on her.

'Do not worry, the earth will fight back.'

She picked up a cut flower from a simple arrangement on a marble table.

He noticed that it was a wild flower, from the forest which he was clearing.

She mused on it.

'He is tall and handsome,' she added, 'yet his heart was broken and smashed years ago. He is an empty husk, possessed by ghosts.'

She dropped the flower on the floor, the stem was broken. It laid there, a symbol of what was lost.

Her glance encompassed him and her daughter.

She spun like a creature at a ball, and then she pointed at both.

'He wants you,' she added, 'he thinks he can marry and become the new ruler of this glorious house.'

She touched his pocket. It always contained the jewelled knife he loved.

'He wants to steal the grain from the peasants, like the old lord.' She laughed gently, and whispered in his ear. 'You want to cut out their hearts.'

The whisper was so loud that everyone heard it.

Silence fell with a thud; everyone held their breath.

Then Lucia rushed forward, apologising profusely, and blushing horribly red at the implication that Victor desired her.

He *was* a handsome young man, but she didn't suspect him of improper intentions at all. Besides, there was something loathsome about him.

Victor left.

He went off to pillage elsewhere, and ignored the princess for a long time.

*

Maria giggled when they had gone. She seemed delighted at the effect she had had. She even quoted bits of Ophelia's speeches, and declared how much she enjoyed Hamlet.

Lucia wondered how mad she really was.

Her mother had drawn Victor out, and overwhelmed him.

Victor was intelligent, and accepted the setback.

He recognised that he had a lot to learn and he had not given up. He had possession, now he wanted to own the souls of the people too. He was angry with himself for being too confident, although he had learnt an important political lesson, which he never forgot.

He permitted the two to go out riding on their two hacks, which were not strong enough to bear soldiers and their arms, while he planned his next move.

*

In those last few weeks Lucia and Maria rode around their estate drinking in every tiny last tree and path.

'Just in case,' they would say, daily. 'This might be for the last time.'

The place was changing.

Peasants ploughed up their park and extensive kitchen gardens.

Lucia and Maria were saddened by the loss of their flowers and dismayed when their rare trees were cut down. Their summerhouses, follies and garden statuary had been demolished.

The rubble had been left in a monumental pile; the rubble had been used to fill the ornamental spinney which they had planted.

Lucia tried to complain; Victor explained that this land was wasted and useless as it was. Who had ever walked there other than the two of them? Was it ever a park for the people? How was it fair that the two of them owned all this land?

Lucia felt pretty bad about it all.

She recalled how last summer, two peasants had stolen into the spinney for a romantic tryst at night. She knew this from the gardener.

She had instructed him to tell the adventurers that they were trespassing and could go to prison unless they desisted.

She began to understand how easily the attitude of their dependents had turned to hatred.

She was revisiting her earlier flirtation with Nazi ideology. She had always trusted in aristocracy and the science of superiority had appealed to her. She was a modern woman and believed in the rule of science. She had always assumed superiority and now realised that she did not do much.

However, she never mentioned the cult of the superior man to Victor. She was beginning to comprehend the total power this slight young man wielded over her life. She was learning to fear.

Perhaps her mother had not run the estate at all, as Victor implied. She was no longer sure of the need for management.

Victor seemed to understand that Lucia was resisting the orthodoxy of equality.

He wanted to proselytise, and demanded her quietude when the spirit of revolution took him. He would sit her down and harangue her for an hour or so each day.

He would wax eloquent, and strike poses from the posters now hanging up in place of their old masters. The soldiers would hear him shouting and thumping his desk, and they would creep in and listen admiringly.

Sometimes they clapped when he had finished.

'Wonderfully explained,' they would say to her, while his main listener tried not to evince her acrimony at the nonsense he spouted.

'Comrade Victor is a great orator. Even the stones are moved by the truth of what he says.'

Sometimes the soldiers would get so emotional about the rubbish he talked, that they would slap her on the back, and sometimes even kiss her on both cheeks. They stank of vodka and onions.

It was the worst part of her day.

Victor was a good public speaker, and often asked Lucia her

opinions on his orations.

She exaggerated and distorted what he said until it became nonsense and drove him into a flaming temper. It was fun, although extremely risky.

Secretly, she was slowly being brought under the simplistic allure of his politics.

He attacked her with the science of the dialectic, and since Lucia had never done much at school, she could not argue back.

At Tseder she learnt that it was unfeminine for a woman to be too clever, it hinted at lesbianism, and it would harm her marriage prospects. As a result, she did not have the resources to refute his arguments.

As she lost confidence in her own superiority, she was less able to answer his logic.

Both ladies, already dominated by a vicious elderly paedophile, were overcome with remorse.

Victor had reported tales of old Peter's crimes against young girls as young as 12, and their beliefs in the innate superiority of aristocracy had gone into free fall.

They were no longer sure of themselves, particularly as their tenants and their servants had started to talk of mother and daughter as class enemies.

The local people had been completely won over to the idea that aristocracy was evil.

The servants' complaints about the princess and her daughter were not unfriendly, and they regarded the ladies as mistaken by their education.

Every time they mentioned a 'crime', they would add, 'the princess is a fine lady. She can't help it.' And they would sigh over her misdemeanours.

Victor was a clever manipulator of people and he continued in his efforts to revolutionise the countryside by manipulating rumour and fomenting strife.

This type of backstabbing was outside Maria's experience. In any case, she was not told much anymore.

She had never experienced such lack of status, and she was slowly learning how frustrating it was to do things for herself.

7.

Louvinka Spring 1940

The princess exuded charisma and confidence. Together with her husband she was director of a complex enterprise that centred on the palace. There were stables, pleasure gardens, parks, wild and tame herds, aviaries, game, dogs, delicate trees, conservatories, dairies, kitchen gardens, wine cellars, farmland, and immeasurable lands, consisting of thousands of tenants.

The cycle of the seasons consisted of parties, hunting, celebrations, visits to tenants, repairs to their properties, fishing, pickling, storage of the generous harvests, stock rotation, cleaning, and all finance and maintenance. It ran like clockwork, with everyone knowing their task and trained to it from childhood.

They were figureheads, steering this mighty ship with the minimum of obvious direction. She knew *how* to do things, without *actually* doing them. Unhappily, she could not dress herself, and her clothes were full of complex ties and hooks which could only be attached by a maid. She had little idea of how to physically pickle and smoke the meats, and she had never slaughtered and butchered a domestic animal.

It was a genuine shock for her to learn about life at the bottom of the pile.

Labourers faced a life of unremitting labour. They moaned, survived, and did not enjoy wealth or leisure. Numbers of beggars, vagrants and gypsies scavenged around the estates, living from charity and feuding over the scant resources available.

Village holidays and festivals provided a respite; and lamentably, often ended in vodka-fuelled violence.

There was little justice. The enforcers changed allegiance to a new regime. These men, who she remembered as well-behaved, were thoroughly self-serving, sycophantic to the strong while abusing the weak.

The new ruler, Victor, manipulated the different power groups in the area with ease.

He set the 'people' against the successful, who always cause resentment.

'Kulak' farmers, who owned a great deal of land and modern machinery, melted away.

Their farms were distributed among the landless, and soon fell into rack and ruin.

Carefully horded winter stocks were wasted, their herds killed and eaten, and carefully hoarded brandies drunk away. The talented businessmen, who Count Peter had so resented, had already sallied forth into the wilds of Eastern Russia.

Their businesses had been taken over by the 'people', which had an immediate effect. There was no electricity. Water purification plants were only partially working. The area fell into disarray.

The 'people' needed scapegoats.

Victor proffered class enemies and the counterrevolutionaries.

He spread fear.

He reshuffled everything, purposely fomenting discord.

He staged multiple pantomimes, always singling out some hapless victim as the oppressor of the 'people'.

Tenant farmers received coveted items, such a sharp new ploughshares, only to find that their grain store had been removed and handed over to their bitter enemies.

*

At last, the master of ceremonies had created sufficient chaos for true revolution.

The remaining populace, consisting of townspeople and villagers, were 'invited' to a general meeting in the town square, attendance compulsory.'

Attendance was mandatory.

*

Two impassive armed soldiers escorted the Ladies to the meeting ensuring that they arrived early and were seated until Victor turned up.

Maria carefully selected what to wear, selecting an impeccable riding habit in a dark material, a crisp white shirt and a smart feathered hat.

Her daughter wore a matching outfit. It necessitated arriving on horseback.

Chairs had been laid out in the square, and theirs were reserved, opposite Victor's modest red felt podium. What were they to do with the horses?

The soldiers shrugged.

It was not their job.

They rode to the local stables, but discouragingly, the ostler had already been warned, 'Do not take the princess's horse.'

They clip clopped around the town with sinking hearts, finally tethering their mounts to a dried up municipal fountain dedicated to their ancestor.

The horses needed to be rubbed down and watered.

More people were arriving.

The two women provided an interesting spectacle. The princess, hot and stressed, was no fool. This was a test.

She spoke French to her daughter.

'You must help me. That bastard Victor is trying to show us up.'

She actually swore! She turned to her daughter and shrugged.

'Whatever, we are not incapable.'

Maria found her allocated seat, Lucia following docilely. Her mother was boiling with rage, though to those who did not know her she seemed quite cool.

She stripped off her hat and riding jacket and neatly folded it on her chair. Her daughter did the same.

They strode to the well. Fortunately, it was not a complicated affair, although it took some moments to work out how to use it. They succeeded in the end.

She and her daughter dragged the bucket to the horses; they drank thirstily.

They loosened their saddle girths and the beasts trotted docilely towards the stables nearby.

The princess dragged out a small bale of hay to the horses.

'It is communal,' she said loudly. 'It is for all. This is a communism.'

The ostler did not dare say anything.

There was silence as the two sat down.

Though dirtied by the work they had done; they were flushed with their success and looked magnificent.

The fine cut of their skirts was unaffected by the strands of hay and rolled up the sleeves of their gorgeous shirts. Maria tried not to feel too triumphant.

Together with the remaining local gentry, they had been seated slightly apart, and the sun was directly in their eyes. They greeted each other ostentatiously and chatted, fanning themselves in the hot spring sun.

People were arriving in large numbers.

Most of them were dishevelled, begrimed and dressed in dreadful rags.

The gentry were taken aback at the obvious beggary of their vassals. They had never noticed the poverty of peasant working-clothes before. They normally met the peasants rigged out in Sunday best.

Maria muttered in French, 'they make us look as if we give them nothing.'

She was wrong.

There was no need. The peasants were miserably poor, and assuredly had been given nothing.

Victor arrived.

The entire square rose to sing the International, followed by a song claimed to be the Ukrainian Soviet anthem.

As far as the local aristocracy could make out it was about revolution and oppression. It was popular and the people sang with gusto.

The local newspaper took photographs as the young revolutionary struck poses like Lenin in the November revolution.

A village cretin got up and staggered toward the princess. He spoke loudly.

'Clath enemieth!' He shouted, and danced lightly to the music.

The princess had no doubt it was stage-managed.

She got up and tried to calm him down, but he became agitated.

He had been coached, and did not want to stop. He repeated his accusations louder and louder, until, at a sign from Victor, he was gently drawn away by his mother.

*

Comrade Victor called the meeting to order. He introduced

113

important communal matters.

Workers had to pull together and make the generator work.

Unfortunately, the head foreman replied, the engineers had all left for Siberian climes.

Victor brushed this off and discussed the allocation of tractors and modern agricultural tools. It was time they were shared out fairly.

There was a mutter of assent.

Lucia was deadly bored.

The interesting people had all vanished entirely and only the most boring were left.

Instead of survival of the fittest, revolution favoured survival of the most mediocre. She noticed that soldiers were at every corner trapping everyone in the square; even the children, playing in a crèche under the care of a deaf old babushka.

Victor fancied himself an orator, and Lucia was reminded of deadly afternoons at the place, as he practiced speeches on her.

The crowd was vacantly attentive. He ranted, as usual, about equality and the redistribution of wealth.

Sadly she had heard it all before and zoned out. When she felt witty she called this speech 'municipal bullying'.

Lucia heard the familiar phrases which he had practiced on her.

'The land will not belong to the kulaks or the aristocrats!' he shouted. 'It will belong to the proletariat, to all! To the women! The children! And to the men who work in our factories!'

*

There was a freezing in the audience.

The atmosphere turned deadly silent. The rustling of the trees and chirrup of birds seemed like noise.

Victor had reached the core of revolution - the collective ownership of land. All land henceforth belonged to the Soviet.

Every peasant loves his land.

It is his wife and mother and baby. The peasants had been with their land for thousands of years. They had lived with it as serfs, preferring to say that the land owned them if that was what it took. The peasant grew out of his land.

There was silence.

It was followed by a loud cheer from the soldiers.

'Long live the revolution. The people will never be defeated!'

The soldiers shouted slogans. They poked those nearest to them with guns.

'Cheer comrades,' they warned. 'This is revolution. You are being freed from oppression. Cheer!'

A rugged hurrah rose up from those parts of the crowd nearest the guns.

It was more like the growl of a dog, warning its master to leave the bone.

*

Victor had done all he could.

He had spent time creating discord among the people. He had divided social groups and turned master against servant and vice versa. He ensured that the essential agricultural tools stolen from the kulaks were fought over. He tried to demonstrate that a collective would bring all this acrimonious in-fighting to an end.

Every act of the play had been carefully planned, and this was the finale.

He finished in sullen rebellious silence.

No one spoke against him.

There was no unified opposition.

The princess quietly got up and left, followed by her daughter.

The soldiers raised their guns at her; the captain barked peremptorily.

'Comrade Orloska, no one is to leave.'

She walked on.

There was a murmur from the crowd, more like a rumble.

Victor wanted a peaceful revolution here, where he hoped to settle. If anyone rose to assist her, there would be a massacre.

He signed to the soldiers to let her go.

'Let the oppressors leave.' He joked.

No one laughed.

'Let those who want to exploit the people join them,' he added warningly.

No one followed them.

*

115

Victor enjoyed the game of revolution - a game with moves played out in words and staged scenarios. He could not afford trouble early in his career.

He was enjoying his new power, and had gathered quite a few trappings of wealth in his commodious room at the palace.

He formulated different plans to make something of their departure later.

'He who holds the press, holds the town,' he thought grimly.

*

Revolution had come to the countryside.

Victor had successfully divided the community into factions and no one could depend on their neighbour.

They needed a collective.

He talked for a bit longer, to make sure that the departure of the two women was a discrete event in the people's minds.

He spoke of the oppressors and the criminals who had made this town poor. He linked the broken generator and the princess in the same sentence several times.

After a few more laudatory speeches about Stalin, the meeting broke up.

The divided people left, muttering darkly.

'It went well,' he acknowledged. Fighting had broken out in other parts of the country. Many had been shot.

'Revolution,' he told his captain, 'is rarely bloodless. We have been lucky to day.'

*

He planned to put up a poster that collectivisation had been agreed by a unanimous vote in the next few days, putting a heavy spin on the fear and discord he had engendered and how this decision had brought it all to an end.

Peace at last, now that our enemies have left!'

No one had actively objected, which was almost the same as agreement.

First he had to eliminate potential leaders, on whom opposition might focus.

He had made much of the fact that the princess was a recluse,

116

and had circulated the news that she had lost her mind.

Her actions at the meeting were popular. She seemed able to draw on inner resources he had not anticipated. She had leadership, skill and glamour.

It was time for her to go, or the people would gather around her.

*

The two women had fallen into a pattern of repacking every morning, then going out to ride.

Each afternoon they sat alone in their shared room and re-organised papers, burning private correspondence and reliving memories.

It became a routine.

In the end, two long days after the collectivisation, they suddenly received the order that they were to move out that afternoon.

The order to leave had come through.

Victor claimed that the Princess had recovered her wits and was strong enough to travel.

The whispers of madness had been refuted at the meetings, though he would ensure that they resurfaced. She would be expunged from memory.

*

The Orloski women were popular. They were a sporting, horsey pair, not particularly enticing, brilliant with animals, tall, blond and handsome. They were much admired.

However, they did not know it, and felt entirely alone. Victor had successfully isolated them.

Victor did not risk alienating his new subjects by treating his elite prisoners badly. The village had a great deal of sympathy for Maria, holding to the primordial idea that the 'lady' represented the land.

He would to deal with that primitivism later.

A large covered truck arrived to take the ladies to their new land. The ancient army truck had a bright red star painted on it and the only new khaki paint was that covering the Polish flag.

Victor allowed Maria's weeping maid to help them on the transport and to say a long goodbye.

He intended to gain a merciful reputation in the villages around.

*

When the two ladies belatedly left the land for ever, they had been allowed to take a great deal more than three suitcases, and still did not bring anything useful for their new lives. Victor, who made a study of them, noticed that they took oddly inappropriate things like mink stoles, fur coats and long evening gloves, photographs, and even love-letters.

When they had gone he would investigate everything thoroughly. He would manage the land, though not in this primitive way with a 'heart' and 'love'. That was spiritualist nonsense! He would use science to subjugate nature and show it who was boss. .

He would impose on it as master, and control it with science.

*

He heaved a sigh of relief that they had left beyond recall.

'You have had time to pack and to say goodbye,' he told them loudly, as a local photographer recorded their departure, including their pile of stolen 'loot'.

'You have seen what improvements we have made. The land is in good hands at last. You have plundered it for long enough.'

Lucia gave a long sulky and sarcastic cough which was drowned out by the sound of the starting engine.

Several neighbouring ladies were already in. They stood up and curtsied, as if in a drawing room.

'So adorable to meet you.' they cooed. 'Yes, unfortunately in desolate circumstances. Do you know what happened to the ----s?'

They chatted about local news as if in a drawing room.

They had no idea where they were headed, and everyone was fearful, but they bore up in each other's presence.

The military aspect of aristocracy was keeping them all afloat.

Victor watched the princess.

He had not defeated her, despite his best efforts. He esteemed her skill. She taught him a great deal.

*

Victor prospered. Over the years, he became a fat apparatchik[10]. He saw himself as an aristocrat of the revolutionary vanguard,

---

[10] A loyal full time member of the communist party, who followed directives without question

one of the pure.

When Maria left, he claimed that she had wanted to marry him. He related that she was glad Peter had died and was complicit in his murder.

He always told this marvellous story when he was drunk.

The little paper knife, which he retained as a keepsake, figured in different ways depending on his audience.

Either

Maria or Lucia had tried to stab him with it when he had rejected their advances.

Or

The count had used it to murder young children.

Or

It was used to torture peasants by killing their children.

Or

It was an ancient symbol of the power of the aristocracy created by a master wizard, and had been handed down from generation to generation.

*

Louvinka was not razed like many other estates. It was used as party headquarters.

Later on the Germans used it to house their officers. When the Russian army returned, the stables became the headquarters of the NKVD.

In its ultimate incarnation under occupation, the palace became a rest home for party members.

Maria's modern gas stove and electric lighting survived well into the 1990's.

The cook stayed with the house until she died. The cook's daughter worked there, when it became a luxury hotel after the fall of the Berlin Wall.

*

Victor never forgot the lessons he had learnt from her, and survived all the purges by falling into sickness and even madness when necessary.

He had many imaginary complaints which he wheeled out at key moments.

His biography states that he had two nervous breakdowns - both coincidental with political crises.

A ruthless and successful politician, he played all his required roles with passion and assurance.

His experiences at Louvinka were formative.

After Maria departed, he had ceased to believe in communism, only in the spectacle of power and the value of words.

He used his skills to manipulate others and became a masterful orator, applying himself to the drama of rule.

*

When the Soviet Republics disintegrated, he took a large part in the independence movement, and, at the end of his long career, becoming a senior statesman and powerful Ukrainian politician.

8.

Marseilles 1940

Marseilles was a hive of paranoia and resistance, and the French did not welcome strangers with German sounding accents and exotic looks.

Despite having plenty of money in a country which was resisting German advances, the Brauns often felt uncomfortable. They were no hicks or uncultured oafs, yet they were ostracised.

Just before May 1940, Izaak got wind of the invasion and took a train to Marseilles.

It was the nadir of their adventures. In later life their stay in that city was never mentioned.

*

It is hard for most people to imagine what it is like to be shunned.

Most people know their place in society. They know when to hold their head high and when to keep a low profile.

A whore or a drug-dealer could feel horribly out of place in the streets of suburbia. Nevertheless, in the narrow roads of slum dwellings they are safe and welcome.

They have a place.

As Jews, the Brauns were not safe anywhere.

Not even the drug addicts and pimps wanted their money in exchange for a place to sleep.

They had nowhere to live and nowhere to go. There was nowhere to stay in safety.

They faced the stomach-churning fear of being altogether unwanted, of knocking at the doors of strangers and being told to go away.

Under this extreme pressure they had to admit that they were considered unwanted dross.

Perhaps they *should* die?

They were invisible and alone, waiting for their sons to come, hoping to hear from their son in Germany. They were alone, unconnected with the world.

They changed hotels frequently. Servants were openly rude and hostile. People shouted at the in the street telling them to be off and worse.

Rebecca could not bear it. She often collapsed into hysterical tears. She was in a panic about her son and his young children.

'Why are they still in Germany?' She wailed about her eldest boy and his family. 'Where is Izaak Jr? 'Why do they not join us? Izaak, get them! Send couriers! We have money. Use it!'

The larger hotels no longer accepted them and they stayed in boarding houses. They remained at each place for a short time, departing before the booking ended in order to prevent eviction.

'What is wrong with us?' wept Rebecca, 'they are ignorant savages who used to come to you to beg for work. You were always kind, Izaak. You were a *socialist*!'

If either of them felt uncomfortable for any reason they would turn round and leave, moving between hostels and boarding houses like unwanted refugees from some uncultured hinterland.

'My wife is a little ill,' Izaak explained. 'Here is the money just in case we cause an inconvenience by departing so soon.'

*

The news was worse and worse.

It seemed that his eldest son would not be able to leave at all. His younger son, David, was trying to escape Hungary. Where was he to go? It was not safe, even in France.

Emigration became a distinct necessity.

Discussion in the family ranged around what to do and where to go - England, Spain, and USA? No one seemed to want them, with a Polish passport and German name.

'I am sorry,' the embassies apologised, 'emigration to this country is not possible for,' a pause, 'Poles.'

Prices for everything they bought rose.

Quite unimportant and inferior service providers wanted payment in gold or diamonds.

'We take gold,' the cleaner had stated to Madame Braun, and added, 'even ill-gotten.'

She laughed like a magpie.

The general opinion was that Jewish people were all thieves.

'After all,' the poor reasoned, 'these Brauns are Jews, rich with

122

ill-gotten wealth, why shouldn't we get some it for themselves?'

9.

Lvov Uprising 1940

Lvov was in the grip of a sweep. As interrogation continued, Janek betrayed everyone he knew, duly making things up to satisfy the paranoia of his interrogators.

In the following two weeks, the majority of opposition was wiped out in lightning raids and arrests on the basis of his information.

Approximately one third of the purged victims were random middle-class individuals with a nodding acquaintance with the traitor. Among them, he gave up Ella, a sweet young girl who adored him, and several innocents, simply because the mention of their names lit up the eyes of his questioners.

Ella was no rebel, but a delicate woman. She was an intellectual socialist who had entrusted him with troubled questions about the regime of fear.

It didn't matter; Janek had no mercy for anyone other than himself.

*

For the Maslows, the 'call' arrived in the form of loud crashes, shouts and heavy steps upstairs.

The 'visitors' thundered upstairs, crashing into neighbours' doors and ensuring everyone knew a 'visita' was taking place.

They did not have time to open the door. It came crashing off its hinges.

The NKVD were inside.

'Come with us,' they commanded. 'Immediately!'

They gave no one time to get dressed, even put on slippers, dragging panic-stricken sisters and their mother out of bed.

Hearts beating, skipping and jumping close to an attack, they were dragged and fell into the waiting limousines and sped off to the Town Hall.

*

No food, barefoot and in nighties, they waited in the hallway of the Town Hall.

The doors opened to blood-stained sofas and beaten men were

124

dragged past them in the hallway.

Distant screams could be heard now and then.

They shivered silently, not even gazing at each other in case this would harm their 'case'.

Sofia held on to her rosary beads. When they were snatched and broken; she prayed quietly for each atrocity she witnessed on an invisible string of beads.

*

After an unknown length of time (the building was always shuttered and lit), they were taken to different interrogation rooms.

Katya was unafraid, even fascinated, having no idea then of the danger that they were in (she later learned that interrogators never discovered innocence, it was impossibility).

She was taken before a young man, intelligent and as attractive as she.

There was an attraction; she could tell.

He was polite and kind.

'Sit down,' he asked.

She could not help noticing that the chair had cuffs and had been smeared with blood.

'Cigarette?'

Katya did not smoke.

'Now, this is clearly a misunderstanding. Tell me all about it.'

Katya was not stupid.

'Say nothing,' she told herself firmly. 'This is a trick.'

In any case, she had no idea why she was there.

He lit a cigarette, and exhaled rapturously.

'Tell me why you are here.'

Katya had no idea.

'Do not argue,' he adjured in a gentle voice, 'You do not want me to call my friends.'

Katya definitely did not.

She had the clearest sense of the bloodstains and the smell of disinfectant barely covering up the smell of piss and shit. People had clearly soiled themselves in the chair and she wriggled uncomfortably.

'What do you want to know?' she asked, trying to imitate his friendly and courteous tone.

She could tell he was enjoying the sense of power he had over her. She could tell that he found her attractive.

He liked interrogating women.

'Tell me about your friends,' he inquired. 'Who are they? What do they know?'

Katya listed the girls she knew at university, impressed that he knew them all. He knew which ones harboured seditious thoughts. He knew about the pseudo peasant-born aristocratic maidens too.

She told him about them first, hoping that this was what he wanted. She mentioned seditious talk of defence and resistance.

It did not interest him. He already had enough to incriminate every single university student if he cared to.

He turned to her religion. '

You are a Catholic,' he pronounced contemptuously, 'like your mother.'

Katya was on firmer ground here.

Members of the church congregation were counted in and out at every service. She was aware the congregation had been photographed on the first few Sundays after the fall of Warsaw. Attendance had fallen sharply. Of course, her mother went, joined by her family on rare occasions.

Katya was ready to reject her church.

'I do not care about Catholicism,' she replied. 'It is true that god sees everything we do. I know I should not sin. Actually, I do not believe in the church.'

She stated this sincerely, knowing that her mother would weep at such apostasy. It felt rebellious and, fun.

'Do you study science and engineering?' he asked.

'Of course.'

'And you are top of the class, or near the top, in the subject?'

'Yes'

'And in mathematics?'

'Yes.'

'You acquired a scholarship to one of the top schools in Warsaw?'

'How do you know?'

He overlooked her surprise. '

'You want to be an engineer?' he asked.

'A good job for a woman,' he added quietly, 'and you want to rebuild your Soviet?'

She felt intimidated, not knowing where he was going with this.

'So why is someone so clever and so brilliant,' he sneered, 'so foolish as to believe in God? Do they not teach you science in school here? Do they not teach the dialectic? You are a primitive people. We have a lot of work to do here if the cleverest are so stupid.'

'My mother,' she stammered, flustered at his despising tone.

'Your mother?' He almost shouted. 'A naive peasant! Babushka!' (So they had watched and followed her family for some time.) 'A crazy old fool who will work out her penance for the Soviet in the fields of Russia. But you! Your country's future? There is no excuse for such philistinism!'

Katya broke down completely.

Stockholm syndrome is at its most intense at the moment of greatest terror. It overwhelmed her higher consciousness and instead of feeling hatred and resentment, she gawked at her interrogator with new adoring eyes.

He spoke sense to her troubled soul. She idolised him, his little glasses and his spotty pasty complexion. Her hero, a saviour who would protect her from the blood and shit that threatened,

'Yes,' she wept, in agonised obeisance, 'my mother must go! Kill her! Shoot her. I no longer believe in god, only in what you say.'

He focussed on her with compassion. He was familiar with adoration. It was deserved, if it was for the Party.

'You are a good girl,' he asserted in a fatherly tone. 'You will do well. Follow your superiors in knowledge and you will learn.'

She goggled at him fawningly.

'The Party knows what is good for you. It may be a prison sentence...'

She had folded so fast! In less than half an hour!

He need not have bothered to check through the notes on the family. This was a straightforward case.

He enjoyed his work, gaining converts for the Party.

He relived the submission of his victims before he slept, using his hands while recollecting the power and glory that accrued for his meagre revolutionary efforts.

This one had been easy. Tough ones were more fun, only their blood and lamentation wore him down a little. He always urged the vicious guards to create lasting injuries for the truculent and brave. Let the bastards who resisted reprogramming; remember their moment of subjection in their crippled body.

'I will do anything.' she sobbed. 'Just let me go. Do not kill me. Others must die. I will tell you everything!'

She clung to his knees and covered his hands with kisses and tears.

Some broke that fast, he reflected, excited by the energy she released. He drank in her devotion and sucked on submission like a vampire.

A knock on the door severely discomposed him.

He was interrupted at the very apotheosis of interrogation. It had better be a good reason.

Katya blubbered a confession of abject stupidity and begged forgiveness as the junior official whispered in his ear.

'Please finish off quickly, this case was solved and they were busy.'

The interrogator walked out in a huff of annoyance, taking a last, long look at his victim, gripping her by the shoulders and breathing in her soul.

*

So ended Katya's first cross-examination. She had wet herself

Sister Anya had waited for ten minutes in an empty interrogation room.

She disregarded the spatters of blood and the howls of pain and, after about twenty minutes, she had strolled out of the unlocked room to attract the attention of a passing guard.

'Tell them I know everything! If it is about the gold and the safe! Tell them I know where it is. Tell them I know the combination too.'

It had taken precious minutes to confirm the subject of the interrogation; then wake a dozing senior interrogator to find out if on-going interrogations were to be interrupted.

*

In that short time, Katya had taken a very specific turn.

She had betrayed everyone to ensure her personal survival. She had turned on those she loved most. She accepted the ideology of domination and taken the first steps towards the war crimes that she would later perpetrate.

*

The sleepy senior party official hated interruptions for minor matters. Unluckily, there was a long queue. Janek had proved very helpful, and this was a minor affair.

'Ok,' proclaimed the senior official. 'Hold it. We have a lot on. Let them go home. Pick up the gold. If any is missing I will know.'

*

Katya later excused every deed in her life based on events in that chamber. She claimed that there had been no alternative.

'God let this happen to me. I had no choice.'

Unhappily, it was not quite so simple.

Lviv was not a good place to be; she had dropped into a hell where options were strictly limited.

Decisions *had* to be made. She had concluded that anyone, no matter how close, could be betrayed. She had done this without so much as a threat or a blow.

'God left me alone. That is why I failed.'

Later on she added the premise which directed her life.

'Those who are tortured deserve it. God does not care about them.'

Katya had already started carefully forgetting what had happened, when with a jolt of fear and joy she saw her interrogator rush up to Anya.

To her humiliation, he was visibly excited with hands in pockets.

She was ashamed to see him leering at her. He sneered sneering at her mother, praying for the lost souls who passed through this inferno.

She gazed at him adoringly, but he looked away. He had no time to savour his victory.

Instead he turned to her sister, Anya.

'So, quite the little sly minx we have here. Just look at those foxy little spy eyes!'

129

He chucked her under the chin. 'I should have started with you,' he murmured sexily, 'It would have been more fun.'

Anya stared back fearlessly.

Katya's wept at this betrayal. She saw his spindly legs and spotty face, his silly glasses. How could she adore him? He despised her.

Sofia had a black eye and her mouth was bleeding slightly, one hand hung uselessly beside her, but she had not told a secret which was not hers to spill.

She thanked the Lord that her daughters had been spared. She had already forgiven Janek for his betrayal. Who knew what he had been through?

She vowed to go on a pilgrimage praying for the survival of her children.

*

Janek did not disappear. He owed his survival to the infatuation to Basia, a Russian maiden he had met at his drinking sessions, where he leered at her, too drunk to notice her moustache and a large eyebrow-wart.

The daughter of an army captain, she had joined other good communist girls following the army, with a view to settling pure thinkers among the newly freed population.

This young lady ensured that instead of a prison sentence followed by deportation, he gained job security for life.

Despite his excellent work in betraying family, friends and acquaintances, his party rank remained low.

A complex hierarchy of officialdom developed around him at the post office. He was a cypher, ignored.

10.

Lvov 1940

The Maslows returned home at 10.00 am on a cold March morning, observed by every neighbour.

The front door of the apartment was off its hinges. It would not close. A small card was pinned to the door, written in a slightly school-ish hand.

'Do not enter,' it declared, 'under investigation.'

Everyone knew the letters NKVD scripted under the card.

To make it even more clear that they were pariahs; they were escorted upstairs under guard, in the unearthly stillness of multiple eavesdroppers trying to catch every sound.

The safe crashed from the wall of the library, and was carried off by burly policemen. The combination was with the NKVD, and woe betides Anya if it was incorrect.

The library had a gaping hole in the wall.

Silence fell. Mother and daughters sat quiet for hours, adrenaline coursing through their systems.

Katya threw her nightdress away. She was a coward and a traitor, her spirit broken under the lightest pressure.

The next three days were a wall of shame.

People crossed the road to avoid them. There was no service in the shops.

Sofia sat alone in church, whole empty pews distant from the nearest parishioner. Ladies crossed themselves as she passed. The priest prayed distantly at her. Confessional was closed, just in case.

Sofia, unshriven, did not feel able to attend communion.

*

They packed and waited, knowing that they would be deported.

After one day of degradation, Sofia was taken away. Her sentence:

'Maslow Sofia, 12 months' jail for theft from the people and the Soviet''

It was carefully typed on card and taped on the door.

Her suitcase was packed, searched, ransacked, and repacked. Prisoners were permitted a strictly limited amount.

The girls remained a further two days, eating rice and millet, which they had little idea how to cook, rancid butter and stale bread.

A new card had appeared at the door.

Maslow Katya 10 years labour and re-education on Soviet Collective
Maslow Anna 10 years labour and re-education on Soviet Collective'

Katya had a minor nervous breakdown and howled all of the last night, waking the neighbours, and greatly enhancing the reputation of the secret police in the process.

On the third night, the soldiers returned at around midnight, rumbling up the stairs like a tank with boots.

Katya wet the bed.

As foretold, they were given 15 minutes to pack.

They were being deported to Russia for re-education among the people.

A small card stated that the apartment was to be

'Confiscated for Soviet comrades.
Long live the Party, defender of the people'

As mama advised, they wore winter coats and boots. They wore as much as possible, in order to leave room in the suitcase, even though it was not cold.

The NKVD searched their cases for stolen goods before they left, throwing out vital provisions when the rumpled suitcase no longer closed, and removing whatever they fancied.

As the girls left, the looters shouted at them.

'This den of thieves is at last cleansed of its corruption. Long live the union of Soviets who heal the land of vermin.'

Their cries, uttered in the jeering tone of vicious gangsters, left an almost visible trail of fear in the remaining occupants. Doors opened to watch them leave

No one waved good bye.

*

They were driven to the Town Hall and left with other disheartened deportees, many from outlying rural areas.

Several eminent aristocratic ladies were already there. Katya was sure she had betrayed at least one of them and recognised Angela looking brave and confused.

Her mother, the haughty and aristocratic Countess of the tea party, was attempting to maintain a cool civilised air, but even her facade was beginning to fail.

There were others there too, bearing the injuries of interrogation. Many had diarrhoea, making the single available toilet untenable, even the basin was full of vomit.

Anya was revoltingly calm, even excited. She had been bored at home. She joined other young girls in the stable attached to the Town Hall, whispering and giggling quietly.

Katya wept for her skis, and her bicycle. Soon she would be in Russia, yet could not ski in the snow or cycle the steppes. She wept for her new bike and her future.

People prayed to god, sang songs and made light of the situation.

Those broken under interrogation watched the world with wan, jealous eyes, willing the others to cry and wail as they had done. They were a people apart.

The deportees were escorted to the train through the town, carrying their suitcases.

It was early, but their humiliation was noted by town gossips.

The terror had begun.

They did not see Janek again.

Part 3.

Vengeance.

The cycle of revenge turns over and over, until the spirits of vengeance are satisfied, or are cut short by forgiveness.

1.

Kazakhstan 1939

The Soviet State was not yet at war, but Kazakhstan was already a place where ideology killed children and extinguished hope.

The Kazakh tribesmen on the steppes were descendants of Genghis Khan's hordes. Their foothold on the land had been gained by raping and murdering the original inhabitants.

The remnants of the Horde combined Scythian animism and a version of Muslim faith. The tribes practiced divination through shamans trusting that their spirit enemies could be silenced by spells, sacrifices and sorcery. They had no concept of forgiveness. They executed women who bore deformed children as witches, and sent childless females and old grandmothers into the snow to die.

Their kidnapped brides, stolen from neighbouring tribes, prayed for the rapists in an effort to ensure the survival of offspring.

Until the birth of the new Soviet, they had evaded karma by sacrificing sheep to the vengeful shades. The past was not forgotten, and ghosts breathed of retribution in the wind buffeting across the endless waves of grass.

The chains of history could not be avoided forever.

*

The Soviet, established in the 1920's, had been imposed on a predominantly nomadic population.

The revolution was building a better world using the science of their dialectic.

Stalin had convinced his party hopefuls that they were safeguarding the legacy of Lenin. The Kazakh Soviet would be transformed from a backward rural economy into a superpower equal to any of the industrialised nations. Work would make the nation supreme and revolution would surely spread.

The nomads had been forcibly settled into collective farms.

'Hand over your herds and start farming the land. The steppes will become the breadbasket of the new state.'

In response, most of the 'kulaks' [11]simply slaughtered their flocks rather than give them up. Their leaders fled East with their ponies and a few sheep.

Their new masters were undaunted. They sent out parties to hunt down the counter revolutionaries and deported several hundred of their relatives.

'Harden your hearts to the enemies of the Marxist-Leninist revolution!'

*

The bleached bones of those holocausts lay in mounds, a shadow of massacres of yore.

'We must kill backward superstition!' the revolutionaries assured the tribesmen. 'The vanguard has arrived to dispel false consciousness.'

They shot any herdsmen with over 100 sheep, regarding them as ignorant savages riddled with kulak ethics.

Stalin had declared huge communal farms were the backbone of the revolution, providing food for the proletariat.

Kulaks, hand in your secret hoards.'

Yurts had been certified counterrevolutionary; as a result, herdsmen shepherding the diminished collective flocks regularly froze to death.

The improved windowless mud huts melted in the spring thaw and disintegrated in the heat of summer.

It did not matter, purity of ideology was more important than expertise.

'Comrades,' the shock troops of collectivisation informed the people, 'this is a depersonalised optimum land area. Tractors will cut through it like butter and we will have grain. Down with tradition!'

The revolutionary vanguard executed grand plans based on out-dated texts for farming in Belorussia.

The beneficiaries of the new order struggled to eat birds, boiled berries for food, ate mud, river slime, and raw potatoes to stave off

---

[11] In Soviet terms, a tight fisted and well-to-do peasant.

the pangs of hunger. Their spirits of the dead whispered in the unceasing winds across the majestic wastes while the descendants of the horde died in droves.

Before their forced settlement, nomads had carefully skirted the areas where the heads of the hordes' enemies had been piled high. Now the spin of history was against them and unquiet spirits roamed the steppes once more.

*

By 1939 the party had once again been ripped apart by strife over the interpretation of revolution.

The party members, who had ordered the initial struggles for revolution were long gone, disappeared into the wastes of outer Siberia.

Almost weekly, the party caucus declaimed the theories of Lenin as re-interpreted by Stalin, and ascribed disaster to the party faithful for errors of understanding. Even these instructions were contradicted daily, as their chairman became more paranoid under the threat of war with Germany.

Most recently there was to be an *aggravation* of class struggle. Their superiors had sent young Partkoms into the wastes, almost teenagers, exhorting them to stand firm against the kulaks, who had superhuman powers to wilt the grain and consume the expected harvests.

'Enemies Destroy our Harvests!'

These youthful tyrants were oblivious to the spiritual warfare that blustered across the ancient landscape, and the wraiths of past injustices. They were fired by the spirit of revolution and the hope of a better life than the privations and paranoia of the capital.

Few of them lasted long in that wild place. They were either promoted or disappeared. The Kazakh collectives were not a prosperous or successful posting.

*

In 1939, the collectives were under the control of three Partkoms: Andrei, Vasily and Mikhail, supervised by Anatoly. They had been promoted in the vacuum created by recent purges and had little experience of rule.

These prematurely balding, damp handed adolescents had total control over an ancient nomad culture. They were builders of a new and better world, peddling ideas which would slaughter millions until the spirits of vengeance were finally appeased.

Anatoly was 22, the rest even younger.

The Partkoms watched each other warily in case they became infected by illegitimate ideologies affecting the countryside, polluting utopia.

Icons of Stalin hung over their bed; they sang revolutionary songs to sleep. Only Comrade Stalin understood it all.

They worshipped their great leader's wisdom in awe.

No matter how often the little gang (backed by heavily armed soldiers) concluded that they had grasped the ideology, the very next day, a new directive sent them into confusion.

Posters screeched ferocious revenge on such capitalist collaborators, with caricatures of demoniac Kazakhs stealing upon the fields at night, even spreading the cocoons of the moths which blighted their bean crops.

Anatoly, the Partkom secretary, showed his assistants reports detailing tons of grain produced by other collectives, for the furtherance of revolution.

'Enemies Destroy our Harvests!'

His juniors strived unwaveringly to bring forth a harvest.

'Remove all the degenerate enemies of the cause by any means possible!

Things were improving every day as the dregs of the old Capitalist System were dislodged. Nevertheless contradictory and nonsensical directives resulted in famine.

Strive against counter revolutionaries.'

They were certain that hoes, sickles, unsuitable seeds, and a few tractors would tame the unruly steppes, even though it would be almost impossible to get a decent harvest from those endless plains without massive machinery.

Never mind.

If the dialectic required death, starvation and mass deportations, then let it be done.

'Forward with Collectivisation!'

By now it was obvious that the collectives had gone disastrously wrong. New mounds of dead rotted hidden on the steppes, joining the spirits of those massacred long ago. Stalin's smiling face declared

'Socialism in One country'

It depicted a crowd of peasants behind a hammer and sickle, yet eerily resembled a pile of skulls.

Forward with the Vanguard! flapped a relatively recent notice.

Mournful notices flapped on the notice-board of the village halls, which regularly had their roofs blown off in winter.

'Only 10% of the produce is to be retained.'
Feed our Proletariat Brothers'

The Partkoms[12] ignored the keening winds. The nomads had to learn that the new world was here.

Another poster, and its tacked on list, waved eerily in the breeze, only half attached to the notice board

'Brothers! These men owe money to the collective.

An almost illegible list of names followed - mostly people long dead or fled from these inhospitable climes.

The people say: Hand in your ill-gotten gains.'

Behind this notice an ancient poster depicted profiles of healthy peasants holding a hammer and sickle, improbably fat and sturdy, stretched out their faded arms.

The wet and wind of the steppes had faded them into ghosts.

The Party did not make mistakes. Success depended on

---

[12]   The party hierarchy was organised into Partkoms. Each Partkom was headed by a party secretary, but each of the heads of the Partkom departments held immense power. They were not known by their complex titles and were called Partkoms for short. The head was 'The Secretary.'

ideological purity; Revolutionary slogans drove the fervent faithful forward.

'Efficiency today will bring rewards tomorrow!' declaimed a sorrowful notice.

A broken and rusting old tractor rotted alongside it.

'Exterminate the Mad Dogs of Capitalism!' hung over the door of their compound.

Posters of healthy peasants sitting around a table piled high with food and drink hung all around. They were garishly coloured, and the reds had started to leak, like blood.

'Collectives are the backbone of the revolution,' opined another, 'we feed the Proletariat.'

It was only here that the revolution was not working, claimed Anatoly. There were extensive gains for the people elsewhere. However, for some reason, the Kazakh collectives barely made enough to feed themselves.

Central Party had kindly offered them more labour, despite the fact that they could not feed their own farmers.

The poorly-educated young Partkom secretaries were ravaged by guilt.

*

Evening drinking sessions, and dialectic struggle kept their revolutionary fervour pure.

'It is,' Anatoly explained, 'something like this. Russia is not perfect. It is not the best place for the revolution, but *our* glorious proletariat was chosen to lead the world and we succeed. They look up to us. Lenin showed us the way and comrade Stalin is leading us into prosperity. Long live Marist–Leninism!'

A toast to the young chosen followed.

His slogan was enthusiastically taken up by his crew.

They poured tumblers of vodka and toasted their gods with libations of peasant blood.

'The young Soviets are riddled with class enemies who refuse to do the work; they have to be weeded out so the seeds of revolution can grow. We follow in the steps of our Great Lenin!' another toast.

Toast after toast, until they were drunk with alcohol and enthusiasm.

'Some individuals in the great Soviets are corrupt and have to die. Torture is too good for them. Most are true proletarians. They simply need re-education through work. We can help class enemies learn, as they build our future Utopia.' And so they drank their conscience into submission.

Great work had still to be done!

Instead of promoting good agricultural practices, the Partkoms concentrated on creating good revolutionaries. They deported anyone who they could not control. New deportees arrived daily in an attempt to dilute the existing culture and practices.

2.

Kazakhstan 1940

Lucia and Maria Orloski arrived at the collective in Spring, when there was little food but pleasant weather.

The steppes looked beautiful; a mass of flowers for miles waving in the breeze. The place did not seem as bad as they had feared.

Since they were from a wealthy landowning family, they were stronger than the city dwellers and were selected to work on one of the successful collectives.

The pair were an instant success. They were twice as tall as the tiny Kazakhs and were at ease with the animals. They knew many traditional horse remedies, as well as most of the herbal remedies used by generations of Poles to cure wounds, rheumatism and bruising in livestock.

Only one tractor still worked, working with parts pirated form the others. Everything else was horse-drawn, since the bitter winters had destroyed any machinery delivered to the collectives.

The pair had grown up with horses, and Maria's Przewalski horses were similar to the steppe ponies.

Maria made an excellent impression. She patted over a horse at one of the meets knowledgably. She pointed out its defects immediately, and even pushed back a strained hock on another. She bound it up expertly with material she tore from her skirt.

Murmurs ran through the crowd.

They were impressed.

They learnt each other's words for horse diseases and muttered their approval of her understanding. The leaders spat in their hands and so did Maria. Respect was sown.

The Princess introduced herself to the village headmen with the confidence of leadership and discussed horse training and breeding knowledgably.

This was regarded with great awe, and they were viewed as honorary wise women even though most of their remedies were already used by the local shaman.

Despite the barriers of language, they found it easy to make themselves understood, having talked to peasants for years. They shared common interests.

When the two ladies proved to be adept at the local sports of chasing after headless sheep (a sport, very similar to polo, never normally played by Kazakh women), they became legends. They were greeted by name by total strangers, their fame going before them. At gatherings, they would be introduced to new-borns and sons with the village elders. Every Kazakh would laugh and joke with them. They had exchanged some of their luxurious furs for a house to themselves. They were trusted and admired.

The Kazakhs were hospitable, fond of singing, and wildly sentimental. They recited long poems to each other over fermented mares' milk and wept over stories of love lost. They wore silly hats, giant felt constructions which looked like they would be blown away in the steppe winds, yet never were.

Their ponies acted like pets, ridden by voice. They animals were small and dog-like in their devotion to their masters. Anyone lost in the steppe grass without a pony would certainly never get out. Horses could be sent to search for their masters, and would often find them, even in snow storms. It was said that the nomads had slept in the yurts with the horses. Countless tales of 'horse saves man' and 'man saves horse' described the closeness of the relationship.

Lucia and Maria had brought no sensible garb, having packed sparkling tiaras and long ball gowns, two mink stoles and luxurious Siberian fox fur coats. They had silk stockings and high heels, tiny leather mitts and long evening mitts. They were chilled, even in the summer evenings on the steppes.

Poor ladies, they shivered and never complained, and wore priceless French chiffon day dresses to the fields with felt boots which they had bartered for their silk stockings. They were ridiculous, and at the same time highly chic.

Maria appeared to be managing her captivity, but she was frail. She had rebelliously chosen her spouse at a time when marriages involving property were arranged. She blamed herself for his misdeeds. She recalled her father's words about being rooted to the earth.

She had been torn from her natural habitat and planted into a wild land. She felt responsible for the destitution of her children and her existence revolved around protecting her remaining child.

The princess found loss of status supremely difficult, and was more depressed than she appeared. She found it hard to maintain a sense of her own identity. She alone despised communism when all around her accepted it as god's truth. She performed menial tasks, and mixed with rude and coarsely spoken people she scarcely understood. They swore and spat in her presence. They commented on her body and breasts as if she were a horse.

She was an attractive woman, and a Kazakh village leader was making overtures for her to become his second bride. Maria was horrified and insulted. She refused his earliest advances with dignity.

Then she received a visit and gift from his first bride.

'Do not be worried mistress,' the woman had announced, 'I have agreed with his choice. We can work together, I will help you make butter and yoghurt and I will teach you how to skin the sheep. I can help you, and you can help me.'

She hugged the princess warmly.

'Join us. You may have fine children.'

She patted her belly.

'You have fine wide hips. I am sure you will have many boys.'

Maria was horrified. She was without resources or support. She had woven her life around children and estate.

She avoided staring tragedy in the face, and denied anything was wrong. Instead of dealing with her own problems, she tried to protect her daughter.

Unfortunately, Lucia had easily adapted to her new way of life. She enjoyed her new freedom and felt strangled by her mother's warnings of eh dangers of mixing too freely with Kazakhs.

Instead of supporting the princess, Lucia gently advised her mama to accept her lot.

'You should marry, mama,' she advised, 'you will be much happier.'

The princess could not imagine being second wife to a man she did not honour. Such marriage involved cutting away her past, discarding everything she had achieved, denying her sons were good men, and admitting she was an oppressor. She had to forget her culture, her horses and her clothes.

Maria imagined spirits of vengeance hovering above her. She was intimidated by the wily old man and even more scared to ask the Raikom for support. Her daughter did not defend her and she was utterly alone.

She denounced herself.

She had made a great effort to be a liberated woman, and had won a few battles for personal freedom, but she had not disseminated her victories. She knew it would be difficult to surrender her hard-won liberty. There was no foreseeable future for her.

In this land of death she contemplated suicide, yet chose to stay alive for her daughter.

She dreaded the future. The Kazakh lecher stank of kvass - a kind of fermented mare's milk drunk by the men. His wife would share his bed and massage his tired feet. She had to touch his unwashed privates and let him into her body. And then, at 40, she had to bear sons, because a woman without sons was considered a witch.

Maria turned down the offer, stating that her daughter had to be disposed of first.

The village leader nodded wisely.

He understood, and withdrew to wait for his bride.

However, she was dismayed to learn that her daughter aspired to the slavery of the women of the steppes. Lucia was being courted by a fine-looking tall-ish young man called Dania.

Maria loathed Dania. He, in turn, regarded her independence as a sign of irrationality. She nagged her daughter about the negative character traits of Kazakh men, and drove her into a fury.

'Trust me' she had maintained, 'the tribal Kazakh are the ones our family fought. They are our traditional enemies, heathens and savages. Remember the painting of great grandfather on the wall of the palace?'

She referred to a great victory over the horde hundreds of years ago. (The painting was no portrait, just a romantic fantasy.)

'You are tempting fate. The spirits of the steppes are seeking redress.'

Lucia's burgeoning hormones disdained every word. She was in the throes of adolescence, and searching for romantic escape from the drudgery.

She had hopes of a new future among friends. She decided mama was insane, and protected her as she had done during their last days at Louvinka.

She often interrupted the princess.

'Mama does not mean that,' she chimed in when the princess spoke in broken Kazakh. 'She does not say what she means. It is her temperament. She is not herself.'

She berated her mother, even for innocuous conversations.

'Mama, you are being retrograde,' she insisted, 'harking backwards to the old ways. There has been a revolution. We are building a new world. Grow up.'

For the moment, she deferred to her mother, and avoided betrothal.

'Ok, mama, I accept your idea that I should wait until I understand things better, but you are locked into the past. You need to change.'

Nevertheless, she foresaw a rosy and romantic future in this exciting new culture. Life as an aristocrat had been restrictive and boring. Although pretty, she was not outstanding and poverty had affected her marriage prospects in Warsaw.

Here, among the Kazakhs she was a star with all the attention a woman could possibly desire. She was slightly annoyed that her mother received so much consideration among the elders. All the same, she reflected, even her mad mother might calm down in marriage.

3.

Summer 1940

Anya and Katya clung on to each other as they were herded to the deportation trucks.

Deportees were loaded on to cattle trucks, 50 to a truck, no matter how fat or thin, families separated if the count went against them, although it was possible to swap.

It was unbearably crowded and there was no food or water. Babies cried and old men needed the toilet. They were told to allocate one corner to sanitation, and the door was locked.

After an hour in the increasingly hot sun, the train set off, idling slowly and jolting over ancient points.

It was dark and there was nowhere to sit except the floor.

Everyone needed their morning ablutions and toilet. No one wanted to use the floor to defecate.

It was only when several were truly desperate that the stampede began. Then the smell in the truck was unbearable and pee rolled over the floor, wetting insensible old people and children. It soaked into those who had stayed up all night and lay in frazzled unconsciousness.

It was vile and humiliating.

And then that evening, the trucks were loaded with more people. There was no room to lie down.

Shifts were organised for sleeping. The shitty corner had to be occupied, and the foulness and stench became unbearable.

People vomited, fighting broke out. Children wept uncontrollably.

At the next station, music played, and Russian political speeches sounded at them as they waited in stinking heat.

The trucks were a living hell.

Yet for all of the horror of these conditions, the deportees merely shared the fate of millions of cows and sheep travelling in identical conditions, to certain doom, every day of every year.

It was part of the dehumanisation process.

Those close to the gaps in the wooden trucks read out the Cyrillic names of train stations passing by.

Every so often the train halted to change engines. Tinned music and speeches was piped to the prisoners for their education.

Guards came round with water.

'Comrades,' they shouted, 'water is available for the next 10 minutes. Form orderly queues under your representatives.'

Occupants fought over water in frenzy, until they learnt that it could be spilt and lost.

Then they queued dejectedly, shuffling and moaning like domesticated cattle.

Guards added fresh straw to the trucks. They asked deportees to push out soiled straw and 'any dead'.

There were none for 5 days.

Thereafter each truck produced at least one body, hiked out like a crowd-surfer, shoeless and coatless; in underwear only, with cries of 'god bless him,' or 'god bless her,' 'She will go to heaven,' 'Have mercy on her soul'.

Prayers were met by jeers from the guards.

After a further two days people were allowed out at sidings outside the railway stations.

Deportees descended; many falling over, stiffened from being in one position for so long.

Giant posters of Stalin and Lenin and Soviet flags fluttered at the sidings.

Old peasant women who brought prepared the food to the guards watched them warily, saying absolutely nothing.

Food was laid out in oil drums, and they queued for a ladle of soup, some containing meat and grain; others containing only watery fat.

Everyone was starving and loathsome, the smell horrific. The slightest infraction of unknown rules resulted in random shootings.

Old ladies knelt in front of the guards and begged, 'tell us where we are going? Please kind sir?'

They were kicked or pushed aside, perhaps because the guards were disconcerted.

Occasionally, peasants brought food and cigarettes for barter. At other times they passed through stations where piles of fly blown carcases lay naked and unburied from previous deportations.

Dejection spread through the entire group.

Babies were born and babies died. Corpses were thrown to the heaps like old socks onto a pile of laundry, often without prayers.

*

Then, randomly, the pattern of halts changed.

Partkom officials materialised at each station accompanied by skinny and hard-faced peasants dressed better than most they had previously seen.

Occupants were piled out and stood in rough lines.

Rifles were trained on the criminals as the visitors checked them over. Several from each truck were selected and signed for to work as labour on the collectives.

They were led off to shouted farewells through the wooden slats.

*

The liveliest dismay greeted the selection process. Each Collective could only take a limited number of human livestock to work the collectivised land.

The unhealthy fared badly. Families hung together with begging eyes. Mothers and children tried hard to look like they would work hard together, often to no avail.

'Have mercy' they cried in Russian, having carefully learnt the words, 'do not separate us!'

If the mother were weak or the child small and puny, separation was inevitable.

The wails of remaining family members on the journey out of the heartless sidings were horrific.

Abandoned children were inconsolable, and regularly died within days.

It was easy to die, because the heat in the trucks meant drinking was vital. Refusal to drink at two consecutive stations ensured death from dehydration. Many died, either by intention or from depression.

*

At each stop and selection process, Katya and Anya hung back; it might be dangerous to leave the train. In any case, they were thin, weak, female and clearly unsuited for farm labour. They only seemed a good prospect once all healthy, able-bodied men had been taken.

At length, the train became pleasantly empty.

Lying down on clean straw was possible. The occupants could keep themselves relatively clean.

Everyone got used to the stink. The girls looked better and stronger, rebounding from deprivation with the strength of youth.

The train continued East, and the weather became hot and humid. Steppes surrounded the train. Tall grass waved like the sea in the wind.

They had reached Kazakhstan.

*

It seemed deportations were universal, in every Soviet.

The party caucus had long ago ordained to dilute the cohesive populace by deportation and relocation of ethnic groups, presupposing that ethnic ties would stifle the revolutionary spirit.

The dregs of the Poles and a fair admixture of other nationalities were joined by rows of newly deported Kazakh peasants.

The exiles waited on the siding patiently, heavily guarded. Katya and Anna watched them as they waited in the sun. They had few spare clothes and no suitcases, how would they fare in the winter?

Four men appeared.

Two were educated, well-spoken Partkom secretaries from central Russian soviets.

They were accompanied by high cheek-boned Kazakh party representatives.

As usual, the deportees were lined up.

This time, Anya and Katya were among the twenty selected.

As twenty Kazakhs were loaded onto the repulsive trucks, the new arrivals, almost twenty women and one baby descended. They knelt and bowed to their new masters in obeisance, hoping for kindness from their future masters. As far as they could understand they were to work in a Kazakh collective farm.

Their new owners led them off. They rode steppe ponies so tiny that their legs almost touched the ground on either side of their mounts.

The captives stumbled behind, none used to walking, and blinded by the sun after the dark of the 10 day journey.

4.

Kazakhstan Soviet 1940

Katya and Anya had arrived in the middle of the latest terror aimed to stamp out kulak revisionism and create better harvests. Whole populations were being transported across Russia in an attempt to break down resistance to the Soviet way of life. As the new arrivals disembarked, introductions were made, and Tatars, Balkars, Lithuanians, Poles, and Turks attempted to communicate in broken Russian which was the *lingua franca* of those attempting to survive the next winter.

Over the next few days they were assessed by the three young men in charge of the collectives. Each Partkom and Primary Party Organisation (PPO) representative had a 'fair' chance of choosing fresh labour. Each representative selected what new recruits could be used for, discussing their potential in an altruistic spirit.

The strong and muscular were universally agreed to go to the more successful functioning collectives, as they would work hard and eat more. Other collectives, containing a thousand peasants and deportees each, were unlikely to survive the winter. They had failed to raise wheat from the barren soil.

The fact was that they did not have the correct machinery to sow at the required depth. Most of it had withered and died in the scorching sun and wind. No more grain was forthcoming. No winter feed had been collected for the cattle.

They would die.

The two slight and weedy sisters were the best of the remaining train survivors. It was agreed to send them to the least successful collective.

They were to act as helpers, or servants, to the head of the collective and his wife, a short, attractive woman with strong black hair greased with fat. She had woven carpets on the walls, taken from a rich man's yurt, magnificent tribal rugs, worth a fortune in today's antique carpets market.

They were to act as house servants and also clean the paths, repair fences and perform general labour of the poorest kind.

They were mostly forgotten by the half-starved inhabitants. At least they were warm. They slept on the floor of a solid house, the walls packed with leaves and grasses to keep out the wind like a yurt.

*

The leader's wife was fascinated by the girls' skin and faces, inspecting them like rare bugs, stroking and poking them as if they were pet kittens.

'Look! Little teeth!' she would say, 'and they speak! Say something, do!' smile, poke, encouraging smile.

She had a fire in the centre of the house and cooked sheep and goats' cheese, products not generally eaten by Poles. Both parties heartily despised each other and regularly insulted each other in their respective languages, smiling all the while.

'You ugly little toads,' the leader's wife would say, nodding in a friendly way at Katya, 'you look like a rotten cheese. You could not even pick up an empty bucket and carry to the well. How do you expect to catch a fine husband, let alone any husband at all?'

Katya would nod right back at her interlocutor, replying in Polish. 'You have put butter on your hair; do you think frying your head would make you less savage? Your face is like a squashed piece of sheep dung.'

Both sides despised each other and enjoyed their conversations mightily, each laughing at each other for what they had just said.

The girls learnt to eat grated raw potatoes lightly fried, a toxic snack designed to quell hunger pangs. Nothing could allay the hunger. They searched for scraps on the floor after a meal, and talked of nothing other than food. They tried not to think of past meals, and food which they had rejected in the past. It would cause an almost physical longing and pain.

This was localised famine, confined to the specific collectives. No relatives or neighbours could help out. Neighbourly assistance was counterrevolutionary. The Partkom secretaries believed in work as a magical force. If the workers had the right attitude, the harvests would be good. If the harvest was bad, they deserved to starve because they had toiled badly.

The collective knew that no subsidies were allowed. Death was inevitable. Many took drugs from secret plants on the steppes or drank blinding vodka. Dinner talk was of poison and suicide, of giving children away to neighbours, of escape to Afghanistan along the old nomad silk routes through the mountains.

A few whispered of uprising; but famine was a strong depressant.

Children wept for hunger; mothers drugged them to keep them quiet. The starved continued to weed the parched fields and watch the wilted crops. They tended the dying cattle and made invisible cheeses. They built barns to store invisible produce and sang revolutionary songs to make the crops grow. Then they went to bed praying that something might yet save them.

Katya and Anya laid plans to get away.

Membership of the party was their only chance, as party members had food.

Joining the party was not easy. It was elite, even if the privileged were demons and lunatics. It required faith in the ideology and dedication to the dialectic. Their only chance was to demonstrate to at least one Partkom secretary that they were party material.

5.

Internal Plotting

The Princess and her daughter were highly regarded by the tribes, but they had enemies.

The ancient and wizened medicine woman who managed the health of the tribes resented their incursion on her power base.

Katya hated them, because Lucia had thoroughly forgotten her.

'Hello,' she said, offering her hand. 'My name is Katya Maslow. We were at Tseder.'

Lucia watched her blankly, not hearing a word.

She was talking to a tiny steppe pony, which looked back at her adoringly.

'Tseder?' She replied. 'Oh yes, I was at Tseder. It had a high reputation. Lamentably, they didn't teach anything useful. You wouldn't have liked it. It was all sparkle and puff.'

The pony frisked around her and she stroked its neck.

Katya did not press the introduction. She was already offended that the ladies blanked her and Anya at the village-meet when newcomers were introduced. The Orloski ladies were the centre of crowds of eager Kazakhs fascinated by the wild giant women of exotic origin. It proved that Lucia's friendly overtures at the school had been totally insincere.

'Did you live in Lviv?' Lucia pattered. 'I wish I had seen it one last time before it fell. Which part?'

She nuzzled the steppe pony, without listening to Katya's reply. This type of conversation went on at cocktail parties, by remote, neither party listening to a word. Lucia had no clue who she was and spoke very little to the drab thin girl.

Katya was offended. She was treated like one of the servants on the estate!

Moreover, the air of the steppes suited Lucia. Her blond hair had bleached in the strong sun. Suffering had refined any coarseness in her features. She was no longer a slightly plump, spoilt aristocrat.

*

Some weeks later, Katya was given to the shaman for several days

154

in exchange for spells required by the village leader's wife. Work had taken the place of money altogether and the healer did little work, expecting visitors to pay for her services with labour.

A brilliant judge of character, she immediately divined the malice in Katya's heart. She also perceived that the girl had the strength and power to be a witch.

'What is it that you most desire?' She drooled.

It was the traditional opening between master and apprentice.

Katya asked her how to escape the doomed collective.

The fortune-teller threw her stones, tossed herbs on her fire and muttered under her breath. She spoke in a whining, lilting voice.

'Your doomed collective was built on an ancient site, where skulls piled high to demonstrate the inexorable retaliation wrought on any enemies.'

She paused, and sang an ancient funeral dirge without consonants, more of a tuneful howl than anything else.

'Exorcists sacrificed there to calm the unquiet spirits, and still demon communists built the collective in these cursed places. They have raised the ghosts of revenge.'

She spat on the ground and muttered to herself; spat on her palms rubbed them together and clicked her fingers rapidly, clearing the empty air.

'They called it superstitious foolishness.'

She was contemptuous, and picked up a pinch of powder from one of the jars and bowls laid out on the floor. She threw it on the brazier. Flames burned blue, green and orange.

A sharp metallic smell filled the cleverly erected tent inside her hut.

'May they be cursed forever,' she sniffed, 'unto the tenth generation.'

Katya was shocked at the weird chanting voice and frightened by her talk of curses. Her life was already fragile; she did not want to die. She knew from history class that Genghis Khan had been through here, and that the Kazakh were the remains of his 'horde'.

The steppe was dotted by Scythian burial mounds which reputedly contained the corpses of hundreds of slaves and horses who had followed their leader to the next world. At night the area was punctuated by lights of all kinds, mostly ball lightning and electric storms; and also mysterious lights which were inexplicable according to the science she knew. The locals called these elementals and dead souls, and claimed that they must be placated. Their houses and their beasts were covered with amulets and blue beads, and they themselves wore all manner of magic wards, to avert the curses which could devastate the land.

Over the next two days, the shaman showed her simple spells: how to curse someone, how to get rid of warts and such like.

'How can I escape my fate?' begged Katya.

The old lady wanted the two tall women out of her way. They were rivals. Most of the educated exiled derided their hosts, but Lucia and Maria had wholeheartedly embraced their new culture. They were learning the language of the steppes and its customs. They were going native.

It had to stop.

'By finding souls to exchange for your own,' the soothsayer replied.

The Shaman had hypnotic powers. It was therefore perhaps the result of auto suggestion, that Katya selected Lucia and Maria as perfect replacements, two women for two women. They were easy to denounce in a sociopathic communist universe where anything out of the ordinary was dangerous.

She returned inspired by zeal to betray the two innocent ladies who had befriended the Kazakh.

*

The Partkoms were children of the revolution, genuine proletarians educated under Lenin's rule.

There was no trace of good breeding among them. They aggressively picked their noses and wiped snot on the walls. They scratched their bottoms in public and never washed before meals. They burped and farted in front of women. They made coarse jokes, swore indefatigably and cursed everyone.

For all that they were delicately built and not strong.

This 'perfect vanguard of a new society' enforced the will of the people, and tortured men, women and children to death. They participated in the deliberate isolation and starvation of 'kulaks', slaughtered herds of beloved ponies and decimated the population - all in the name of revolution and progress.

As elite, leaders of the revolution, they were weak and greedy. They believed that they deserved the wealth of the land in the name of a dialectic, which they recited to themselves at every wobbly moment.

These users of women and despoilers were not men anyone would want to attract. They lived the lives of power-crazed megalomaniacs, yet they only tortured in the name of progress, for the People.

Katya had already heard how they had collected the famous Silk Road carpets which decorated the Khans' yurts. They'd urinated on them, and piled them on to a gigantic bonfire of ancient carved yurts.

And yet, their eyes had the faraway stare of those who see salvation and know the location of heaven. Their faces bore the thin and ascetic expressions of monk inquisitors. They were sociopaths who worked in the name of ideology

Katya focused on Andrei, the weediest Partkom; a short pimply youth who picked his nose and ate the snot.

At 20, his fair hair was thin and wispy, showing signs of baldness soon to come. His slightly receding chin was covered by a thin Leninist beard and moustache. He stooped, probably from malnutrition as a young boy and looked as if he came from a genuinely poor and malnourished background, perhaps beggars or street vendors in Moscow. (This was in fact the case, his father, a spy for the Mensheviks, won fame as a runner in the revolution.)

Andrei's credentials were the highest, and he needed to prove his revolutionary fervour, based on the fact that his father may once have spoken to Lenin.

If Katya had been comely, or sexy, Andrei would have arrested her for approaching him. He had a deep-seated fear of being seduced by a seditious counterrevolutionary. Fortunately, Katya really did not fit the bill.

She approached him as he delivered the latest instructions on herd management to the leader of the collective.

The Partkoms had concluded that the imminent starvation was due to the Kazakh incompetence in animal husbandry. His wisdom

157

was extracted from Stalin declaration that 'one revolutionary was worth ten experts' when implementing new technology.

The Kazakh elder listened with dignified seriousness, to measures which would give sheep hoof rot and decimate neighbouring flocks.

The old man was wondering how to implement the new measures without lasting damage, when Katya entered with tea.

*

The revolution had not helped women's rights in any way. Although 'liberated' by revolution, women were not allowed to speak or expected to have ideas.

Their freedom had improved in so far as employment as low grade workers and all-round drudges. Working women were still responsible for all housework duties, and their babies were placed in state nurseries, to be brought up by the People.

Abortion was free, and was the main form of contraception available. Divorce was simple, and state orphanages overflowed with abandoned children.

Katya contrived to open the conversation on her own. She had interrupted important man-talk, and Andrei turned on her with blazing eyes.

Before he said anything, she spoke. She already knew that he prayed to pictures of Lenin before going to sleep.

'Comrade,' she uttered quickly, eyes modestly lowered, bowing as to an aristocrat, 'please explain to me where I can obtain a picture of Stalin? It may help me to sleep if I look at his sweet face last thing at night.'

Andrei felt a shudder of understanding. He had left for a boarding school for young party cadres at the age of 13. It was indeed a significant honour to his revolutionary parents, but he had been deeply lonely.

Photographs of parents were deemed bourgeois and weak. He had cried quietly until given a photograph of Lenin, which he kissed before going to sleep.

'I think I may be able to obtain one for you, comrade' he replied, and for the first time, noticed the plain proletarian face, shining with love for the revolution.

Katya was excited to speak to a man. She was a normal teenager, and craved admiration like any other girl. This was her chance of status, the best she could hope for. She needed to get his attention, and revelled in sweet success.

'Lucia has an icon,' she stated humbly. 'I want to show her how much more spiritual it would be to have Stalin over my bed than any silver and jewelled puppet. '

It was a direct hit. Andrei reddened. He too, admired tall and loose limbed Lucia, striding through the steppe in her flimsy dresses and voluminous felt boots, sometimes wearing a mink stole in an attempt to stave off the cruel winds. He dreamt of her quite inappropriately and was conscience-stricken by his desire. Now he learnt that she was a worshipper of icons, almost a counterrevolutionary. Where would this lead?

And so the first step in the exchange of souls began.

Katya worked through each Partkom secretary, carefully raising her revolutionary profile while shattering the reputation of two innocent women whom she intended to take her place on the altar of doom.

*

The brief popularity of Lucia and Maria fell away. People were afraid to talk to them in case they were deemed part of a counterrevolutionary clique.

Having obtained copies of Stalin's speeches, Katya was easily able to undermine the women using the same directives which the Raikom was forcing on the hardened and tough old nomads. She also found nameless traitors and conspirators, and fuelled their paranoia, encouraging them against starving families when they were faint-hearted. She helped identify those who had hidden grain or who used primitive traps to supplement their diet.

In all this, she steadily grew in power, even obtaining free advice from the frightened Shaman. She became a power to be reckoned with, and a vicious opponent to any who crossed her, causing deportations of whole families on a whim and gaining the reputation of a first class informer.

6.

Loucki Prison 1940

Sofia was taken to the Lvov Penitentiary, Loucki, which was not yet a chiefly political prison.

Right up until the invasion of Poland, it has been a penitentiary for criminals, populated by working class women who transgressed the male-dominated laws. They included lesbians, abortionists, forgers, and gypsies. Their crimes included running away from abusive husbands (and thereby stealing), criminal insanity (for demanding freedoms only available to men), theft, fraud, child murder (abortion), and prostitution (tempting men).

The regime was harsh. Food was scarce and physical exercise out of the question. There was a slow walk around a narrow sunless yard for one hour per day, no running and no talking. Eight women spent the day in a tiny cell with a bucket of shit, bored out of their skulls, with only maggoty food or the rattle of keys to pass the time. Their limbs were stained with chilblains, nit bites, scabies and impetigo. Their minds were driven into the darkest extremes by close confinement. The place was ruled by bullies who mirrored the intimidations of the outside world.

Since the invasion, it was increasingly overcrowded, filling with middle class women.

*

Sofia arrived at the prison still sporting a vicious black eye from her recent interrogation. Her left hand was useless with several broken fingers. She was raped by one of the guards and brutally strip-searched by a further two. She bore it meekly. Every blow she received and every humiliation faced was something she had spared her family.

She was moved into a cell full of hardened women who hated her on sight. Sofia was, and looked like, a cultured and educated Jewess. As such, she personified change, progress and industrialisation. She, like the rest of the Jewish population, was held to blame for its effects on the rural and illiterate populace.

She was shown a soaked and stinking cot. It had been moved

close the large latrine bucket that the inmates shared. Each inmate spat in her mug and one wiped her befouled finger around her plate.

She prayed for her accusers and torturers in an attempt to gain strength and overcome her feelings of shame.

She was overheard by one of the inmates.

'A Jew is praying to Mary.'

'Jesus killer!'

The women fell on her, kicking and ripping and scratching her, venting their frustration for the injustices they faced.

*

During that long first night in prison Sofia lay on a stinking mattress with two newly-broken ribs, added to existing injuries. She retched uncontrollably at the smell from the bucket and from memory of fellatio performed on the prison guard.

At around 3.00 am, a long shuddering sob left her pain-racked, sleepless body.

*

The tight, suppressed sound reached out to Magda, self-appointed cell leader and newly elected 'People's Representative for the Women Prisoners of Loucki'.

The prison PPO[13] had selected Magda as representative. She was adept at spouting communist cant, having learnt how important it was to say what customers want to hear. She did not care what she did, and this suited her new employers.

She was the meanest bitch in the block.

Magda guessed what had happened to Sofia. She too had been strip searched, and raped by the same guard. As a street walker it had not bothered her at all. As a working girl she had long given up ownership of those heavily abused parts of her body. She was able to let her mind wander off.

She did not care that Sofia was a Jew. She respected every race and every range of belief in her line of work, provided they could pay. If not then would turn into a foul mouthed racist, spouting the vilest insults.

At heart, Magda was no sociopath, she simply did anything

---

[13] Primary Party Organisation

necessary to survive. It had been a long time since she had encountered someone unsullied by crime and degradation. And the suppressed sobs elicited unwanted memories of her childhood when she too had faced such despair.

She hadn't thought about her past for a long time. Now for some reason, these unwanted memories stole into her mind. At 7, she had been a typical plump, blond Polish girl with long blond plaited hair and rosy cheeks. She remembered the beatings her mother had endured to protect her children and a heavy sigh stole from her.

One fateful night, her mother had ordered her to sleep alone in the children's room, taking her other eight siblings to her bed.

Magda slept fitfully. The oil lamp left burning in her room kept her awake. Silence felt like a stifling blanket without the accompanying snores of her family.

Most workers were asleep in the large semi- derelict apartment block by 2.00 am when her waiter father returned. She could tell he was slightly drunk by the way he bumped into the doors

He was not alone.

She pretended to sleep, covering her head with the sheet.

'She is a pretty one' she heard her father say, 'worth every penny.' He giggled a little. 'Unbroken and a virgin, quite pure.'

The intruder interrupted.

'I will take a glance,' He sounded Lithuanian, and addressed her father in the servants register.

Father gently lifted the sheet from her. He lifted her nightdress too; a clean one mother had insisted she wear.

She pretended to be asleep, eyes tight shut.

The man turned her over gently and sighed, 'Yes, she is a pretty one. I will take her.'

And they both did.

First the stranger, as her father whispered he would kill her and her mother if she so much as whimpered, and then, her father.

That was the end of childhood. She was sold to a local brothel where her happiness was sucked out in acts she carefully avoided detailing to herself, although the darkness left behind by the deeds had etched into her soul.

She recollected the quiet serious intent of the elderly paedophile

162

as he added her young life to his conquests. She still remembered his elderly face. The energy stolen from childhood gave him the weird sheen of an elderly vampire.

As to her father, his expression was utterly merciless. He viewed his daughter as a commodity to be sold when a suitable offer came up.

From there on she was sullied and her father sold her into prostitution. She remembered entering the local church where the priest noted a child-prostitute in her garish overly-mature dress and gaudy ribbons. The priest had ejected her – terrified that his parishioners would discover that he visited child-prostitutes.

She watched Sofia pray silently, her good hand telling the beads of an imaginary rosary. It harked back to her mother's rocking her to the peaceful rhythm of forgotten prayers.

She regretted her lost youth. At 25, her body was wracked with alcohol abuse, her once pink and white skin was sallow, her hair mousy and lank.

She had been imprisoned just after Lvov had fallen into Soviet hands. She had stolen a cake!

Her 'crime' occurred on a quiet evening as she wandered the streets in a drunken haze.

She noticed a fancy patisserie in the window of a fancy bakery. It looked delicious; she wanted to buy it.

The fancy shop catered to the wealthy, even though she had money.

Surely she would be allowed in now that there was a communist government?

It made no difference, she was not welcome. As they hustled her out she picked up the cake and bit into it.

She tried to pay, but they claimed she had stolen it.

By that time she was shouting and drunkenly abusive to the proprietor.

He pressed charges.

The Soviets were keen to establish order on the streets and they did not approve of affray and immorality. She was condemned to four years in prison for theft and intimidation; an example to keep her sort away from the people.

Sofia was bourgeois, betrayer of the people oppressor of the working classes, but she was also like her mother.

Would her mother approve of what she had become?

All at once, Magda regretted her every act of infamy. She wept for the first time in years. She cut her arms and bled tears of remorse for the young girls she had pulled into the ghastly trade in flesh, in revenge for what had been done to her. She decided to become a good communist and make the world a better place.

*

The next day she stared balefully at the pinching and slapping which normally took place over breakfast.

'Stop that right now. Is this how comrades act to one another? We are here to learn to be better communists.'

She ordered the Jew was to be left alone.

The entire cell block felt a relief from bullying. It rippled through the cells like fresh water, turning lives into new channels. The cells were lighter and somehow cleaner. The new inmates had no idea of the horrors which they had been spared.

A few gypsy crones started a dance, tapping the cell bars to a famous gypsy tune.

Later an old nomadic woman sung her weird mouth music and did not get beaten as the foreigner she was. Unknown to the inmates, she sang an old Kazakh shamanistic song for the exorcism of evil spirits.

It worked.

*

Sofia spent her sentence in relative peace. Her food was stolen or made foul. She was kicked and spat at. She carefully checked her bedding every night for lumps of faeces and dead rats, yet she was not turned over to sadists who crippled middle class inmates in their madness.

If she witnessed acts of injustice she broke into prayer for the wicked.

Amazingly, this inspired the perpetrators with deadly fear of the afterlife.

'Don't bother with her', said the bullies to each other. 'She's not worth it.'

*

As the prison filled with middle class women accused of crimes against the state everyone gradually found places in the prison hierarchy. It was a key to survival.

Sofia remained outside these cliques. The Jews hated her because she was a Catholic, and Catholics hated her as a Jew.

Bizarrely, her high-minded spirituality gained her a couple of bizarre allies.

The first time she baffled a direct offensive from a crass bully by praying at her, the ancient shaman grasped her by the hand and muttered in a foreign language, indicating that she would join her. And a fat gypsy fortune teller hugged her like a sister.

They ate together thereafter and walked close to each other during exercise.

'Let them be,' ordered Magda. 'They're just lunatics.'

They were mostly left alone.

The trio had an aura of otherworldliness which frightened the guilty. No one wanted to be remembered for multiple hidden crimes in the afterlife.

*

The political committee soon heard of this tiny corner of primitivism in the den of punishment.

They weren't initially sure how to deal with it. Eventually they found a solution.

The three were moved together into a cell into which twenty five selected injured and dying inmates spent their remaining days in a cell built for eight.

Those with terminal injuries from torture were sent straight to 'Cell number 9', as were the sick, the cancer-ridden and the insane.

Sofia prayed, the Shaman muttered spells, sung hypnotically and the gypsy laid out the dead.

It was a corner of peace for those who ended their days in that particular hell.

*

Sofia was deeply traumatised by the injustices in the overflowing prison.

165

She felt guilty for surviving and made amends by sacrificing herself for others in the time-worn expiation of the abused. The remainder of her life would be a pilgrimage for the safety of her family.

*

At the end of 12 months, she was released, subject to deportation.

Magda heaved a sigh of relief that the saintly prisoner had gone. She had secretly asked Sofia to pray for her and felt that this was a betrayal of her new god of communism.

She had mixed her miniscule understanding of Christianity with communist ideology. She combined naiveté with a new-born kind heart and sincerely believed that Stalin would bring peace to the world.

For Magda, prison was an opportunity for re-education rather than punishment. She was assured of the truth that it would re-educate those who were sick and unwilling to work.

She denied the torture and forcible re-education of political prisoners, and the guards wisely kept her out of that department.

Such things could not happen under Soviet rule.

The NKVD told her absurd lies, and laughed at her sincere shock at what prisoners had done to themselves under questioning. She worried about prisoners falling downstairs because they were drunk or resisting the guards.

She warned political ladies to be careful not to injure themselves and waved inmates off to labour camps, believing that they would learn new skills in the fine open air.

*

She succumbed to the trials of the 50's.

By that time, she was a committed Christian as well as a socialist. She died in the uncompromising belief that her party was honestly mistaken.

Comrade Stalin was a good man, misled by evil advisors.

She was shot quietly lest her idealism infected audiences at the trials. She is remembered as a hypocrite and torturer while the true perpetrators live in quiet retirement on prison pensions.

166

7.

Marseilles 1940

Marseilles was filling with Jews on the run from all over Europe. It was also filling with Germans, apparently soldiers on vacation.

The Brauns had moved to a modest and almost empty hotel close to the port. They had stayed there nearly a month and the staff were used to them. There was another family of Jews at the hotel and they often came to tea. No unpleasantness was discussed with these neighbours, although the men often talked of emigration.

Rebecca had located her younger son, David.

He had abandoned his business interests in Hungary. Even so. it had still been extremely difficult to leave.

He had spent every sou on escape. He had two young children and very little money as he had been unable to sell much. His young wife was pregnant and travel had proved very difficult as everyone was sure that they were carrying gold and contraband. They could not afford to move quickly and had walked much of the way.

Rebecca was ecstatic when the bedraggled family arrived at the hotel. She booked a new suite and ordered an opulent meal, inviting everyone they knew.

About 20 people descended on the hotel and they stayed up to 2.00 am.

*

Unfortunately, with the arrival of their son and his family, the family were eased out by rudeness and hints from the management.

'This is not a Jewish hotel,' the patron had said, 'we cannot be seen as one. It is bad for future business. There are too many of you. We had German visitors yesterday, they explained why we cannot do this, and I agree.'

It was clear that even here in the poorest part of town they were outcasts. They were an island in a sea of hatred, weighed down by suitcases of fine clothes, jewels and gold.

These educated people of haughty demeanour had become the unwanted. They could not go into cafes, bars or theatres. Even in museums, people murmured and stared.

Where to go?

They considered returning to clear their name, but were prevented by the shadows cast by fleeing Jews.

There was an atmosphere of panic among the entire Jewish community hiding in that part of town.

Rebecca talked to other women on a regular basis. Izaak and his male friends called it hysterical gossip. The women had heard distressing gossip of yellow stars, which Izaak advised his wife to discount. He had no doubt of the innate hysteria of the women; even he was becoming pretty worried.

He controlled his own fears by attacking his wife.

'Rebecca, you are hysterical,' he cautioned. 'This is a temporary blip on the political landscape. I have been very lenient with you. You must learn to control yourself.'

She reported that women were giving their children away to goys in the hope that they would survive.

Izaak paid no mind, until he met men desperately searching for refuge for their families in France, without success.

He knew of arrests, and disappearances in German occupied territory; now there was talk of arrest even in 'Free' France.

Their business had gone overnight, Izaak Jr had vanished. They only possessed what they had with them.

By December 1940 panic gripped the hearts of the remaining Braun family.

*

There was no community spirit among the fleeing Jews. There could not be.

Rumours of Jewish conspiracies abounded and were openly discussed in newspapers and radio.

Jewish bankers behind financial collapse of 1929!' hollered one of the headlines
Jewish socialists proved to have made Peace of Versailles' implied another.
Jewish Bolsheviks congregate in France'

It was said that large numbers of foreign Jews congregating or even meeting in secret, risked arrest for conspiracy. So they avoided each other, pretending nothing was wrong.

'Jewish Conspirators hide in Paris,' claimed the papers.
'Bombing of Eiffel Tower planned'

Something in society had irrevocably broken.

'Socialist refugees planning to take over our government.'

They had dropped from the normal world into a universe of silence, hostility and isolation.

Jewish people were fleeing with nothing; people were dying because they were Jewish, they were being beaten and robbed for no other reason than being Jewish.

It was not the faith, but the race, something intrinsic and unchangeable. It was an indefinable biological difference which made them inferior.

Conversion and belief made no difference. A Jew was a fundamental and inescapable aspect of who they were. Nothing could change the fact that they were unwanted and hated.

'What is Jewish?' they heard a little boy say, as they passed by. 'Is it monsters?' mama hushed the little boy as he turned and stared at the exotic couple in the street.

8.

Kazakhstan Winter

The Shaman succeeded in her plan.

The Orloski ladies were forced to transfer to the doomed collective and the by now feared Katya and her sister moved into the home of evicted counterrevolutionaries in one of the most successful collectives, near the Raikom headquarters.

Winter came and starvation strode into the collective.

Lucia was young and full of hope. She had a chance to grab at life among tragedy, and grabbed it eagerly.

She and Dania came together in a bid for survival in the dire circumstances.

The intensity of their affair was the bond of two people facing death. They went out in the dark nights in the autumn snow checking traps and digging in the frozen ground for hibernating voles and rats. They slept close together to keep warm.

Dania endangered his own life to save his girl and their differences were swept away in the urge to live. It was a torrid affair, and Dania accepted her as equal because it was essential to survival.

The combination of Dania's native cunning and her astute judgment hacked a small band of survivors from the doomed collective. They famously rustled a whole cow from a neighbouring collective one snowy night. No trace of it was ever found despite severe questioning. Lucia was beaten, yet as she constantly repeated,

'Logically, how could we have done it? Where is the proof that we dragged such a heavy animal some 50 miles across the steppe?'

A clever woman, Lucia had kept her wits under questioning.

Furthermore, she severely undermined Katya's credibility in the process.

'I expect Katya made this ridiculous suggestion. She likes to spread rumours, and she is a clever lady. Have you asked her about the cow? It would realise a substantial sum in the black market.'

For all their successes, Maria persisted in distrusting Dania. She observed the way he led Lucia, and noted his resentment of her independence and skill.

'Mama, I have waited as you asked, and now I have given you up. Dania is perfect. He believes in freedom for women. He told me so.'

'He will turn you into a slave!' claimed the frantic mother. 'Do you know you will be killed as a witch if you do not bear sons within two years? Please don't do it darling. I was a slave to your father and I bore the insults *he* deserved. Don't do it, my baby!'

Her mother's deep suspicion of her suitor created an incurable rift.

'What are you talking about?' Lucia complained.

Lucia was not interested in the past, and she had rejected all the stories of roots and the land. 'I know Dania loves me, and you hate him. He is not an old-fashioned man like father. You are over-imaginative and hysterical. Dania thinks you are unbalanced. I have told him what happened at Louvinka. We both agree that this is more of your instability.'

She avoided her mother - her starved and grief-stricken expression was unbearable. Her mother was prejudiced and revisionist.

Dania was different. She was the first free woman and a true revolutionary, the heroine in a story, and a warrior maiden in a Russian fairy tale.

She had sparkling dreams despite the death surrounding them. She imagined her face in a Socialist broadsheet.

'Heroine saves collective!'

She was full of passion for Dania in those romantic winter nights.

She learnt the Kazakh way of life, their exotic way of training horses, hiding in the snow, how to find the way home in white wastes. She learnt how to hunt and to throw a lasso.

She also more than half-believed the dialectic, and was keen to prove her working class credentials. She imagined her famous face on the propaganda trains and planes, demonstrating treasures of revolution to the people.

She would be a new woman, healing the rift between cultures.

'Comrade Lucia leads the Kazakh people to revolution'

All the while parent and lover engaged in a relentless war of ideas.

171

It was no contest.

Lucia took Dania's word that mama was erratic, counterrevolutionary and a class enemy. He had a real hold over the idealistic girl, who already resented her mother's dignity and charisma.

Maria related horror stories of women burnt and starved, beaten like horses and killed when food was short.

'Mama!' Lucia remonstrated, 'you are looking backwards instead of to our glorious advances. We are the future! You mistake him absolutely.'

Maria recalled her blind faith in Peter and sighed,

'I know that you worship him, and I would not seek to crush that.'

She could see how captivating Lucia was by the fugue of love. She wanted her happiness above all things. If she was sure of her daughter's future then she could deal with her own.

'You must also realise that he is very different and holds totally different views of women. That kind of love does not last. '

'Oh! I can change him mamma.'

'Men do not change. Women do.'

There was another heavy sigh.

'Mama! You sound awfully depressed. Cheerlessness demonstrates a lack of revolutionary spirit which drives progress. We must show our revolutionary spirit. We will drive on to build a new future.'

Maria sighed again and tears filled her eyes.

Lucia bit her lip; mother was proving a dreadful disappointment.

'Denial of progress is counter revolutionary. Everything is improving! This is revolution! Do you remember the dreadful life of our poor comrades under the Count?'

'No,' replied her mother sadly, 'only those in power have changed; nothing is different. You are surrounded by death.'

Lucia coolly observed her stooped and saddened mother.

'Dania told me you are a class enemy, and I think he is right.'

Her mother did not reply. She understood that her daughter did not share her aspirations for the future of the land.

She glanced at Lucia speculatively; and was shocked at the hatred in her eyes.

They confronted each other in silence; Lucia flounced off and did not speak to her mother for a long time.

*

After a month's absence Lucia visited her mother.

Dania stood a little way away, supervising his girlfriend, apparently uninvolved.

'Mama,' she had a proposal to heal their relationship. 'Perhaps you *are* crazy. Comrade Victor said so and Dania agrees. They must be right because they are good men.'

Maria watched her daughter, bemused.

She was sinking into deep despondency, having lost home, husband sons and friends in one short period. She needed to regroup.

'Dania says that there are fabulous re-education programs out East. You can register for one. You will return to us healed; maybe you could marry when you return. Dania says a woman must marry or she goes mad. Don't you think that might be true? And you did refuse everyone. You need time to work out wrong thinking.'

Maria turned away.

She walked away slowly saying nothing.

*

Dania was reassuring.

'Don't worry Lucia my sweetness. The old lady will come round. You have told her nothing but truth. She will listen unless she is utterly insane.'

Maria overheard Dania's words as he drew his girlfriend away,

'Counter revolutionaries need time to learn that there is no alternative. She needs to be left alone.'

Her sparkling tears went unseen.

*

Bleak spring frosts took hold of the steppes.

In that time Maria became a 'goner'. Starvation and depression ate away her soul, and she rarely spoke.

She, who had always considered herself the equal of men, was overborne by a world of extreme sexism.

In meetings of the collective, alternative plans for survival were

173

discussed endlessly.

Maria opened her mouth to speak. She had a plan for escape.

Male leaders made allowances for the countess. However, her own daughter hushed her, convinced she was insane.

'Mama,' she maintained afterwards, 'you sound touched. You are not actually mad, just everyone thinks you are.'

Lucia crushed her mother, and her hold on life wore thin.

*

Lucia had trustingly reported her mother's opinion of Dania to her boyfriend.

Dania carefully argued against every single one. And his girlfriend was convinced of her mother's insanity.

'I was worried,' he told his companions, 'Lucia seemed to think I owed her mother some kind of duty! At long last she has realised that her mother is cuckoo!'

By this time Maria was completely isolated. She no longer maintained her aristocratic self-confidence.

She started to mutter to herself.

'Maybe I really did exploit the peasants? May I really am an evil person.'

Perhaps she really was an evil exploiter? She became uncertain, without purpose, and doubtful that she was worthy to live.

She refused to eat food better used on others and made personal sacrifices for the people, without gaining recognition or attention. She was becoming a hungry shade.

*

Traditionally, unmarried women and the childless died in the snow to save others, and several had departed already.

Dania beckoned food away from her in the evenings; she was expendable.

The mother needed to be eliminated.

Without her mother's backing, Lucia could be excluded from meetings, and prevented from interrupting her husband when he spoke.

She would become a proper subservient wife.

*

Maria left death until the last possible moment.

174

She was enchanted by life, the untrodden beauty of the white late spring snow, clear morning light and spectacular sunsets. She traced the exotic patterns made by the dirty straw of her bed. Even her pangs of hunger were signs that she wanted to live.

At last, one clear moonlit night, she heard a cracking chill outside.

Death would come quickly; no one could survive outside in such extreme cold.

The starving slept in tight groups as she carefully unpacked her remaining possessions. She had given away everything except her treasured fox fur, and silk underwear. The remainder consisted of standard Kazakh winter clothing and boots.

She crept out in her underwear, almost turning back.

There was no wind, and the freezing moon shone so brightly on the half melted snows that she was almost blinded.

Dania and her daughter slept alone in another hut, like newlyweds. They were endlessly fascinated with each other.

Maria accepted that she could not change fate.

Lucia wanted this.

She left her fur coat and boots at the door of their hut.

Her body ached to live as she sat outside the compound for a moment.

She could not feel her feet or hands.

She tried to think of a useful purpose in living. She revelled in the wonderful beauty of the night landscape.

She had a sudden realisation of who she really was, feeling intensely alive.

There was a loud crack in that icy silence. A wolf broke her neck as she stared at the moon.

*

Maria was one of millions that perished in the winter of 1940-41. She had been careful to leave her Siberian fox fur coat and felt boots by her daughter's door.

Her body was never found. She joined the ghosts haunting Louvinka, and the spirit winds of the steppes.

Dania wore the fox fur in their next night's hunting. He resolved that his new wife should make him a cap and cuffs from it.

It was a modest dowry, yet suitable. He generously allowed her to trim a coat for herself with the remainder, though he could sell the fur.

*

All through winter, the Partkoms faced rumblings of unrest from the other collectives. Survivors left corpses of their starved children outside the compound by night, which was unnerving. Old grannies taking the traditional option of walking to their doom in the snow, rather than watch children starve, headed for Raikom headquarters, sometimes dying stuck to the door.

They had to be kicked off, leaving bits of skin on the woodwork.

It was impossible to bury bodies in the frozen ground and by spring the corpses became an inconvenience.

At one point Partkoms ordered the corpses to be burnt.

The pyre left a stinking pall of acrid smoke over the compound, and, in any case, they did not burn properly.

The smell hung around for days and the roasted flesh attracted wolves who howled all night.

In the end, the maddened comrades ordered the remains to be dragged to the station some 50 miles away to join the counterrevolutionary trash ejected from the trains.

Nevertheless, the young leaders still kept faith in the ideals of revolution.

*

In April, when at least half of the collective had died of starvation, they provided the remainder with emergency rations.

Lucia and her small band had pulled through. A handful of the survivors died of spongiform encephalopathy, caused by eating human flesh, which Kazakhs called the curse of the dead spirits.

*

Now they were safe, and Dania single-mindedly prepared to cure Lucia of independent thinking. He dreamed of becoming a clan leader. An obedient, exotic woman would raise his status when he escaped to Afghanistan with the survivors in May.

Dania contemplated different schemes to break her before the journey.

He had to have complete authority.

'A few beatings,' he mused. 'She will come round because she

176

adores me. Or I could marry a second woman. Two wives will fight over me, both learning their place. A little jealousy is a good thing,' he speculated with satisfaction. 'She could beg, like woman should.'

He forbade Lucia to chat to other men, and insisted that she cover her blond hair in a traditional scarf.

She did her best; they had been through so much together, he was impossible to resist.

Then he started threatening her, and even slapping her. When she expostulated, he insisted that women were 'like cattle'.

*

Lucia accepted a great deal.

She wanted to live among the Kazakh and to be a good communist. She insisted on coming to at least one of meetings planning escape to Afghanistan.

She crept in, to the glares of men. As Dania made plans to leave, Lucia joined in.

He interrupted her rudely. 'You will travel apart,' he ordered, 'and sleep with the women, escorted by the boys. My aunt will act as chaperone.'

'No,' said the provoked Lucia, 'we will be together as before! We are always together, remember?' she shook her golden head petulantly, and golden locks crept out from under her scarf. 'I will not go.'

*

After the meeting they were left together.

She could have been persuaded otherwise if he had coaxed her.

She had rejected almost everything of her past, and may indeed have become the perfect bride. She gazed lovingly into her boyfriend's eyes as they entered their hut.

She was intimidated by his expression, and wavered.

'What did I do?'

Dania's pride was wounded by the fact that his kidnapped bride had used the word 'No', and in front of men!

It was a cultural matter; the word 'no' is masculine.

It was a dangerous word among the Kazakh, betokening impending conflict, a word with knives in it, and *never* used by women.

177

He slapped her face.

'Do not talk to me like that, bitch. You have no right to question me. Who do you think you are?'

Shades of her mother's warnings returned.

She drew on the remnants of Valkyrie training and resisted him. She refused to contemplate departure.

'I can do what I want. I will not go!'

The mood changed to a cold violence.

Dania beat and kicked her.

'Come with me or die like the dog that you are!' he growled through clenched teeth.

He took off his leather belt and whipped his woman in the traditional way, like a recalcitrant donkey.

'Say sorry, bitch. Do not ever speak to me like that.'

She tried to answer back.

He re-assaulted her with strength and violence.

He was furious!

If he had only used a little kindness and love! Instead, he let anger take rein. The resentment she caused when speaking out of turn at meetings overtook his normal wits. It had to beaten out of her.

'Do this again,' he roared, 'and be sure that you will die!'

He was serious and capable of murder. She had dishonoured him in a way which she did not understand. He was implacable, and held a sharp knife to her throat to silence her.

She feared losing her life by breaking rules she could never grasp.

Her most pressing need was to survive. She apologised, knelt before him and allowed him to subjugate her with sex.

Even as he raped her into submission, she knew that that their union was doomed. She could not give up her freedom like this.

He left, and she kept quiet.

*

He had been careful to bruise her in places which would not show – though he would boast of this to his friends. They would watch her painful steps and laugh to themselves.

'Breaking in a horse,' they called it.

She adulated Dania, but finally admitted they were irrevocably different.

Shocked and scared, she was not broken in.

She remembered her mother's words in her head as tears poured down her face.

9.

Marseilles 1941

Even in Marseilles in the very south of France, where sailors of every race and colour lived together; there was talk of yellow stars. The Brauns knew that they would not be able to move once the census had taken place. They lived in fear of registration, followed by arrest and detention.

They had to leave.

Unfortunately, there was nowhere to go.

*

As rich exotic Eastern Europeans, it was impossible to avoid the conclusion that they were Jews. People commented plainly on their appearance and their wealth in a sneering tone. Old men and women spat at them in the street.

'Dirty Jews!' they muttered.

They were accused of theft, war, and money frauds which had caused the depression. No one showed kindness or sympathy. They asked for none.

They avoided the radical Jewish self-help organisations which were regularly firebombed. They shunned the Zionists leaving for Palestine with boatloads of children.

A young boy approached Izaak one day, and asked, 'is it true that you took all the money from the Bank of France in the night and that this why mama has no money? If so can you give it back?'

'No it is not,' Izaak replied, 'here...'

He tried to crouch down and talk to the child, who was around 7 years old. The boy was terrified, and ran away crying for his mother.

If they went to a restaurant people left, or they were asked to leave. Waiters were openly hostile.

They lived on bread and cheese and wine purchased from shops in a furtive manner.

*

They found a cheap pension on the dock front for top hotel prices. The patron of the pension was rude and haughty. She randomly raised prices for things like baths and hot water, saying

180

'You can always go somewhere else,' in a jeering tone.

During one of the heated whispered discussion of what to do and where to go, the youngest boy, Malachi, a precocious four year old, had piped up.

'We should go to Brazil!'

*

In those days Brazil was like Africa, a place of steamy jungles and Amazonian wilderness.

The child had been read bed-time stories about the place. He was referring to little Lola who went up the Amazon in a boat and made friends with the jaguar and the anaconda.

South America was a dark continent an unexplored wilderness. There were swamps, cities full of bandits, dictators, coffee plantations guarded by men with guns.

The idea took hold. Jews had already gone there and survived.

'Should we literally leave for the ends of the earth?' he asked Rebecca.

Luckily she had already been to Egypt and was more adventurous than he.

'He is just a baby! And yet,' she replied, 'perhaps there, no one would care that we are Jews?'

Nevertheless, there were serious problems. How could they get there?

*

The complex enquiries cost a lot of money.

There were discussions with smugglers and wharf rats - people old Braun would rather forget. These were people he would never have noticed in Poland. He would not have considered giving them work. They talked down to him! He was obliged to respond with humility lest they walked away.

After an extensive search, and many bribes, he located a creature from the criminal underworld of Marseilles. The man was hideous. He carried a dark cloud of death about him and was clearly armed, with henchmen on call.

Izaak, in a fine tailored suit and carrying a large sum of money, asked him for a route to Brazil. He handed over a large cash bribe.

'I'm not sure, old man,' whined the bully, carefully counting the

181

money and secreting it about his person. 'You are a criminal and a refugee from justice. Of course it will be expensive.'

'I can pay.'

'Not enough old man, not enough.'

Izaak was sure he had lost the money.

He walked away aware he was being watched by hidden eyes. They would never get out now.

He did not argue and cursed his wife for insisting on this slender hope.

He had just parted with a huge sum. Why risk further?

*

Luckily, the old bandit was not unsympathetic. He too was a refugee from some long forgotten colonial vendetta in Morocco. He called after the retreating bent old man.

'Come back here tomorrow, 3.00pm. I'll see if I can find someone.'

Izaak was unaware that the criminal underworld, from all races of Europe and North Africa, had sympathy for the accursed.

The reasons for the delays were due to the fact that these criminals were creating a complex escape network which would later carry thousands.

The pair stayed in touch via bandits passing notes requesting sums of money.

Izaak tried to bargain. So did his wife. Every time a bandit left, Rebecca pressed a piece of jewellery into his hand.

'For your boss's wife,' she whispered. 'Keep my children safe.'

After 6 months of tension, they were told of a boat leaving for South America, Argentina to be precise, from Nantes.

The old bandit leader had built up a complex escape network. They were to board a ship. It was a long way from Marseilles at a tiny port, and it was not passenger ship, just a cargo boat containing corned beef for the troops and returning with mining equipment.

The trip would be dangerous. There were U boats waiting to prevent the shipments, and there was a risk that they would be robbed and thrown overboard.

The whole plan was fraught with danger. They were to go disguised as peasants and leave their valuable suitcases behind. Their possessions would be taken along in barrels. It sounded like a recipe for robbery.

Izaak was extremely hesitant, but his family were far less brave about continuing to live in France. They had bonds, diamonds, gold, jewellery and furs, much more than many who were fleeing now, and the danger was increasing daily. They did not want to die and put extreme pressure on their patriarch.

Still Braun hesitated; he did not want to lose his remaining holdings and his bank accounts. He had extensive investments in the industrialisation of Eastern Europe, both monetary and emotional, maybe they would be returned.

'Rebecca, you are an idealist. I have a Swiss bank account. They are all thieves. They are trying to frighten us and steal everything. We should not give in.'

He found it hard to abandon all that he had worked so hard to achieve.

Surely the Germans were rational people? After all not everybody in Germany could possibly be this imbecilic.

He had lived there when building his most recent factory. He knew people.

The rest of the family were at their wit's end. The reports were increasingly dire.

'You must talk to papa-in-law,' David's wife urged, 'he respects you. He listens. He let you go to Egypt. You must save our children and preserve the family line.'

In order to expedite matters, David offered to stay in France among friends in the Marseilles Jewish community. He would secure the business, keep an eye on their factories and be ready to recover anything that remained if the war should finish. After all, surely this madness would soon be over?

They were sat on a bench by the waterfront when a beggar approached them. Instead of asking for alms he spat at David.

'We will be rid of you soon,' he threatened. 'Your time is up.'

Finally Papa Braun grasped the danger.

He spent a nail biting three days debating whether he or his son should go. David was keen to stay and convinced him.

'Leave the limousines with me. I can sell most of them and keep one to travel to our businesses. People have said I don't look at all Jewish. It will be fine.'

Izaak was relieved. He left his son a briefcase full of bonds, the papers to the factories and a lot of clerical files as well the limousines.

Daniel would change his second name to Jacques Brodeur. It should be easy to find a forger.

*

The details of the departure were complicated.

Argentina! Followed by a long, dangerous journey to Brazil? It was far from civilisation.

On the other hand, his son assured him, civilisation had temporarily left Europe.

His wife and daughter-in-law spent almost every day in tears over the appalling rudeness and unkindness of perfect strangers. The exotic appearance and fine clothes of the women were stared at in the rude way French people reserved for anything out of the ordinary.

And the low-life of Marseilles was taking an unwholesome interest in their progress. Their every move was watched with suspicion, their tooled leather suitcases sparked jealousy and greed.

Bandits were all around.

They were treated like criminals who had stolen from the poor. People trod warily if they arrived, even in tiny local shops. They were unwelcome. Still Izaak wavered. He would be losing everything he had worked for.

*

Izaak finally accepted the reality of the situation. In August 1941, the family left Europe for ever, boarding the freighter Vitoria, paying in diamonds and the finest jewels. The cabin was cramped, the smell of beef pervading and repulsive.

Each cabin contained a family of Jews; the captain had sold his single berth cabin to a family of 10 for the same money as he would normally earn for his whole trip.

10.

Lvov 1941

In March 1941, Sofia had completed her punishment.

However as a social misfit, there was a further test; she still had to learn the meaning of working for the people in the new towns of Siberia.

This time, trains were more crowded and the conditions worse. Food was scarce for anti-social class enemies.

The deportees starved, and their guards were even less keen to show counter-revolutionary compassion. They threw new born babies off the trains and randomly shot prisoners for no ostensible reason.

'No mercy for the state Enemies!'

The scientific premises of Communism allowed man to manage his god. Agitprop posters showed full bellies and wonderful harvests, using great machines, built by science.

'Forward with Marxist Leninism!'

Social justice would only come once the class war was won. No one could be allowed to harm the birth of this fledgling scientific paradise. Defection and escape was equally impossible. Only re-education was an option.

'Forward with the Proletariat!'

For all the talk of freedom and progress, posters everywhere encouraged persecutions, driven by history.

'Root out Class Enemies!' showed cartoons.

Communism was every bit as strict as the most extremist deist faith. Those who did not believe in the universal triumph of communism, died like the martyrs of old. Class enemies accepted their fate, took the blame, and flocked to their doom.

'Death to Fifth Columnist and Wreckers!' posters proclaimed.

Soviet Russia had not progressed a great deal from a country of unquestioning serfs who trusted government propaganda. The deportees were considered the sole cause of the problems facing the new regime. Their fate served as a warning and an example to the rest, and the putrefying corpses were viewed with same distaste and fear as corpses of heretics during the Middle Ages.

'USSR Symbol of Peace'

Sofia watched through the cracks in the cattle trucks as the Soviets prepared to defend themselves against Germany. The stations were packed with troops. Everyone had to prove their rectitude. No one was safe. People could be accused by anyone, or professed outcast by the party priesthood. Children could denounce their parents, underlings could report their supervisors.

The guards on the trains to Omsk feared that they would fail the class struggle, as much as their leaders did.

'Beware of False Consciousness'

Everywhere pictures of Lenin and Stalin watched over them. Speakers endlessly repeated key speeches set to music.

'We must rescue our youth from these malevolent petit bourgeois influences,' they were instructed, *'we should eliminated the bloodsuckers as quickly as possible.'*

Posters and slogans guided the people in the paths of their new faith. Lack of food, poor quality of production steel, shortage of decent housing, was the fault of the people, for insufficient rigour. They needed to be firm with the slackers, class enemies and counterrevolutionaries in their midst. Those in the trucks lived in fear, as they were left in sidings without food or water, and begged passers-by for snow to drink.

'From each according to his ability, to each according to his needs'

The mad dogs of capitalism could be put to good use in the brave new world, working in the inhospitable, yet rich territories at the frontier. They would be used for the salvation of mankind as a whole.

Each one had a number, and criminals were strictly differentiated from politicals.

The long journey was a nightmare of starvation and discomfort. Deportees fell into despondency. They had betrayed Uncle Lenin. Even those who felt the injustice of their sentences soon showed signs of mental illness, expressed in destructive behaviour, self-harming and suicide.

At each station a few some deportees were taken off. The train stopped near the collectives where her daughters were held.

Sofia was lined up with the rest and checked over by Andrei, who did not give her a second glance.

On the way posters depicted Stalin leading the new Soviet economy to victory of the proletariat.

'You will earn your release.
Make sure you meet your Work Quota.'

Stalin spelled out his message in gigantic letters at every opportunity. Massive poster declared:

'Liberation comes through Honest Toil.'

His gigantic face warned the enemies of the people that they were to be used to construct the Promised Land, even though they were not worthy to enjoy the fruits of their labours.

11.

Siberia 1941

Sofia remained on the journey to Siberia, where the train debarked its contents at Irkutsk.

The next leg of the journey, to Magadan, was to be undertaken by forced marches, resting overnight in camps.

The convicts were to press on to Port Vanino, or Vladivostok, headed for labour ship transports to the worst gulags, extracting metal out of the permafrost.

*

The gulag projects had evolved from a penal system to a scientific and social experiment, designed to re-educate the lazy and wrong minded, and to get rid of those spying, sabotaging the industrialisation process, or contaminating food.

The massiveness of the projects in Siberia required monumental resources. Prison labourers were allocated to various projects, where towns, mining concerns, canals, roads and railways were already under construction.

The Dalstroy, the Far North Construction Trust, was an economic venture requiring a massive labour force where the climate was too inhospitable for easy life. They had a slogan.

'Wealth of the Motherland for the People'

Its officials were provided with goals, deliverable and timescales to use up the useless dross.

Theoretically, such socially-sick and mental individuals could be useful in the construction of a new world, and, after a chosen period of service to their country, they could be released back into society.

In fact, the prisoners were to be used up, scientifically finished off. Their productivity and inevitable demise was one of the deliverables and a part of planning.

To this end, the transports unloaded a mixed group of unhealthy labourers for the gulags at Magadan.

The wind was biting. Sofia had no winter clothes and no convict number. As a result, the selection panels from the camps were able

188

to judge that she was not an official prisoner. Magda had neglected to put her name on the list of deportees, therefore she did not exist.

No one wanted a labourer who was going to die after a day's work. She would count as an unfilled labour quota, a body to dispose of, and extra paperwork.

As the column of bedraggled peasants, criminals and political prisoners parted to different destinations, Sofia was left with those who had already been proclaimed dead on arrival.

Those left on the platform were already officially deceased.

*

Sofia was close to death from exposure, and set out to walk the half mile to town and search for work.

There was not a rag to be found on the few naked corpses thrown off the train, so she sat behind a storage container and washed using spittle and leaves.

She picked off the worst of the lice and prayed for the dead, lying in a tragic little heap. They did not appear human, frozen stiff, with glazed fish-like eyes. Cold prevented the pile from decomposing.

Sofia knelt and prayed silently.

Some stragglers watching the disembarkation wandered over.

One severely weakened woman had already been carried off by two men on a makeshift stretcher.

'We are taking her to hospital,' they winked to Sophie. 'We will nurture her, never fear.'

The woman did not resist.

The remainder were greeted by crow-like men dressed in rags, with hands bound in tattered cloth instead of gloves.

The men chatted to the severely weakened individuals, and then led them away into their distant huts.

Their hovels were built from the most bizarre collection of scraps, broken pieces of steel, tarpaulins, branches, wool stuffing, old springs, broken pans all piled together in a sort of igloo made of rubbish. Sofia avoided them as she cleaned her hair and hands.

As the depot quietened down, one of the remaining men, who had quietly waited for gulag-bound groups to entirely disappear, approached Sophie in silence.

He seemed impressed by her praying. He addressed her in broken

189

Russian, with a German accent. She replied in fluent German with a Yiddish accent.

'Oh,' he conjectured, 'a native of Germany?'

Sofia explained her origins.

'I am German,' he claimed in an upper class accent. 'I have been here for 10 years, a free man.'

His face was ancient and grey, his skin like parchment.

'Are you praying for the dead?' he spoke in a snuffing shifty way, glancing around with madly rolling eyes.

He invited Sofia to come and eat at his simple home near the depot.

*

She had nowhere else to go and they set off together, arriving at a hut surrounded by piles of old bleached bones and skulls.

The door was down a piled snow tunnel, just like an igloo. Inside was dark and fetid, stinking of glue made from rotten bones. The smell was fearful, like a crypt in a church, only fresher.

'Please. Sit down,' he said, 'I do not often get visitors. Welcome. I am Ivan.'

She guessed it was not his real name. He had lost that long ago, in an attempt to prevent random beatings as a German spy.

She sat down, panicked by the smell like an animal about to stampede at the smell of fire.

Every instinct suggested this place meant death. She prayed for the other stragglers, presumably seated in similar huts.

'Food?' he offered. There was boiled cabbage, raw cabbage, and meat stew.

Sophie was starving, and had been for a long time. She took a taste of the stew, filled with lumps of meat not often seen in that time of starvation.

She gagged.

Her body revolted at the taste, her throat closed in an instinctive reaction to the taste of human flesh.

'No thanks,' she replied, 'I am a little sick.'

'Perhaps some cabbage?'

That too tasted of death. She refused it.

She offered to cut up cabbage and onions and eat them raw.

190

The man murmured assent.

He was mumbling to himself in an odd way. He did not seem to see her as she diced food in the repulsive den, terror gripping her being.

She prayed for the Lord to bless her food and to forgive the man. Suddenly he leapt up.

'I am a sinner!' he squealed, frothing at the mouth.' I have eaten my brothers! Forgive me. I am a ghoul, a vampire. Forgive me sweet spirit.'

He knelt at her feet.

'I saw you praying for the dead,' he disclosed. 'We are returning to strip them down when we have killed you lot. Look!' he pointed to piles of wrapped white beads, which she realised were teeth.

'We get gold from the teeth, glue from the bones which we sell to the factories. The party representatives let us keep the liver and kidneys to sell in the market. The clothes left by the guards are ours to keep.'

He knelt down and confessed, 'I am a miscreant.'

'Angel,' he gripped her knees. 'I could not prevent it. They caught me as a spy in 1921. I was sent to Siberia, to the infernal wastes. I have been in this cold hell for 19 long years. Now can you forgive me?'

He was shaking and grinning in a mask of pure horror.

'The Cheka took my nails. There!' he pointed at his stubby nail-free hands 'they took my toes, they burnt my skin. I betrayed friends and people I did not even know. I did my 10 years. I served my time in the white hell, where can I go? This is the devil's den. The pile of corpses grows ever taller, yet we have to live. The Russians will not deal with me as I am German. Save me please?'

The man's wild eyes rolled around like a maddened horse.

Shudders shook his skinny frame. He frothed and gibbered. He repeated the same story endlessly. He had been a spy, agent, imperialist informer for the White Army.

He did not seem to have any reason or purpose in spying and had no doubt been arrested during the Civil War. The Cheka persuaded him he was an evil imperialist.

Sofia had seen tortured prisoners come to her cell in Loucki,

191

convinced that they were imperialist agents, German spies, counter revolutionaries, imperialist courtesans, or any fantasy that their interrogators had imprinted on their broken minds.

She knelt with him and prayed aloud.

They intoned German prayers she had never heard of, about angels sitting by the bed, at the feet and at the head.

He reverted to prayers and lullabies his mother sang when he was tiny.

He wept and gibbered.

'Forgive me!' He frothed.

At last, he calmed down a little.

'Come, holiness' he begged, 'I have a coat, and some fine boots. I have been saving them for you.'

There was a false wall at the back of his rotting hovel, containing a patch of rags which seemed less bedraggled.

He removed a coat from the little cache.

It had clearly been stolen from a deportee, although not recently, as it was well-made in an old fashioned style, possibly from a middle-class political when Russia was prosperous. It was patched, but warm and functional.

He handed it to her. 'I have been saving it for someone special like you. Tell god I gave it to you. Tell him I was good, and you forgave me.'

He reached into the shreds of wood making up the walls and located a pair of nearly-new felt boots. He piled fresh wool inside so they would fit.

She took them gratefully. He did not have such a fine pair himself.

'I would take them to market,' he averred, 'they would say I stole them. I would be sent to the gulags.'

He shivered uncontrollably, 'not there again, god. Please.'

He sang lullabies and childish prayers in a singsong rasping voice, like a drunken man, smiling vacuously at some blissful vision.

She crossed herself; evil stalked the hut.

'The devil rules in Siberia,' he said.

She hid her fear and smiled gratefully, desperate to leave. He seemed deranged.

In fact, Ivan *was*. He had been infected by a CJD variant common to those who eat human flesh. His fits were getting worse. He faced paralysis in a grin of horror, then rigor mortis.

The rest of the knackers and vultures in the camp had already abandoned him. They did not dare risk infection, thinking the disease to be contagious.

Sofia begged to leave.

After gibbering for some time, he released her.

She travelled on to Magadan in a fine coat which would set her up for the winter ahead.

*

Sofia began her new life in a place where even a kopek was wealth. An un-patched coat was a rarity and most felt boots were second-hand and ill-fitting, which was positively dangerous in that freezing climate.

Inhabitants wore a weird selection of clothes as if they had rifled through corpses and taken whatever fitted. Several people seemed to be wearing all their clothes at once, at least three hats and two coats, as if they expected their clothes to be stolen if placed down for a moment. The place stank of dirt, greasy cabbage and fat, even in the open street.

Most inhabitants had been worked out, like dray horses retired from a brewery.

They were known as 'husks' or 'dust', so emaciated that they looked as if they would blow away in the harsh Siberian winds. Their age was indeterminate. They could scarcely walk and suffered from multiple diseases.

At first, Sofia thought that there had been a terrible plague in the country; she later learnt that the 'dust' of Siberia eked out existence rifling corpses and selling everything possible. Prisoners judged absolutely useless for labour were judged expendable and freed. It cut the mortality rates and allowed the administration to utilise rations more effectively. They would die in the cold and could not escape.

Their capacious pockets contained mystifying items, including human kidneys and livers, love letters and last wills, carefully washed out so that the paper could be resold.

Sofia remembered Ivan kindly and sought for him when she went outside. She prayed for him, thanking god for the coat and boots.

*

Ivan had a brief moment of clarity after she had left. He did not remember much of his fits, and they were becoming more and more frequent quite rapidly. The prions had already eaten large parts of his brain.

He remembered little of Sofia, although he was certain that she had somehow cajoled him into giving up his most precious possessions. He confused her with the interrogators he had met long ago, thinking she was the 'soft' one who had teased out his secrets. His troubled mind proclaimed she was a demon in disguise. He cursed himself for meeting her.

He gibbered all day in his room and shrieked by night, claiming that angels and demons were fighting for his soul and his coat and shoes. He began to severely disturb his neighbours in their adjoining igloos made of rags and bones. His erstwhile companions resolved to kill him as soon as the creeping paralysis took hold, which they knew would happen soon enough.

It was in truth a mercy as he would otherwise starve to death paralysed in a grin of horror.

It never happened. Shortly after meeting Sofia, the fits took him most severely, and he strode into the night without proper clothing.

He died of exposure in the arctic winter cold of Siberia.

It is to be hoped that he found peace and clarity in his last few moments.

God rest his soul.

The remaining knackers fought over his meagre possessions like the vultures they were.

12.

Kazakhstan 1941

Katya's status improved. As an informer, and later on as a trained interrogator, she enjoyed the thrill of power, her ability to inspire fear.

She hid her excitement behind an impassive wall, and often could not sleep, intoxicated by the fruition of her plots.

Secret wrongdoing stimulated her, and she came to believe that hidden deeds would go unpunished.

The sisters observed the scramble for concubines dispassionately.

Anya was 15, young, defiant and plain. Katya was older, and plainer.

They did not want to be separated.

*

When it became clear that the captured brides were assured of food and warmth, Katya calculated how to foster a liaison.

She singled out Andrei, a thinker who spent time deconstructing every party announcement in a way which bored his fellows. On the contrary, his tortuous manipulations of ideology fascinated her.

She decided to pander to his vanity. She begged for pamphlets, and asked him to explain obscure statements which she did not fully understand.

She always pretended conversion to his view.

Now and then, he kissed her chastely, holding her hand in a clammy grip.

'You will be an excellent Partkom member, comrade.' He claimed, 'I will recommend you as representative for minority peoples. We discuss it tonight.'

She visited the medicine woman for love philtres.

She had no need, yet wanted to discover the tricks of smoke and mirrors.

The old lady handed them over without any charge.

She had cast the girls' horoscopes, using hairs she had carefully collected from Katya's head at her last visit. The horoscopes predicted annihilation for many at Katya's hands – the girl was possessed with the spirit of vengeance. The Earth spirits whispered that curses of the dead could not be evaded.

The divination proved correct.

*

As the collectives stabilized and survival more likely, Germany invaded.

Stalin's wavering economy, battered by ideology and permanent revolution, was forced onto a war footing that it was incapable of delivering.

The Kazakh Soviet reeled under the demands expected of it.

A wavering steel industry was expected to build tanks and guns.

Stalin had lost control of the grain baskets of Belorussia, so the barely surviving collectives were expected to support a standing army.

Their remaining cranky tractors, used to plough up the steppes, were requisitioned for purposes unknown, and labourers used hoes and wooden spades to break up frozen soil.

Central committee instructed them to produce crops unsuited to the weather conditions.

The collectives were required to increase production while sending men to the front.

*

The remaining Partkoms 'debated' the closed orders.

Mikhail wrote to head office, carefully detailing the situation. He disappeared in a black sedan and did not return.

Andrei's task was to persuade recalcitrants that party requests were just, and only White Army recidivism prevented their execution.

He was sent to a specialist training academy which had studied the latest scientific German interrogation methods. He was trained in psychological pseudo-science for two whole weeks. After this, he knew how to seek out the weak minded and the slightly insane among the populace and utilise them to cause increased pain in others.

These men beat and tortured his victims while he supervised. His task was to wait for the moment when a mind broke and the victim hearkened to the inquisitor with subjugated devotion.

His new job was to rebuild their minds. He learnt how important it was to break prisoners even if they had already confessed.

It was part of re-education of the proletariat.

Ever since he had undertaken training Andrei had changed. He was no longer a weedy youth, just a creature who walked in a cloud of darkness.

His power-crazed blood lust repelled most people. His secretary 'vanished', rumoured to have committed suicide.

Katya was fascinated. She remembered her orgasmic moment of capitulation and wanted to understand how it worked.

After several weeks of stalking by Katya he confessed his feelings in halting and confessional tones. He had recognised the appetite for the souls of helpless victims in her and fell on her in a frenzy of lust. They had sex against the wall of the NKVD building, in the empty car park. He relived the tortures inflicted on poor souls, taking her again and again, openly gloating over his power to harm.

She had won him.

'Come. Work at the NKVD' he panted. 'You are the right sort.'

*

Katya joined Andrei as a denizen of hell.

Shift by shift, she worked in the shuttered inferno. Among the broken souls and shattered bodies, they constructed unlikely conspiracies to appease Stalin.

Backed by a new staff in the NKVD building, the two lived in constant arousal.

They got their high from broken dreams extracted from hapless victims, returning home to have sex, often alone, fuelled by the despair they engendered.

Drugs were freely available to specialist workers and they and their henchmen used methamphetamine.

Like other interrogators, Katya could not sleep, waking up to vile nightmares.

Sleeping pills had little effect and she and Andrei often took drugs and discussed stoned nonsense interspersed with wild sex, until too weary to stay awake any longer.

They lived in the black night of the soul, disregarding the details of the passing menu of humans, like vampires on a killing spree.

Katya moved in with Andrei, although she visited her sister regularly.

Anya had the best of everything; her apartment was filled with gifts and offerings from terror-stricken locals. She never enquired about her sister's role, and no one enlightened her.

Andrei kept faith in the truth of every conspiracy extracted under torture. He trusted the lists of conspirators, as if inspired by a communist god. He was convinced that the barren steppes were Russia's breadbasket, second only to Belorussia. He adored Comrades Stalin and Lenin and suspected Trotsky of masterminding every shortcoming in the state. He always called Trotsky 'that evil Jew,' causing Katya's heart to jump as she, too, belonged to that accursed race.

Their passionate affair was punctuated by arrests, deaths and disappearances.

*

The stronger Kazakhs continued to flee to the mountains, trekking through high passes on old silk routes as far as Afghanistan, sleeping in secret caves.

Starving babies and children were left outside their apartment, accompanied by offerings and spells written in an old forgotten tongue.

Children queued outside, panhandling.

Soldiers dragged them away. Still they did not leave easily, begging and wailing from hunger.

Locals treated them as demons to be appeased and carried charms, place them over the door, with little scraps of pamphlets wrapped in herbs.

It drove Andrei wild.

'Primitivism!' he howled in despair. 'Read the works of Lenin and learn from history! You do not need to starve.'

As he closed the door Katya often heard him moan.

'The cost of revolution is so high. Our little father tells us that they have to learn.'

*

One fateful day, the old shaman turned up at Katya's door with a tightly wrapped bundle.

'For you, my dear,' she crooned in a gentle sing-song voice.

She sang a fearsome mouth-song as Katya opened the bundle, which revealed a repellent doll.

Its face was made up of what she knew to be her own hair and skin, bound with wax, and dressed in scraps of her clothing. Indescribable horrors hung from its gaping stomach, pins in its eyes and heart.

Such things were produced by dark witchcraft.

'A curse for you, my dear,' sighed the old lady. 'Nothing can evade it. Signed in blood.'

Countless interrogations had allowed Katya to hone an impassive expression.

'I think I uncover conspiracy,' she stated quietly, 'headed by you, evil one. You are the focus of crimes against the people, and do not frighten me with superstitious nonsense. Leave before I call someone to arrest you, or bear the consequence.'

The shaman hummed her uncanny mouth music, attracting spirits to witness.

'You are a liar, and charlatan,' Katya replied.

She spoke calmly, as if to the spirits. She hatched out a conspiracy centring on the old lady which would involve at least 6 months of investigations.

The old woman was unfazed.

'You *are* a witch,' crooned the old lady. 'I could have trained you if you had asked,' she sang. 'You showed promise, and understood the work.'

She rocked back and forth hypnotically.

'I knew you were herald of darkness,' the old woman droned, 'revenge for the sins of Genghis and our Horde.'

She drew close. Her cross eyes, (one eye on the other world, as required for a Shaman) somehow both fixed on Katya.

'Your name is in the vendetta cave, signed by the brethren, my pretty. We will wreak revenge on the Soviet army and its secret police. Your deeds will be remembered by our children and our children's children. We will maim and kill your young. Revenge is coming!'

*

She left before Katya could call for guards, at a good speed for an apparently decrepit old lady.

She was not seen again, presumably hiding in mountain caves, and moving to Afghanistan, where the final stages of this vendetta played out in the 1970's.

The soothsayer's dwelling was burnt down and witchcraft was outlawed as revisionist voodoo.

It had scarcely any effect.

The communists, riding their ponies through the steppes, often came upon shrines containing curses and dolls, evidence of a return to animism.

13.

Siberia 1941

Magadan, a Siberian frontier town, operated a feeble barter economy based on food brought in by the indigenous population, in exchange for a variety of stolen objects.

The main currency was cigarettes, vodka and kopeks.

Despite her emaciation and lousy condition,

Sofia was in better health than those who had outlived their sentences. The coat alone made her employable.

She obtained work as a maid in a boarding house. She cleaned the immaculate rooms and luxurious, clean fittings at the Dalstroy Hotel. She picked up leftovers and ate well. She and the rest of the maids slept by the clay stove which ran the central heating, waking up in turn to stoke it at night and chopping wood to maintain it by day.

*

Life in the hotel was debauched.

Everyone apart from Sofia drank heavily.

They became even more raucous as the war went against the Soviets. The maids collected leftovers and scraps from the wasteful wealth of the hotel.

They sold their gleanings in the market to augment wages.

Sofia gave away her share among the city scavengers. Daily, she went to a corner to drop bread among the 'Vermin' and their 'shrapnel' children.

As soon as she arrived, women and children rose up and clustered around, quacking like ducks.

The weakest lay on the ground, waiting for hand-outs. 'God has forgotten us,' they sighed.

'How can he let such injustice happen?'

'God is dead in Siberia.'

Like crows, old ladies homed in and snatched her charity from weaker babies, warning her briskly, 'kindness is punishable by death. Do not be kind to anyone, dear.'

They out-stared women and children who had arrived too late to obtain bounty stuffing the scraps into their underwear.

Unknown to Sofia, the queue was chargeable and in control of a mini mafia. They skulked in the shadows and pried the food out of children's hand, leaving them scraps.

*

The hotel was dedicated to Dalstroy officials and controllers from central headquarters supervised the great scheme to create an industrial superpower, while cleansing the state of contamination.

Central Office created the schemes. Every month, officials from the central party caucus travelled to the hotel to receive reports of results.

A permanent staff dedicated long hours to produce a perfect paper trail detailing progress. As always, success was based on the purity of the vanguard; failure was a mark of counterrevolution or political instability.

There were bridges to build, factories to construct, logging quotas, coal to be delivered, and metal ore to be mined. There were furniture factories and even toy manufacturers.

Each of these industrial concerns were fuelled by forced labour. Each work area was surrounded by camps of inmate workers. The workers were broken down into teams. Each delivered a specific 'work quota', irrespective of the tools and infrastructure available.

Each project had two aims: firstly, to build the country into an industrial superpower, secondly, to winnow out politically debased elements from the People, leaving a politically pure population.

Visitors from central office, wearing starched and sparkling peasant uniforms, arrived regularly.

Large and red faced, they appeared innocent of the atrocities they supervised and discussed camp inmates as if they were recalcitrant children.

'We can't be soft on the beasts; no omelette was ever made without breaking eggs.'

They and gave affectionate bear hugs, even to those who they had already elected to execute.

Every aspect of the labour camps had been calculated in advance, from the amount of space allowed to each inmate to the precise layout of the buildings and latrines.

Workers' lives were controlled by Central Office thousands of miles away.

Inmates were rewarded with food and shelter - provided they had completed their quota.

In accordance with Stalin's sanitisation policy for the Soviets, food intake was measured to produce 80% death rates among inmates, over 6 months of 'hard' labour.

Labour was calculated at an average of 12 hours per day, which could take up to 15-20 hours, depending on the strength of the individual and unforeseen problems like the weather.

The workers were untrained and under equipped prisoners. Nevertheless projects were expected to match industrialised countries using sophisticated processes.

Stalin's Soviets had to outdo the capitalists in every way.

'What shall we do with these lazy fellows?' the controllers asked genially, when things went wrong.

They drank immense amounts of vodka, talked of Papa Stalin's 'gentle hand on the till of state' as freezing winds around the toasting luxurious hotel brought death to thousands.

*

Each project had been broken down into deliverables consisting of man-days and man-outputs based on a two, four or five year plans.

However, these could be modified depending on Comrade Stalin's mood. Camp leaders needed to adjust or face consequences.

The bluff officials winked genially.

'*I'm* not blaming *you* for failure,' they smiled, like sharks with bared teeth, 'sadly; Central Office might not like it,' they sighed and quaffed mugs full of eye-watering spirits, 'ha, ha. We do what we can.'

Camp commanders backed away from them as with royalty, promising to do better.

They exhorted the recalcitrant inmates and acted with sadistic cruelty. Whenever figures could not be reconciled, 50 or so saboteurs were discovered and executed.

Once every month grey, dark suited auditors arrived, trailing darkness like invisible smoke.

Quality control was unnecessary, providing everything added up, and had been counted and delivered. They observed the luxurious trappings distastefully, and drank sparingly.

They checked *output, throughput* and set *reviewed and amended goals*. Camp commanders attempted to hide discrepancies in their accounts to no avail.

'The figures do not add up,' the auditors complained, circling anomalies. 'The monthly figures cannot be signed off unless correct.'

Terrifying commanders trembled.

'It can be sent to Central with the problems highlighted, if you like. Is that what you want done?'

No one did. Figures always added up in the end – they had to.

Matters were simple. Inmates were 'throughput'. Throughput was never right because it varied according to numbers of incoming prisoners. There was a limit to how new convicts could be utilised and excessive survival rates were a problem. 'Your throughput is too slow,' meant that too many inmates survived.

Miraculously, deliverables were frequently achieved.

14.

The Partkoms

At nearly twenty-seven, Anatoly was the Partkom secretary and the most senior party member, in charge of a region the size of Britain.

He was attracted to Dania's girlfriend, and reasoned that the group he led would be denounced before long, falling foul of the drive to mediocrity. He saw how she tried hard to be a good comrade, to be equal to others and to help the distressed. She did not shirk her tasks and did everything with a kind of joy which was extremely attractive.

The sun had bleached her hair into the finest gold. She was very skinny, healthy and tanned. Even the traditional peasant clothes fell in a pleasing and stylish way over her body and she walked with strength and elegance, like a tiger.

Anatoly knew everything about her from his spies.

He grew increasingly obsessed as he saw her young body grow sensual and open to Dania's passion.

Her affair scorched his heart. She represented forbidden fruit, a possible counterrevolutionary, a black hearted bourgeois, expiating her sins in labour.

He wanted her to look at him adoringly like that, with her sparkling eyes and flashing white teeth. He also wanted to know Dania that he could take her. She, like everything else on the steppes, belonged to the conquerors and not to these unenlightened fools.

He did not admit to the sickness of love, and he did not seek her adoration, or her soft consent. He wanted victory over her refinement. He wanted to squeeze out the life she had stolen from serfs in the Ukraine. How else could she be so beautiful? He would suck out that allure on behalf of the proletariat.

*

Anatoly already knew of the planned escape and was waiting his moment to snatch up the rebels.

He visualised the scene when she would offer her soul to him in exchange for Dania's life.

He would take it from her and leave a shadow. He wanted her to hate him, tremble before him and, and despite all this, to offer herself.

He prepared the scenario in advance, how he would vanquish her, and kill Dania afterwards, so that she knew that her abasement had been in vain.

As soon as he heard of her maltreatment from his spies, he hastily changed his scheme.

No one but he could break her and extract her essence! First he had to check that his prize was unharmed. Only then could he plan precisely how it was to be done.

The very next day after her punishment at Dania's hands he called her in for an official meeting.

His soldiers 'visited' the hut, where she lived with other single females. Lucia had returned to talk to other Polish girls, confused and anxious about the future. Vague memories of her mother's words echoed in her head; she worried about freedom and liberty, large words which she had never truly esteemed before.

Anatoly was being shadowed by the escapees, and Dania knew of his visit almost immediately. At the same time as armed guards escorted her to the compound like a prisoner, shadows flitted about and made emergency preparations to hide in the long grasses of the steppes.

Betrayal seemed imminent.

*

Lucia stood defiant and resplendent before Anatoly.

She had arrived in Kazakhstan a spoiled brat. Since then she had been thinking about the great principles behind life.

She had discovered sensuality and sensitivity to others. The beating had done her spirit no harm. Every tribulation refined and improved her.

'How you hate me,' he gloated. 'And even so, you will give up yourself freely.'

She was defiant and proud.

'This is how I want you' he thought to himself, 'defiant and haughty. Give in to me, or I will leave you to Andrei's ministrations.'

*

Lucia was relieved not to be in the interrogation room. Anatoly looked down at his papers.

He hid his feelings of relief and triumph - addressed her officiously.

'Comrade Orloska, you write Russian?'

'A little,' she replied. She spoke the Ukrainian language which was very similar.

'Can you read it?'

'Of course.'

'You use a Cyrillic typewriter?'

'Yes.'

'You are selected to work as a secretary for the Raikom, starting tomorrow, a high honour for a deportee. You must to sign these papers.'

Ostensibly, he needed someone literate and educated to work as secretary. They both knew that this was arrest.

She knew that they were discovered, and Dania was in danger.

Her feet twitched to run and tell the band to be off.

He turned his back and waited.

Lucia accepted. Her hand shook as she signed. She was betraying romance.

Anatoly exulted, and knew perfectly well that she might change her mind. He folded the paper carefully and placed it into an official-looking briefcase.

He signalled his men to arrest Dania and his crew.

'Follow me,' he commanded the proud creature before him, 'you have new quarters starting from today. You have one hour to pack and you will leave with me at 4.00.'

Soldiers were posted outside as he visited the collective alongside her on spurious business.

*

Sadly, the birds had already flown.

Lucia packed and was escorted to the compound.

The collective watched her departure silently. It would cause scandal among the tribe. She feared a knife to the heart from Dania's kin if he was arrested.

In the next few days Lucia heard that Dania was sleeping on the steppes hiding among sheep and drinking the milk of mares.

He was waiting for her.

She refused to run, instead offering to spy on political directives and save his people.

Dania blustered that he would snatch her away; after all, they were officially betrothed.

Regrettably, carelessness on his part meant that there had been no betrothal. She had been a mistress; and, he realised with a sinking heart, he had already openly threatened to liquidate her if she shamed him again.

However, she was a valued piece. He proposed an honour killing to the elders.

Perhaps he may have gained his wishes at another time, - but the collectives were in turmoil. The steppes were full of shadows as families debated whether to stay or run for Afghanistan. An affair involving a non-Kazakh was a minor issue when the elders were debating the relocation of the heart of the tribe. It was a trivial matter.

It was adjudicated that she had been a concubine only and irrelevant. Besides, her information could help escapees.

Dania was at first shattered by this loss of face. On the contrary, the affair had raised his status, and several men offered him their young daughters as consolation. He chose a 12 year old child to take on the perilous journey.

She would never talk back.

*

By the late spring, at least half of the collectives had melted into the steppes.

Anatoly was seriously discommoded by the loss of so many workers. He knew from his spies that they were hiding nearby. His troops searched the tall grasses. Although soldiers often passed within feet of Kazakhs lying on the ground many times, they found no one.

Anatoly was distressed that they had deserted, and taken a few fat sheep and horses too.

However, it was a minor setback and no disaster. They were due to be shipped east anyway and new deportees were arriving all the time. He gloated over stealing the most attractive female from an oppressed people - an appealingly tyrannical act.

At the same time, the new secretary concerned him.

She was no peasant. He was vulnerable to attack from rivals until he re-educated her.

Desire conflicted with his pragmatic ideology. He hated her clean strength and pure ideals. He loathed the way she had innate sympathy for the people, while he despised, cajoled and tortured them.

His ideology had been twisted and turned by the machination of the central party caucus. It irritated him that Comrade Lucia impelled him into admitting the dark political realities of power.

Moreover, Lucia was not sufficiently passive.

Anatoly read Nazi superiority into every expression. He disdained her good manners and refined speech, and tried to break her with countless humiliations.

'What's with the posh voice and the long words, girl? Anti-Soviet activity? Take care that you are not deported east.'

He slapped her in public, which she learnt not to resist. At the office, he regularly called her in, and shouted at her when she opened the door.

'Get out woman. What are you doing here? Wait till I give you permission to enter.'

He secluded her, and relentlessly persecuted anyone she befriended.

Her friends learnt to avoid her.

'Why are you talking to her? Are you plotting?'

He built on her penitence at abandoning Dania, calling her harlot and traitor on every occasion.

'Are you going to betray everyone like you did with your boyfriend? Can you ever be trusted?'

She became timid and apologetic.

She no longer strode about, and sat quiet, instead of throwing opinions around.

She strove hard to get rid of her class roots. Even so, her new delicacy and frailty made her even more attractive to him. Sorrow for her lost suitor left her face wide-eyed and ethereal.

He hated her for making him forget his faith; and almost felt he would betray the god of power in exchange for her soul. He touched her and brushed past her all the time. He slapped her bottom playfully and she shuddered in disgust.

*

One day, it was late, and he was overcome by her nearness, he spilt out his desire.

'Come to me, delightful princess,' he muttered huskily.

His breath stank of vodka and his uniform was unbuttoned. He held her by her waist and grabbed her by the hand. He tried to kiss it.

'Sneering demon!' She snapped. 'What have I done to you that you torture my soul?'

She wept copious hysterical tears for her love.

'You took my rue love from me,' she wept.

'I will have you,' he fulminated as he licked her disgusted face. 'Those tears, I will drink them up.'

He fumbled at her uniform. He was always armed and his soldiers were within call.

'I could kill you now, and no one will care.'

She looked at him with contempt.

She was well aware how close she was to death. After all she daily typed lists of those to be shot, deported and taken in for questioning.

Death did not matter anymore. She trusted in romance and heroism, an honourable way out of hell. She drew herself up in a new sorrowing dignity.

'I may die. But you are a dead man,' she whispered, 'there will be a day of vengeance when Evil will tremble.'

He slapped her hard over the face many times.

'Shut that crap, shut your face!' He rapped coldly.

He had no faint heart in the face of miserable primitivism. If he had no fear of shamanic curses why should he be scared of a girl? All the same he wanted total resignation from her. He wanted her to hate him, and still submit.

She sported two black eyes for days afterwards as re-education continued.

*

Her friends suffered new agonies as a result of her resistance. He brought her best friend, Anuta, in for questioning.

Lucia learnt of friend's arrest in shudder-some horror.

'Do you know how Andrei works?' he asked 'Shall we go see?'

Lucia was shattered by the things done to Anuta. She whimpered for mercy behind the glass alongside her friend.

Andrei knew she was watching and put on a fine show. They had quickly broken her spirit. Yet it went on for days.

Anuta betrayed the private things they had whispered together, the way the girls laughed at and Andrei, the little names they had for each Partkom, Lucia's attempted escape, and the private things she had said about Dania.

Later, much later, the broken young girl, invented plots which could send her friends for execution many times over.

Andrei and Anatoly did it for fun, giggling about it over their evening drunken bouts.

Lucia fell sick after that, with the dread steppe influenza. She sweated and froze by turns and lay delirious in her cot in the compound.

Anatoly came over once or twice and poured vodka down her throat.

She got better.

*

When another of her friends was arrested, Lucia begged for her release.

She came to Anatoly and admitted that she was resisting his advances out of superiority.

The choice was between sexual servitude and suicide.

Her friend was merely deported, for which Lucia was snivellingly grateful.

And so, after three months of struggle with her conscience, she became his mistress.

Anatoly had to be satisfied with his lesser victory. Dania was not there to see her humiliation and his triumph. By this time, he had already successfully escaped using information she had passed him.

*

The tribe remembered her doomed affair.

They surmised that she had stayed behind to ensure Dania's safety. Such self-sacrifice was the stuff of legend and romance and did her no harm.

Anatoly stayed obsessed with his conquest.

She slept beside him in tormented sleep every night. Even so, it was not enough.

He desired her innocent soul and dragged her into perversion. Instead of making her foul like him, he wiped out her selfishness and expunged her debt for unwitting cruelty to her mother. She discovered new truths, and understood Maria's dignity and motherly love.

She did her best to like this man, and gave herself without resistance.

Enragingly, his body did not satisfy her ardent passion, and his lifestyle did not conform to her newly awakened socialist ideals. He felt a failure.

Like Dania, he considered killing her and expiating his self-disgust in her death.

In the meantime he waited. He needed her stricken warmth and disgusted adoration. Her tears cleansed him from the ghastliness of his days.

*

As it became clear that Lucia was Anatoly's mistress, it inspired his comrades to emulate. The Partkoms sought out new secretaries, who had to be educated, young and attractive.

There was a scramble for the most attractive Lithuanians and Poles.

Resisters were deported.

A Lithuanian schoolteacher had set up a classroom in her hostess's home.

This had to stop.

Besides, she was full bosomed and swayed attractively as she walked. She was attached to a young Kazakh man, and ended up at Vasily's office where she typed the young man's deportation orders.

The original Russian secretary, an older lady who had left Moscow with the young men, complained to the party caucus.

She was disregarded.

Wife stealing had spread like wildfire through the Kazakh Raikom.

Some of the more senior apparatchiks acquired several mistresses, living the life of Eastern potentates, smoking hashish in hookahs and sipping mint tea, as they received supplicants for the populace bearing gifts.

Their shocked juniors said nothing.

Power had diluted the purity of the vanguard.

Part 4.

Whispers

The biggest crimes are too difficult to understand.

People simply fail to believe that such things could ever happen.

1.

Lvov 1941

Janek returned to his family apartment with his Russian wife. Basia, who had saved him from certain destruction, had taken a fancy to the grand rooms and lavish furnishing.

As a known informer, Janek lost all credibility at work and among his social circle. Furthermore, he was shattered by the effects that his betrayal of his family and friends had on his social standing.

He tried to bluster it out.

'They tortured me,' he began.

People just turned away.

He was alone, with only Basia for company and her crowd of rowdy heavy drinking and uncultured friends.

He attended the party meetings though he had little to contribute. He was not a committed party member. Instead he took to going to bars after work to drown is sorrows, apparently tortured by the fate of his mother and his sisters.

Basia had a token secretarial job, and waited for him every evening in full makeup and furs looted from Poles. She dragged him to bars full of Russian speaking military where his broken Russian accent caused a lot of derision and back-slapping.

He hated being seeing with the soldiers and his wife was increasingly annoyed by his refusal to swagger around the city.

*

Basia grew in confidence. She attended the city beauty salons and began to wear rather garish makeup. She had the benign cyst on her face removed by Lvov's top surgeon. She staggered around in high heels on the cobbled pavements.

She was unimpressed by her husband's mild-mannered weakness, and contemptuous of his braggadocio when drunk.

Over the year, she became domineering and superior to the inhabitants and to her husband. There were constant arguments over his failure to enforce his authority over shopkeepers and taxi drivers.

"Janek, we need to show these people who is boss."

She was the new ruling class and felt she could do better. She claimed to be a pure blooded Ukrainian freeing the minority of Ukrainians who lived in the city from Polish oppressors.

*

Hers was a tenuous superiority, as invasion by Germany threatened the new born Soviet.

Basia became increasingly hysterical.

'Why do you come home so late? I could be murdered at any moment. Can you not protect me? You are weak, and I do not think that you deserve me.'

She cried theatrically, like the sensitive woman she was.

'Don't you know that the Germans are planning to invade?'

She began loading some of the more vulgar ornaments in the flat into packing cases. She and her fellows were stripping the country of the last vestiges of value.

Janek did not know whether to be relieved or upset when they divorced shortly before Operation Barbarossa. He was afraid of the Germans, knowing that they were violently anti-Semitic. Nevertheless, he was equally afraid of his future under Soviet rule.

His ex-wife was swept up with the army and left for Russia alone.

'Father says to leave you behind. You disgrace our revolutionary family.'

*

There was some resistance to the invasion.

The population of Lvov was divided again, into those who welcomed the Germans and those who resisted or ignored them.

Most Poles and Ukrainians trusted that nothing could be worse than communism and did not put up much of a fight. A few of the Jewish militia attempted to resist and were cut down, leading to the Jews being publicly blamed for the thousands of political prisoners executed by the Soviet in the last few days of occupation.

The German military didn't bomb the historic areas believing that this would be their promised land.

Janek did not get involved in further collaboration of any kind. He kept his head down, intending to survive.

*

Lvov had become a frightening place.

It was hard not to be deeply cynical. The city had been occupied by two thoroughly opposing ideologies within a short space of time.

Soviets had killed most of the powerful people in the city, and before leaving, they eliminated remaining political prisoners.

Germans purged the universities and any remaining intellectuals who had supported the outgoing regime and systematically attacked the large Jewish population in public pogroms and violent purges.

The thud of tanks driving to war reinforced military domination. Germans swaggered about in smart uniforms, and drove impressive vehicles.

They conceived that they were a superior 'Aryan' race of tall blond people, despite mostly being quite short, fat, and dark while many Poles and Ukrainians were blond, and even pretty tall.

It was wise to cower.

Everyone was treated with contempt. Jews were especially singled out, openly beaten in the street, shot and arrested. It was common to see piles of Jewish corpses and groups of well-dressed Jews cleaning the street on their hands and knees.

The invaders fomented anti-Semitism as far as possible.

Anti-Semitic advertising was everywhere and the remaining abject Jews sported a yellow star.

No one wanted to share their fate.

Every single minority race in Lvov, and there were several, felt the danger and oppression of potential extermination. Jews were an example of what could happen; a horrific example to keep the rest in line. Even before the Germans arrived it was clear that they intended to make a clean sweep of the Jews, and equally obvious that even children had little chance.

The entire population became obsessed about racial purity and right to existence.

Asiatic-looking Georgians and Armenians were randomly beaten and taken to concentration camps, in fact, anyone foreign or exotic looking was in imminent danger.

People of every racial origin scrutinised their mirrors and worried about the shape of nose and chin. And out of all this chaos a febrile Ukrainian nationalism emerged. Ukrainians wore national costume and carried stout canes to beat outsiders cheered on by Germans.

Soldiers randomly closed off markets, swept up the people, and segregated them by appearance. Those judged inferior were never seen again.

*

Janek was Jewish by blood. He was very tall, and quite mousy, if not blond. He worried about being recognizably Jewish, and avoided Germans, knowing that they had devices for identification. He had taken to wearing a hat in public and stooped to ensure he was shorter than passing invaders.

*

He was not alone in worrying that he would be identified as a Jew.

Despite his concerns, he let rooms out at a high rent to a family of Jews. He was one of several prepared to take in such obvious refugees.

He knew Reuben Schmidt to speak to and had agreed to take him in once Basia had gone.

They were extremely nice people and no bother. They paid Janek weekly and he lived on their rent.

Reuben had been a senior accountant for a Warsaw government office and had retreated to Lvov in 1939. He left his post as soon as Germany invaded.

He had a beautiful Nordic-looking wife and four young children of 13, 12, 9 and 2 years of age. He didn't have anywhere to go, the area was locked down. It required extreme daring to attempt to escape in a hostile countryside with his large family.

Reuben had the brown hair and slanted eyes common to most Ukrainians. His delicate wife was mousy blond, and refused to leave the apartment in case she was arrested in the street. They changed their name to Jelinski.

The children were dainty, and none of them were particularly alike.

The family thanked god for every new day. They celebrated Sabbath, and prayed in Yiddish, quietly. They and were more religious than had been before the invasion. They relied on God for survival.

The mother was to be his maid, and after much discussion he

agreed to claim the youngest child as his daughter, in the event of a raid.

*

At night, Lvov was a quiet and secretive hive of activity as people attempted to move around, escape, and pass around illegal food, resources and information. The Germans had a habit of tucking in for the night, believing that their job of intimidation had a finite span, and leaving the evenings for entertainment.

By night the market was full of Jewish mothers attempting to sell their children on the black market. Unluckily, the Jelinski children were too old, except for the youngest child, a plump, pretty girl with potential for another life.

The mother had already offered her pretty blond two year old girl in the market place to citizens who looked kind, but they had chosen another child, because a better bribe was offered. Mrs Jelinski tried not to be grateful, because she idolised her and spent every moment with her as if she knew that they would part soon.

The older children were quiet and traumatised. They could see what was going on from the windows occasionally and heard the shouts and screams of the victims from the main square. They were living among strangers, without any idea of the horrors awaiting deported Jews. Their parents conspired to keep them ignorant while, at the same time, warning them of the perils of talking to outsiders.

Janek regretted taking them in. he had unwisely agreed to take the daughter if the worst came to the worst.

The Jelinskis trusted him implicitly, and he was stupefied by it, knowing himself to be a traitor. He was particularly upset that they had unwisely promised him their remaining money for their little daughter. It made them a living incarnation of his honesty and he became closely involved as he tried to rebuild his shattered integrity.

The racial superiority of the Nazis was no longer something he could believe in. he had bonded with the Jelinskis as people, as friends, and as Jews.

*

As the German war effort stalled, the population returned to a barter economy. Tasteful niceties which once cost a lot become worth very little. Food and heat become expensive. Buying and selling was done in the old market place by day and night.

Items were laid out, jewellery, books, personal things, lace, nighties, socks, clothes and hats of all kinds laid out like apples and potatoes. People carried lamps and firewood to market, in exchange for food. Those with money strutted around like millionaires.

Janek did the shopping, working from a long list provided by his maid. He had no idea how to barter and had no idea how much things were worth. It was humiliating and immensely difficult, as the market place was full of gossip and questions.

'This,' shouted the stall holders, 'is worthless. Was your mother a Jew?'

They laughed raucously, in order to bring the price down.

He regularly turned to Eva, a fat peasant girl with food to sell. She had a kindly and friendly manner and did not humiliate him, while other marketers denigrated his offerings.

Eva was rapacious, yet never rude. He trusted her. She made money out of middle class fools like him, and sold his stuff for double or triple what she gave.

*

Eva had recently arrived from the countryside where the German scientifically based land clearance policy was killing thousands. She had escaped her doomed village.

She spoke Russki and her peasant background and wits served her well. She sold goods to peasants who travelled to Lviv by night and settled in holes and cellars underground, in exchange for potatoes and grain. She collected edible wild foods and prepared salads using sorrel and geraniums, mixed with lettuce grown on hidden roofs in the city. These, served with kasha or coarse brown rye bread, sold well as ready-meals. There were queues at lunchtimes, mainly middle classes who had previously relied on servants. She bought holed socks for a song, darned them and sold them for 5 times the price.

Eva knew about the Jelinskis. One day she gave him a little extra bread and salad.

'For the boys,' she winked. 'They liked it so much last time. Tell the Jelinskis it's from Eva.'

Janek did not bother to deny it.

'Thank you.' he replied.

Several days later, Eva spoke to him again.

'Maybe I should take a commission for selling your things,' she offered. 'I can come round and assess what you have. You have no idea what sells. Some things are worth more on particular days of the week. I know who comes in and what they want. I can help.'

Janek heaved a sigh of relief. He was selling Jelinski property as well as his own and had no idea of value. After discussing the matter with the Jelinskis, and several free meals, he agreed.

Eva came round with delicious food made from very little. She made instant friends with mama Jelinska, and petted the children.

In the normal course of things, Madame Jelinska would never have spoken to a common peasant. Under these conditions, the two women spent hours gossiping, despite their very different backgrounds.

Eva picked everything over. It was noticeable that she set aside things with a Jewish flavour, advising immediate sale.

Within a week she had moved in, without direct permission from Janek. He could not object as she slept on the floor in the children's room.

She proved a sparkling addition to the household. The house became lighter and more peaceful, with less underlying panic. She grew plants in the attic and on the roof, sprouted wheat and grain in the basement and sold everything. The place became a workshop, with the children cooking and peeling, sorting stuff she had got in the market, teaching Mrs Jelinska how to darn. She taught them peasant songs and dances and directed sing-songs during the work on market business.

They learnt that she had been sleeping on the street and had been seeking somewhere to spend winter. She laughed coarsely at the crap Janek had been selling. She only accepted it because she felt sorry for him. He was such an idiot.

Janek had taken to going to church. He had brought the little girl with him every Sunday, hoping to bring the rest of the family once they understood what to do. It was the best way to prove that they were not Jewish.

That first Sunday, Eva accompanied him. She was very quiet on

221

the way there and back, unlike her usual coarse self, which was full of slaps, pinches and peasant tricks. Janek noticed that she had little idea of the order of service and no knowledge of the prayers. He assumed that she was Eastern Orthodox.

Eva had been in the apartment for about 3 weeks when they heard that Germans were raiding the ghetto.

The occupants of apartment subsided into a quiet terror which killed appetite and song.

The sounds of shooting and screaming rocked over the silent city as everyone stayed at home. Mama Jelinska prayed quietly for her fellows. She rocked her little baby. The older children played silently, guessing that something was up.

*

They were betrayed.

Their absence from church had been noted by Mikhail, the spiteful concierge, who reported the suspected Jews to the Germans, in exchange for a bounty which provided him warmth all winter.

The raid consisted of three Jew-hunters with scary-looking cases, and two armed soldiers. They beat on the door. Janek ran to answer. He did not want it knocked down again; it was not properly repaired from the last visit.

Janek haltingly explained that he was not harbouring Jews. He was a widower with a young child and they were in service to him. The lady was a maid to his baby, and the peasant woman was cook. He was certain that they were no Jews, as they did not look it and had no accent.

He wished that the Jelinskis had denied their origins but the petrified family admitted it immediately.

Surely they could have made up a story of some other religion or ethnic origin. No one knew what evidence the Germans were acting on.

These were gentle guileless folk. They gave up hope.

Despite their confession, they had to submit to humiliating measurement of their nose and body proportions to prove their racial inferiority.

As the visitors proved that the proportions of their victims were uniquely Jewish, Janek became unsure. Maybe there really was some difference? He could see nothing quintessentially Jewish in the cowering family's demeanour. Maybe there was? They were experts with a higher knowledge. If so, then he was petrified that they would notice his racial impurity.

He could not leave his friends to their terrible fate. In a burst of recklessness, he looked the Jew-hunter in the eyes and repeated that they did not look like Jews.

'Oh!' averred the squad leader, with a knowing smirk. 'It takes an expert to find them. You are not to be blamed, fine Aryan-looking man as you are.'

He scrutinised Janek with an expert eye. It was clear that he liked what he saw. Janek was uncomfortable under his perverted intrusion, with something sexual about it.

'I am not surprised you were fooled.' He opined smugly, 'They hide among decent folk you see. They tell evil lies and may even have worshipped in your house. We will need to search for their magic paraphernalia.'

The other one interrupted.

'They trade on the good-will and naiveté of young Aryans such as you.'

He raised his eyebrow questioningly. 'German mother?'

Janek nodded miserably. He was no less Jewish than the Jelinskis.

It was impossible. His resemblance to Grandpapa Braun was startling. He had his mother's nose and she was always considered to look quite Jewish.

'I thought so. The Poles here have a good mix of German. We are adopting some of the children into good Aryan families so that they can be brought up in a superior culture.'

He turned to the tiny little blond child who was being carefully distracted by Eva.

'What a fine child!'

He turned to Janek.

'Your daughter could go to a good Aryan family home. You can see instantly that she is of pure blood, unlike these little goblins.'

Janek broke down in tears. He tried to tell them that his daughter was all he had left of his wife, and she was well cared for by his peasant cook.

Mrs Jelinska tried not to look towards her baby, in case she betrayed her child. He wept for the Jelinskis, for the mother who could not say goodbye to her own daughter.

Seeing the raw emotion in the man, the German dropped his callous offer. He sneered at the little girl's brothers and sister.

'There is a lot of ethnic cleansing to be done here,' he revealed to his mate. 'This is a city of beasts and animals. It will be purified.'

Everyone was silent.

Janek needed the toilet and also felt sick. He thought he would faint. The grief-stricken parents were hugging their remaining children.

The Germans kicked them gently into a corner.

One smacked papa Jelinski on the cheek.

'You, dear Jew,' he accused, 'have traded on this poor man's kindness. You had no right to be here, you belong in the ghetto with the other rats. Never fear, you will be taken to a work camp where your labour will make the German nation great. Otherwise things will go very wrong for you. Don't worry.' He added. 'We can even use dross like you.'

The raid lasted a further half hour or so, although it seemed like they were there for days.

The Jew hunters left with their prey. As the group were marched off, their leader winked at the remaining occupants of the apartment.

'Don't worry,' he reassured them. 'We have got rid of your vermin.'

2.

The Eastern Provinces

It was impossible to escape the truth that Russia was in the grip of defeat. The party had requisitioned seed-grain, troops, tractors, guns, felt boots, iron and lastly old men and children from the poverty-stricken collectives. The Soviets could not defeat Germany alone.

Stalin would certainly have toppled if the Allies had not committed to aid the ailing dictatorship. Even so, did supporting his regime shorten the war?

If Stalin had fallen; the party would have re-organised to drive out the invader. The ensuing confusion might have given Germany the upper hand.

The Allies did not want to condone the invasion of Poland, which had started the war in the first place. One of the conditions of the Treaty of London was the release of some 1.5 million detainees to join the Allied armies in the Middle East.

*

News of the defeats and German advances reached the Raikom. The Eastern provinces were to be the centre of government, defenders of the revolution. It spelt a huge change to the running of the Soviets as the Siberian projects confronted a very real industrial power.

Their meagre produce was to sustain the war.

Senior NKVD arrived in the remote corner of Kazakhstan driving an impounded German transport. Andrei and Katya were demoted, relegated to espionage, uncovering conspiracies among retreating party members, who were to blame for soviet defeats.

All able-bodies men were recruited to fight for their country. The remaining workers were involved in back-breaking labour which would fell a horse. People moved across Russia in stupendous numbers. Each day consignments of labour arrived, diluting the Kazakh population. Whole families melted into the steppes by night. A few were caught and executed. Most succeeded in finding a new life out East.

Party directives contradicted themselves daily.

The revolution was over.

*

The original vanguard struggled to survive in this new atmosphere of frenzied reorganization. They lacked the increasingly psychotic commitment required to rule by fear. They followed every twist and turn of policy, tying themselves into ideological knots in order to hang on to power.

They had once believed that the Russian peasants and workers were the best off in the world. However, this belief was increasingly difficult to maintain this certainty as the people struggled with massive overcrowding in the immense land.

Andrei changed from the heady days of early interrogations, when the old guard strode about like heroes. He became unclear about his role in the party, and faced existential angst each morning, needing vodka and pills before he got out of bed. He was incapable of believing in the latest conspiracies.

'The Kazakh are simple folk,' he whispered in the dark of the night. 'They are incapable of acquiring sophisticated intelligence about party intrigues involving people far away.'

He was finding the deranged directives of their great leader particularly difficult. He supported every twist of policy, even when it was contradicted within days, but began to show signs of instability.

He hung on to his faith in a future socialist nirvana and still relished reading his beloved pamphlets, yet did so in a tired, flat voice.

Sometimes his soul engaged and he started to question the wisdom of wanton destruction in the name of progress, and fell to groaning remorse.

'Perhaps we are creating a new world,' he averred doubtfully, 'I am not sure if it is right to take *all* the food for war.'

Katya did not support him. She had never credited any of it. She did not accept the ideology; though its lies and machinations fascinated her. In the privacy of her own mind, she compared the luxury of bourgeois life in Warsaw with her present condition.

'This is all lies,' she concluded. 'If wealth were shared equally, people would be richer than this.'

She was oblivious to slogans like 'destruction before construction' and other nonsense. She felt above the doublespeak which brought food to the table and victims for her hunger.

Andrei was a believer. He was struggling to reconcile alliance between the pure Soviet nation and tainted British and American capitalists.

'Comrade Stalin has a plan for these sly democrats.' he tapped his nose significantly. 'He is up to something.'

He got more drunk than usual and wept aloud.

'We have betrayed the cause. That Jew Hitler has caused mother Russia to eat her children. What have we done?' Andrei sobbed. 'What have we done?'

Katya watched him without compassion. He was twitchy, unwashed and regularly vomiting. She would have to leave him soon.

*

Fortunately, a new directive gave him hope.

Communist Poles were to act as the new vanguard, propagandists in the Capitalist Desert. Any brothers and sisters in the party could depart for the West. They were to act as fifth columnists for the glorious revolution.

'We have a secret plan for revolution. Comrade Stalin will be elected President of America,' he suggested. 'Then those fat capitalists will release their ill-gotten wealth.'

In accordance with the terms of the treaty, every able bodied Pole was permitted to leave. However, only good communists would obtain transport to the Allied armies. The dross had to contrive their own means to reach the holding camps for the New Polish Army. They had until late Autumn 1942.

Andrei was happier. He lay in bed dreaming of future revolution, as imperialist nations consumed themselves in war and their proletariat rose up.

He discussed Katya's future in the West.

'You will be able to explain how to do it,' he gloated. 'You will be a glorious leader in the inexorable victory of the proletariat.'

Some of his old confidence returned and he turned to his photo of Stalin,

'Little father!' he wagged his finger at the photo. 'You had a plan all along!'

*

Andrei's old enthusiasm for communist ideals revived, although there was a hollow note in his voice.

He found it hard to hide his sympathy for the starving Kazakh and his loyalty was in question.

He still dutifully discovered saboteurs, although becoming less and less convinced of their conspiracies.

Copious amounts of vodka mixed with Dexedrine made him imagine insects crawling in his skin. The apartment stank of various detergents and insect killers, and Katya would wake to find him pulling off the sheets.

'They are here!' he shouted, 'they are all over the bed. Bugs! Numbers of them! Katya, why is the maid not cleaning properly? Get them off me!'

He had deep gouges on his arms and cheeks, where he had tried to drag insects out from under his flesh; they were hiding there, conspiring.

Despite his paranoia, he attempted to guide his mate. She would have to work with the dialectic among primitive and savage capitalist economies.

She stroked his skinny neck, of course she would.

'You will be shining light in the West,' he told her, weeping uncontrollably. He was giving his divine girlfriend away for the purest revolutionary motives.

'Good party members will be working for international socialism. Go,' he pressed her, 'go,' he said, hugging her tight and weeping.

He discussed her future endlessly, hopelessly assured that the collapse of capitalism was imminent.

*

Internal party directives were sending tendrils of fear into every provincial Raikom.

Since the exiled party had moved east, party officials from larger Soviets, with better connections, struggled to find a decent purchase among the remaining party echelons.

It was dog eat dog.

The weakest would fail, and Andrei was weak.

*

He had a precognition of his imminent denouncement and death, and hoped it would happen after his beloved girlfriend had left.

It could not be long.

'You must marry,' he sobbed, as he contemplated lonely nights ahead.

Katya hid her excitement at the idea, regarding him dispassionately. She might be attached to Andrei - survival was more important.

'Marry a bourgeois, and convert him to the revolution. He will cherish you, I know, but not as well as I.'

He drowned in sentimentality as he presaged his own lonely death.

'I will die here. Please, never forget me.'

Katya murmured assent. The fact was that she had already forgotten him. She was coldly aware that he was doomed, a party dinosaur, and that she would fall with him unless she left with the first cohorts departing for the West.

She scarcely remembered the old days in Warsaw. Still, she imagined balls, and tables piled high with food and diaphanous dresses, and waltzing on the arm of a handsome young plutocrat.

*

Everywhere, idealists were being replaced by pragmatic men who believed in less and therefore achieved more.

The party faithful attached great weight to the Marxist dialectic, and its ideals. It was increasingly obvious that Stalin's political and imperial ambitions meant that he had to relieve the country of derelict idealists within the party who clung to internationalism.

People like Katya were the perfect new party members. People who were prepared to say can do anything in the name of the party, whose political affiliations were directly to the party caucus rather than some ideological straight jacket.

Had Katya remained in the Soviet, good things awaited her. She welcomed greyness, repetition and boredom, and the uncompromising tastelessness of the ugly concrete blocks which replaced the peasants intricately carved wooden houses and delightful yurts. All that mattered was power and control.

To good party members like her, dullness indicated all was well. It meant that the dead were lying peacefully rather than screaming vengeance. It meant that there were no ghosts, no God, and, more importantly, no Satan, to drag them to hell. Because late at night in the dark she feared the shaman's curse and worried that perhaps there was a god after all.

*

Good party members like her no longer sought out revolutionary spirit. They were on the alert to quash enquiry, spiritualism or search for truth. They scoured schools and universities in order to thwart every move towards redemption or justice. Even possessing a rare old icon was a sign of rebellion.

3.

Soviet Allies

Stalin had agreed that any Polish person fit to fight could leave to join the Allies. It was not until May 1942 that Katya and her sister were booked for departure.

By then thousands of Poles, who had obtained passports and permits, or *propisky*, aimed for Iran, Egypt and Afghanistan where borders were open to receive army conscripts.

Crowds of starving refugee women and children walked on the roads, hitching rides on buses and trains, despite being in terrible condition. Many died on the road.

*

Lucia was trapped. She did not obtain the required signatures because Anatoly claimed to be unsure of her revolutionary purity.

He knew that she wanted to escape and he wouldn't let her have such happiness.

In any case, he did not want her to leave. She provided him with something to torment. Unlike most Russian peasant women, who just sighed and got on with life, she fought back. She was elegant and attractive too.

He threatened to marry her, because married Poles were officially Russian.

He thought he had defeated her many times, but she recovered from the humiliating tasks he set her. She drew on ancient myths of knighthood and warfare and honourable death. No matter what he did, she maintained her courage and defiance. She was thinner, with huge haunted eyes, and graceful as a swan.

Nevertheless, he would not doubt have succeeded in the end. She would have broken down if there hadn't been the potential to escape. The chance to get away provided her with hope and she was determined to get away and reach the Allied front in Cairo.

She spent all week contriving a plan.

If it failed, she would commit suicide.

Meanwhile, she appeared inconsolable, begged for mercy and appeased his sadism, while plotting escape.

231

*

The transport was due to leave early Tuesday morning and Anatoly had arranged to keep his girlfriend close.

Lucia anticipated this.

It would not be sufficient to get him drunk. She intended to drug his vodka with valerian, an herbal soporific which she had diligently collected for weeks and boiled down. Her mother had taught her a lot about herbs as she often dosed the peasants in her care with herbal infusions.

She knew that Valerian would work. She had been brewing and distilling it for weeks.

*

The transports arrived, ready to load up those with papers. They had gathered selected Polish men and women from collectives and party offices all over Kazakhstan. The occupants were healthy and strong. Some were still in Party uniforms.

Anatoly had got up early to show her the troop carriers loading up Poles in the mist.

She hugged him and told him she worshipped him - when was the wedding?

He laughed heartily.

'That's a good joke, you strumpet!' He sneered. 'You are dying to meet all your bourgeois friends, go to balls, wear silks.... *you* never will. That's for Katya.'

Like all Party stalwarts, his vision of the West was based on prohibited Hollywood gangster movies. He imagined her swanning around in ball dress and getting involved in gun battles with other criminals.

He grabbed her arms and wrapped them round his body. 'You are mine.' He pushed her hands down his pants. 'Don't worry. We will marry, only when I want to.'

He turned to the bottle of vodka on his desk and drank half a tumbler. It was his usual morning pick-me-up. 'I had better sign the transport off,' he grumbled.

He signed the forms, took another stiff drink and went to the door with the paper.

'You, my dearest darling, had better stay here while I take these

232

papers to the carrier.'

His legs got weaker and weaker. He started to feel sick and puked down his shirt. He cursed her violently.

'This is not good. Clean it up bitch.'

And he collapsed, asleep, right by the door.

Lucia flew towards him, checking he was unconscious, prepared to cosh him with the heavy, Lenin-shaped paperweight if necessary. He was out cold.

She carefully moved his legs out of sight, dragged him to his desk and leaned him drunkenly against it.

Finally, she stamped a new form with her name on, forged his signature, and left, slowly shutting the door behind her.

'Comrade Anatoly is dozing,' she disclosed to the staff in the office as she handed them the sheaf of signed papers. 'He must not be disturbed.'

This was quite normal. Anatoly often had a nap in the morning. His staff took the calls, unless it was a senior party member phoning about a difficult matter.

She went downstairs and took her duffel bag out of the stationery cupboard. She was in charge of stationery and kept the key.

She had packed it with crumpled waste paper, because it would be odd if she had no luggage.

She went out of the back door and walked to the front, right away from the office window and gave the papers directly to the drivers.

*

Not many people were about.

Raikom staff kept late nights and most officials drank themselves to sleep.

She avoided transports containing local girls and climbed into the last one, explaining to the driver that the others were full.

She observed her companions, many in cadre uniforms with red kerchiefs.

No one was fat; though none of them had starved, unlike the columns of walking refugees.

Most of them were tanned and healthy.

There was an undercurrent of carefully subdued excitement among them.

233

Everyone was quiet, in case there was a last minute change of plan. Some were frightened, suspecting that they were off to Siberia. Others were quietly exuberant, and reassured their companions in hushed voices.

*

They set off through open countryside.

Tashkent was two day's journey in the hot sun.

Even so, no one got off at first - they were terrified of being shot. After a while a few careful Poles slipped down to relieve themselves at each stop. They crouched near the rear wheels and held on to the hands of those on board. As they got nearer to their destination more of them got off and walked a short way to stretch their legs. No one strayed far, and half of the group remained on the transport at all times, keeping an eye on the driver.

Those walking near the truck loudly proclaimed how they grieved for mother Russia, and praised Stalin at all times.

The convoy lumbered on.

Lucia was petrified almost every minute of the journey, certain that Anatoly had woken up and called ahead.

She half expected to be dragged off the transport, and had resolved to run into the open grasslands and be shot, rather than return to interrogation and torture.

*

In the event, Anatoly was not discovered till midday.

His staff were fooled by his drunken stupor and the glass of vodka Lucia had left by his side. They thought he was drunk.

Lucia had prepared a strong dose of valerian, which might have killed a less heavy drinker.

Her boyfriend merely benefited from a long sedated sleep. He was worn out, altogether overburdened by the presence of nomenklatura breathing down his neck. He slept like a baby for four hours, waking up deliciously peaceful and cosy - to the anxious faces of his staff.

'We tried awfully hard to wake you, comrade. Then we suspected *she* had poisoned you,' one of them whispered.

'We did not know what to do. We called the doctor and he said you were sleeping.'

'He pronounced you well, and left you to sleep it off. He was of the opinion that it might be – that you were – tired.' ('Tired' and 'sleeping' were common terms for drunken and comatose.)

Anatoly rubbed his sleepy eyes.

'Who?' He asked - jerking up as the adrenaline kicked in to his sleepy body. 'What poison?'

The office staff were young men and women with all decisiveness winnowed out under evolutionary pressure.

The independent ones had either disappeared or moved to the heights of party membership. They looked at each other impassively, kept quiet.

'Who?' snarled Anatoly more authoritatively. His voice required facts.

'Lucia,' they all chorused together. 'She has gone - on the transport.'

Anatoly jumped up, regretting it immediately; his head reeled and he lurched alarmingly.

The office was a hotbed of gossip. Everyone knew what had been going on.

'The bitch poisoned me.' He shouted. 'Find her. Arrest her. No. Shoot on sight. Ring the transports! Stop them! There is a fugitive on board, a terrorist! Get her!'

'What shall I say? Is she a fugitive, or a terrorist?' asked a prepossessing youth with a death wish.

'Tell them my secretary has stolen state papers,' roared the abandoned paramour.

*

At that very moment Lucia was regretting the crumpled papers in her rucksack.

They scratched her as she tried to use it as a pillow.

'Anatoly will claim I stole secret papers,' she realised. 'He will have me shot.'

Just like man and wife, the two were thinking in parallel, even though hundreds of miles apart.

She was still terrified of him, though she felt stronger and angrier with every passing mile.

'Never fear Anatoly, you old bastard, I will be questioned first, to

235

discover if there is a plot among the Poles, and I will implicate you - and probably everyone else on this transport.'

Still she rued her foolhardiness at taking the papers. 'I should not have done it.'

She schemed how best to lose the rucksack at the next stop if she could.

'That shithead, he thinks he will finish me off, but I will finish him. I could take him down with me,' she schemed. 'I will say he told me to take the papers. He is an agent and obligated me to spy. I will kill them all. I will have vengeance. I will at least bring those bastards down with me.'

With such intimate knowledge of each other, they instinctively understood each other's' thought processes.

Almost at that very moment, Anatoly was screaming for Lucia's head, then stopped short. He knew that his girlfriend would do her best to implicate him in some kind of plot.

It was a scary time to be alive, even for terror-bringers.

He stayed the young hothead eagerly reaching for the phone. Local officials would link him with a wide range of their errors if he owned up to even the smallest mistake.

'Wait, I will check what has gone.'

He retreated into his office and tried to think, although his brain was befuddled.

'Oh I am in trouble!' he realised, 'if any apparatchiks has done anything, I am fucked. If anything goes wrong today, even as far away as Moscow, I will be blamed. I have just done myself in.'

*

Anatoly was justifiably petrified.

Stalin saw rebellion in the tiniest gesture, smile or word, and his paranoia permeated the party.

Party members needed to explain the army's pitiful performance on the battlefield. And officials sought to pin errors on to the nearest scapegoat.

He rubbed his head.

If he admitted to a mistake, however small, to do with lost papers or orders - he would be the fall guy for everything, including lost tanks and incorrect battle plans.

He simply could not afford to make any mistakes. Mistakes demonstrated lack of devotion to the cult.

'Yet,' he surmised, with some relief, 'the executive are fully engaged with Stalingrad. They won't notice if I lie.'

He deliberated fast. 'Better to make out that I deliberately let her go,' he decided.

Feelings of rage overtook him.

'The bitch planned it all along.'

All this thinking gave him a blinding headache.

'Wait,' his hands trembled with fear at the extreme danger of his position. 'I had better check that she didn't in fact remove any papers fast. I had better check.'

He shot around the room, his head reeled. He was drunk and immobilised.

He tried to think straight despite his numbing headache. Would she have taken anything? Could he take the chance?

'That noble bitch!' he remembered. 'She is just that - honourable. She didn't take a thing. I am sure of it'.

Waves of affection flowed over him. She was too high-minded to bring him down.

'Unless, unless, I went for her. She would not hesitate then.'

*

He emerged from his office.

The young boys, not sixteen, watched expectantly.

'Nothing is missing.'

He tugged at his collar.

'I was unwell.'

He glanced significantly at the empty tumbler of vodka.

'I forgot. I sent her off. She was no good to me. She wanted to marry me, a good working class hero like me.' He made an obscene sign. 'Capitalist whores all of them.'

They coughed and smiled politely at his crudeness. As good communists they were intensely prudish, since their cult controlled every basic act and necessity. They were perturbed at his rude reference to carnal acts.

*

He had to make a good story of it.

237

He waxed sentimental.

'She did not want to leave, until I insisted. She loved Stalin. She was broken-hearted and did not want to go.'

There! He had covered every eventuality.

His drunkenness was easily explained. Everyone in power spent most of their time inebriated. He could easily say he had overdone it, because he regretted the loss of his secretary.

*

Lucia had played a poker-type game, for high stakes. She bluffed her way to a win based on the fact that Anatoly could not afford an error on his record. He would cover up her escape to save face.

4.

Siberia 1942

It was not until the very last transport were leaving in for the North African Front in August 1942 that Sofia prepared to leave Magadan, along with 5,000 starved ex-prisoners serving sentences for imaginary offences against communism.

The journey of thousands of miles required preparation, and logistics. June was already too late for most of the refugees to leave.

She had a bag of food and her earnings, and headed for the freight yard for transports leaving for Irkutsk.

There was a flutter of hundreds of Poles in all conditions standing on the flat platform and around in the cool autumnal air.

Some sat on the chilly ground, huddled together for warmth, too weak to stand. Ghouls watched the concourse of heaving flesh patiently; confident at least a few would be left behind. She tried not to worry, and to discount the bone igloos in the distance.

Approximately half of this particular group would ever make it to the near East.

*

The refugees had all manner of ragged packs with them and whispered to each other in Polish, sharing their experiences in the gulags.

Most discussions veered to their Polish origins. Everyone was carefully re-establishing their status and caste.

There was a high level of excitement. After all, Russia was at war and being defeated. Plans were made; there were estates to reclaim from confiscation.

Information flowed through the crowd in waves, followed by silence as everyone drank it in.

'There is a battle for Moscow and Stalingrad.'

A flood of queries and hopes rushed back.

Another wave swept through.

'Germany is losing.'

This was known for sure.

Rumours flowed like waves blown over water.

'Poland is free; Poland is invaded'
Then
'Poland has risen up.'
The crowd exulted. Withered and frostbitten skeletons shouted hoarse war-cries.

Fight for the motherland!

Pitiful fists rose in the air and slashed imaginary bayonets at the invader.

Names shuddered through the multitude. Any Jablonkis? Sikorskis? Kaminskis? Wysockis?

If there was a yes, then replies would shoot back, genealogies, addresses, locations and first names.

There were joyful meetings, loud weeping, cheers of elation as families struggled through the sea of people to hug and wail at each other. They huddled together to rebuild relationships.

Sophia sent out a shout for Anya and Katya Maslow.

There was no response from the throng.

*

The host moved as one body, instinctively recognising that the only hope of survival was in the herd. They made plans, shared food and prayed for a transport column which could take them all. Everyone had arrived well before dawn.

They waited patiently, freezing and starving in the frigid wind.

The days were getting short. Half an hour before a transport was due, staff arrived and lit lanterns.

There was upheaval as individuals jockeyed for position so as to get a decent space on the transport.

They waited most of the day.

*

As the bleak flat area got darker, monstrous, armoured American trucks and lorries heaved into the yards. They were mostly hauling open trucks, not the wagons which the people had hopes for.

Aid from the West was arriving at the Siberian ports, to be loaded on trains where tracks had been built. Corned beef and army supplies were guarded by armed soldiers, as were live ammunition.

The transport was massive, and consisted of timber, tanks freshly

240

painted with red stars, guns, ammunition, and food supplies. Trucks and crates were directed for the front.

The drivers got off their cabs and watched the tumult impassively. They allowed Poles to clambers over the cargo, unless soldiers drove them off.

Poles clambered into every available space. Struggles broke out for comfortable positions.

Families or groups working together fared best.

Sophia got under a tarpaulin covering a large American tank painted with a red star.

She was accompanied by a lady and her daughter, as well as a typhus-ridden man of unknown age.

His bald head had been shaved recently, and was covered in scabs. He had been bound for the ships crossing to the gulags, yet insisted he was Polish. He spoke a little Polish, and the guards did not check.

He was feverish, and scarcely made it onto the low loader carrying the tank.

He had laughed at Stalin's picture while drunk, and had been sentenced to two years of hard labour. His two week stay in a Lvov prison with other lousy jokers had left him with typhus. And he had not qualified for decent food rations. He was a husk.

'I am Polish.' he insisted, 'Polish, Polish. I am a free man. I love comrade Stalin. He is my father and my brother.'

He repeated this endlessly as his fever grew worse.

The 'joker' kept everyone awake for the first night, until they got used to it.

When he woke up and shouted, people quietened him automatically.

'We know,' they hushed him. 'Don't worry. Comrade Stalin is a good man.'

The two other occupants were Teresa and her mother Greta.

Teresa had no fingers on her left hand, lost in a saw early on in her working career.

Her remaining fingers were frostbitten and stiffened by swelling; she walked like an old woman on account of a prolapse from the back breaking labour.

Greta had been dragged out of the Gulag furniture-making factory by her daughter.

She was dying.

*

The four slept close together under the belly of the tank. The tarpaulin fitted tight and they were warmer than expected. Where there were draughts, Teresa crawled around under the tank, tucking in the tarpaulin and tearing off pieces for covers.

'It was hard, hard,' she moaned, 'seven women unpacking pallets of timber. Do you have any idea how big the pieces were? They were longer than this tank. And we had to move them all before we could eat. It didn't matter how long it took. They would keep us working until the day's quota was complete. 'Do not come back until you have finished,' they ordered. And the stakhanovite[14], criminal! He would drag younger girls into the forest, and send them right back to work after, it was hell. God forgot about us.'

'God forgot about us,' echoed Greta, like a soughing in the trees.

'We are free mama,' she would always add. 'We will join the Free Polish Army and fight for our nation.'

'We will fight,' echoed Greta.

As if.

Their recruitment into the armed forces was a whisper of hope. They were severely weakened by overwork, with short stubbly hair growing in tufts among the silver shadowed scars of the shaving process.

They had been working for three months and had just enough strength to reach the trucks.

*

The convoys moved forward slowly, and it was two weeks before they reached the huge freight yards where the produce of Siberia and imports from the West where sorted for the front.

Peasants came by to sell watery potato soup and gritty bread, and remarkably, people were carrying goods for barter, copper chains, medals, and rings. They had been used as currency in the camps.

---

[14] Shock workers who oversaw the others in exchange for better food rations.

More Poles arrived until it was quite uncomfortable under the tank.

It was difficult to get food and water because everyone was afraid of being left behind. Frantic screeches and desperate chases of those left behind haunted the remainder.

At Irkutsk, an ever-increasing horde of emaciated Poles waited hours at the depot, sharing morsels of food, freezing in the wan summer sun, boiling in the afternoon when it got warm, and starving alongside supplies from the United States of America.

After a while they were forcibly removed and many were forced to seek out alternatives.

*

A massive Siberian armoured train rolled up.

The massive front was iron, heavily armed and windowless. It was designed to intimidate.

It carried timber, arms and aid from the West, coats and boots, guns and tanks to Stalingrad.

The train had a few passenger cars, carefully screened off from the common multitude; these carriages also contained Poles, only these were NKVD members and ex-party officials.

No one saw them. No one asked.

The bedraggled crowds were permitted to clamber over the freight.

The tanks were unhitched and connected to the train bound for Stalingrad. Sofia stayed under the tank, knowing that she would not be able to fight for the cattle trucks loaded with food supplies.

Refugees scrambled on top of carriages, hid under tarpaulins and even hung on to open loaders, hoping rather than expecting to survive the journey.

For those on to the roof of the trains, falling asleep meant certain death as the hundred or so carriages and trucks jolted slowly through the steppes.

*

The train came to a standstill in the wasteland twenty four hours later.

By that time the crowd were in an appalling state.

No one wanted to disembark. Water was short, and a young

243

water carrier appeared from nowhere selling fresh, tepid water from a sheepskin.

He moved from truck to truck giving out tiny cups for a price. A few got up to defecate.

A shout arose, and they rushed to get on and the train lumbered on for a further 4 hours.

This time they heard the train was to stay in place for longer and passengers slowly descended with stiffened limbs and reeking clothing. Everyone hoped to improve their location.

The sick under the tank did not move and Sofia resolved to look after them.

As they moved west, the food got better.

Peasant women sold black bread and thin cabbage soup containing streaks of fat.

The crowd haggled for bowls which had to be returned for the next in the queue.

The women overcharged the famished refugees. Their humble fare was like the highest luxury and caused severe and agonising cramps in starved guts.

When this had been devoured sorrel soup and watery pickled cabbage arrived. The herd consumed everything. They bartered American rice and cans of corned beef stolen from the loaded train.

More refugees turned up.

They settled on top of carriages and precariously balanced on the tarpaulins covering tanks and trucks. With each additional group, Chinese whispers seeking friends and relatives began.

The noise garbled names, still everyone played, in the hope that someone they loved was nearby.

'It's me!' shouts reverberated in the quiet moments of the journey, 'your brother.'

'Praise to the Lord,' shouts of joy and whistles rang through the train. 'They survived.'

People sang the Polish National anthem and folk songs weeping sentimentally for motherland.

Poland has not yet perished
Just so long as we still live

What the foreign force has stolen
We shall yet with swords retrieve

They sang Polish songs and even declaimed Pan Thadeusz[15], a popular Polish story in verse.

"O Lithuania, my country, thou,
Art like good health;
I never knew till now
How precious, till I lost thee."

It was a merry group, even though each stop deposited a few dying and dead by the track. Each station added men and women from collectives dotted around the steppe. These emaciated individuals were a deal stronger than the shades from Siberia. It was obvious that the land was in the grip of famine.

*

After many delays, it became unpleasantly warm.

The train was unloaded. New carriages were added and others were removed, to the confusion of scurrying refugees.

Hundreds of boys aged between nine and eleven waited on the platform.

These were new recruits headed for the front. Each boy bore a prominent red star, hastily sewn on to his clothing in order to distinguish him from enemies.

The station was a mass of confusion, weeping and tears as armour was attached to armoured trucks bearing frightened children and heavy American artillery to the front.

*

Old Greta clung to her daughter, too sick to move.

Sofia, who was by now fully rehearsed in the role of victim and scapegoat, promised to stay under the tank, so that she would die in kind hands as Teresa started for a new life.

'Bless you,' affirmed Teresa, 'my mother is going to die in good hands. You have saved her. You are a saint.'

---

[15] A love story about two noble families, and an uprising against oppression. At the time Poland and Lithuania were united. (written by A. Mickiewicz Translation by Kenneth Mackenzie)

She wept loudly and told everyone of what she had done, as she was ushered away to survival.

As Sofia's sacrifice became known, the underbelly of the tank was loaded with more sick and dying.

It assuaged the guilt of those who abandoned their fellows; the living could not afford the burden on the remainder of the journey to the refugee camps of Iran.

'Bless you,' they cried, as they abandoned their dying and terminally sick.

'A saint!'

Then they turned their backs and left. Tears would have to wait.

*

The refugees waited for a transports going South. Sofia never saw them again.

She headed to the wrong part of Russia, into the thick of battle.

She trusted the rightness of her choice. It was correct in terms of every religious tenet she clung to, in the thick of temptation to curse god and die. She would sacrifice her life, in exchange for the survival of her children. She would die for others, in the best traditions of the Christian faith. Her forgiveness was assured.

5.

Kazakhstan 1942

By the winter of 1942 there were only boys of 12 were left in the Kazakh collectives. Women and children did the work of adult men twice their number.

Anatoly called a mass meeting of the collectives under his control. Attendance was compulsory and everyone was rounded up from 6.00 am. The peasants shuffled in and sat in family groups. The meeting appeared to be full of geriatrics and young children, although a few burly women were notable among the starved crowd. At 11.00 am the square was surrounded with large limousines and armed NKVD officers in plain clothes. Glorious music played as a fat senior party member stood up at the podium. He gave along speech about the victorious Soviets, progress and freedom. There was a film showing German atrocities and Russian soldiers putting up brave battles. Stalin's smiling face beamed down on them from posters. Everyone waited for the denouement.

'Comrade Stalin calls for our sacrifice to save communism,' pronounced the grey man who led the meeting. 'All those in favour of sending boys from 10-12 and men from 65-70, raise their hands.'

Loud wails rose from the remaining assembly. Everyone possible had already gone to war, mostly dog tags returned, or letters for the wives and mothers of heroes.

NKVD officers strolled through the crowd, checking that that the vote was unanimous. A mother refused, bellowing hysterically. Too old to have more children, she had lost three sons to the war already. An officer approached her and whispered quietly in her ear. She wept silently and shook her head.

She was gently ushered from the crowd and shot in the hearing of potential waverers.

Several others were led away.

More cracks of rifle butts and shots rang out as mothers tried to drag back their skinny, absurdly childlike sons.

The vote was unanimous.

The crowd was silent bar the quiet muffled wailed goodbyes of the boys' mothers as they quietly marched from the crowd, heads held high.

'Wonderful!' remarked the senior official, 'the vote is unanimous.' There was silence.

'Forward with Stalin!' he yelled. The NKVD howled a loud response. Triumphant music blared to cover the silence.

He turned to his secretary and declared, 'collectives 1, 2 and 3 have voted to send their sons to defend our motherland. Praise to the Soviets!' he rose again. The dishevelled crowd scraped their feet tiredly, there was more?

'And so, to other business, we have heard that there is grain in this collective. Grain which could be used to feed our troops on the front!' The NKVD around the crowd booed, as if it were a pantomime.

'Comrades! Let us offer it to those how fight for us on the front!' the crowd muttered and whispered, as NKVD moved among them raising recalcitrant hands by force, scraping shins and breaking ribs if necessary.

'Another unanimous vote!' he cried delightedly. 'Comrades, this sacrifice for the motherland will be remembered by future generations. You have voted for freedom, peace and the motherland. This great sacrifice is the work of a heroic people who are prepared to fight for revolution and progress. Long live Stalin!'

No one moved.

The party faithful, anticipating escapes in the night, rounded up boys from the meeting and led them to waiting cars and transports. They were going straight to the front.

The music droned on as the soldiers packed up and the commissars piled into cars for the next meeting.

6.

Siberian Winter

By 1942 a huge part of Russia had been occupied and the Siberian projects were under increasing pressure.

A memo arrived:

'Production levels and quality will improve by 15%.'

New reports were prepared for deliverables, outputs, throughput, and returns per prisoner. Everything was counted and signed for. If it could be counted, that was fine, it existed. There was a flurry of meetings. Piles of canapés, buckets of caviar, and gallons vodka were laid on for the soft cops, who had to be suitably fortified.

The Camp commanders arrived.

'Eat, Eat!' The bluff peasant leaders ordered, softening their victims for the terms to be delivered by the auditors later. The victims struggled to stay sober while pressed to partake from lavishly piled tables.

'To Stalin!'

It was impossible not to drink.

'Drink!' pressed the fat people's representatives. 'Plenty of time for business!'

Once visitors were 'softened', the hard part commenced.

'News from the front comrades! Stalin holds Russia together.'

Another toast to motherland and leader!

Their corralled hirelings struggled to stand with the quantities of pure alcohol in their veins.

'Pull together in revolutionary comradeship. We will win!'

Another toast; accompanied by hard glances to check for waverers. Noses grew red and faces flushed by ice cold vodka, so pure that a drinker had to breathe out or choke on the fumes of evaporating alcohol. Choking betokened dissent.

'Let us be serious. Stalin has increased work quotas. We must push those lazy saboteurs a little harder, brothers in revolution. Push forward to victory.'

Another toast.

'Construction of the railway link to Magadan is proceeding far too slowly,' asserted the fattest representative. The maids, who gossiped endlessly, already knew the railway line was behind schedule. They'd been discussing it for weeks.

Everyone stood away from camp leaders in charge of the work.

The blood in the room, heated by alcohol, almost froze.

The bluff and hearty officials smiled reassuringly and hugged the doomed commander.

'We must pull together. Divert new convicts to the work!' they ordered. 'Put them on 24 hours shifts if necessary. The embankment must be constructed. It does not matter how.'

The maids had effective radar for upcoming decisions, knowing the outcome long before the camp commanders.

'Them upstairs,' they used servants' vernacular about the guests, 'are saying, that there must be a proper throughput. If more come in then more have to leave.'

They looked at each other significantly. 'For the afterlife you mean?'

'Yes.'

They were right.

Stalin had ordered an intensification of deportations. The effect was instantaneous.

'We've got an extra 12,000 coming in on Friday,' officials explained. 'There's no space.'

The auditors had already calculated how to arrange the culling.

'An extra 20 dead in every hut by Friday,' the camp leaders giggled drunkenly. 'Our guards will arrange it. We will find more class enemies.'

'It's done then,' they agreed.

*

The camp leaders staggered off; inured to the quirks of their leaders. They were only obeying orders.

The visitors slept their drunken sleep; they were executing orders too.

A word from the top, and the next day guards shot prisoners for plotting attacks. They had sold their souls for survival; a few extra deaths were nothing among the crimes they had signed for.

Sofia told God what had happened. She hoped the place would go up in flames.

It did not.

*

Central party directives became contradictory. Paranoia riddled the whole country.

'How could the Soviets lose this war?' the party demanded.

The answer was obvious:

'Progress is being deliberately delayed by espionage and counterrevolutionaries.'

No one was concerned with results, only with demonstrating that Central Party Directives were carried out. Projects were completed on time, even when steel and cement was as much fiction as the existence of working bridges and railways. The work was riddled by negligence. When cement was unavailable, mud was mixed with concrete to build walls.

'Sabotage!''
'Wreckers' crimes will be expiated in Blood.''

Timber replaced steel supports in the bridges. Branches were used as concrete reinforcements.

'Spies and wreckers attempt to destroy the work of the proletariat!'

Starvation was caused by reactionaries and counter-revolutionaries.

'Workers' food is poisoned by traitors!'

It was always someone else's fault.

7.

Stalingrad Autumn 1942

Sofia, accompanied by the sick and dying, trundled inexorably to the Stalingrad battlefront. She had attempted to get free of the bonds fettering women, but had only become more trapped in their coils. She hoped to still escape. Her sacrifice assured her of a place in heaven.

She watched the crowds fade into the dusty horizon believing that her death might ensure that she was finally considered a good person.

It certainly worked in the short term. The guards knew of the group and tacitly allowed Sofia to collect food from the tureens that fed increasing numbers of boys conscripted from collectives.

Sofia was mother, sister and wife to those whom she tended under the stinking tarpaulin.

The sick died one by one.

Greta held on to life, confident that she and her daughter were headed for freedom. Sofia got to know the estate, and used details to ensure that Greta was happy.

*

As they approached Stalingrad, the sounds of battle, like distant thunder, were unmistakable and awe-inspiringly ominous.

'Teresa! Greta whispered. 'Autumn storms around Krakow! We are nearly home. It is there, the house and the stables. Rufus will be so pleased to see us. He has taken care of the estate as promised.'

The roar of battle surged.

Sofia quaked with fear, while caring for the survivors fouling the area under the gigantic American tank.

Finally the transports shuddered, and screeched to a halt. The tarpaulin was whipped away in a blinding flash of daylight.

Hardened and battle weary soldiers making the tank ready for battle were surprised to find sickly invalids living beneath like cockroaches.

The soldiers' faces were a horror of dirt, dust and blood, wild eyed and sleepless from battle drugs, with pin prick pupils.

'What have we here?' they jeered. 'New troops?'

They had no time for the dead and dying and dragged them off like meat to Sofia's meek protests.

'Have mercy!' she cried, 'this could be your mother.'

'And what of it?' jibed the soldier, as he pulled old Greta away.

She was blinded by the unaccustomed light, and persuaded that she was in heaven.

'Hundreds more like these lie dead and dying on the streets right now,' he said. 'She can join them.'

He pointed to a pile of ruins not far off.

'Crawl to one of the holes over there and be quick about it. We have no time.' he pointed to the tank which was being unloaded at speed. 'This is needed now.'

Men leapt into the vehicle, and started the engine to a load roar.

The tank shuddered into lurching movement, remorselessly crushing remaining dead bodies in its way, and missing the hallucinating old lady and her typhus-ridden companion by a couple of feet at most.

An exhausted soldier addressed Sofia, who was kneeling by the remaining sick people.

'We are off to fight to the last man, and you should be warned. If you get in our way, darling, you will die.'

Heaps of wounded lay on the ancient bombed and defunct siding, waiting to be evacuated. Only severely wounded, missing limbs or eyes seemed to make it.

Sofia later heard that walking wounded were loaded with explosives and sent to the front, to blow themselves up at tanks and artillery.

The sleepless captain glowered at the women. He shouted some codes and numbers, whistled, and scarecrow creatures appeared from nowhere and dragged Sofia and her companions off.

*

They were dragged to a cave-like basement of a partially demolished house. The entrance was camouflaged by a bedstead and curtains.

In the cellar soot-covered refugees sorted piles of German uniforms, lugers, helmets, watches, bracelets, and what Sofia suspected were gold teeth. They were warming soup on a brazier and offered the sick a bowl each.

Sofia made sure that the dying Poles were lying comfortably among the scarecrow scavengers. There was water, and a latrine. The noise of howitzers and the trembling ground did not contribute to a feeling of safety, but it was warm and dark, punctuated by candlelight.

The old lady had fallen into a coma.

Sofia ate and cleaned up.

In a continuing spirit of sacrifice, she headed to the surface to tend to the wounded soldiers. They were abandoned, in great pain, and very thirsty. Yet there was plenty of water and even food. Most had been acquired from Germans, judging by the German writing on food packs lying nearby. Rolls of bandages and disinfectant lay on the ground.

Battle raged, well past dusk and continued through the night.

*

As she scurried among the wounded, Sofia noticed the child recruits being handed rifles, pills and arms. They were bundled into groups of twenty, trained to shoot and led off by hardened troops waiting for reinforcements.

Most of the soldiers laughed at the young boys, several of whom had soiled themselves. They talked callously of death and pointed out mutilated German corpses which had been placed nearby to harden new troops. The children were needed in battle and there was no time for sympathy.

An army captain was in charge. The boys shot their oversized rifles, sobbing and shaking. Several were injured by the recoil. All of them were deafened by the noise of the shot and scarcely able to support the weight of the rifles and equipment.

'Kill one for one. If you die make sure that your death counts,' instructed the captain. 'You will die for mother Russia. This is glory. If you kill two of the enemy you will get a medal. Your mother will be proud. She will get her own house and a pension from comrade Stalin himself.'

Several of the boys looked exotic, as if they had come from the wild outlands of the Soviet Empire. They clearly did not speak

Russian. Sofia could only guess at the wild Russian tribes they had come from.

One of the lads investigated complex and highly dangerous equipment in a suicidal fashion.

The captain ran up to him and kicked him away.

Then he picked up a rifle and shot it at one the boys.

He chose a weak child, almost an infant, who was unlikely to make it to the front. He was dead anyway. The boy crumpled down bleeding.

'See,' he announced, pointing the rifle at the cowering children. 'This kills. *Kills*.'

He had their attention as he turned the dying boy over. The child whimpered and frothed blood.

They boys stared at the child, fascinated as he drew his last breaths.

The captain walked away and the boys followed him like sheep.

He showed each group how to line up the notches and shoot at training targets. He demonstrated how to throw a grenade by blowing up a maimed German cadaver. Limbs flew skywards; the boys laughed dutifully, as drugs kicked in to their tiny frames. They were having fun.

'Do this and blow up Germans,' he commanded, showing them how to remove the pin.

He was talking more slowly and gently now that he had control of his audience. He instructed children how to kill, using the voice and mannerisms of someone telling a bed time story.

'Remember your poor mother. Yes, your own mother will be proud of her hero son. She will get bread, bread with your name on it, with lashings of thick soured cream. Imagine that.'

He passed out guns and grenades to a group of boys, who were marched off almost immediately.

He addressed the next group.

'Your mother will never have to work again.'

A young boy shot the target; the boys cheered.

'Think of your proud father, and your sisters. You will be hero for papa Stalin himself.'

He patted a boy whose rifle was almost as large as him. He knelt down and smiled at the child.

'Comrade Stalin will hear your name.'

Later he crouched down and hugged a young lad in tears.

'Do not worry.' He pinched him on the cheek as he handed him a string of grenades. 'You will be famous all over Russia.'

He laughed theatrically at the sound of distant explosions. He held his ears and laughed.

'This is a glorious war.'

He ignored the wreckage around him. 'Comrades, you are men, here today, Men who Russia depends on. You are heroes of the Soviets.'

The young troops raised a ragged cheer. Although weakened by their long journey and missing their families. This seemed like a game.

More wounded were arriving all the time, their groans pitiful and unrelenting.

The boys regarded them apprehensively. Some were praying to Stalin, others recited lullabies and half-remembered songs.

The loudest cries were for water.

*

Once the soldiers had marched off their contingents the square emptied.

Sofia decided to get water for the wounded. After several hours she was worn out by the trips she had taken to a pool of water leaking out of the ground nearby. She could never provide enough, their thirst was unquenchable.

She tried to staunch some of the worst bleeding with bandages lying nearby.

Unfortunately, she had little idea of what to do. She prayed for each one, soothed them, shrived and baptised the dying, and enacted the role of loved one where necessary.

*

It was very dark and a wintry moon had risen.

A group of doctors and nurses arrived. They carried dressings, many already blood-stained, probably removed from German soldiers.

They had drugs, principally morphine, which they administered along the rows of wounded, reusing hypodermics.

They alleviated the suffering of the noisiest dying, and concentrated their efforts on those who had a chance. Even then, they offered rudimentary relief. They stitched what they could and cut away the rest, moving quickly through the hundreds of wounded. They bandaged and made good, although their work was hurried and the nursing inexpert.

Those who passed the test of the commissar in charge of the medical team were moved to their field hospital or to transports waiting nearby.

Those who could walk were sent limping back to the front.

The sky was punctuated by flashes all night, the noise was continuous. It was clear that the battle would drag on, no matter what.

The nurses took their break.

They offered Sofia food, vodka, morphine and Dexedrine. She ate.

There was an unspoken camaraderie. The men would mostly die, yet they continued to do everything possible. It was a desperate situation.

The nurses left.

*

The weather was quite mild, although the nights had been very cold, Sofia slept outside, on a stretcher and under a pile of blankets. She woke up whenever she could to administer more water.

She had committed to spend the day there, while the nurses and doctors slept, despite being warned that the place was unsafe by day.

'Go', they advised. 'Do not stay here by day. There are bad men here.'

Sofia learnt why as she woke up to the hard glare of the recruiting captain.

'Still here, little saint?'

Sofia gawped at him. Close up, she surmised he could not have been more than 25. He looked older.

She was not sure if he had slept. He did not look like he had. He acted insane.

'Well, my dear. It is time for you to learn about war then.'

He dragged her to a corner of the station, where piles of rubble covered with blankets provided a rudimentary bivouac.

She struggled all the way. She fell to her knees and he yanked her along, cutting her badly on the rough ground, without hesitating as she frantically tried to pick herself up.

She ended up leaned against a wall, severely bruised and altogether petrified as he carefully stripped away her clothes, making sure not to tear the rags further.

He was careful of the clothes, though not of her, treating her body to more violence as he stripped her like a rag doll, bending arms and legs painfully to avoid damaging fabric.

Finally, she stood before him, naked and shivering with fear. Her knees were bleeding in tracks down her legs, and she suspected he had dislocated her shoulder.

He threw her down pinning her under his knee as he neatly folded her clothes, as if making them ready for sale to the scarecrows.

She did not stir. She was savouring her last minutes. Time moved slowly, as if she were underwater.

She had been raped before, on the train to Siberia and, before that, in the prison.

This was even less humane and more deliberate. He intended to humiliate her, and did so effectively.

She did not weep, it would make it worse. She prayed silently, aware that she did not want to die.

He defiled her everywhere.

Afterwards, she lay there quietly, turned away from him, avoiding his mad eyes.

'Crawl back to the shelter, little martyr of the revolution,' he remarked coolly. 'Or you will die. This place is not for good people. No kindness here. Go back to where you came from.'

He knelt over her and turned her head in order to glare into her eyes. His eyes were bleak and dead.

'Get out of here or I will kill you. No sweethearts here,' he slapped her hard. 'Leave now.'

She struggled to dress. Her knees and knuckles were severely grazed. Her thighs were badly crushed, her body polluted. She was shaking, and kept tripping and dropping things under his basilisk gaze.

He squatted down and lit a cigarette, observing her efforts without comment, analytically. Then, when she was half-dressed, he stripped her with the same scrupulous care for her clothing, and despoiled her again.

He was determined to vanquish, obliterate, and force her to join him in hell. It was not just her body he wanted to erase, but every part of her life and soul.

She forfeited her body, while gripping on to her soul. Moments ago she had seen herself as martyr; now she became blazingly aware that she wanted to live.

She pleaded with the almighty.

Her body enacted gross things, while she was curiously absent.

When it was over this time, she covered herself with the blankets and fell torpidly asleep. She was paralysed, lethargic and needed to turn off. The long hours spent trying to satisfy the thirst of the wounded soldiers on the train platforms had wearied her; she was prostrated by the struggle to withstand him.

*

She was out for a long time, and when she became conscious, he had gone. She got dressed, her body drained and in pain.

She was degraded in every way, and learnt that she wanted to live. The captain had tried to extract all hope. He had attempted to prove that there was no reason to survive. She had fought a desperate battle for life, making a bargain with her beliefs so that she could live.

One thing was certain in her mind. She did not want to ever return to another man-made hell.

As she crawled around the shelter, in considerable torment, she recognised that she had expected to die when agreeing to go to the front.

She had believed her sacrifice would secure a place in heaven. Now, as she slowly remembered how to dress with stiffened fingers, she reversed this decision. She elected to live. There had to be a way to heaven which did not involve pointless death.

She found scraps of food lying around, and, after deliberation, made herself eat.

Curiously, her body was hungry. She ate with pleasure as nutrition flowed through her body. She couldn't walk properly and hovered behind the ruins, scanning for signs of soldiers nearby.

The entrance to the cellar was across a wide plaza. Perhaps she could cross it unseen.

*

There were signs that more recruits had passed through. Another German corpse had been blown up and targets had been shot away. There was a pool of blood where the weakest boy had been sacrificed, his body dragged to some nearby pit.

Rats scurried away when they saw her - not far, she was unarmed. The piles of rifles and grenades had diminished. She had slept through it all.

The square was apparently deserted; yet felt watched and overlooked.

She limped towards the underground den, marked by the bedstead and curtains. She brushed off the looseness and nausea in her body, added to the burning pain as the scabs on her knees broke open.

She made a good start and began to feel confident, making no noise as she flitted from cover to cover.

Suddenly he was behind her, like a demon from a horror movie. She fell shuddering to the ground, cowering before him.

The body exhibited the signs of extreme fear, her spirit was unafraid. She had passed a supreme spiritual test. She trusted in god's mercy. She would get away from hell somehow.

'Hah!' he jeered, 'running away to your little den? Not so brave now? Not *such* a good woman, are you? See? I knew you were a hypocrite. I knew what you were.'

He jumped at her, kicking her legs apart. She tried not to flinch, and gazed into his demented eyes calmly, fully aware that he was armed and killed without a thought.

She tried to make her expression courageous; her body trembled like a traitor and her bowels opened.

She remained silent.

His mood swung alarmingly.

260

'Look!' He snarled. He was in the middle of some psychotic episode. She was not even sure he could see her. 'Are you going to abandon them?'

He pointed to new piles of wounded who had been brought to the station during the day, while she had slept like a corpse.

He dragged her up by one arm. He pushed her violently towards the wounded on the platform.

'Aren't you going to assist? Are they going to die alone?'

Appalled, she noticed some of the young boys of yesterday among the wounded.

She forgot her own pain and humiliation and hobbled towards them.

They were gruesomely disfigured; several of them had been badly burnt. Presumably the Germans had used flame throwers to eradicate a nest of hidden soldiers, and the boys had been among them. Their lungs were burnt by the flames, and their cracked lips and their throats were hideously parched. They moaned for water.

The captain motioned to the pool of water she had used the day before. 'Get to it,' he admonished her.

*

She spent the rest of the day and part of the night getting water and trying to make the wounded comfortable.

She acted the parts of a number of people, sometimes several at one time.

When a weakened and dying soldier said, 'Dania, Nita, Natasha, Anya,' or any other name, 'is that you?' She would assent.

By the end of her shift, she had claimed to be so many people that, when at length she fell asleep among the wounded, she had forgotten her own name.

*

She had eaten with the nurses, and remembered nothing of it, other than that she was no longer hungry. She dreamt that she got up to answer pleas for water; her legs did no more than twitch.

'Don't worry.' She spoke in her sleep, 'I have come across Russia to be with you.' She was speaking to a faceless soldier, blinded and maimed by a flash grenade. His skull was exposed and she could see his teeth through his cheeks. 'I am here,' she whispered, 'you are not alone.'

*

She woke up under her pile of blankets surrounded by wounded and their endless groans for water.

The sun was shining and the crack of warfare continued unabated. It had not taken long to be immunised to noise, and she only noticed sounds of conflict if they came very close. She no longer cared about the battle.

More dishearteningly, the captain was back.

'Not left yet, sister of the revolution?' he sneered. 'I told you to leave. I warned you.'

This time he just violated her as she lay among the wounded. She twitched in pain, and did not stir.

'There now,' he alleged. 'You enjoyed that. You should know that there is no way I will let you go. Join me in hell. I will see to it.'

He fixed her with mad rolling eyes. 'Come with me,' he exhorted. 'Not here. We need to go.'

She struggled up quickly, doubting that she would survive another dragging across the square. Her knees were covered in puss and the blood had not congealed properly. She hurried after him although her legs could scarcely carry her. She was frightened of the gangrene and putrefaction around her. It might be contagious.

The previous night, the nurses had asked her if was safe to come out during the day. She had hurriedly replied it was not, shivering with shame. They glanced at her bruised face speculatively, and nodded.

It was not safe.

She followed him to his den, her stance begging for mercy. He grabbed her and pushed her in.

She noticed the soldierly bivouac. Incongruously, pot plants had been arranged around it. They were sprouting in the spring warmth. He pushed her into the space, took her clothes off in his neat way, and molested her again. Then he threw some blankets on top of her naked body.

'Don't get dressed.' He urged. 'I am coming back soon. Sleep now. You have work to do later.'

She lay down shivering and sobbing drily.

She wanted to run for it. Her body refused to cooperate. She heard him addressing a new batch of recruits, using identical words to the first time she had heard him.

She was too intimidated to try to escape, fearing she would become an example killing in front of the young recruits. She heard the shots, the laughter of young boys, and the explosion of grenades. She tried to blank it out with prayer, and could only think how much she desired to live.

She was prepared to be his slave, anything to survive.

He returned.

*

She had not moved. She was a coward, yet could not agree to this death. She pretended to be sound asleep. He did not try to wake her, just turned her over gently.

He un-plaited her long black hair, which she wore, coiled around her head. He laid it out over the blankets, and checked over her body carefully. She was delectable, with clear olive skin, and long black hair.

She kept as inert as possible; his touch made her sick with fear and she tried not to cringe.

He shook her; she opened her eyes, trying to pretend she had been asleep. He did not notice, and pulled out a gaudy necklace he had found in the ruins. It was placed round her neck as if it were the finest diamonds.

'For you,' he whispered in the rasping voice of a demon, and had sex with her.

She asked god why this was allowed to happen.

He grabbed her face and stared deep into her eyes. She was forced to look back, and gently checked if this devil-torn creature was human like her.

She was prepared to care, and tried to smile kindly.

Surprisingly, as she felt for his soul, she saw a hidden person, driving a demented machine of a body, loaded with drugs and out of control. She reached out, one life calling to another, begging to live.

The meeting of eyes seemed to last forever, as he tried to dominate her.

263

It was like out-staring a lion. She did not waver. He was an unhappy mortal, possessed by the spirit of war. She sought to find some empathy.

In response, he pinched her intimately and wrenched at her body beneath him. Tears crept out of her eyes; and she slowly detached her mind to a place of safety.

He withdrew. He got her up and helped her to dress.

He clucked disapprovingly over the bruises, bites, and cuts on her body.

'Look at this!' he complained censoriously, at a vicious bite on her thigh, as if she had done it to herself.

He pushed her out of his hide.

'Off you go,' he directed, slapping her rear. 'Feed the dying and the dead. Give them something to be happy about.'

She did not move immediately, expecting another demented change of mood. On cue, he spun her round, grabbing her violently.

'My name is Sergei,' he confessed. 'Remember it when I am there.' He nodded to the pile of wounded being offloaded onto the station platforms. 'Sergei,' he repeated.

Unexpectedly, he kissed her.

*

The next night Sofia fell asleep among the wounded again. She had not an ounce of energy to spare and she was dreadfully bruised. Not even a direct hit close the square roused her.

It seemed like minutes had passed when the captain started shaking her awake.

Her heart beat wildly as she tried to work out where she was and why she felt so afraid. She had been dreaming of life in Poland and did not immediately realise where she was.

This time he picked her up and carried her to his lair. He was gentle and kind, careful of her bruised body, like a different person.

They had long, slow sex. She lay in his arms passively, feeling a lot safer. Like all captives in extreme danger, her subconscious had bonded with her captor, seeing this as chance of survival. He held her close, and talked about himself. He was from Kiev, and had recognised her Ukrainian accent.

'I heard you talking to the dead over there. That's why I didn't kill you,' he whispered softly, and stroked her cheek. 'You reminded me of home.'

Intent on survival, she asked him questions, attempting to find common ground.

He opened up to her interest, and related details of home, with maudlin tears over what he had lost. He seemed to relax, and leaned against an empty ammunition case, smoking a cigarette, like a hero in a movie.

His face and stance had changed as he talked of his past, and she realised he was handsome and possibly likeable.

He turned to see her soft curiosity, stubbed out his cigarette, and lay down beside her again.

They made love. He stroked her long black hair and as they lay naked together, murmuring sweet words into her neck.

'Remember me kindly,' he said, afterwards 'I don't want you to forget this.'

He seemed to have changed completely, and sighed deeply. 'Don't plait your hair,' he asked. 'Remember me and don't plait your hair.' He snuffed at the long hair on her neck. 'Do it for me.'

They sat in silence, thinking about their own situations. She was reminded of her elderly husband, who had also liked her long black hair. She had located an island of calm in Sergei's psychotic mind and was secure for the moment; though she could never be safe, negotiating a perilous path between love and death with a madman.

He tucked blankets around her.

'Sleep now,' he counselled, 'I was berserk for a long time. It was not me.' She dozed in his arms.

Abruptly, he returned to his old self, grabbed her roughly and barked.

'Don't move an inch. I will know. Stay here!' he shook her awake.

He kissed her for a long time. She could feel the conflict within him, as he alternately bit her lips and neck viciously; then stroked her face and body begging for forgiveness for each yellowing bruise, cut and bite.

He wept muttered and ranted.

She made no attempt to remonstrate, aware that this was something he was battling alone.

After some time, he got up and strode off.

*

When he had gone, Sophia fell into a black unconscious torpor and had no idea of time.

She had a clear, highly visual, nightmare. She was saying the Lord's Prayer in her sleep, as she tried to get away from a demon attempting to drag out her soul.

She recited the words slowly, agonisingly, as the tormented creature clasped her tightly and begged for water at the gates of a fiery lake.

'I cannot go for water,' she explained, 'unless you release me.'

'I cannot release you,' he replied, 'I will fall if I let you go.'

She stretched out for the water, far away on the platform, slowly enunciating the Lord's Prayer, which she struggled to remember. She was convinced that they would both fall into flaming hell if she stopped, and the words were supporting them, as he dragged her down with all his weight. She kept forgetting the words; and they were wrung out of her soul in the midst of evil.

'Have faith!' she cried, as she prayed. 'You have a choice.'

He grabbed her praying hands, and peered deep into her heart with horrific red eyes. She could feel burning in her chest, and fought to get away.

'There is no choice,' he contended. 'Join me in hell.'

Clawed toes ripped at her flesh, and the skin on her legs came off in strips. Her legs were bleeding and scorched.

She refused to give up. She was surrounded by gore, and still she wanted to live.

After a measureless struggle to move across what felt like a real impediment, though it was probably her blanket. She managed to give him water which, dreamlike, appeared in her hands. He drank thirstily, in the same way as the dying wounded.

'Help me.' He begged, and at last, much more quietly. 'Stay with me.'

They lay at the edge of the pit, enervated by the struggle. She held him by the arm, which lay heavily across her chest. They lay together in tranquillity.

At this moment of peace, that she became aware that she was

266

praying aloud. She heard her own voice speaking and woke up with a start.

*

Sergei's arm was across her naked body. It was cool and immobile.

He had shot himself next to her sometime during the late afternoon, and she had been too shattered to notice the noise, or to hear his explanations and confessions.

She had slept through the distressing process of a man talking himself into suicide, and then slowly choking to death with half of his brain gone. Bits of bone and brain matter were everywhere, although for some reason she was only spattered with his blood. Presumably he had been facing her as he shot half his brains out. The new recruits had been and gone. The soldiers had visited Sergei's lair. They had seen them lying together in a pool of blood and assumed that they were both dead.

She carefully removed his arm, in case she was still in her dream. She contemplated the remains of his smashed up face. She was repulsed by her antics with this barbaric soldier, but dutifully continued with the prayers she had commenced in her sleep.

As she moved his arm she noticed a live grenade lying at her side. He had been trying to blow them both to smithereens.

She lifted it carefully and laid it aside. The pin had been loosened; not pulled. Perhaps he was weakened by the grip of death, or had changed his mind.

She was shocked and confounded at how close to death she had been and lay in the blood until it started to scab and crack on her skin.

After some time, she cleaned herself up and went to help the dying on the platforms.

*

It got darker.

She tried to help the thirsty wounded, yet moved very slowly, as she tried to make sense of events. She kept checking the skin on her legs, uncertain if she were awake.

She searched for the flames she had seen on the edge of the abandoned platform. It was difficult to distinguish what was real.

267

She had no idea where to go and could not imagine what was to happen next.

Sometime later, the nurses arrived.

Stalingrad had lines of communication which were complex and effective, so they had already heard of Sergei's death.

They made no comment on her survival, and told her that he had been notorious, having raped and murdered several nurses before they realised that he was a psychotic and deranged killer. He was the reason they worked at night.

The captain had been extremely unstable. At regular intervals, he shot every wounded soldier who made it to the Red Cross area, claiming that their moaning drove him mad.

*

The area was surrounded by snipers who picked off those in the plaza. Disembarking recruits were sitting ducks.

After each 'delivery' of reinforcements, dead and wounded lay all over the square. The fact that the captain survived added to his fearsome reputation despite the fact that the snipers had probably decided that he was working in German interests.

For weeks recruits had been dying in this way in large numbers. There had been a lull when the trains disgorged boys in their hundreds. No doubt snipers balked at shooting children. Perhaps their youth was part of military strategy.

The medics wondered at her survival, while Sofia sat deathly quiet.

She felt responsible for his violence.

*

Sofia's faith had changed. Everyone here, herself included, was a sinner according the Catholic Canon, yet she was certain that god did not blame them.

She tried to remember Sergei's last words, regretting that she had been soundly asleep when he died.

The nurses quietly handed her a uniform, and she joined the staff.

8.

Spring 1942

Andrei committed suicide shortly after the departure of the young lads for the front. He overdosed on Pervitin[16], which was arriving in large quantities as the German army stalled at Moscow and Stalingrad. No one was sure if he had intended to kill himself or had simply not understood the power of the ills he had taken. To be sure he had taken a whole bottle.

*

Anatoly fell deeper into darkness. He finally admitted to himself that the party was an empty shell full of lies. Every trace of idealism left him forever. He hated socialism and depended only on the pleasures he drew from power. He became a brilliant architect of the reformed war party.

He never forgot Lucia's anguished frowns as she tried to give herself up to vileness and failed. He gnashed his teeth over the way she had successfully preserved her soul from Hades.

How he had determined to quench her youth! He had dreamt of driving her into madness on his behalf. He wanted her to join him in the inferno and never ceased to regret that he had released her!

*

After the war he made Lucia a scapegoat for every mistake he made. She was a Mata Hari, a master spy and an evil seductress. He was an innocent, taken in by her wiles.

When the purges began, Anatoly made countless confessions to the party elite. He had fallen for a class enemy, master-spy and Jezebel.

He was reprimanded and sent for re-education to summer camps in converted dachas and country palaces. Senior officials hectored juniors and were paid back by admiration and flattery.

Mostly they extolled Stalin, and had to write reports on the leader's wisdom, so it wasn't precisely fun. At these 'jollies', Anatoly

---

[16] Pervitin was a battle drug devised by the Germans it was based on methamphetamine

wept at how this evil spy had driven him into sin.

He survived by attributing all manner of poor performance and mistakes to her influence.

*

The revolution was entirely dead.

Whole villages could be swept away, and Agitprop[17] provided logic for their disappearance.

People were starving, many of them as a part of deliberate policy for minor infractions by their party representatives.

Propaganda trains and planes visited towns and hamlets carrying information about Marxism and Marxist economics which explained why they were suffering such hardship.

Posters explained that class enemies, nationalists, spies and saboteurs had been behind any temporary disasters.

No one considered truth anymore.

---

[17] Department of Agitation and Propaganda designed to teach the people revolution through art and literature.

Part 5.

Beginnings

Those living in peace and plenty provide support for ideological sadists.
They make heartless decisions about others' lives, sufficiently distant from their own compromises.

Armchair socialists talk of the wonders of the collectivisation process and the bountiful new world in the Soviets knowing that they would never choose such a life for themselves.

They shore up the regime and bear some part of its crimes.

Those who suffer from such hypocrisy are mostly children.

1.

Tashkent 1942

Stalin's elite Poles were destined for Egypt to join the desert war. They headed for Cairo which harboured an international force of well-fed and fighting-fit troops with proper equipment, clothing and good food.

Tashkent was a major stop on the way. It was warm and humid after the chill winds of the steppes. Under the flood of newcomers, the old city blossomed as it had not done since communists had strangled its natural vigour. It hummed like any Middle Eastern city, although people remained careful and wary. Pomegranates, grapes and dates were sold in the party shops, and on the black market. Hotels opened by magic. Forgers, tailors, and street vendors of every kind flickered in and out of existence in a bewildering way. It was a comical sight to see markets appear in five minutes and vanish at the same speed if danger threatened. Woe betides anyone who handed money to a stall holder just before he rushed to gather up his goods. He dematerialised, almost in a puff of lightning, the money with him.

Party refugees glowed with happiness at their release from throes of dictatorship. They revelled in modest luxury, ate blinis and caviar, and drank tiny glasses of vodka.

The real refugees, starving, sick, dying, and carrying every kind of disease, slept in cardboard cities outside the town.

Communist control was still present although the sun warmed it up. Movements of troops, tanks roaring through, armour and food aid dispelled stagnation.

Party members slept six to a room in hotels meant for two people. They chattered constantly about Poland.

'Oh yes,' one of them would screech 'I once met your father!' Or: 'That's right; I went to the school in the very next town!'

They hugged each other like the oldest of friends, and carefully avoided talk of what had happened in the last three years. No one mentioned the self-reproach racking their souls. No one wanted to share their recent past.

Katya recognised interrogators and NKVD instantly. These

heavy drinkers and drug addicts, were grey from living indoors and being up all night. Lack of strong stimulants affected their motor skills and they stumbled and suffered from shakes. Their actions did not sit well in daylight. They mooned around one particular cafe, from morning till late in the evening, no doubt brooding on their future.

Katya felt no such guilt and avoided them. She too was coming down from the drugs, but blamed her shivers on a light fever.

Anya joined crowds of giggling girls, relishing their freedom, checked out male talent. The singled out a good-looking chap, who Katya recognised was wracked with guilt.

He sat solitary in the 'NKVD' cafe, no doubt wondering why the alcohol was so weak and watery. He was trembling, probably coming down from heavy stimulants and could scarcely imbibe the thick black coffee which he needed to stay awake.

A healthy young girl, who, judging from her hearty peasant beauty had been a Party official's ex-mistress, whispered to a friend.

'He has been so dreadfully tortured poor thing!'

The rumour was taken up with enthusiasm. It was a perfect cover story, with the reassurance of familiarity. They needed to create new stories to explain their lives in the USSR and slowly built them up, carefully adding layer by layer.

*

Katya's personality had been shaped and defined in Kazakhstan. It was honed in Tashkent, under threat of discovery.

She did not feel guilty for what she had done. There were a myriad excuses for what happened. She had been young; she never touched anyone, being the one who asked questions nicely. Her decisions were logical and normal. She had been forced into her choices by a stony god.

Science had proved that there was no spiritual world and there was no god and no fate. And even if there was a god, he did not care about her victims or he would save them.

'I did nothing. God could have saved them,' she repeated to herself.

The fact was that she had been a good interrogator, because she was cool-headed and dispassionate. She could extract any story;

273

because she was assured that her quarry knew nothing and it was all nonsense. It was just a question of breaking the mind and rebuilding it again.

She had no sympathy for her victims. Every time she saw a victim shattered in mind, it reminded her of her own interrogation, and hardened her to others' grief. She had never needed to ingest so many drugs as the others. Instead, she took light naps between interrogations until she could drink in the buzz from a broken spirit. Then that alone kept her awake and lively for the rest of the night.

She held on to her faith that her actions were minor transgressions, easily forgotten, so long as it was never recorded or noticed. She clung to the dialectic for proof. Life was nothing, just a specific configuration of cells. Death was the end. The alternative was red screaming terror, the curse of the shaman and Satan with his teams of lesser demons.

From now on, she cultivated the semblance of an ordinary, plain person, inhabiting a routine world. She created a facade, and once in place, maintained it for the rest of her life. She never asked questions, never held an opinion, never loved or hoped or dreamed. Drabness ruled her soul.

*

Anya despised her ex-interrogator sister. Having come through the deportation unscathed, she firmly believed that she was a better person.

She watched Katya's shaking hands, and dry retching as she came off Pervitin.

'Katya,' she insisted, 'You cannot say where you were all the last two years. And I do not think you should mention Andrei, or the NKVD.'

'We must keep this whole affair a secret, just between the two of us.'

Katya merely waved her away. 'Just keep us safe. I did it for you, now you do it for me.'

'You should be ashamed of yourself,' replied her sister.

Anya was popular. She was full of amusing stories of the primitive Kazakh tribesmen, of the starvation and deprivation on the steppes and how they had survived.

Katya spent much of the day lurking by the river, in the shadow of her sister. She affected not to remember much about her collective and relied on her sister to fill in details.

'Oh don't mind Katya,' said Anya, 'she's just shy.'

*

The healthy Poles swam in the river Chirchiq. The water was not cold. They swam in dresses and shorts which dried in the sun.

Every day the riverbank filled up with excited and delighted youths splashing in the water. It was heaven after the careful, dreary seriousness of the collectives. Tiny fish nibbled at the feet as they paddled in the water of the mud bank in the middle of town, reserved for hotel members.

The beach-goers were mostly young people from the party cadres. There were also a few light and guilt-free souls like Lucia, who had stolen onto the transports despite having little connections with the party.

Katya, sitting with her sister, noticed Lucia almost straight away. She didn't betray her.

As ex-NKVD, she needed to keep a low profile. She and Lucia affected not to see each other, and sat at opposite ends of the beach.

*

Lucia was recovering her health and wellbeing fast. She made friends easily. No one asked questions about where she came from and what she had been doing. Their questions were always general and vague. Freedom from her past abuse made her feel sparkling and insouciant.

Her feeling of relief did not last long.

She hadn't had periods for years. Somehow, she was pregnant!

Her body kicked into gear to build new life inside her. The tiny foetus tickled as it leapt and jumped around in its amniotic sac. Her breasts grew and her body shape changed.

At least Anatoly did not know!

Her first intention was to get rid of the child. Abortion was easily available and the most popular method of contraception in the Soviets. Unfortunately, authorities would question her about the father.

She had to wait until Cairo, where the child would be more

difficult to get remove, having established a kingdom within her womb.

Meanwhile she grew sublime, more rounded and curved than her friends. She danced and swam, and tried to ignore her body.

Above all, she still needed papers. They were vital if she wanted the right to live among the chosen ones. The Party paid for accommodation and food; there were no shortages and the elite had money and spare clothes.

She sought out a forger, which was a formidable risk. It cost her duffel bag, money and clothes stolen from her peers. There were forgers everywhere and anything could be had for money or for barter.

She was loud in her complaints about thieves in the hotel rooms and sympathetic party cadres gave her replacements.

*

One morning, as everyone settled onto the beach, a harvest of ripe peaches floated by.

Few Poles had eaten fruit in captivity.

Here, in the warmth of freedom, they had recently gorged on grapes, hanging from vines which provided much needed shade in the narrow streets. The market was full of dates and pomegranates because under collectivisation, people had taken to growing food in their courtyard gardens, even in the courtyards of grand old Kasbah houses.

Sunbathing youths watched them pass by.

'We can't eat them,' they decided, regretfully. 'There is cholera and typhoid on the edges of town. There is famine. It is dangerous to eat anything from the river.'

No one really mentioned the cardboard city on the edges of Tashkent. There, a swarm of Polish refugees encamped on their way to freedom, riven by starvation and decimated by typhoid, typhus, tuberculosis and cholera. Those living in the shanties never met with the chosen ones who stayed in the centre of town. They were connected by the flowing river which occasionally carried dead bodies downstream.

The shanty dwellers were headed for Iran and Lebanon, hoping to be conscripted into the Free Polish Army.

Only a few of them could possibly make the grade. The remainder would eke out a troubled existence on the charity of the French and British armies. As many as possible were conscripted into the Polish army battalions, where they spent at least a year recuperating from their sojourn with the Soviets.

A heedless few swam out and grabbed the fruit, sat on the shore sniffing at it hungrily.

A few pealed the skin and bit into the peach flesh.

Katya grabbed one.

'Don't do it, dearest,' warned Anya.

She bit into the peeled flesh.

'I don't care if I die,' she said, foolhardily.

Somehow, the peaches represented freedom of the flesh, apples of temptation.

'I am having it.'

It was delicious.

There was a flurry of splashing as several good swimmers swam into the middle of the river and picked out the rest, intending to bring them home and wash them carefully, first checking with the locals that it was safe.

Others, including Anya, disdained the peaches. They had the sense to take no risks.

*

Later that afternoon, a pair of naked bodies floated downstream. They were skeletally thin, almost dried up skeletons, eyes already eaten by the fish, and fingers and toes nibbled to the bone.

Katya regretted her foolhardiness. For some reason she remembered the shaman's curse.

That night, those who had eaten came down with fever.

Katya had griping diarrhoea, and stomach pains, which she told herself, were from overeating.

Anya called the doctor but otherwise kept away.

As soon as it was discovered that the victims had eaten fruit from the river, the doctor diagnosed typhoid.

Katya was overcome by fever.

Every time she closed her eyes, horrific sights loomed. Devils were dragging her to hell and as she begged for mercy her pleas came out as nonsense.

She was sedated with morphine and taken to the local hospital for treatment.

The rest of the troop moved on to Cairo.

2.

Tashkent

All in all, eight of the Poles who had sat on the beach that day fell sick with Typhoid fever. They were taken to a Party-members-only hospital in the centre of town.

The hospital was an old-fashioned building with wards opening onto quadrangle gardens filled with orange trees and bougainvillea. A directive permitted Poles for treatment, on the condition that they should report the perfections of Soviet healthcare. Specialists of all kinds did very little other than cure diseases of overindulgence, while soldiers at the front were tended by inexpert field nurses and peasant herbalists.

After two weeks, the fever broke. Shaven headed, and severely debilitated, she became aware of her perfect, Hollywood-movie surroundings.

The hospital was a miracle of fineness, a dream place, staffed with the best doctors from Russia. Each bed had crisp, clean sheets, changed every other day. Even the nurses were chosen for their beauty. The wards were cooled by ceiling fans, patrolled by pretty nurses in pure white outfits and blue pinstripe dresses, who took temperatures and soothed the patients with quiet, kind words.

Katya savoured the tranquillity, care and the excellent food. She showed signs of addiction to morphine and the nurses decreased the doses gently, clasping her hands at night when she had bad dreams.

Finally the nightmares receded. She returned to her grey self.

*

The nomenklatura had retreated to Kazakhstan for this period of the war.

There were several generals at the hospital, and a few war heroes from Stalingrad, who required the finest care. They had been selected in order to be decorated by Stalin for their actions, and to have propaganda films made of their heroic deeds in that great battle.

Twenty or so severely injured across two wards had each been involved in acts of extreme heroism.

279

Nurses hovered around them excitedly, whispering about their valorous deeds.

*

The great man himself had requested a short visit. The mother of her great leader's wife lay in a dedicated ward in that great hospital.

She was surrounded by fresh flowers and had constant attendance, having caught scarlet fever.

In the following weeks the hospital became very tense, preparing for the august leader. No one was to leave overnight in anticipation of the visit and to ensure the highest level of security.

The hospital was on high alert. Each ward was locked down. There was an armed soldier guarding the occupant of each bed, fully armed, rifles cocked. Wards were cleaned twice over, disinfected so that they stank of carbolic, and every patient and nurse was strip-searched by senior NKVD officers, every cavity checked.

On the day, the hospital corridors were filled with flowers. Everyone was intensely nervous, not the least, Stalin's soldier guard.

The great man arrived, as Katya noted from the terrified hush which filled the hospital.

*

He visited and left.

Everyone breathed a sigh of relief.

Stalin had seen the wounded men in their cots. He had complained to the doctors, 'why are we wasting beds on these heroes? Every one of the soldiers fighting at Stalingrad today is as great a hero as them.'

That afternoon, the wounded were quietly shot so as not to embarrass the hospital further.

*

The last transport for Cairo was coming through the next day after Stalin's visit. After this, there would be no more opportunities to leave. Any remaining Poles would have to stay in Russia, or take their chances with the real refugees.

There were two Polish women in the ward. They were required to walk to the transport unassisted. It was a requirement to leave.

Katya's limbs were entirely wasted by fever. Shaven headed, she was almost bald, as was her companion. The weak and wasted creature stumbled about, making sure they would reach the transport unaided.

On the day the trucks arrived, every single Pole made it out of the hospital, some crawling along the ground. Determination to get out of hell saw them through.

3.

Cairo September 1942

Troops of all nationalities buzzed in and out of the desert war around Cairo. The African theatre of operations represented a clean war - if there were such a thing.

The refugee Poles entered a different world, full of celebrations, parties, dates, outings and drunken roisters under the hot night sky. There was progress, and optimism as opposed to defeat and disaster. Compared to the extreme hardships and starvation in Kazakhstan, it was a dream.

There was a shortage of females.

Pretty women, who included the curvaceous Lucia, were mobbed. As well as Canadians and British troops, there were international brigades of Free French, Czechs, Hungarians, and Yugoslavs.

Lucia encountered several of her peers and cousins. They had deserted well before the invasion of Poland.

Her cousin, Bartosz who had escaped to England before the invasions. His father, the younger son of Warsaw Orloskis, had a small estate near the Louvinka.

Bartosz fawned on her sycophantically.

'An Orloska of the house of Orloski,' he announced, clicking his heels in a Nazi fashion, holding back from a full Nazi salute. 'You are of the noble line direct. Your mother was Princess Kamienska of Lithuania,' he confirmed.

Lucia looked at him askance.

His dapper, arrogant manner, coupled with extreme effeminacy, made him slightly ridiculous. Moreover, her last memory of her mother was of a starving, angst-ridden lady warning her not to go to Afghanistan.

'Rank is of no importance,' she stated, with what she hoped was dignity, as he pranced around her. 'We have no land, no castle, and nothing to rule anymore.'

He strutted like a turkey. 'Breeding will always out,' he replied.

Lucia smiled at this class recidivism. They had travelled such different paths that he was almost a foreigner.

'Surely we are *fighting* Hitler?' she rebutted quietly.

Bartosz was flustered, 'I do not refer to Hitler. I refer to the fact that we are perfectly bred natural born rulers,' he excused, 'We are descended from kings and rulers and defeated the heathen.'

'Don't worry. I know what you mean. We *were* brought up to rule, but the world has changed. Surely you have noticed? We have to start again.'

Her cousin simpered.

'Everyone recognises our superiority. Never fear,' he explained smugly. 'We shall recover our dominance in society. The British aristocracy will welcome us where we belong.'

Lucia avoided him as much as possible; even so he hung around her, boasting that he knew the prettiest girls in camp. He introduced her to slobbering men, and egged them on like horses in stud. It was abhorrent.

*

It wasn't just her residual belief in equality which set Lucia apart. Pregnancy gave her a withdrawn serious air.

What was she to do about the baby? She was often to be found in the bar earnestly discussing the future with some older chap.

She had not yet given up the idea that she could be equal to men in all things, considering Dania an aberration and Anatoly a misguided fanatic.

She believed that she was free to have her own opinions and to do what she wanted.

She was fascinated at the comic-book idea of communism was available to the West. Stalin was universally respected as a leader with heart.

'Stalin is killing the Kazakhs, and deporting millions. There is famine and people are starving!' She complained to an educated Polish officer.

The man appeared absolutely British and had a hefty flying moustache. He was a famous 'ace'.

'He is a bad as Hitler.'

'Well my dear, you could be mistaken,' he remonstrated. He had an English accent in Polish! 'The Kazakh are savages. The county is making progress and its people are very backward. They need to learn about the modern age.'

'Not by torture!'

'Now look here, Miss,' he interrupted, getting up. 'This is political talk; if it goes on I might have to report it. We are searching for fifth columnists. You might be one.'

He avoided her thereafter.

*

No one cared what was happening; they clucked disapprovingly at the quality of the Polish army in Iran without analysing how the refugees reached their condition.

It was frustrating, because, once Lucia attempted to disabuse senior officers; they accused her of being a 'commie spy'!

In the end the captain warned her to stop talking politics.

'If this goes on, Miss Orloska,' she warned, 'you will get a reputation. We are at war and you are affecting morale. This is sedition and you may be arrested as a communist.'

Lucia interrupted, 'how?'

'Silence! I cannot take interruptions. This is your final warning! We do not incarcerate women here - it might be time to make a start. If you serve time, you will receive a dishonourable discharge and will have nowhere to go.'

She accepted the rebuke, realising that the freedom of the West had strict limitations.

The Poles were already avoiding her.

They were anxious to fit in, and desperate for somewhere to settle. The old Poland was finished, even though they fought for it. They were abandoning the sinking ship.

*

Everyone had to choose where to go, England or Canada or France.

Lucia hoped to settle in Canada if possible.

Canadian French was similar to the drawing room French spoken in Eastern Europe - nothing like the language spoken in France.

Once she stopped talking about the situation in Russia she had made friends with Canadians, drawn to their fondness for exercise and slow ways. She learned English from the young men, who buzzed around her.

She met Caleb, a tall, dark individual whose high cheekbones and slanted eyes betokened a fair mixture of Indian blood.

He was, in fact, half Indian, and renowned for his remarkable skill at ice hockey, which was a Canadian passion during long boring winters in the white wastes. Perhaps because of his fame as a sportsman, he had a magnetism which drew eyes.

Caleb was fascinated by her glamour, good looks and class.

The girls giggled at the smouldering way he watched Lucia. He noted that she was unaffected by the sexually charged atmosphere of base and saw her steal off to be sick on more than one occasion.

He realised her problem.

*

One night she approached him at the bar to ask him what he was staring at.

He took her gently aside by the elbow.

'You are pregnant,' he stated quietly, 'you should not be drinking. It's not good for the child, or the mother.'

Lucia burst into tears, prompting one of the men at the bar to ask if he was bothering her.

She said no.

Was it that obvious? 'How do you know?' she asked.

'I can tell,' he maintained.

She had to laugh. The staring had not been a chat up line. She had got him entirely wrong.

He settled her at one of the side tables the bar owner set out for intrigues of every kind.

'Do you need to talk? Is there a Mr Lucia?'

His eyes searched her face. 'I guess not,' he said.

She decided to trust him. He was the sort of person who had secrets of his own. 'I suppose I was a kind of kidnapped bride - in a way,' she explained. 'There was nothing I could do. I escaped when the chance offered. At least, I got away. I took something with me.'

She patted her stomach. She had bonded with the child. 'Do you know about bride stealing? I mean in Kazakhstan?'

He smiled He did not seem to mind the implication that he might be as savage as the Kazakhs.

285

'No,' he remarked, 'I get the picture. Were you married? In Russia I mean?'

Lucia blushed red, from her toes upwards. 'No,' she admitted. 'I was not.'

'What are you going to do?'

'Well, you can't be pregnant and in the army. When they find out I will be kicked out. I have nowhere to go. I am thinking about abortion.' Her eyes filled with tears, 'I don't want to kill my baby. It is part of me.'

He looked at her steadily, and drank off his drink. He got up to leave.

'I like the way you tell the truth,' he stated. 'I like that in a woman. They mostly lie, you know. I don't think you do.'

He touched her on the shoulder and smiled. 'I'll see you again.'

He left.

*

The girls laughed tipsily on the way home under the stunningly bright stars of the desert. They teased her that she had made a conquest. They were afraid of the dark giant, Lucia was not.

She felt warmly affirmed, that someone liked her and knew who and what she was, and *still* liked her.

'You know what I think?' she told her friends as they left the bar, joining in the giggling about Caleb. 'Canada is perfect.'

That night, she remembered her experiences in Russia, and cried all night.

She was sick in the morning, and passed it off as the result of getting drunk.

The girls in her dormitory commiserated. They remembered similar hangovers, discussing remedies until Lucia begged them to shut up as she ran off to be sick again.

4.

Stalingrad September 1942

Sofia joined the nurses remorselessly repairing wounded warriors for the front, as battle rampaged through the mild autumn to depth of winter. She was taught basic field surgery, stitching, cauterisation and injections.

Snipers of both sides watched every move in the square, and poking a head out of the ruins was a sure way to excise brains. The medics were exempt.

Since the death of the captain the nurses had once again started to work in shifts. They treated men and boys, sending many back to the front at the behest of the commissar. They moved among the wounded with military precision, staying out in the open where their Red Cross uniform was visible.

They spent nights in heated bunkers, leaving the injured to fend for themselves in spacious, double-insulated American hospital tents.

*

Sofia changed. She cut her long hair to shoulder length, reneging on Janek Maslow's moralistic strictures on vanity. She resolved to leave it loose and voluptuous.

She took interest in people around her, and confided in them. She crept out of her repressed shell, acting like the other nurses, and joining in the nightly sing songs, accompanied by the rattle of machine guns and punctuated by explosions. She even danced, in an inhibited, middle-class way.

She drank vodka, although it made her morose.

*

The medical team were tightly bonded. Every member looked out for others and knew each other's phobias.

'Let me take this one,' they quietly took over when a member of the team was overcome by tears.

They protected each other from Valentin, the commissar. Opinions were hushed up and quarrels were always settled in secret.

The doctors were treated like generals. If they declared a man a

287

'goner', no one except Sofia bothered with them.

Sofia had withstood Maslow by retreating into faith. Her disturbing liaison with the crazed Sergei was a different thing altogether. They had laid bare their tortured souls for a moment and shared spirits. One sane moment at a time when madness was essential to survival had ensured his demise.

She was hideously aware of cradling his body in affection and enjoying some of the sinful pleasures they shared. She could still feel his cooling arm on her body, the lump of a grenade lying under her waist, and the cold, congealing blood pooling around her.

She had flashbacks: treading on bits of brain and bone as she stole from the hide, the swirls of his blood in water as she washed her face and body clean. Her encounter with the captain had strengthened her belief in a forgiving god.

*

Sofia owned her victimhood. She combined her faiths into one which would fit the world she now inhabited. She still felt that she was a receptacle for the sins of the world, but now believed that self-sacrifice did not mean wasting resources and skills. It was important to do something useful and level up, away from the hell of this particular incarnation.

Her life had to mean something.

Her father had demanded total obedience from his women. He had used religion and race to bludgeon her into obedience. She rebelled.

Maslow had made her feel that women were dirty and her time in prison had shown her that she was intrinsically tainted. Psychotic Sergei had shown her warmth and kindness just before he died.

Was this because she was evil? If she was, then she could try to expiate her wickedness by doing good. She continued to pray for Sergei, deciding that suicide *was* sometimes the right way forward.

*

Over the next two weeks, her self-recriminations turned to stomach-churning dismay. The tickling and leaping in her womb was unmistakable.

She was pregnant with a monster's child.

*

All of her life, she had reported injustices to the Lord, while searching for things to praise.

'Find one bad thing, find one good thing,' she repeated daily.

It kept her sane, although it had not protected her.

This unwanted pregnancy was not justice!

She sympathised with those victims who lost their battles with conscience and cursed their fate.

'Why did god do this to me?' She whined.

The brutal Sergei - even if he *had* sought absolution - was a vicious murderer. She had momentarily reached out to a psychopath. Her moment of sympathy was punished tenfold.

'God, I trust in you. I believe in you. I do what you ask. Why do this to me? It's not fair.'

Her punishment made sense with a vengeful god, but Catholic teaching forgave sins.

Was she unforgiven?

Doubts piled in. If god so loved his people, then the deaths of children dragged into war made no sense - countless wounded boys, dying for no reason in intense pain.

*

As the most junior and inexperienced, she was generally given the dirty and dangerous tasks and administered to the dying. She often left the dark safety of the Red Cross tents in order to vomit. Still she beseeched her lord on behalf of her patients, gave the dying water, and recited what she remembered of the last sacrament.

Her kindness and sympathy for the dying were noticed by Valentin, who kept thick dossiers on each member of the team.

The shortage of nurses was acute. Still, he promised to deal with this spiritualist recidivism at the first opportunity.

Sofia saw his narrowed eyes and ugly looks as she blessed the dying and pretended to be their loved ones. She knew that he wished her ill. Having encountered Sergei she cared less than she should have.

*

After six weeks, she settled into routine.

Yuri, the doctor in charge of her team, sat beside her on their break. He was originally from Tibet, and had fled his country in a fit of socialism.

He was a short, bespectacled man with a small grey Leninist beard, which he sported as a criticism of Stalin's policies. He resembled Trotsky.

'Sofia? That's right isn't it?' he asserted, as he sat down beside her. 'I heard that you turned the captain round. Instead of killing others, he killed himself.' He smiled in a mild mannered way, and added, 'The commissar thinks you are a witch.'

Sofia grimaced uncomfortably. She was afraid he meant trouble. 'If you are pregnant,' he stared at her belly in an expert way, 'I can get rid of it. Is it the child of the killer?'

Sofia was alarmed; she protested quietly, 'the child is innocent. Everybody has a chance to redeem themselves'.

Her unborn child had so far only heard the sounds of war, the groans of the dying, and evening sing songs.

The doctor sat closer to her and took out a cigarette.

'Christian?' he asked confidentially.

She nodded.

'An interesting faith.' he mused, 'I suspect it adds something to our native wisdom.'

He lit up and exhaled.

'Why does your god let these things happen?'

He pointed at the disfigured city and the tragedies unfolding before their eyes. '

'Have you asked yourself that? Do not worry. Your face replies.'

She felt her lack of faith keenly and had nothing to say.

'You know,' he warmed to his theme and scarcely noticed her. 'Most people seem to believe that the underworld is elsewhere, which is a strange idea, because where would god put hell other than here? Why does God need to build hell, when we build it ourselves? We do his work, and create heaven and hell for ourselves.'

He had identified what troubled her.

He went on, 'If there is hell, then, of course, it is here.' He gazed at her seriously. 'We create our own hell you know.'

She said nothing. The sounds of gunfire and warfare were never far away. It was undeniable that man had created hell for himself.

'The question you should be asking is - why are *you* here?'

She was silenced.

He got up and announced loudly.

'Break's over comrades.' He turned to her and winked, 'back to hell.'

He was a heretic and a heathen, yet she was intrigued.

He had read her mind.

*

The nurses discussed the old doctor.

'Guess what? He ran away from Tibet to join the revolution. He was a Buddhist. He will drone on about it if you care to hear,' complained Juta. 'So boring.'

'Yuri is a counterrevolutionary,' whispered Danuta. 'He does not love comrade Stalin, only don't tell anyone. He is a nice old man and I would hate to see him leave. He does the tiniest stitches you ever saw. It is like embroidery.'

Irka, the last team member, added, 'he thinks we are being punished for sins in a past life. It is so stupid don't you think?'

Irka was the perfect nurse, never having known peace. Born into the Ukrainian famines, death by violence or starvation was normal for her.

Sofia agreed with each view, and noted that he was both a good man and a good communist. He never complained about ridiculous party directives, and carried out orders uncomplainingly.

He duly sent severely wounded men back to the front, checking with Valentin before he did so. He deferred to his authority, saying 'if comrade Stalin says this is right, then I do it.'

*

Yuri was conscious of the rules of equality and applied them circumspectly and neatly. He had confidence in communism, and tried to live by its precepts.

He spoke to every nurse in turn.

When it was Sofia's turn, he asked again if she wanted to keep her baby.

'You cannot stay with this unit if you are pregnant,' he explained. 'We insist that nurses abort. The Party cannot bother with babes during revolutionary war. Babies come later.'

Sofia replied that it was against her faith to abort. She had no intention of killing a child.

'Your primitive belief in the sanctity of new life persists among this carnage.'

She said nothing.

He sighed. 'You will join the homeless. The baby will die. It is tragic waste.'

Sofia acknowledged that this was likely, but she trusted in god.

'You are savage and unscientific,' he accused. 'Yet,' he added speculatively, 'You tamed the devil. You have a strength that you do not yet realise. Maybe you will both survive.'

They did not speak for a spell.

He took out a cigarette and lit it.

Then he asked, 'Have you pondered what I said? Why does god let this happen? Why does he let the innocent die? Maybe even your baby?'

Sofia started in consternation. She visualised forced abortion and shrank away. She explained that she would rather leave.

'No one here will compel you,' he reassured her, looking at Valentin significantly.

He was never far away, and sat opposite, flirting with Danuta.

'You have not answered me,' he insisted. 'Why is this happening? Even to good people, like you?'

Sofia was silent, miserably aware that the Catholic Church held nothing sensible on the subject.

Yuri broke the silence. 'I like your religion. You seek to forgive those that harm you and love your neighbour.'

He touched her stomach.

'Did you love him? Like a neighbour I mean?'

Sofia jumped. Her last sexual encounter with Sergei, who subsequently blew his brains out, had been the closest she had ever been to a man.

She recoiled.

'I love my baby.' she replied hollowly. 'I trust in god.'

Her response lacked the sincerity she would have liked.

'Well,' he announced reasonably. 'I see you are unsure how to answer. God gives us multiple chances, and this is what we do with them.'

He waved his hand toward the desolation around them. There was a reverberating boom nearby; the ground shook as a building tumbled to the ground.

He turned to her.

'This is not your first life. You try to be good.' He laughed, 'and you fail. Jesus spoke of reincarnation you know. He is one of the sons of heaven, seated with the supreme one. He visited Tibet, as was written in our scrolls. Such holy ones sometimes return to earth in order to help sinners to learn the Way.'

She was astonished at his story, and that he even knew who Jesus was. He did not seem to believe in communism after all.

'You can get to heaven,' he claimed, 'after you have lived out your lives.'

He got up, and they returned the endless task of tending the wounded and dying.

*

Sofia's faith was evolving in the absence of priests to vanquish her spirituality.

The doctor's explanation worked for the incidents she had experienced. She was increasingly influenced by Buddhist ideas.

Subsequently, she never openly acknowledged reincarnation, and followed Catholic liturgy in so far as she remembered it. She adhered to the spirit of the New Testament, and kept faith in Christian fundamentals: forgiveness was vital, because, together with love, they prevented the cycle of vengeance from growing ever more violent. Her Christianity was mixed with a heavy dose of Buddhism and she never forgot the idea of hell being on earth, created by men for men. She fully believed in reincarnation and spent the rest of her life ensuring that she would at least level up.

She had to admit that Stalingrad demonstrated reincarnation without forgiveness at its most bestial.

Children were being given rifles to kill nameless men, and dying pointlessly. No one in the city knew anything of the causes of war. The generals outside the cities planned the annihilation of millions.

Man had indeed created Pandemonium.

5.

Cairo 1943

Pre-war elitism had survived in the Allied camp, un-dented by communist ideology.

Several refugees reverted to pre-war arrogance. They simply switched values without compunction, contriving to retain status by any means possible.

Others lost faith in everything and had to rebuild who they were all over again.

*

Everyone was finding their place. Only Lucia was in deep trouble. She had no idea where she fitted in to this new world.

She had to admit she was pregnant soon, and as mother of an illegitimate child, she had no hope of emigrating anywhere.

She contemplated drowning herself.

'I would probably float,' she thought miserably. 'The Nile is putrid and stinking.'

She celebrated on every possible occasion, believing that each day might be her last, particularly if Caleb told on her.

The desperate carousal helped shut down the problems droning in her brain.

She avoided Caleb as much as possible, while cheered that he knew of her situation.

He still watched her antics with a sombre expression.

Her flush of beauty faded as the child ate away at her bloom, using up energy to build new life. The parades and roll calls of army life took a toll. She felt miserable, dispirited and ill.

Her friends were concerned. It was a tricky deception because morning sickness, noticed even once, would have given everything away.

She and her tight circle of friends visited the picturesque old town, where there was a wonderful market. They drank strong black coffee and discussed boyfriends.

'Where is *your* intrigue?' inquired Ella, suddenly. 'You are the only one who has no sweetheart. What is going on? There is a secret, I am sure of it. The quiet ones are the most dangerous.'

'Oh she has a heartthrob! I am sure of it,' her friend broke in. 'She is keeping it quiet. And we have guessed – she moons about like a lovelorn creature.'

'Who is it?' chorused the girls, giggling and bridling at the open admiration of passers-by.

'Is it that tall, dark Canadian guy?'

'There he is!' they all shouted. 'It's him.'

They saw Caleb walk into the square and laughed uproariously. Lucia tried to appear nonchalant. Unfortunately, the upset brought on sudden nausea. She rushed off, saying she had forgotten something.

She staggered to a narrow alley between the extensive old houses in the old quarter. The walls on each side were the blank, windowless walls of the zenana, whose female inhabitants were not allowed out unless covered and escorted.

There in the squalid alley, Lucia puked her guts out, hidden from the curious.

Caleb was seeking her. By the time he found her; she was miserably aware of being at her worst - why it mattered she did not know.

'Oh,' she said as lightly as possible. 'Sorry about the mess here. Were you coming down this alley for something special? Careful you don't slip on that.'

She laughed phonily to hide her retching.

'No,' he attested in Canadian French. 'I was looking out for you. I asked Malina what you would be doing today, hoping to talk to you.'

He observed her seriously. 'You have been avoiding me.' It was not a question.

Lucia blushed.

'I met them just now. They told me you had turned back. Did you not see me? What is the matter?'

Lucia had nothing to say, although she felt annoyingly delighted to see him. Perhaps he *was* interested in her!

'Are you ok? You look pretty awful these days, you know.'

She laughed hollowly. It made her head swim and she felt faint with trying not to be sick again.

'What are you going to do?'

'Drown,' she muttered, not quite succeeding in making it sound like a joke.

He hugged her, and she sank into his chest with a feeling of comfort, and delicious safety. He held her as she emptied the last of breakfast coffee and croissant into the alley.

He patted her gently on the back and she felt better.

'There now,' he remonstrated. 'No death. There's been too much of that.'

He stared into her red watery eyes.

'Was Mr Lucia a Kazakh?' he asked. Very direct, she realised. 'I've been hearing about them. '

'No,' she replied. 'He was a communist bastard.'

The angst in her voice reflected the humiliation and pain of her last year with Anatoly.

'He tried to kill Dania, who was my man, and Kazakh. I was nuts about Dania,' her voice broke.

She didn't cry. She had hidden pain away and tried to make light of it.

'He got away,' she added, 'to Afghanistan. I could not leave.'

Her body heaved with overpowering emotions.

She was sick again, bringing up the bile of repression. Her eyes watered as mind and body were racked by confusion over the past. Her decisions seemed right at the time, now she doubted herself and had no clear idea for the future.

Lucia feared Caleb, no matter how physically attractive. She was a foul creature, besmirched by war. Her story sounded weak and hysterical.

'You don't understand. I know. I did not belong with his people. I just couldn't run.'

He listened intently.

She faced him, 'I know you think I am feeble,' she protested, 'it wasn't that, it truly wasn't. I am not a cook, and I will not waste my life preparing yoghurt from yak's milk as a Kazakh housewife. I am a person, not a chattel to be confined like an animal.'

Her voice raised a tone as she remembered Dania's threatening attitude. She straightened slightly. 'I have to be free.'

She stared at the blank, prison-like wall of the zenana and sighed for the women inside. Her friends speculated on what life was like behind them. She knew.

'He wanted me to be like them,' she shrugged at the wall. 'I am not like that.'

She imagined life with Caleb, cooking cakes and sitting at home. Part of her wanted the idyll like a good little housewife. Unfortunately, her life had taken a different direction from birth. She had been trained in the tradition of the warrior class, and grew to adulthood where all adults worked. She could never be a housewife. It would kill her.

His closeness appealed to her senses. Memories and images of snowy steppes appeared in her mind, horses' hooves covered in felt to leave little trace. They had rustled a cow from under the Partkoms' noses using brushwood to cover their tracks. She had faced torture rather than give Dania up.

Yet she was not prepared to be mastered and broken. She would resist Caleb's allure. Maybe her way of life was dead and she was a fossil. It made no difference; Anatoly had exposed the nightmare of life as a trapped woman.

She felt frustrated by her fate.

'I am a person. I play polo, I bred horses. I even read books for fun. I was supposed to go to university. What's wrong with that? Why should I be hidden away? It would never have worked. We would have been so unhappy.'

There was a long silence as she worked out her ideas. She was rebuilding herself at last.

'He would have killed me, you know,' she reflected.

He stared at her impassively, and she lost the thread.

'Still - I did love him.'

She wished the word had not been uttered. It hung on the air sultrily.

Lucia recollected the dark nights, hidden under piles of half-cured furs in the badly constructed village hut. The sound of crickets somewhere in the room, and the stove slightly warm beneath them as the dawn rose. Her refusal to follow Dania sounded hollow.

Love should overcome all difficulties.

For a moment she was lost in memories of bliss, and then she returned to earth.

'You have no idea how hard it is for women to endure being menial, even for love.'

She could never accept the Kazakh way of life, their innate sexism, and many wives. Her face was a mirror of her conflicting emotions. Her eyes filled with resentment. 'Women are not cattle.' She argued, 'even if we are like cows.'

He watched her in his sleepy way. 'No one owns man or woman. The heart is free.'

She had wasted time discussing freedom with men on the base. This was the sort of trite nonsense which emanated from those who knew nothing of deportation and slavery in the name of progress. She had earned a reputation for political activism. Still she could not let it go.

'Pretty words!' She spat. 'Oppression comes in many forms, all of them couched in fine language. You should know that.'

Women had lived under a yoke for generations and she had both witnessed and experienced injustice.

'The worst oppression is in the name of good, ideology or religion. Here we are in Cairo, talking of freedom while ignoring what is happening a couple of hundred miles away, or behind this harem wall.'

Her memories floated to the facts of her escape. In the desperation of flight, she had overlooked the inconsistencies of her life story.

The truth was that she had abandoned her true sweetheart in order to avoid subjection, only to submit to a sordid relationship as a humiliated slave. She had made bad choices, and lost.

She was a strumpet.

She sobbed loudly twice as she admitted it to herself, swallowed and carried on.

'Anatoly would go after Dania unless I went with him.' She cowered in shame at her past self. 'I did what he wanted. I was a coward.'

It was true.

Anatoly made her feel that she merited punishment as a class enemy. There had been a long period of subtle denigration before he commenced his sexual abuse.

She shivered. Ten years older than her, he seemed an old man. She had consorted with a demon. 'He was vile, old, a murderer. I screwed up. I am disgusting.'

She shuddered at the memories. Sex was perverse. Her body had responded, to her mortification.

'I am carrying his child.'

Caleb was silent.

'The child is innocent.'

The baby was stirring most of the time and she felt a lot better for once. It was intensely comforting to talk at last. 'I can't keep it. I have been in denial.'

She snuggled up, wiping her dirty face on Caleb's pristine, starched military sleeve. He smelt clean and masculine. She gloried in a feeling of safety in his strong arms, just for a moment.

Unbeknownst to her, her words struck a nerve. He admired her lack of bitterness and acceptance of destiny. A path she walked alone.

'You know,' he enunciated slowly, even slower than usual,' in my tribe...'

'Hah! She twitched involuntarily. Of course, that wild stance; he would use violence on women, lock her up and drive her mad. The shades of Dania's possessive violence suffused her body. She drew away.

He held her tighter, insisting she listen.

'We *honour* women like you. You need suitable warriors who understand your need to be free.'

Her story appealed on many deep levels. He was sure that she was right for him.

'Return to Canada and bring the child. It will be my own. We can have more.'

Lucia stared wildly at him, unaware that he was the offspring of a union between white man and unwilling Indian woman.

She pulled away from him. She had lived with the concept of suicide for weeks; it was hard to let go.

'It's a bastard,' she stated coldly, 'a communist bastard. And I am a fallen woman. What is more, I am covered in puke. Leave me alone.'

*

She skipped home to the base, imagining a future with a child and lover. She fell asleep in bewilderment at this turn of events and dreamt of starting again.

She woke up as the others were returning to camp. She washed her hair and put on make-up, feeling herself again, and not so pregnant at all. Caleb liked her, despite her sordid story.

It did not last.

She was vile, friendless, and didn't speak his language. He would never understand the complex paths her life had taken.

She was completely wrong.

To him, she was half-wild, beautiful and brave.

The life of an Indian at that time was similarly full of compromises and lost hopes.

People in war made split second decisions. There was no time to procrastinate, and no time for courtship. He might die, or be called away.

*

She thought about him in the hot desert night, and the rest of the day.

That evening, she stayed on base, in case he saw her hungry eyes.

Caleb deserved a better woman than her. She tried to think logically; the idea of being with Caleb prevented her from thinking straight.

The next day, she made an appointment with the doctor, allowing the weekend to explain.

Belatedly, she pulled together. She could be as uncompromisingly noble as he. She could not keep this child even though a late abortion was dangerous. Her awful past precluded happiness. Besides she knew nothing about him, and he probably did not comprehend her sordid history.

She put on loads of makeup to cover her wretchedness. She wept for her unborn baby, soon to die, wriggling like a maniac in her belly, and for her broken heart.

300

She left for her appointment, heavily-painted and grief-stricken, and ran into Caleb almost immediately.

He had been waiting for her.

Her whole body lurched about with sweet adrenaline. She moved like a puppet, stepping back in exaggerated surprise, like a Shakespearian actor. She had to act a part.

'Oh! This is a surprise.' She alleged. 'What are you doing here?'

'Waiting for you,' he hugged her lightly and kissed her lightly on the cheek.

'Oh drat!' her stomach lurched, 'I wish you wouldn't do that.'

She held on to his proffered hand. Dumb happiness conflicted with the calamity she was enacting. Luckily, she remembered her words.

'We are not suited,' she began, in a carefully rehearsed speech. 'We are too different...'

She choked on her lines.

His eyes were smiling and soft, and she stumbled over her speech.

They stood intimately close.

'It will be ok, the baby will be mine. We can marry, and have more. Come back to Canada.' He held her hands together. 'They are allowing us to bring back brides. It is a wild country.' He pulled her to him. 'Consider yourself kidnapped.'

The two of them were full of desire; little else seemed to matter. They couldn't keep their hands off each other. He walked her to a hotel near the base which catered for such interludes, thereby making sure of her.

Such dazzling temptations were normal. Soldiers faced annihilation every day at the hands of behemoth machines and wonderfully engineered instruments of annihilation. Those in the theatres of war savoured every moment, in case of oblivion tomorrow.

Everyone fell into love or lust in order to better appreciate their last hours.

6.

Stalingrad January 1943

Sofia was thinking independently of religious dogma for the first time, and it seemed the right thing to do. The doctor came to her in the night and she took him in.

*

At a time when opinions were better left unstated, Yuri discussed philosophy and religion with Sofia.

He had been coerced into acknowledging that Trotsky, hero and engineer of the survival of the revolution, was traitor and class enemy. As part of the purges, he had been sent to the front to learn humility. He faced regular re-education sessions with Valentin, and no longer had the option to heal patients, except under direction of his commissar. Like Sofia, he had discovered the urge to survive.

Sofia triggered his memories of the Tibetan culture, and he revisited the precepts by which he lived.

'Power is a corrupting force in society,' he acknowledged, 'those who seek it find darkness. I have been observing you, Sofia. You struggle to forgive and love those around you, and often succeed, even with the vilest monsters. That is the key to escape, yet it eludes me.'

He had left Tibet because its people used theology in order to do nothing. The country had become stagnant and primitive in their obsession to reach nirvana. It was falling apart; he predicted it would be invaded soon.

'Our leaders had knowledge to succeed. We are an ancient and learned people. Instead of wisdom, our leaders seek stasis, and even try to cheat death.'

'I wanted to bring change and justice to all. Infant mortality is high in Tibet. We have diseases which could easily be cured by modernisation and inoculation. Instead our people are taught the calm of prayer and meditation while the world around us decays. '

One of the rich upper classes, he had wanted to help his people and was driven out by conservative powers which strangled the country. At 22, well into medical studies, he left for Soviet Russia, ostensibly to finish medicine.

That was in 1923. He had never returned home.

Yuri treated the nurses as his harem. He did not just visit Sofia, but all the nurses, and she suspected that he employed a strict rotation, for the purposes of equality.

She resented it deeply, because he was hers.

*

They spent a lot of time discussing their different religions, a cross-fertilisation process that changed her beliefs forever.

He would bring a little device to listen to the foetal heartbeat and do checks on its growth. 'Healthy so far,' he would say, 'both mother and baby are well.'

Throughout that winter, Sofia regarded herself as Yuri's wife, and was jealous of his other mistresses. She remonstrated with him about unfaithfulness; he simply kissed her lightly and said, 'Yes dear, we have so little time together. You are my wife, carrying our little child.'

Over time she learnt to be more independent, and to accept her lot. Her pregnancy scarcely showed because she worked so hard and was extraordinarily thin. The only sign was the tiny round belly on her frail form. It could easily have been wind.

'You are right to hold onto the child of death,' Yuri stated one night. 'Perhaps the baby holds the solution to the puzzle of existence.'

He was struck by the simplicity of her faith. She told him that Jesus had come to earth to be a witness for the truth and that there was no way to get to heaven except through the path of love and truth.

Yuri asserted this was impossible.

They spent weeks arguing as to its meaning.

'We are blinks on the eye of history,' he claimed, 'how could we ever know truth? Better to trust in science, which has eternal validity.'

He explained dialectic materialism. She accepted the laws of science, though she believed that they described a tiny fraction of god's creation.

As to blind faith, her father had poisoned religious dogma for her with paternalistic religion, which enforced subservience of women.

As far as she could see, here in Russia, Communism was a blind faith, and Catholicism had also proved to be disappointingly paternal.

She modified her faith to encompass a female god, who considered love as supreme. The destiny of those who heard his word was to witness forgotten crimes and stand up for the forgotten. That was the path to Nirvana.

Yuri disagreed. There was only science. As to truth; lies were revolutionary necessity – tools to achieve the highest political truth. He happily used American and German medipacs, and accepted Valentin's claim that they were fashioned by revolutionary hands.

Under pressure, he admitted that the Soviet lies had grown larger and more pervasive.

She pointed out that 80% of the tanks being used in Stalingrad were American. Russian industry was old-fashioned and bankrupt, although recently, effective Russian tanks were arriving in numbers and they worked well in the extreme cold.

Sofia told him that industrial successes in Siberia were based on death camps utilising political prisoners. People were being killed and tortured for stating scientific fact.

'The biggest crimes are too difficult for people to understand.' She told him, 'How could anyone comprehend the scale of death in the gulags? Or the cold brutality of those who participate in their organisation? The perpetrators are assured that they will get away with this. Who will remember what happened if everyone involved is dead?'

She was passionate in her defence of the helpless. She pointed to the piles of corpses - soldiers who had recently died were stacked up outside in a special tent. They were burnt with old fuel outside the station in a distant siding.

'All this death is needless! This battle will be described as Stalin's great triumph. He will claim that the soldiers were brave and patriotic. They will lie about it, because no one who was there will survive. The few who live will be afraid to tell the truth.'

They argued long into the night, making love and talking about matters which had sat in their hearts for a long time.

Their discussions dug deep into the crimes of the regime and demonstrated why Stalin was right to eliminate idealists, religious and moral beings from his Utopian tyranny.

Idealists were certainly more dangerous to totalitarianism than criminals.

*

Valentin was the commissar for the medical unit.

He did absolutely nothing, other than control ideals and mentor all decisions. He did not even carry medical packs.

On at least one occasion they had to burn medical supplies in case they fell into German hands when he could easily have picked them up. Valentin had observed the destruction of essential supplies dispassionately.

She had seen him step over wounded so many times she scarcely noticed.

*

As it became clear that the Germans could not sustain their advances, Valentin started to interfere in their politics. There were painful discussions where revolutionary spirit was tested. A newly arrived secretary took notes of what was said in self-criticism sessions, recording who stayed silent.

Stalin was incapable of error; war time failures had been due to sabotage; it was important to eliminate class enemies in their midst.

In the urgency of battle, Valentin had always determined which of the badly wounded were to survive, the rest were given an overdose of morphine and died quietly of respiratory failure. As the conflict receded, Yuri found it increasingly difficult to murder those with a good chance of survival.

*

The child soldiers had shattered the last vestiges of Yuri's revolutionary fervour.

A crisis arose over a legless young boy, who was doing well, and talked hopefully of returning to his collective to work as a tractor driver, using specially adapted manual controls. A sweet and sensitive child, he was the only son of a widow, who would be hopelessly lost without him.

Sofia had emboldened Yuri to revisit his Tibetan origins, and the young Uzbek had the high cheek bones and slanted eyes of the

305

mountain-dwellers of Tibet.

It would be romantic to say that Sofia had changed Yuri's heart and made him more sensitive. In fact, she was just one aspect of a volatile situation. Yuri was already a dissident, and a suspected Trotskyite. Sofia did no more than hasten his inevitable clash with the party.

He resisted the order to kill him until it was obvious that the child was recovered.

'The boy is totally healthy,' Yuri confided, 'killing him is murder.'

*

The commissar wanted him dead. He would have little economic value to his village and his injuries might affect morale. That was not the point. Above all, the slightest sign of rebellious thinking had to be crushed. Yuri was showing independent thought and that was something dangerous.

Valentin called several emergency meetings where the doctor had argued for the boy's life.

'He is strong; he will live and contribute so much to the village.' He had protested. 'How full of life and happiness he is! He is a good Socialist and glad of making a sacrifice for Stalin.'

There had been a major investigation of this refusal to work for revolution.

Meetings went on for days. With threats and careful instigation, everyone had identified Sofia as the class enemy and a saboteur. She was the one who had polluted the doctor's mind and perhaps even worked for the Germans.

The doctor crumbled.

He had already betrayed Trotsky, his shining star. Under extreme pressure, he confessed that Sofia advocated respect for life and therefore undermined his faith in revolution.

Valentin was triumphant.

*

The Germans were in full retreat, and the commissar called Sofia in. He reported the unanimous judgment of the group - she had to leave.

'Listen,' he announced, 'you are no longer needed here. We are moving out tomorrow and we do not need such a large team. No one likes you. You are a troublemaker.'

Sofia was distraught that her friendly and confiding behaviour had been judged so negatively, and collapsed into rueful tears.

Valentin was smug and triumphant.

The Party could be generous and merciful in victory he declared. She had undermined the tight control he had over the medical team, and now he had regained it.

He looked at her conspiratorially. 'We can find a place for you in revolutionary Russia, can't we?' (Oh yes, he thought to himself, the party could easily disposes of such a dangerous enemy to Party control.)

'You have tried to undermine the revolutionary fervour of our doctor Yuri, and he insisted that you be shot.'

She was stunned to hear that the doctor, who she had thought of as husband, disliked her. Nevertheless she did not consider his betrayal. She hid her love for him and sobbed.

'The party has decided to show compassion.'

He paused with a generous smile.

'Do you want to work as a nurse?' he asked.

She nodded.

'I have a new placement for you,' he offered. 'It is East, in the deepest countryside. You will not bother anyone there, and they need medical assistance. You would be welcome. I have sent off your details and there is a place on the next train out. Do you agree to go?'

She was being returned to Siberia!

She asked to think about it and reply tomorrow.

'The train leaves tomorrow afternoon,' he stated. 'Come in and see me before then. There are papers to sign.'

She left. No one spoke to her. She was a marked woman.

*

The nurses liked Sofia and warned Yuri that she was to be 'dealt' with.

That night, the doctor stole into her room, deeply upset. He kissed her forehead. He was sweating with fear, while desperate to save his lover. She had provided an outlet for moral qualms, and before her arrival he had already contemplated suicide.

Sofia hugged him and hushed him. She was certainly being watched.

'I was ok with Lenin,' he whispered, 'even though he ultimately betrayed Communism. Triumph went to his head. Lenin could not wait for true revolution.'

He gulped hard at the thought of what was happening, at the betrayal of everything he believed in.

'Stalin is creating a military superpower, to follow in the footsteps of tyrants, and become tsar. He hides his crimes by killing all witnesses.'

He tried to justify his betrayal of the cause, but Sofia refused to accept or deny his decisions. She did not want to take on his sins, a Buddhist concept which she admitted.

'I accepted the killing of the wounded. They were collateral.' he confessed. 'The snipers were injuring our soldiers in order to damage morale.'

He hugged her belly and groaned.

'Your actions made me doubt. I cannot accept experiments on babies.'

Her heart fell.

He sighed. 'Stalin has ordained that the party will beat Hitler at his game. There is a new super-warrior program in Kazakhstan. Your baby is to be utilised in experiments.'

There was danger to her unborn child? Fortunately, Sofia was galvanised. She sat up recognizing the need to escape instantly, without fear of the dangers.

*

Yuri had made his one heroic act of resistance, to rescue what could be saved. The legless boy would die, so Sofia and her child *might* live, as a symbol of freedom and rebirth.

He had been planning for this eventuality for weeks, anticipating the excision of truth that was occurring as the history of this great battle was being rewritten. It had been fought without compunction or morality, utilising the lives of men women and children in their millions to uphold the opinions of a vicious tyrant.

Now, it was being hailed as a heroic last stand of the Russian Soviets, and none of the dark deeds were to be revealed.

He had brought the blood-stained clothes of a youth, which approximately fitted her. 'I could not get you women's clothing,' he explained, 'you would stand out. Put these on. I took them from the wounded this morning. We must cut off your hair.'

They both snipped at her hair with shaking hands.

Even with short hair, Sofia did not achieve boyish at all. He dirtied her face and her hands to make her less obvious, kissed her and made to leave.

'The door at the end of the hut is open. It is always locked, they are not guarding it.'

He provided detailed instructions. 'At four in the morning Juta and I will have a serious argument. She will howl that she has dumped me.'

He gave her a last farewell kiss, 'By the way, everyone sends their best hopes.'

He turned back again and clasped her hands.

'Do not worry about me. I will confess to my sins. I will be forgiven. There are not enough doctors here. They will need me for some time yet; if necessary I have my end upon me.' He patted his breast pocket. 'I will never betray my friends.'

Sofia fell back on her bed when he had gone. She could not sleep, and was in a hurry to be gone. She sat fully dressed by the side of her bed until she heard the crash and shouting.

She opened the door and ran into the freezing air.

No one followed her.

*

The city was remarkably quiet, with only a few shots and rumbles in the distance. The battle had retreated.

Yuri had planned Sofia's escape well. Her departure was unnoticed until daylight.

It was clear to everyone that she had been using this secret door to communicate with German spies for many weeks.

Yuri explained that he had suspected her for some time, and she had influenced him into a counterrevolutionary sympathy for the child.

Valentin may or may not have been fooled.

It did not matter; he had gained his main objective, which was the complete subjection of the doctor.

*

Yuri survived the darkest days of the revolution.

The escape of Sofia was his last, secret act of defiance. In his mind, this one action justified all of his subsequent submission and his lies.

He killed the young Kazakh boy, judging that he might affect morale in his collective after all.

The doctor's part in the battle was written in the finest prose in Valentin's latest report. He was a hero.

Yuri did not die in the purges of the 1950's. He pursued and long and eminent career in medicine. He fully recanted his earlier Trotskyite sympathies, and shaved off his Leninist beard.

He married Juta, who later trained as a doctor. They had a son and daughter and lived out their lives in a luxurious Moscow apartment.

Both of them were adamant that Sofia had been a German spy. She had killed the recruiting captain and many wounded heroes waiting for treatment at the station.

The injured had been shot brutally when no one was there to see.

Her final act of wickedness had been to poison a legless boy as she disappeared into the darkness

7.

Cairo 1943

Katya arrived in Cairo in January 1943, two months after everyone else. She had boarded one of the last transports containing healthy army recruits for the desert forces.

By this time the British were aware of the condition of the refugees coming in to Iran and Afghanistan and felt obliged to accept her in a weakened condition.

The last few transports included several Poles who had been trained as spies. Each one had a detailed history and their acts of heroic resistance were a background to Katya's dreams as she dozed her way to Cairo. They discussed escaping from Siberian internment camps, fighting Germans and facing torture for their beliefs.

These individuals were confident in the rightness of the communist cause. Their ire against the West had been formulated before Soviet invasion, and nothing had shaken their belief in future revolution.

Volunteer fighters against decadence and corruption, they were destined to become agents in a shadow world of espionage. They claimed identities of individuals who died in gulags and torture chambers and rehearsed their stories before their involuntary audience.

'So,' one would say to the other, 'you fled the evil committee running the gulag and walked across enemy lines, carrying messages for the troops. What did you do before that?'

They questioned each other painstakingly, watching Katya to see if she was convinced by these unlikely tales.

'Where were you born?'

'Who was your mother?'

Katya made reassuring noises, and took care to forget what she had seen and heard.

*

Apart from these conversations, the journey was quiet and uneventful.

They were met by a wall of noise as they disembarked in the dry

311

heat of Cairo, full of allied troops, fighting against Germans with brilliant engineers and superior weapons. The allies needed all manpower available, employing conscripted troops from the British Empire and adding every defector and refugee who made it to Allied shores.

The city was stunningly different, even compared to the relative freedom of Tashkent.

Crowded markets offered food of every kind. Cairo was as poor as they had expected, although no one seemed to be starving, not even beggars.

They had been told that the West was full of untold wealth, with bourgeois tyrants battening on poverty-stricken denizens. The mixture of absolute luxury and destitution in the city reinforced this opinion; its inhabitants were ready to sell almost anything; they locked up women and kept myriad servants.

Police, even secret police, seemed more interested in German spies than Russian fifth columnists.

The Russian agents moved around freely. They had detailed histories to relate, and no one questioned their stories of daring-do. They were lionised. No one breathed a word about collaboration. Soldiers did as they liked on leave, and openly criticised their leaders, even the evil dictators Churchill and Roosevelt.

It was easy for the healthy refugees to fit in with the Polish troops who had reached England in 1939, and most of whom had been involved in fighting.

British officers had maintained a professional army for centuries. They believed themselves to be experienced in assessing the men at their disposal. As a result, several would-be spies obtained senior positions in intelligence. In general, the soviets obtained every piece of information they required.

*

Among those who had escaped Poland in 1939, was Katya's brothers, Casimir. He had successfully regrouped with the army in England and was in Cairo!

Casimir, engaging and jovial, had inherited a puritanical streak from his mother. He smoked a pipe, and affected air-force mannerisms, although he did not get involved with drinking and womanising.

Without regard to his foreignness, which normally mattered to the imperialist British soldiers, he was popular with his squadron, and with the ladies. He organised outings to the pyramids, and cast ashtrays and plaques out of spent shell-casings.

His engineering degree from Poland, allowed him to work with bombers and spitfires. He refused to work on bombing runs, and worked in the control towers, claiming he could not bomb locations where his family might be living.

According to military records, he had a pacifist streak, defined as 'lack of courage'. He lacked killer instinct, and was unlikely to fire a shot in battle. Fortunately, he provided an excellent addition to the logistics team, playing his part with dedication and aptitude.

He was overjoyed that Katya and Anya had arrived safely. The three of them formed a strong bond and spent time together.

Anya reported their arrest as a result of Janek's boasting and did not elaborate. Neither sister provided details of events in Russia, agreeing with general opinion whenever possible. Details of life in captivity had come from starved and diseased refugees streaming across the borders.

'I don't want to talk about it,' Katya insisted, with tears in her eyes. Anya was equally silent, watching her sister carefully.

Casimir respected their need.

He was dismayed to hear that Sofia had been sentenced to Siberia, and doubted that she had survived.

*

Katya changed her political stance, though she did not change her heart. She felt her loss of power keenly.

She had been content living in grey dictatorship, where people picked words with care at all times.

She despised the lack of central control in the West because it left her without a role to play. As a woman her only chance to get into power seemed to be to marry. No other options were immediately available.

She tried hard to think of a way to find a willing and subservient partner in this completely different milieu.

She and Andrei had occasionally watched American and British movies, mostly of upper class women having tragic affairs in divine locations and wealthy country houses. Perhaps she could be like one of these?

Several Polish girls were engaged after two weeks of arriving in Cairo. Katya observed them enviously, imagined herself in a long silk gown, shouting at servants and torturing them if necessary.

Unfortunately, the dream was slow to materialise.

Neither Katya nor Anya could speak English or French and they were both shy and retiring. They were invited to parties and outings, and should have been spoilt for choice among the randy men around them.

Somehow they were not in the centre of the pairing game among the rich and the successful and were scarcely noticed despite the shortage of women.

The refugee community also had parties. These were much quieter affairs, during which heavy drinking went on and very little dancing.

Anya had already met a handsome young ex-Komsomol member. The two spent long hours alone, whispering together.

Antek was shy, and rarely spoke to anyone other than Anya. He was a passionate idealist who had worked in a show collective close to St Petersburg. He had seen Comrade Stalin in the flesh and admired him greatly.

He had not seen starvation and had never heard of interrogations. He did not believe any of their stories and suspected that the Poles in the refugee camps were saboteurs who deserved punishment.

'They must have been responsible for all manner of crimes,' he whispered to Anya.

She agreed.

*

Katya was less successful in finding a mate at either type of gathering.

She felt alienated from the festive atmosphere of an army on leave, and was guided by Andrei's stories of the balls and parties, which were not too far from the truth.

Few people talked to her, even at the quieter gatherings of refugee Poles.

She had something repellent about her, mostly shadows of the despair she had wrought.

*

Katya still hoped to find a young duke or count to woo her. There were certainly plenty of upper class British chaps in Cairo and they seemed relatively persuadable and rather unintelligent.

A visit to see the pyramids was a chance to meet men in surroundings which could show off her taste and erudition. She would mention that her grandmother had been inside and explored some of the newly excavated tombs.

She signed up to a tour by camel. A party of British officers had arranged it and she made every effort to attend, even paying another much prettier girl to cry off so that she could take her place.

It was not a success.

Most of the party were dead bored and complained all the time.

A stuffy young fellow rode a camel by her side. He completely ignored what the guide had to say and decided to explain the monuments to Katya.

'Pyramids you know,' said 'Very, very old, and all that. Built by some pharaoh type. Not very nice you see. Got chaps dragging those blocks on top of one another in all this heat. Must've been pretty terrible.'

He turned to the guide.

'I say, old chap,' he shouted, 'got a drink? Whiskey and soda? This young lady's gasping for a drink.'

The man shook his head.

'Bloody uncivilized here. Can't get a drink in all this heat.'

He ran a finger under the collar of his pristine white shirt.

'Let's be off. This was a stupid idea. Bloody boring in my opinion, what? Just a pile of rocks. Can't think why they make so much of the things.'

She tried to tell the party that her mother had excavated in Egypt, but she had a thick Polish accent and most of the party just shouted at her in a similar way that they shouted at the guides, believing that shouting made them more comprehensible.

'Very nice, what? Better than anything you have at home in your mud hut eh? This is a bottle. Bottle. You twist the cap like this.

315

Water. Drinkee. Good. No drinkee water except from this bottle, understand. Water here bad. Very bad."

She and the guide exchanged knowing looks and looked away in embarrassment.

She was beginning to understand the exclusive nature of the class system, particularly in Britain, where it was compounded by colonial racism. As a Pole her chances of gaining a British officer to wed were slim. As a very plain young woman, her chances of finding any man were almost non-existent.

*

Katya had been in the upper echelons of power and she was not giving up that easily. She had learnt what drove people, through her skilled interrogations. That had been difficult; this would be a piece of cake. She was sure that she could regain her footing in the West. It should be relatively easy.

She redirected her search for a husband to the Poles who had escaped the rigours of occupation and deportation. Anyone else might guess her history.

Aristocratic Poles were thick on the ground in the new Polish army. They left Poland before it was invaded by Germany and Russia because they had the resources to do so.

The pilots and officers were highly Anglicised, and did not give plain Polish women a second glance.

Polish ground crews had strong affiliations with the countries whose armies they had joined and formed tight social groups. They were always delighted to drink and dance with most Polish girls, although uninterested in Katya.

She rejected working class Poles, who showed little interest anyway.

Polish Jews were mostly fundamentalists, preaching of a new Zionist state in Palestine. She avoided them. In any case, she had started to go to church again. It laid Partkom rumours to rest nicely.

This left the party crowd - men and women who had promiscuous relationships. These heavy drinkers hid dark secrets hidden behind aggressive drinking and flighty romances. They wore a desperate air, and looked as though they would break in battle.

*

She searched for potential targets and singled out Bartosz, an effeminate aristocrat from the Polish base in St Andrews in Scotland and Lucia's cousin.

He was handsome, foppish, and clearly influenced by Nazism. He had not joined the German Nazis, because the Polish Nazi party had been extremely nationalist.

Bartosz worked as a fitness instructor and trainer. The recruitment office had formed the opinion that he was a Nancy boy. The British army was heavily homo-sexualised, disapproved of an open avowal of gayness. The British were not used to the extravagant effeminacy of Polish rich.

His role was to foster morale on training exercises and he took it seriously, dancing around sweating trainees on assault courses, shouting words of encouragement as they crawled through imaginary trenches. He enjoyed his war. The rumour of his bisexual tastes did no harm, as most girls enjoyed the company of gay man; a horny creep with wandering hands was a worse proposition.

The man had every arrogant vice of aristocracy, except an appetite for political power. He regularly got drunk, boasting of oil millions, his Ukrainian estate and his eminent lineage.

He was confident of the future. Stalin would fall. Poland would be free once more and he would own the world.

He was clearly a fool, which meant that he would be easy to manipulate. The fact that he was Lucia's cousin also made him desirable. It would annoy her rival.

He was a useless fop. In her caricature understanding of wealth and power, this made him a high aristocrat. She was impressed by his wild behaviour and swagger. It was what she expected.

*

Katya introduced herself as Lucia's friend at school.

She became a committed admirer and acolyte of his appalling jokes and camp behaviour. She was careful to promote her virginity and her faith in Catholic teaching on marriage and abortion.

She played the innocent, while deliberating how to arouse him. She had plenty of experience, because Andrei, like most who believe in perfection, was ridden with vice. He did not hesitate to try out the perversions elicited from the interrogated. Katya participated, yet regarded loss of control, even in orgasm, as dangerous.

However, he proved harder to attract than she expected. She considered, and rejected, the idea of a threesome. It would not help the virgin story.

She had to try another way.

*

Bartosz regularly got into trouble at the base, and came to rely on her to get him out of caverns of embarrassment he dug himself into. She bailed him out when he ranted anti-Semitic speeches claiming that she had asked him what the Nazis believed. She deflected problems when he annoyed by talk of a superior race.

After some time, he waited for her before going on a binge circuit of bars in Cairo.

He was utterly uninterested in Katya. She realised that she would only be able trap him into marriage.

Katya told Bartosz that she had no periods. He relied on this, since many Polish maidens suffered the effects of starvation. In fact, she had never eaten badly and her periods had re-started as soon as she moved to Tashkent.

The shaman's knowledge and power had centred on fertility of livestock, so she knew about fertility cycles. She taught her pupil how not to conceive with Andrei, who did not use protection. It was easy to apply the same knowledge to ensure pregnancy.

To make extra certain of conception, Katya engineered a sexual encounter in the open desert under a new moon. She claimed she was giving up her virginity on the basis of a long-hidden passion. He was drunk and had no idea whether this was true.

At least he made it. She made sure he remembered it was done, squealing loud enough to wake camels.

Katya was pregnant. This alone was still insufficient for her security. Further steps were necessary.

*

She hid gestation until the baby was impossible to remove safely.

She did not push Bartosz into further intimacy, yet contrived that they were noticed together. She and made it obvious that he was dependent on her cool-headed temper when he got into trouble during drinking bouts. She hung around him, always agreed with him

318

and complimented him - he enjoyed that.

He was a little confused by her - she was not a cool girlfriend in any way, but she treated him like a stud, when he was normally a joke for poor performance. He tolerated her.

Her slight frame did not show signs of pregnancy for 4 months, when she covered the bump with loose clothing.

At six months, almost everyone suddenly noticed her swollen stomach. She had taken to wearing tight uniform and pushing out her stomach.

Katya affected to be innocent.

'What? Pregnant? How?' She was shocked and burst into wild hysterics of an innocent betrayed.

Her brother was up in arms. The rapist must be brought to book. Katya affected total innocence.

There had only been Bartosz, and he had taken every precaution, or claimed he had. She had been enchanted by him and he told her he loved her. She had confidence in him, and adored him so much.

Casimir was indignant and threatening.

Bartosz was cowardly and blustering. He had not realised that the girl would have protectors.

His attempts to get out of marriage were quickly silenced by the threat of being cashiered.

*

It was a shotgun wedding. Katya had won her man.

She anticipated life in a castle, surrounded by servants and loyal serfs. She was certain communism would fail. She would go back to Lvov and rule the land she had helped to destroy.

319

8.

Stalingrad 1943

Sofia's departure in the February snow was noted by the one remaining German sniper overlooking the square.

He scoped her as she ran into the open. He recognised her, smiling at her pathetic disguise.

She intrigued him. He had been watching the square for weeks, and rightly surmised that she was escaping something.

She hid in the ruins around the square until the light was a little better. The silence was punctuated by the distant crackle of gunfire. The darkness seemed full of moving shadows.

She crawled around creaking and unstable buildings and tripped noisily over the piles of rubble.

After an hour spent creeping around his hide, which was in a semi-derelict building, she found a little ante-room. It seemed remarkably warm and intact. She fell heavily asleep in her winter fleece and fur cap with its prominent red star.

*

She awoke to the stare of mad blue eyes.

'Sergei,' she started in abject terror, as she saw the ghostly face in the dim light of dawn.

A gun was pressed into her temple; she stifled her noise immediately.

It was not Sergei, just a young German of 18 or so. His eyes were reddened by lack of sleep, with the pinprick pupils of Pervitin induced psychosis.

He had been holed up in rooms like this for months. She smelt the stink of excreta and rotten food, as he had opened his snipers nest to confront her. He had inhabited it for a long time, shooting at the new recruits.

He motioned her to move into his den in order to view the departing medical convoy. He gestured that he was not going to shoot at them.

'I know,' she agreed in German with a thick Jewish accent. 'No one had been shot for weeks.'

Most of the snipers had been cleared. The buildings were being checked, and then blown up if they were unstable.

'You are German?'

'No.'

'Jewish?'

She nodded.

He recoiled from her as if she were a snake.

'You are a spy?'

'No!'

He cocked his gun. 'You have come to kill me like you did my friends,' he threatened.

She vehemently denied it, explaining she had just escaped torture and execution at the hands of the commissar in the medical convoy.

He accepted this was true, having watched her clandestine departure the night before.

He pointed to the tortured and disfigured naked body of a captured sniper. He was hanging from makeshift gibbet in the square.

'This was the work of Jews and Vandals,' he said. He was heavily armed with finely engineered equipment. He slowly pulled out a vicious sharp knife to cut her throat, tested it on his finger. The knife was quiet and lethal.

She stood as still as a lamb for slaughter.

As he scrutinised her, he thought better of it.

'Wait,' he put away the knife, though he kept holding her in a tight grip by the shoulder. She sensed he could break it with a twist, and did not move.

'Shoot me and you will become a heroine. I have been trying to die for several days. I cannot do it alone. I have no poison and I am afraid to use my pistol. I need assistance.'

The resemblance in expression to Sergei was remarkable - another man deranged by war.

'To be certain of instant death I have to use my sniper rifle. It is the only way. It will blow my head to pieces and I die instantly.' He knew very well how long it took to die from a partially effective head shot, and so did she. He had been thinking about this a long time. 'The rifle is too long and for me to wield alone.'

She was full of remorse over Sergei. And she knew that he was right that it was difficult to kill oneself with a gun. She imagined the Sergei's drawn out passing, which he had faced alone as she slept.

'Listen, heroine, comrade, you can help me die.'

Sofia felt sick. She had vivid nightmares of Sergei asking her for help. She had moved so many steps down the ladder of evil, committing every mortal sin.

Only murder remained, and she was being asked to perform this last transgression. It would ensure her eternal damnation in the eyes of the church.

'I cannot do this,' she protested, 'it is against my faith. I cannot kill.'

He fell to his knees. He did not loosen his grip on her shoulder and she collapsed with him. His eyes were gruesomely panic-stricken.

'I die at the hands of a Jew.' He spat. 'At least I will not perish like my friend over there. I watched his lynching.'

'I cannot kill,' she repeated. Images of Sergei's face kept looming up in her mind. In the poor light, she was no longer sure who he was.

'Jews have no faith,' he cried. He fell to the ground and sobbed. 'You must help me or perish.'

He looked like a child, not a soldier.

It was a nightmare. Her misconduct coming back, just like Yuri had explained - karma.

'Please do not let me expire like them. I beg you.'

She let him finish his fit of weeping, and mused how far she had travelled on the path of reneging her simple faith.

She had administered morphine to the severely wounded for months, unaware that it was a lethal dosage; she had believed it provided comfort to those in pain. Yuri had explained what she was doing during one of the interminable moral arguments in the long hours of the night. Instead of refusing to administer the close, she was grateful when they died peacefully afterwards. She never questioned it and continued to do it even when she knew that she was administering death.

She had slept through Sergei's lonely end. Now she was being compelled to see what she had missed.

She prayed for the young man and for Sergei too.

She could not let him be tortured to death, and his doom was unavoidable. The best he could hope for was to be blown up with the building. However, judging by how easily she had found his nest, discovery was inevitable. His tearful face showed that he did not have the strength of purpose to die alone.

He listened to her praying in Polish, suspecting her of some Jewish curse; he no longer cared. He was not sufficiently courageous to die alone and entreated for mercy.

'I will be finished instantly', he pleaded, 'and I will thank you for eternity. Please help me to pass away in peace.'

He was behind enemy lines, and had to prepare for martyrdom in the Nazi cause.

She acquiesced, hoping that she had made the right choice, and accepting the consequences. She needed to expiate the sin of leaving Sergei to die alone.

*

He set up the complex rifle, and he showed her what to do. He could not reach the trigger and she had to fire it in a highly confined space. After some manoeuvring in the tiny hide, they agreed to go out into the main room. They spent an hour or so setting up.

He was livelier, and seemed to be savouring his last minutes with a clear head and bright eyes.

In truth, he was glad of company. He had been alone for so long. She was a Jew, and he only spoke to her because he was not able to shoot himself dead, still he enjoyed the fact that someone was with him, and debated leaving her with messages for his family.

Nevertheless, he avoided close contact. They kept a distance despite the intimacy of the task and addressed each other in formal German.

He recoiled from a chance touch, and treated her as if she were unclean, although he was rank and soiled.

She did not mind, imagining Sergei's last lonely moments, talking to a heavily sleeping woman, who probably snored.

They earnestly discussed which part of the brain to aim for, balancing minimum pain against certainty of instant annihilation,

323

and the risk of recoil.

*

The shot echoed through the square like a clap of thunder.

Sofia prayed for his spirit and hoped that she was laying Sergei's ghost to rest.

She was not as horrified as she expected to be. She had not seen Sergei die, and, in her twisted morality, conceived that the horrific sight of his shattered head flying against the walls was a part of her quest.

The silence, which she heard through the throbbing of her deafened ears, was the quiet of a hundred soldiers converging on the building.

He had been hours, minutes from discovery.

Sofia saw movement below and ran out of the building shouting, 'Do not worry, comrades. I have killed him.'

Grey soldiers emerged from the shadows. They trained their guns on her.

She shouted louder.

'I shot the sniper, comrades. He was hidden and waiting. I found him and killed the villain.'

Her head was ringing and she was not sure that they had heard.

In her determination to survive she forgot that she was wearing men's clothing. Luckily her cap had a red star. It had little effect other than to prevent immediate execution.

They roughly restrained her as other soldiers rushed upstairs to find the dead man lying in the corner, his brains dripping over the walls.

Almost nothing was left of his head. Some newer recruits were sick, partly from the stench of the hide, which mingled unpleasantly with the smell of gunshot, blood and brains.

Of course, the troops were accompanied by a commissar, who had the directive to report heroic deeds in the battle for Stalingrad.

He turned to her and addressed his comrades slowly.

'A heroine, a daughter, no, mother of the revolution, comrades!'

Sofia wriggled uncomfortably.

'Our Soviet heroine donned the clothes of a dead comrade and sought out this viper, who had been preying on our revolutionary

324

comrades. She shot him with his own gun while he slept.'

The men murmured their admiration. They slapped her on the back and offered her strong vodka, which she sipped.

'I will send this story in my dispatches comrades.' He beamed at her. She had provided a notable tale. 'You will be famous.'

'Is your husband dead?' he asked, as he led her away.

She nodded.

'Shot by a sniper,' she stated. She could not explain how Sergei had died by his own hand.

'Wonderful!' He crowed. He would make the front page of the news. The tale might even get Stalin's approbation.

'Come with me.'

Sofia had her photograph taken next to the dead man. Her name and details were noted; she changed her name to Bogdanova, Sergei's name, judging it to be common enough to be untraceable. She was cheered and feted by the soldiers, most of whom had not seen any of the bitter fighting around the square.

*

Sofia was worried that her name and description would come up soon, and that she would be arrested.

Luckily Yuri had worked hard on her escape, and as far as the commissar knew, she had been wearing nurse's uniform, and his vague description was insufficiently accurate to make the connection. The men were on the watch for escaping German spies; it was to her advantage that she had just shot an enemy soldier.

The commissar wove her pregnancy into his romantic tale. 'Young Bogdanova was carrying the child of her dashing young captain, whom she followed to the front disguised as a man.'

His dispatch related how the two fought for comrade Stalin together.

'The captain had died heroically after many brave exploits. His mistress had no time to mourn. She thought only of her Soviet. Snatching her boyfriend's rifle, she hunted down the evil man who had shot her dearest and tried to damage our Socialist dream. The heroine had located the sniper in his lair and, after a great battle, shot him.'

The commissar was delighted by the valorous story.

Meanwhile, Sofia was disheartened and afraid.

It was not a good idea to be noticed. Under this regime it was not clever to be good at anything, because no one was meant to be better than anyone else.

Even a fine appearance hinted at class recidivism. It was wise to be one of the grey masses.

In any case, that night, the scarecrows alive in the caves under the square crept out. They enlightened the commissar as to Sergei's demise. He was a hero, they claimed, who had shot himself for this Jezebel.

She had absconded on his assassination, only to resurface when the fighting was almost over, and in man's clothes.

The commissar hastily reconsidered.

The story was a good one and should remain. As a trained communist, he had no interest in truth. His advance through the ruined city had shown him that Stalingrad was no heroic battle, rather a heartless war of attrition which killed most of the city's civilians.

Sofia must disappear.

He told the scarecrows to stay underground, intending to blow up the building, burying the whole lot and their tale with them.

Sofia was sent to the battlefront, with a note that she was a suspected German spy.

*

Sofia duly left the camp. At a safe distance, she opened and read the message. She breathed a sigh of relief at her escape.

No one would seek her. No one had guessed who she was and she was alive.

She found bands of refugees and exchanged her man's clothes for a woman's rags.

She joined the gangs of invisible beggars, scavenging for food and metal scraps in the ruins to sell to the advancing army.

9.

Lviv 1943

Janek mourned the Jelinskis. Eva found their money, hidden under a floorboard, where they had told her it was. That night he sought refuge in her bed and cried.

He confessed that he was half Jewish, railing against the Germans.

She consoled him.

They married shortly after and obtained a birth certificate for their daughter. The neighbours assumed that Eva had been his mistress for some time and accepted the situation without questions.

Mikhail, the concierge, who had a picture of Hitler in his tiny office, occasionally muttered about immorality and Jews in his apartments. However, since the visit of the Nazi hunters he had been far more subdued.

This was because the Jew hunters had scrutinised him very carefully when they arrived at the apartment.

'How did you come to be aware that these people were Jews?' they asked.

'Because they never attended church,' he boasted proudly. 'I knew it.'

They looked him over suspiciously. 'Have you seen many Jews?'

His hooked nose and nasty limp had not bothered him much before this meeting, now he became shufflingly aware that he was not a fine specimen of humanity.

Under Soviet occupation, he had become proud of his ugliness. It showed his lowly origins. Now he began to tremble.

They took his papers and read them through painstakingly. 'Who was your mother?'

They went over his origins for at least an hour, and his voice cracked as he realised that his peasant Ukrainian origins were doing him no favours at all. He was made aware that he could not possibly pass any test of superior breeding.

Their lips curled as he explained that his great grandfather was a serf. They picked up his icons and laughed over his ancient samovar which he had proudly brought from his village 30 years ago.

'How proud these unter-mensch are of their primitive artefacts,' one of them remarked to the other as if he were not in the room.

'Yes,' his friend had responded, 'this specimen is the height of their civilisation.'

He laughed derisively. 'We have a great deal to do here.'

'We will be back soon,' they declared. 'This apartment block needs *cleansing*,' they threatened ominously as they trooped upstairs.

*

The baby missed her real family for two weeks and then completely forgot them. They doted on her so much that it was hard to imagine she was not their birth child.

The family attended church services every Sunday, where Janek cursed god for what had happened.

Eva rehearsed Catholic prayers and learnt about dogma. She imitated a Catholic peasant very precisely.

Winter fell.

They had enough, and were warm and comfortable.

Eva was an excellent business woman. She went out often, involved in underhand market dealings, selling and bartering all manner of junk in the marketplace.

She overwhelmed Mikhail, who was unfailingly polite to her. Mysterious lodgers came and left with her, and Janek suspected that she was embroiled in the resistance, but asked no questions.

Janek continued in employment, although he was scarcely ever paid.

He worked at the menial tasks necessary to keep the post office running, particularly in delivering Red Cross parcels and letters of comfort.

He no longer aspired to high status. He was happy to do his work, bring up his adopted daughter, and to have good life. His wife kept him down with a sharp peasant tongue. He did what he was told.

*

The effect of two invasions and occupations in quick succession was to make everyone extremely aware of their race and ethnicity. People squirmed under yoke of inferiority, while accepting the Aryan classification.

The persecution of the Jews had a hugely depressing effect. Everyone feared for their lives and shuffled through the snow in the early hours of the morning and late at night avoiding German working hours.

The Germans congratulated themselves on the cleanliness and order. The inhabitants watched them and their collaborators from behind windows with loathing and despair. It was a life under siege, under the constant threat of enslavement and extermination.

*

German policies for extinction of inferior races were extensive and detailed, though they did not get far beyond the elimination of Jews.

They had made a start on Ukrainians and Poles, and achieved little other than to foment deeper hatred between the peoples by judging Poles to be superior to ethnic Ukrainians, for reasons too obscure to fathom.

For the moment, all such plans were placed on hold. Germany was losing the war with Russia.

Bedraggled German soldiers and wounded boys passed through Lvov. They were inadequately dressed for winter; many were wounded and lost. A tragic sight, they had to move in groups of at least three, as lone soldiers were mugged and killed by callous locals.

Eva went out a great deal, returning smelling of streets and occasionally, of gunpowder. She was a vehement socialist, and Janek guessed that she and her fellows were hunting down Germans and, he suspected, in contact with the Soviet forces. She slept with a German luger under her pillow and he knew when her acts of violence and sabotage had been particularly successful, because on those occasions, she was insatiable in bed.

The city dreamt of freedom.

Eva spurred Janek to attend secret meetings at various locations in the city. He refused point blank.

As the battle drew nearer, Eva rushed about carrying messages and supporting the fighting ever more openly.

Janek was a coward, and Eva accepted it. He nagged Eva constantly about her involvement in resistance and begged her to consider their tiny daughter.

*

The rumour that Americans and the British were liberating Europe was good news. The Ukraine wanted to decide its own fate.

Socialists planned their own government, under the protection and support of the Soviets. Troops moved back and forth across the streets with armies and tanks moving this way and that, dragging bystanders into the conflict.

As the battle reached the city, civilians hid in underground dugouts, waiting for moments when shooting abated to return to a barter economy, selling and moving around what they had.

The Maslows inhabited the wine cellar for their apartment with their tiny adopted daughter, surrounded by Eva's market stocks, sheltering a few of the resistance as the battle raged.

Tanks rolled overhead and the crackle of machine gun fire was heard in their street; the two of them prepared to die with a weeping child in their arms.

Eva confessed that she was a Jewish peasant who fled her village, leaving her family to die. She had had no idea about churches and was disquieted by them. She admitted that she had killed several Germans and had their kit in the cellar, and Janek confessed that he had betrayed his family and his friends.

They fell in love among the bombs and the gun battles, hanging on to their adopted daughter, a symbol of their secret origins.

In a frenzy of confession, Janek told his wife the details of his involvement with the NKVD.

She listened carefully, saying nothing.

He tried to explain that the NKVD were not interested in freedom for Ukraine and that many of those he had betrayed were good socialists and revolutionaries. He begged her not to get further involved in the battle for socialism, admitting that every single socialist he had betrayed in the first occupation had subsequently disappeared. The Germans had dug up their bodies to show how brutally many of them had been tortured. He made her promise not to get involved in liberation, warning her that the secret police were absolutely untrustworthy.

He beseeched her to desist for Maryssa's sake.

Eva was very quiet. She was thinking about the party of socialists

330

she knew, and he suspected that she was in with them quite deeply.

She left him alone with Maryssa for a day, and tried to inform her compatriots that the Soviets might object to independent Ukrainian government. She placed herself in severe danger by her attempts to save her friends. Her pleas went unacknowledged.

*

When the violence was conclusively over, and the red-hot shooting and bombing ended, Lvov was not free.

Janek had been right to plead caution. Those who rose up to support socialism and independence were exterminated as the battle moved west.

Eva's friends were dead.

The Soviets returned, and clamped down on the Ukraine harder than before.

The party, influenced by German concepts of Social engineering, re-organised Eastern Europe, which was a patchwork of tribal confederations and races.

The NKVD eliminated the remaining Polish rulers, whose bodies were piled outside the city.

No one cared.

*

Stalin intended to continue the ethnic re-organisation commenced under German occupation.

Poland moved into Silesia and the borders of Ukraine were expanded.

The area was purified by deporting minorities and relocating nationalities. Few fought back. Almost nothing was standing anyway.

Janek, who had no political morality, made plans to re-join the Party, realising that collusion with the Russians was their only chance of survival.

Party membership would give them the right to stay in Lvov.

As a party member with a Ukrainian wife and child, he felt quietly exultant, with high hopes of building some kind of future.

It didn't happen.

10.

Buenos Aires 1943

Before the war, the educated, delicately-nurtured and mothered Jews had been winners. They had no experience of losing. They did not understand the defeated. Winners never do. By now they had learnt what it is like to be at the bottom of the pile, and they never forgot it.

There is a lot of repressed anger in society. Humans are animals, even though they despise the animal kingdom. Animals do not take to overcrowding. Normal animal responses: sniffing people on the street, standing close to women in heat, and preening masculine displays, have to be repressed. Men are not supposed to expose themselves in public, or sniff at women, or beat up drunks.

Those in authority, with control over progress, had refined outlets for instincts: - music, opera, theatre, reading, study, symposia, art, and travel. They released their frustrations in music, art, song and the cut and thrust of polite conversation. Status wars provided intense satisfaction.

The sailors on the Vittoria were the lowest of the low. The crew consisted of Latin Americans and West Indians who were anti-everything. Anti-Semitic was just one of a long list of things, which being far away, they could safely despise.

They were looked down on by almost everyone. They had no higher outlets for their resentments and frustrations. They had no status. They were treated like scurvy knaves in port, and robbed by the whores they frequented to vent their frustrations. Their every move had to be circumspect in order to avoid arrest on land or the brig on board. They lived close together with stinking cargo, bullied by the captain and officers. Such men had a lot of anger to vent.

They knew that Jews were the new scapegoats for society and the presence of the sheep-like victims provided an opportunity to intimidate and scare others. They could not pass up a chance to feel better than someone.

Once the ship left port, the sailors swore and spat on the ground every time a refined passenger passed them by. They rolled their eyes, and swung heavy ropes in their path. They watched the women with salacious glances, and passed comments on their appearance in foreign tongues. They met the new passengers by crossing themselves and passing derogatory comments.

Underneath it all, they were not unsympathetic to the outlaws. They knew how it felt to be despised.

The fact was that the sailors were behaving in the feral, atavistic manner of animals around their territory. They only resented the presence of refinement on board their cargo ship for a while, to establish their boundaries. This stinking cargo boat was theirs. Once they had established control of the decks, they wanted to make peace.

They tried to make friends, with the children in particular.

Unfortunately, their passengers increased sensitivity to all matters of hostility made them imagine all swearing and shouting among the crew, and there was a lot, was directed at them personally, and specifically because they were Jewish. They quieted their children, hid in their cabins, and acted in every way like victims.

'Hush, my darlings,' hissed the mothers, 'do not speak to the bad men. Stay here and play backgammon and cards, we will be on dry land soon. Leave them alone.'

It took a week to reach Argentina. In that time, the passengers spent as much time as possible crowded together in the depths of the ship, ate as little as possible of the non-kosher food, which was mostly out of tins, and supplemented their diet by orange juice and increasingly wilted fruit which they had brought on board, to fight off scurvy.

'It will not be long,' fathers admonished his hungry offspring. 'We cannot eat the same as those rough men. Their food is unclean, it is not proper food.'

*

Argentina was nothing like the grey and war torn country they had left.

It was full of life, poverty, religion and colour. Argentineans were brim-full of vigour, the weather balmy, and the cities luscious and raw.

If the sailors stared and posed aggressively, then the Argentineans did so even more. The port was hot and smelly and might have been fascinating, if the men and women were not grieving for their lost past. To them it appeared as a jungle, full of primitive savages at the edge of civilisation.

Almost everyone in town had arrived to see the unloading of the ship. Virile men unloaded the swinging cargo reach the ground like bull fighters, occasionally spitting on the earth in front of them. Exotic under-dressed women in bright clothing ogled the posturing of the males. In the corner of the dock sat a group of feathered and savage Indians, crouched like statues. Even the dogs scratching at their fleas, watched the goings-on.

As the Jews disembarked, uninhibited babies crawled among the passengers, spreading vile dirt all over their fresh laundered and carefully ironed tropical clothing.

People shouted greetings in a foreign tongue - the new arrivals were silent.

Then, as they set foot on the dock, they heard, 'Shalom!'

A group of Jews was waiting for them expectantly. They were welcomed by a small band of men, wearing kippahs and tallit shawls who hustled them away from the curious crowds.

There was no time to get to know the locals or to assess the culture. They had closed themselves from new inputs anyway, trusting absolutely no one except other Jews.

*

The rabbi brought them home in a ceremonial welcome, where they were introduced to other emigrants.

It was no normal homecoming, nor normal welcome. There were ashes to spread on their heads. They shouted in Hebrew, and did all things Jewish.

The experience was both shocking and emotional. It was their first direct experience of Zionism.

They learnt that Jews in Latin America were free to return to the core of their faith and enjoyed it even as every expression of Judaism was being expunged in Europe.

The women wailed and the men tore their clothes. After the misery, indignities, families lost and dead, it was safe to grieve and to revel in being Jewish.

It was exactly the type of behaviour that the Brauns had hitherto despised.

They revelled in it.

11.

Cairo spring 1943

After six months of engagement, meeting on weekends and sneaking around the camp, Lucia and Caleb were wed with the lukewarm approval of the regiment.

During the two day honeymoon, the two inhabited a cocoon where no harsh reality entered. They were besotted, and had agreed to commit to each other. Marriage brought them together on levels which neither was prepared to explore.

Intelligent, tall and graceful, Caleb was a brilliant hunter and sportsman. He had done well in High School and went to university on a sports-scholarship as a key member of the college ice hockey team.

He worried about returning to the white Baptist community, and wanted to make a new start on his return. He was prepared to take risks in gaining Lucia as a partner and an equal. He admired her pioneering and questing nature and found her deeply attractive. She was passionate in seeking out new things, and he intended his foreign wife to get involved in his attempt to start afresh in Canada, reconciling two cultures which did not gel.

He thought in universals and cared little for detail, such as politics, and what was going on in the Soviets.

As far as he was concerned, his primary task was fighting for freedom in a just cause. He had few problems accepting his wife's baby, since he did not anticipate any involvement in childcare.

He knew that she had regrets and watched her carefully, fascinated by her penitence and her turmoil, which showed in myriad expressions on her face. He had acted from high motives as well as lust, while unprepared to change his lifestyle for a pregnant wife.

They talked little, although to be fair, she was not particularly fluent in French. She found Canadian French very hard to understand.

Lucia left the army and moved into a flat as a married woman. She was entirely dependent on her husband.

He did not include her in his life, and stayed out late, leaving her alone for long periods. He played a lot of games: football, hockey, baseball and poker. In the evenings, he and his mates sat around a tiny screen in the officers' mess watching American sports fixtures, corny war movies and attended propaganda visits from film stars.

At first, she was happy sitting poolside with other brides, who exuded calm and self-satisfaction, and seemed happy to do nothing all day, chatting about washing, ironing and removing stains.

In the evening, she listened to the Canadian French radio, learnt English and got bored.

She was suffering from PTSD[18] and needed to talk about the past, even though no one cared. Everyone from Eastern Europe had a murky past, which they did not want to discuss. Her army mates were out partying. If she talked to Caleb, he listened for a few minutes, and fell sound asleep.

Then she became resentful of the empty evenings. Her life had always been restricted, and her mother had protected her from most problems. She wanted to see the world, to discover the real world and explore. She was in the centre of a great exotic culture and surrounded by history.

She decided to get out on her own and explore.

*

Caleb's dollars went a long way.

She visited the ancient pyramids and took trips down the Nile.

The other wives occasionally came along, although in general they were incurious about Egypt.

She tried to ignore her pregnancy and often returned quite drained of energy. Her husband did not appear to object.

Once she had completed the tourist circuit, Lucia moved on to the Cairo museum.

She read everything written in French, sitting next to desiccated professors who smelt embalmed and learning from them when they spoke to her.

Ancient Egypt was depicted as a cult of death. The musty

---

18 Post-traumatic stress disorder was not recognised as a problem until the late 1960's

museums and libraries contained the ghosts of millions. An awful lot was known about them. She worried that no one would even remember people like her.

'Who will remember this appalling period of mass exterminations?' She brooded, 'And what will be remembered of me?'

She bought antique Egyptian curios from the markets.

The Egyptian government was keen to prevent antiquities from leaving their country; even so genuinely ancient things were openly sold. The process of collecting was cathartic, helping Lucia understand what she had experienced.

Caleb disliked the ancient artefacts.

'Dead things!' he complained. 'It is likely haunted.'

He let her collect.

'It's not good to sleep in the same area as this stuff,' he suggested. 'We can put it into an outhouse back home if you like.'

Most of it was stored in crates to ship to Canada. He let her continue to collect if she wanted to.

*

Lucia was still bored and chose to test her boundaries further.

She wandered around Cairo alone, sitting in westernised cafes used by single army women.

She met a young Egyptian called Haseem, who reminded her of Dania.

He was friendly, and helped her choose antiquities.

They got on well, and he took to escorting her around interesting parts of Cairo which few visited. She was fascinated by his culture which reminded her of the Kazakhs in some odd ways.

He in turn he regarded her as a collector's piece, a rarity, who could cope with the Middle-Eastern way of life. He wanted to show her the good things about the Middle East, which was generally despised by the colonials.

They went out frequently, comparing Western attitudes with those of the Middle East.

He took her to a bar where the men smoked hashish from hookahs and drank black coffee.

She played backgammon, though not for money.

It was frightening and exhilarating. He talked about women as if they were a race apart, or exotic animals, dangerous and mysterious.

'We collect cheetahs; they make superb but dangerous pets.'

He picked up her hand on which she had painted red nail varnish, 'it is best to remove their claws.'

Lucia treated him as a good friend, and flirted with him outrageously.

He became more risqué and invited Lucia to visit the racecourse, where she was feted by the Egyptian men, who treated her like a peculiar specimen. They were extremely friendly and curious; not flirtatious.

They did not find Lucia attractive. They liked soft women, locked in harems and devoted to male desires. To them, she was half man, and not as sexy as a young boy.

She brought some of her friends to the races, who found the Egyptian men scary and intrusive.

'I hated the way they looked at me,' said her friend, 'like a piece of meat.'

'Horrible' agreed her other friend, who had several boyfriends who she played off against each other, 'like I was a slut.'

Lucia argued the matter.

'It is just a different culture. They lock up their women and regard them as inferior. We need to show them that women can be free. Be an example and join me.'

They refused.

They were intimidated by the innate aggression behind the friendly attitudes and insulted by the implication of sexual promiscuity.

Lucia did not see it.

She came to the conclusion that her friends were insular and racist. She had no experience of being treated as an equal and did not notice their superior tones. She drank mint tea and discussed the racing forms. She felt a similar kind of excitement to the Kazakh days.

*

Lucia was getting a reputation for hanging around with Arabs. She was already a little tainted by her strong political opinions and this was another serious matter. Soon she would be shunned, or asked to leave the country.

Caleb remonstrated gently.

Even gentle criticism drove her into a passion.

'I am free!' she shouted, 'you said I could be free. I am not doing anything. You should trust me.'

Lucia did not admit that she was flirtatious, yet her excited laughter and giggles among Arabs shocked the tight community of wives.

They considered her fast and dangerous, and she was suspected of having an Arab beau.

She became quite isolated.

Katya had said that she was a bit of a harlot in Russia and her gossip was finding purchase.

Caleb was unhappy.

He was informed that she was unfaithful more than once.

Still he wanted to give Lucia a chance. He felt sorry for her. When he came home every day, he found her pacing around the tiny apartment like a caged animal. He listened to her complaints of being trapped and beaten and respected that she needed to test the boundaries.

He wanted her to commit to him freely, and Lucia had no idea how close he came to Dania's solution.

'She needs to work things out,' he explained his concerned buddies. 'The Arab companions mean nothing. She is finding her feet after a tough time in Russia. No one knows what happened out there, the refugees don't talk about it much.'

*

Caleb was uniquely capable of understanding how Lucia felt. He came from a tribe in British Columbia who were forcibly educated using only English.

His mother, Akule, was an attractive woman who had been raped, then married to the young son of a trapper at the age of 16. They lived in poverty outside the Indian territories. His father denigrated their Indian past on every occasion while his wife paced the floor in the same suppressed acrimony he saw in Lucia.

He believed in freedom for women, although he had no real idea of what his mother meant by it, since he was born male.

By day Akule sat in the yard with her children, whispering of a life of freedom under the sky, occasionally beating a drum quietly in praise of the Great Spirit and singing softly to the children so they didn't forget their heritage.

She had inspired her son to seek a new way of life, combining two opposing heritages in peaceful union.

He was genuinely attracted to Lucia. She was extremely attractive and high status and at the same time exotic and foreign.

She had the look of one of the lost and he hoped that she would love him.

'If she leaves, I have lost nothing,' he thought. But he sighed deeply. She was his choice of mate and physically, and their relationship was intense and very strong.

*

Lucia was absorbed in regrets. She had loved Dania and missed him still. She believed that she had betrayed him and regretted not going to Afghanistan on such and adventure.

What was it like to be a locked in wife? She was insatiably curious about the life of Egyptian women. Rarely seen in the market, they walked behind their young sons, heavily veiled and in long buttoned coats.

'Why do the women not go out?' she asked. 'Can't I meet them? Is there any way that they can invite me over for tea? Perhaps we can go out to visit the ruins together?'

She begged Haseem to let her meet Egyptian women at home.

Haseem was not keen.

She might be a corrupting influence.

He consulted with his friends as to its wisdom of inviting a Western woman to visit, without the permission of her husband, an idea more shocking that Lucia could realise.

The effects of such a meeting on sequestered women were discussed with his elders. It was not advised.

In the end, Ali, a modern, westernised man who worked in the French embassy, agreed to invite the creature.

'We are more civilised than those stupid kafir,' he claimed. 'They allow their women to be unfaithful and immodest. We should be proud of our superior domestic arrangements.'

He had discussed the matter with his wives, and his mother.

They were just as curious as her to meet Western women. However, as trapped and controlled women, they had to tread carefully.

They professed themselves shocked at the ungodliness of a woman like Lucia. Perhaps their superior example would lead her to see the error of her ways?

*

So it was that a taxi drove Lucia to a house with a stunning carved entrance in the old quarter of town. The door was massive and ornate, lit by a massive oil lamp of exotic design. The walls of the building were otherwise blank. The building occupied an entire block.

She entered a courtyard sheltered from the street, surprisingly cool, and gorgeously tiled. Unexpectedly, it contained an indoor garden watered by a spectacular fountain, surrounded by palms which were invisible from the outside.

The reception area was packed with friends; shouting to each other in Arabic and ordering about innumerable African slaves.

Lucia did not feel threatened; more like a freak. The place was alien and hostile, and it had ceased to be exciting.

As she approached the exclusively male company, she guessed they were saying quite insulting things about her and it no longer felt spirited or flirtations to be among them. She remained polite and well-behaved, trying to act unaware of their intrusive attentions and jostling. She was alone with a large group of men and wondered where the women were.

Young African boys knelt down and offered her mint tea and sweet cakes, Turkish delight.

A hookah appeared briefly.

She showed concern and it vanished immediately. She sat on benches and tried to make conversation.

'Where are the women?' she asked, feeling that their absence compromised her position at the meeting.

But no, begged Ali, at her honourable request all of his women were present.

This was a *tea party* of his family, and everyone was there, even his sons, and his mother.

He pointed to an ornately carved screen.

'They are here,' he declared proudly.

He was a modern man, and allowed his women to come and meet his Western friend. She was welcome, most welcome.

Lucia stared.

Wholly invisible, they sat quietly on the floor behind a heavy carved wooden screen.

Their proximity drove male visitors into frenzy.

'See Lucia,' they shouted in broken English, 'Women, here!'

They pointed excitedly at some heavy screens across the room.

'They are here!'

A strong smell of patchouli and jasmine emanated from the hidden females. The smell of women was intoxicating to the men, who scratched themselves excitedly.

'Ali's mother, and his wife and children are here,' cried Haseem, hugging his friend. 'And even his new wife.'

He gesticulated wildly.

'She asked to come. Ali gave permission. You see them! He is a modern man!'

He pointed at the screen.

There was a moment of silence.

Not a sound came from the heavily carved wooden area.

Lucia asked to meet the women.

More debate and frantic hand gesturing - they discussed her openly. She was so ugly, walking about like a man in the market.

It was agreed that she was too unattractive to damage the harem. None of them could want to be like her.

Ali was beginning to see some disadvantages to the visit. He did not want his women corrupted.

His friends egged him on, after all, who would want to live like her? Her hands! So coarse! Her blond hair, cut short!

Everyone spoke at once, shouting each other down. It sounded like a vicious altercation to the intimidated Lucia although it was a friendly discussion. After several minutes of hubbub, there was relative quiet as Haseem translated for his friend.

343

Of course she could meet all of his wives, he offered unctuously.

Ali spoke to her in French for the first time, he was obsequious, his home was her home, and she could visit anywhere she wanted, as an honoured guest.

Lucia thanked him equally profusely. The honour was all hers. The host pressed her forward touching her intrusively on her back, as if she was a man.

Ali's eldest son, a young boy, about 5 years of age, escorted her behind the screen with the proud, strutting step of an adult.

There was silence.

Everyone strained to hear what was said. Lucia stepped through the dark intimate rooms of the house to the zenana, where the smell of stale perfume and sweets spices was overpowering.

It was quiet and hushed, heavily carpeted, and very dark.

The space behind the carved partition was small, dark and dreary, allowing an indistinct view of events on the other side.

The women sat on the floor in a tight group, like corralled sheep, on ravishing carpets laid out on the floor.

Each woman wore lacy veils and heavy eye makeup. However, the draperies were wilted from constant washing and had the appearance of bandages.

The area seemed dingy and the air was stale and choking. It smelt rotten under the heavy cloying perfume.

The tight group sat away from the partition, which rendered the men almost invisible.

They stared at Lucia with wide, child-like eyes.

The women were surrounded by several children and held babies. The children ran around silently, cared for by African slave-girls who knelt with their heads held low, not looking up.

Plates of sweets lay around, with flies buzzing over them.

Lucia greeted the ladies. They did not reply, instead touching their foreheads, looking down modestly, and giggling, almost silently.

Lucia came closer.

She crouched down to meet the seated women, and suddenly Ali's mother shouted in a loud cackle.

'It is a man!'

The men did not say a word, waiting to see what the wives might add.

'Sit! Sit with us,' the old lady shouted in Arabic. 'You belong here, not with the men.'

She dragged at Lucia's cotton dress.

'Cover up! You should be ashamed of yourself.'

Lucia did not understand the Arabic and was afraid.

She tried to back away. The old lady dragged at her skirt. She dragged so violently that Lucia thought it would tear, and tried to prie it from the women's claw-like grasp.

'Sit with us!' she repeated in a rasping voice. 'Sit!' she screeched, 'sit!'

Lucia was frightened.

'Please stop!' she begged in French, 'let me go.'

There was a murmur from the other side of the screen, which Lucia could not make out.

Being in that prison cell was like under water.

Ali's eldest boy, the fat five year old heir who had escorted her, was ordered by Ali to rescue the visitor.

He entered officiously and smacked at his granny's arm hard. He commanded her to let the man-woman go in a shrill, loud voice.

She did so instantly.

As Lucia scrambled out of the space she was followed by cries of the old woman.

'She is naked!'

She shrieked through the screen in a cracked voice.

'I saw her legs.'

She laughed loudly and coarsely.

'Legs like a herder, tanned and strong. Why did you bring her here? Take her away. She is a bad example to my daughters in law.'

There was an embarrassed silence.

Lucia hurried out and left, blushing furiously.

As she exited, she noticed a very young girl sat slightly apart, not more than 14.

She was the new bride, and she was happy and content. She smiled with the great eyes of a lapdog, a cherished pet.

The older wives looked defeated. They were caged birds, with clipped wings.

They stared at each other with open curiosity until the boy tugged at her hand to leave.

She stared at the women with the startled eyes of realisation. There was no way she could have married Dania. There was an irreparable gulf between the cultures. As a female, she could never have crossed it.

Lucia left the tea party almost immediately afterwards, and the Arab men agreed that the meeting of women was not a success.

*

The wives were warned not to ever attempt to dress or behave like the abomination they had seen.

Lucia finally understood that she and her mother had been treated like honorary men in Kazakhstan.

This was a world where men had a wonderful time, whilst women lived a life of darkness, trapped in cages, and riven by jealousy and conflict.

She felt deeply discomposed, and finally understood why Dania had reacted to the smallest sign of free-thinking.

She was struck by the fear in the women's eyes and knew that they had all been beaten at least once in their married lives. It was normal to them, acceptable, or at least to be borne. She realised that this would have been her fate if she had given in.

Independence in the zenana was unthinkable.

She was silent and thoughtful all the way home.

She never saw Haseem again, and did not return to the racecourse. They avoided each other.

She was relieved of regret over leaving Dania and laid the ghost of lost love to rest.

She finally understood and mourned her mother and realised that a lot of the things she said stemmed from wisdom born of experience.

It was time to turn her attention to the future.

*

The tiny community of wives were a hive of gossip, so Caleb was already aware of the visit to an Arab home.

By consorting with natives she had crossed the line.

He returned earlier than usual, hugged her and sat down to his meal, cooked by the Sudanese maid who came with the apartment.

Lucia felt confused and lost.

The atmosphere between them was strained and fractured. They spoke very little during the meal.

At last they sat down on the ottoman.

Caleb did not know how to introduce the subject of her behaviour. He had married her for reasons of honour. He had agreed to look after her and her child because he saw love as a lifetime commitment.

He was not sure that she was truly honourable any more.

*

'Caleb,' she asserted, 'I have been working things out. We need to be connected to the land. Rooted in it.' she understood what her mother had meant at last.

Caleb looked at her dumbly and nodded.

He had similar ideals without words to put them into.

'The key to freedom is to given freedom to women.'

He knew men should be equal and women too but she was talking radical stuff. Did she mean to take a lover?

Or was this some political stuff? He'd heard she might be a commie. He did not want to be branded a commie.

Tears of regret ran down her face.

'My mother always said that.'

He suspected her mother had been political creature who would cause him trouble.

He looked at her face and thought of the lands his tribe had lost. He recalled the Indian myths taught him by his mother and it made him confused and tired.

'Hmm,' murmured Caleb.

He was already dozing off. He couldn't help it. He was falling asleep.

'My mother was right,' she ranted, 'but, at Louvinka, people were not free.'

Caleb collapsed on the sofa snoring lightly; she shook him awake.

'Freedom is frightfully important. We need to be emancipated and to do what we want. Women do!'

347

He turned over.

What was she talking about? He was not ready to give her any more freedom.

It was very disappointing. She was not committed to the relationship in any way. He could not be bothered with it. He had given up.

She was annoyed.

'The land needs us to be free!'

He was not ready to give her any more.

He turned back to her, hugged her to him and muttered 'gnff.'

They were moving in different directions.

Lucia got up. She could not sleep and listened to the radio until she was sleepy then got into bed. Everything was about freedom.

Her husband stayed on the sofa until about 3.00am and then snuck into bed.

*

He got up in the morning while she was asleep and left.

He looked down on his sleeping wife. She was beautiful, and he fancied her. She was not the right sort, she was a commie and immoral, like all commies. Their marriage was over.

12.

Cairo 1943

Caleb had become morose and silent.

His friends no longer mentioned his bride. It was obvious that the marriage was over and it was just a question on who to cite on the divorce papers.

'Can't put an Arab on the papers old boy. It wouldn't be right.'

Behind his back, they quietly discussed the earlier rumours that she was a hussy with a stranger's bun in the oven and shrugged.

Such things were pretty common in Cairo, although extremely painful for the protagonists. Of course her unfaithfulness could be proven without much fuss, even though such matters would normally take years of sorting in a peaceful world. War-time conditions were intense: love, marriage, divorce, widowhood, pregnancy, and death - all could happen within a day or two.

Caleb gloomily spent the evenings at the bar, nursing a long line of whiskey shots.

Maybe he had got the woman totally wrong. He reflected that she just the kind of female who would not give him a second glance in Canada. That was part of her attraction - that, and the fact that she deliberated over principles.

Perhaps he had not understood her? His ice-hockey team mates had affairs with such pale, ice-cold ladies and described them as utter bitches.

*

Lucia was also making life changing decisions based on what she learnt from her visit to the Egyptian household. She was conscious how close she was to losing him.

While Caleb sat in the bar thinking how to divorce his new-found wife, she was sitting at home, writing draft after draft of notes. She wanted him.

*

That night he staggered home, slightly drunk and knocked.
No answer. He unlocked the door.
The apartment was empty. Without. Minus. She had gone.

349

A note lay on their bed, neatly folded.

I love you, it pronounced, *but we cannot stay together.*
Lucia.

The writing was blurred with tears.

All he could think of through alcoholic fumes was that she *did* love him.

He tried to sober up. Where could she be? The place was quiet, empty and tidy.

He looked through the trash; it was full of crumpled paper. He extracted the crumpled and torn scraps from the bin, and painstakingly pieced them together.

All of them started with '*I love you*'.

For a moment, that was all he could see; words that she had never used, although her body had sighed it over and over again. His heart softened.

I thought I loved Dania, one scribbled, *but I didn't at all.*

He stretched out luxuriously, satisfied. She loved only him. He had ousted the past.

He tried to take in the details in the other notes. How much she pitied the locked-up women in the zenana – how she was certain that Dania would kill her. Blurred and faltering details of Anatoly's beatings and mistreatment, she had been an empty shell for a long, long time.

He sighed. His tribe were silent over such matters - more dignified that way. He knew that this was the experience of many Indian women who left reservations. He understood.

He sprawled at the frail and insubstantial desk, inlaid with rare woods, scented with camphor. Torn and crumpled papers surrounded him; articulating her broken life. He brooded over the confessions earnestly.

She had rebuilt herself; refused to kill her child. She was idealistic, clever, classy and beautiful. She disdained the rampant racism in Europe and had hacked out a set of ideals to live by. She was a woman in a million. Hell yes! He wanted her.

Slightly more sober, he swept away the messages.

He was sure that he loved her. They would heal each other, and undo some the pain. It would be like the dreams he trailed through just before sleep.

*

The past was understood - not forgotten - forgiven and therefore no longer important. He rose with energy and purpose. He had to find her before she was kidnapped by another - possibly better - fate.

He headed for the women's barracks. He was sure she would be among her old friends, the centre of commiserations, plans, comfort and tears. There, nightly, young women sat up gossiping after curfew. They assessed impossible romances and evaluated the latest breakups, smoking cigarettes and downing illicit alcohol.

He strode past couples lying in the dunes copulating and located the semi-official break in the barbed wire around the compound.

He knocked on the window and called her name.

Tomorrow's gossip was breathless and waiting.

There was a tense silence punctuated by whispering.

'She's not here.'

'I know you're there. I need to speak to you. Come out now. Please?'

There was more whispering. Yet no movement.

He refused to leave, and rattled the shutters. It would alert the military police. She *had* to come out.

After a pause the window shutter unlocked and she clambered out.

'Why are you here?' She asked, dangerously calm. There was a break in her voice.

'You claimed you want to be free'. He was still a bit tipsy. The one electric light shone its parabola across the hot sand. It seemed dazzling. He drew on a cigarette to keep cool.

Her face was tear-streaked and defiant. She loomed over him and snarled.

'You hate me!'

'I don't.'

She opened the door and leapt on him like a heavily pregnant panther, no less vicious for her pregnancy.

Caleb clasped her tightly to him, observing her despair in the acid

351

lighting. He kissed the biting, scratching fury wherever possible and she made little headway against his strength. He was tender, hugging her tight and gently transforming ferocity into consuming sorrow.

The girls were staring and whispering from the window. Neither of them cared.

'Do you still love me?' she choked and hiccupped. 'I did so many bad things.'

He whispered words she had guessed, stopping to kiss her as they returned home through the silent base.

The base was silent. The lights in the dorm turned off all of a sudden. Curfew was on and the base shut down for the night.

Window screens were shut, although there was no glass.

They walked back in the dark, staying as silent as possible.

Every now and then Lucia howled out in grief and he tried to shut her up by holding her close.

They wanted each other.

'I want to start again,' she keened. 'I am so sorry. Please can we stay together?'

She nuzzled his neck, imbibing his smell.

'I love you. I always did.' He squeezed her closer. 'You knew, I suppose.'

Despite their intimacy, they had never admitted their feelings. It was a heady mix under the shining desert stars.

*

Afterwards, Caleb spoke in his slow measured way,

'You asked for freedom, Lucia.'

She smiled in the dark. He was the most laconic yet meaningful person ever.

'I wanted to thrash those sleazy guys. They did not respect you.'

Lucia blushed in the dark. She was haunted by the silence in that great riad as she had returned from meeting the women behind the screen. She closed her eyes and buried the past.

'We will start a new kind of life,' he said.

She listened in peace and sleepy contentment to his description of the beauty of Canada.

She grasped at the dream. It felt real. The baby kicked hard and she felt warm and alive.

*

The next day she was in labour.

It was a boy, tiny and blond, with deep blue eyes, nothing like Caleb.

He looked full-term. Both parents agreed he was a seven months babe.

They called him Misha, Misu for short, a name which worked for both Russians and American Indians.

13.

Stalingrad Train Station 1944

Sofia joined the million or so civilian refugees who survived the battle of Stalingrad, homeless and destitute, with little hope of succour. They inhabited storehouses and ruins, scavenging the dead for food and valuables. Most were armed, and killed without mercy. They avoided soldiers. Soldiers were quite capable of using civilians as mules, running messages or carrying timed explosives.

The Soviets were victorious, although there was little confidence in the liberation. People obtained news along the grapevines which had been established early on in battle. Women were still being raped, even grannies, and soldiers were blowing up buildings without evacuating civilians. Citizens were robbed of watches and rings scavenged from dead Germans.

The rat-packs scavenged by night. They did not stick together, and formed and reformed around the battle front as opportunities arose.

Nevertheless there was some sense of community. Packs cooperated to fend off soldiers around crashed or bombed German transports. Large numbers were necessary to pillage in safety. They were merciless to wounded Germans, dragging off watches and food packs, ripping out gold teeth and wedding rings, stripping them naked in minutes. They were beaten to death with rocks or torn apart. The dead fared no better. A warm coat did not remain on a corpse even if covered in gore.

As a kind of peace was established, the groups broke off to create tiny settlements as close as possible to where they had once lived.

Sofia had nowhere to go. She turned South in the hope of reaching Iran. She was too late; most Poles had already left. She could not find transport, and, in her forties and pregnant, she found walking difficult.

*

She ended up back at the derelict station where she had spent most of the battle. It was under reconstruction, the scene of multiple troop movements. Tents had been erected in the square and the building which held the sniper had been demolished.

She stole on to the lines, invisible in a black peasant outfit. She walked along until she found where a track which was in use, hoping to board a train in the dark.

She had not gone far before was dragged to an underground hide by one of the scarecrows.

They did not know her, or she them. The original denizens of the square lay buried by a bulldozer long ago.

'Where are you headed?' They asked urgently. 'Do you want to die? They think we are thieves and wreckers; they shoot residents on sight.'

Sofia explained she was heading out of the city.

'There is nothing out there,' they warned. 'Most refugees return here because at least here we can steal food.'

Sofia noted the American labels on packs of long grain rice cooking in their den. The smell was wonderful and she was starving. Her appetite had grown in pregnancy; she was nearly at term and still only a little swollen.

'I am heading out,' she insisted. 'They will be clearing the city. Rebuilding of the main squares has started. The party want the city rebuilt in order to show it has survived. There is shooting of scavengers in the centre. I am sure it will get worse.'

'Hah! Comrade Stalin can be proud of us. We love Russia and the Soviets,' the scarecrow replied. 'We fought for comrade Stalin. We killed many foul Germans.'

'Maybe we should report to the party?' her companion suggested.

'Not yet,' Sofia advised. 'Wait until the victorious party is re-establishing the city. At the moment they are killing looters. It will be a while before they start searching for survivors.'

The scarecrows spent a long time discussing her suggestions and making plans.

It was agreed to wait.

*

The band split up. Several felt inclined to head out with Sofia to find a safer location.

'Stay here until dark,' they recommended. 'You can board one of the outgoing trains. They do not search departures, only arrivals.

355

Some of us might come with you.'

Sofia ate and fell asleep.

She slept for 24 hours. No one woke her. It was common for people to sleep that long in those days. They had usually been awake and running at least as long.

She woke up hungry but refreshed.

It was night again.

She ate a massive mound of rice mixed with unidentifiable meat which tasted like rotten corned beef. Her stomach digested it gratefully. She packed cooked rice into her pockets and left for the station outside Stalingrad.

*

The dark freight line was a mass of fluttering shadows.

Young boys ran around unloading trains in the dark, stealing food and supplies. They were careful, and amazingly quiet, like moths. They did not take much, and seemed to know the paths which the soldiers took on patrols. Several times, when Sofia came too close to being caught, she was dragged back by hands which appeared from nowhere.

The denizens were tiny, ghostlike children, who asked her what she was doing.

She did not realise that she had been carefully searched. Her pockets had been picked clean of all the money she had gathered, though they left her the rice.

They loaded her onto a train, quietly and stealthily; she had paid for her journey already.

She lay in the dark, wondering if they had betrayed her, and then dozed off all the same. The train shunted off and she headed out of Stalingrad and away from the war.

Dawn revealed a truck full of tramps, children, and scarecrows like her. Some were returning to collectives; others just lived on the trains.

The occupants shared breakfast from pockets, careful to eat just enough to survive. There was probably not a spare pound of fat among the 10 or so individuals. Not one was greedy, or took an unfair share of the food.

The train, it turned out, was bound for Moscow. The hitchhikers were gambling that it was safer than Stalingrad, which was overcrowded with vagrants.

The train shambled on.

Orphaned children crawled around like lizards, clambering up the sides and on to the roof of the carriages, and leaping from carriage to carriage like athletes. Although illiterate, they knew the trains, by the shapes colours and truck descriptions. They fought, bickered and bullied each other.

Sofia, dozing in the corner, woke to hear a child shrieking in agony. He was held down while an older boy burnt an abscess on his leg with a German cigarette lighter.

Sofia intervened, and the tiny rats turned on her, kicking, biting, and intending to push her on to the tracks. They held her at the open door like determined assassins, waiting for a steep embankment to drop her to her death.

Sofia addressed the boy who had the lighter.

'You should not treat his leg in that way,' she insisted quietly, 'he could get blood poisoning. I am a trained nurse. I can deal with it.'

The boy glowered suspiciously.

She repeated, 'I am a trained nurse. I can help the child.'

He spat on the floor.

'I ran away from a medical unit. I am a nurse. I cannot follow the battle. I am having a child.'

The boy felt her stomach expertly and called to his crew.

'Let her go,' he ordered. 'She says she can help Peta.'

Sofia was heaved back from the open doors; the world swam to normalcy as the adrenalin left her system.

'She says she is a nurse.'

He turned to her and snarled. 'Prove it bitch,' he warned, 'or die like scum.'

The children surrounded her savagely. They yelped and growled like tiger cubs, no less vicious for being cute. Her death sentence was not revoked; only delayed.

She requested a knife and was handed a vicious flick-knife, which she carefully cauterised with the German lighter proffered.

Fascinated youngsters crowded round so she could scarcely move. They carried German knives, broken bottles and shanks of

357

every kind, and dressed in an odd assortment of cut down uniforms, jewellery and even formal military evening dress, all looted from German columns. They swigged vodka from hip flasks with swastikas on them.

'Back off,' she asked.

The tight phalanx retreated a few inches.

The tiny child whimpered quietly as she inspected the abscess. The burn was superficial.

She sought for clean clothing and materials in the carriage. There was none to be found.

'This is an abscess,' she told them. 'It is caused by infection. It needs to be drained. It must be kept clean.'

She inspected at the row of dirty faces. They had no idea.

A red track on the child's leg showed that blood poisoning was hours away.

She pushed them back a few inches. The tiny child snivelled and mewled like a wounded animal. She scarcely heard, inured to moans of every kind by her stay at the front.

'Hold him,' she commanded, hefting the knife expertly.

Twenty hands grabbed the boy in an iron grip.

She cauterised the knife again. She asked for vodka, and poured it onto the wound.

The boy howled in agony while in the meantime his companions laughed and chittered in anticipation. They offered him vodka, which she refused to permit, but gave the child a rag to bite on.

'Bite it,' they chorused, like tiny dictators. 'Bite, bite,' they chanted, a rabid mob, anticipating gore.

'It's a minor operation,' she announced.

They purred like predators.

'Operation!' they chanted, 'blood! Cut his leg off!'

The boy struggled - they held him fast.

She took the knife and cut into the flesh.

The abscess was ripe, and out popped a volcano of green pus.

The boy screamed.

The mob collapsed into chaos. Some wept; others fell on her, punching and kicking until stopped by their leader.

It was a minor riot.

'Wait!' shouted the leader, 'the operation is not ended.'

Order resumed.

The howling boy tried to sit up. He was held down as she squeezed out the remaining poison. She poured a drop more vodka onto the area, advising him to leave it open and clean.

'Wash it with vodka for the day. Keep it clean and open to the air.'

There were raucous shouts. Every child had a container of vodka on their person, which they patted suggestively. They were tiny drunks, and many had the old wizened faces of alcoholics.

Regretfully, the boys let the patient go.

'I am cured!' he cried excitedly, 'I feel better. Look!' he shouted. 'I can stand.'

He wobbled to his feet, whereas he had been unable to support himself at all before.

'It will return,' she warned. 'You must eat properly. Keep cuts and sores clean,' she turned to the group. 'Use vodka to clean wounds. It kills bacteria.'

*

She spent the rest of the day lancing abscesses. The children were covered in them, and must have been in a great deal of discomfort.

They laughed like banshees over those in the groin. It transpired that most of them had infected wounds in embarrassing places, so there was no point pretending.

Their leader commanded a level of privacy in the truck.

The clamour died down and they went into the operation corner with bravado.

'I am no pussy,' they boasted. 'You won't catch me whimpering like Peta. He is a complete pansy.'

If anyone squealed or groaned as she cut into the ulcerated skin, there was a cacophonous shriek of derision from the playing children, who yelled insults and obscenities which would have shocked a soldier.

Towards the end of the queue, several boys proved to be girls. They hid themselves and begged her not to tell. It was dangerous to be female. They had boy's names, and were too young to distinguish on the basis of appearance.

All the children were sick and diseased, and over the next day she tried to deal with other injuries, infections and sores. Some had severe venereal diseases which she could not treat. She did her best, although she did not feel confident that many would survive the year.

By the end of the day, the children accepted that Sofia was all right. They piled on to her at night, seeking something in the shape of a mother to get to sleep.

As the train stopped at different depots, trundling along at almost walking speed, they showed her places to steal food. They shared takings with her, and explained which gangs ruled the tracks.

They were little murderers, without morals of any kind. Tramps entered the trucks at their peril - the children pushed violent drunks out of the carriage, using superior numbers against strength. Most scarecrows left, seeking out safer parts of the train.

*

Over the next few days they explained the complex culture of the tracks.

Carriages and trucks were marked with clan graffiti. Encroachers from other gangs were ferociously dispatched.

There were several vicious battles for control of the carriages on the journey. There was even a minor war, although Ivan's gang were only peripherally involved.

It started when a crew of older and stronger youths determined to rid themselves of the children, who interfered with gangsterism. They picked a truck at random, and attacked the children therein.

The disparate child-clans united to fight them off (they always cooperated to remove such threats).

Each truck had scouts on top of the train, and these ran to call on others, clambering across the top of the trains and whistling for assistance against adult invaders denoted by the code-word 'wolves'.

The allied children had strength in numbers and moved fast, while the hoods, heavily armed and slow, wasted time on intimidation.

The fight spanned several trucks. Armed children clambered through the train, passing through and over Sofia's truck, where she cradled a small child who was feverish and dying.

She watched them, scrambling like monkeys; uncover a set of vile weapons from under the boards. Several sported terrible slashes and cuts, as they retreated and advanced. Scouts kept everyone informed of the fight.

'Five wolves in yellow!' they shouted and whistled to each other.

'One in the blue, with luger,' came back the cry.

They scampered around lightly carrying knives, glass bottles and guns. They had no mercy for wounded companions and were unafraid of death.

A hoodlum caught Kiril, a tall strong boy, and an admired clan leader.

'Stop!' he warned, 'or I cut his throat. We can negotiate.'

'Cut out my heart!' bellowed Kiril.

He turned to his crew, 'get him. Kill him quick!'

The barbarous criminal cut the boy's throat. Choking, and bleeding to death, Kiril pulled out a piece of broken glass and stabbed the older man in the leg.

Immediately, the rest of the children fell on him and cut him everywhere. He fell in a mass of blood and gore, and even then the smaller children did not cease hacking at him.

'This is for Kiril,' they shouted, and swearing furiously.

There were cheers and shouts as more children poured through the roof and sliding doors of the truck.

The floor was slippery with blood and they attacked the older man and his slow supporters with no thought of personal safety. They were irrational and totally irresponsible, like mad dogs.

The older gangsters retreated.

'We will get you for this,' they threatened each other.

However, it was obvious that even vicious criminals lacked the berserker instinct required to eliminate the children's dominance over the tracks.

*

Afterwards she listened to the protagonists discuss the horrors with excitement. The men had retreated, after losing several of their companions to horrific wounds.

'Kiril was brilliant. A hero!' they chattered. 'I want to be like him. He died a perfect death.'

361

They sang Russian war songs and the international.

So comrades, come rally
And the last fight let us face
The Internationale unites the human race.
So comrades, come rally
And the last fight let us face
The Internationale unites the human race.

Perhaps they really are the new human race reflected the glum Sofia, as she watched their flushed faces in the sunset.

They drummed on the walls and declaimed revolutionary slogans which they did not understand.

Permanent revolution!

The united clans returned to the scene of the battle, tossed out the dead and wounded and cleaned the floors of blood. They drank large gulps of burning vodka and rolled around drunk and laughing.

'We got a lot of them. Hurrah!' they babbled. 'We showed them. Maybe they will leave us alone after this.'

Victory to the proletariat!

*

The next day Sofia stitched up serious, deep cuts which she carefully cleaned with vodka and bound together until she could find a needle to stitch them.

The children sported their bandages proudly, and incorporated them into their savage costumes. They approached her with tiny cuts, several days old, demanding extensive bandages in order to appear tough.

A couple of hours later, they were tired, hung-over and sleepy.

They wept sadly, and Sofia tried to comfort their tears at lost companions.

'Why did we have to toss Lev onto the track?' they wept. 'Nurse could have stitched him up. Lev will never come back *and* he could write our names.'

They moaned and shivered over their losses. Sofia realised that Lev had been thrown out alive.

'Why did you do that?' she asked Ivan.

'There is no room for mercy,' he replied, imitating the talk of generals in Stalingrad. 'There is no room for dead weight.'

A quiet fell on the truck as they slept off their exertions.

She prepared food and listened to their stories as she travelled onwards. In most cases, their parents had died in war or famine. They were abandoned and without resources, depending on each other.

*

She arrived in Moscow, just as far from any kind of home as before. She joined the wild urchins in their den at the station.

She was their trophy and they kept her from sight, at a rarely visited part of the station depot, she tried to explain that she was heavily pregnant, and had to leave soon.

It was hopeless, whenever she mentioned departure; they reacted with a mixture of panic and violence. They cried, and threatened to kill her for sure. They would cut out her baby and she would die in agony.

Sofia needed a space to safely deliver her baby, yet she remained with the children, recognising their need. Their pinched and diseased faces told of the unlikelihood of long-term survival. For the time being, her role was keeping them alive.

They lived in crates, and cooked out of Billy cans, on fires made of packing material. They wore an assortment of stolen clothes and were ridden with lice and skin diseases.

Tuberculosis was rampant, and the youngest rarely survived. Sofia cleaned up the dens, cooked from the scraps they lived on. It was uphill work.

Fighting and theft broke up meals, and her soup was often spilled, because someone had been insulted. She asked them to steal medical-packs, and attempted to deal with injuries effectively.

*

It was an unstable, engrossing life.

Life-expectancy was brutally short and the children got as much into their brief lives as possible. They were mostly happy and smiling and the atmosphere was hilarious and fun. They played daredevil games, such as jumping and running in front of trains moving between sidings. They drank heavily, and she toured the station by night, picking up tiny children lying dead drunk on the rails. She could not blame them for the violence and their immorality. They were living life the bottom of a foetid social heap.

Sofia learnt that the station was in the control of several distinct clans, who had defined territories marked out by railway lines.

Fighting between clans was common and violent. Stabbings were a regular occurrence. Although everyone had guns, they were not used. Noise would attract attention.

The orphans had myriad connections to the criminal underworld which operated outside the station. They stole guns and ordnance which they passed to fences and vile men, who lived in darkness, and worked on tasks which were never discussed.

In the past, dying children had been abandoned outside the station. Now they were placed into Sofia's 'hospital'.

Instead of being left to die alone, the fatally injured were served strong drink by their mates and she sat with them until they died. Their dead bodies were dragged to a dump outside the station called the graveyard.

Their clan leader, Ivan, came from the South, his father and mother had run away from a collective in Turkestan, seeking a better life in Moscow. They had been shot on arrival as spies.

At 11 years old, he had a faint moustache. He was stronger than the rest, and the clan followed him everywhere.

She tried to teach then to pray, even though they had no idea of what god was.

'He is invisible and all powerful,' she explained. 'He will take you to heaven if you are good.'

The smallest children began to cry.

'We don't want to be good,' they howled. 'We don't want to be taken to heaven.'

She tried another tack.

'God is invisible. You will join him when you die.'

'Oh,' agreed Ivan knowledgably. 'The Grim Reaper, I have seen him creeping about. He steals souls and eats children's hearts. When we come to wake them in the morning, they are dead.'

The children were aghast.

Did she know him? Promise? Could she talk to him? Would she save them from him?

She did not know what to say, so she taught them the Lord's Prayer, which she could not say in Russian, so she made up a version which made some kind of sense.

They chanted it like a nursery rhyme, and treated it as a talisman to keep death away.

When a child fell on to the tracks and died one night. They all crowded round accusingly, 'he recited the Lord's Prayer,' they insisted. 'And the Reaper still got him.'

She tried to explain that the Lord's Prayer would keep him safe wherever he had gone.

After a great deal of discussion and argument they were satisfied with that the Lord's Prayer was a talisman at all times of danger.

If someone died, they assured, 'it's Ok. We said the Lord's Prayer. He has joined his mum and dad.'

Sofia was sure god would understand.

*

Within a couple of weeks things had become a bit more stable and organised. They brought her stolen food, and she cooked nutritious meals.

The children filled out and began to look a little better. The younger ones stayed to help her cook, and made a horrific mess.

She tried to show them how to live and had hopes that they would survive when she left.

It had to be soon. She was eight months pregnant, and although it didn't show too much yet, she was struggling to move about. The children were cleaner and healthier, and the young ones clung to her like babies far younger. She could no longer carry them, but if she sat down they clambered over her like kittens.

One night, Ivan shooed them off. He told her their secret. They had other problems than disease.

*

'Mummy,' he confessed, they all called her mummy. It was a little heart-breaking. 'You know that there are bad men here?'

She nodded. She had seen them lurking around their hide, whistling for Ivan.

'We don't like them, but they protect us.'

Sofia said nothing. She had seen the shivering children return in tears from visits to these men.

'They are doing things to us, both girls and boys.'

Sofia's heart fell.

'We do not like it,' he complained. 'Can you help?'

Sofia wept quietly.

She knew that she could do nothing. These were gangsters and paedophiles, men without compassion, who would kill them all. The children were helpless.

'We should move,' was all she offered.

Ivan agreed, and the little clan made plans to move elsewhere.

*

Even the slightest resistance to forced prostitution had a calamitous effect.

The plans to move went forward in secrecy. But children cannot keep secrets. They laughed and giggled at a new life and talked about a rosy future in Stalingrad. They gathered some of their precious belongings and gave away others. They refused to take on jobs for the gangsters.

A few nights later, as they dozed piled up around Sofia, whispering about the future, the police raided the shelters with a crash.

Winter was coming soon, and the Party declared it was time to deal with the wreckers who lived around the tracks.

In a nightmare of bright lights, shots and confusion, the children were taken away and Sofia was pressed into a waiting police van.

Sofia could hear their sobs and their cries as she sat locked up in the van in a night of horror and violence. It sounded like most of them were raped by the police.

After hours of waiting in a small cage, Sofia was taken to a police cell.

*

The arrested children never made it there, and she never learnt what happened to them. They may have been killed, or sold to the gangsters.

They disappeared from her life, though never from her prayers.

She had decided that her journey through Russia was a pilgrimage for peace and justice, and for the rest of her life, she tried her best to remember the injustice she had witnessed to those babes.

14.

Moscow 1944

Sofia spent a night in the cells with the badly beaten and poverty-stricken tramps caught up in the station sweep.

The police searched for social value in the dregs of humanity they had arrested, among them pianists, teachers and other social inadequates.

Those without social worth were shot.

When they came to assessing Sofia they were confused. She had already learnt to adopt the stance of an ancient crone and humble peasant and looked nothing like a gangster. They could not account for her presence among the gangs.

They debated whether to send her to prison as a Madame, or a criminal master mind. In the end they resolved to free her. They could make it in to a story which justified the raid.

'Sign this report. You were captured by those gangsters who used you,' they ordered. 'You are innocent, captured and enslaved by the evil bandits. They got you pregnant and intended to use the child.'

Sofia signed. She was photographed and finger printed.

The report was sent to head office and amended.

She signed it again.

More photographs were taken, together with weapons and instruments of intimidation.

They filled in her papers. They asked for her address. She gave her name and address in Lvov.

They gave her a passport. 'Go home. Leave town. Go back to where you belong. We have your details. Do not let us ever see you again.'

At long last, she had papers and somewhere to go!

*

Early in the morning, she walked to the station, which she knew well.

Unfortunately, it was crowded with police.

The Party were clearing out the beggars and the refugees who had congregated there during the war. They were using extreme methods, and she could hear the sounds of violent struggle all around.

The streets around the station were crowded with apparent loiterers. There were many in her position, hiding from police patrols, searching for somewhere to sleep

After half an hour's walking through streets, trying to appear as if she had somewhere to go, she approached one of the brand new apartment blocks on the edge of Moscow, new proletarian housing for workers. Each block was perfectly square and plain. Each apartment had a balcony from which fluttered newly-washed clothes. Each block had an underground space, which housed the communal boiler, a large laundry space and stores of wood and other materials.

Sofia wandered about purposefully, and then stole in. It was quiet and empty. She hid among piles of logs and fell asleep.

*

At crack of dawn she woke up to the sound of shrieking. The apartment concierge had found her.

'Thief!' she cried, 'You were stealing our wood.' She would be arrested or crimes against the people screeched the concierge. They were cleaning up the city from criminals like her.

Sofia insisted that she had not touched the pile of wood; she had only been sleeping against it.

The woman dragged her up a bare concrete staircase, knocking on doors.

'We have found the criminal!' she shrieked.

People tumbled out, half asleep before going to work. Apparently, someone had been stealing wood from the commune and selling it in the back market.

*

Sofia was dragged to a tiny apartment on the first floor. It was poorly lit and overfilled with furniture. Antimacassars covered every surface. Someone had been on a crocheting spree. There were plastic flowers in jugs, and piles of aluminum pans hung in the dining area.

Two men sat at the table.

Despite the early hour, they were drinking tea and vodka. There was a plate of gherkins cut into slices before them and rye bread with slices of hard boiled eggs.

'What is this?' they inquired. 'Trouble?'

The concierge shouted her accusations.

More doors opened in the hallway, and mothers and babies, workers in vests and grannies poured out.

The two men were knocking at the doors for an emergency meeting at the commune. Something was up.

In the hubbub that ensued Sofia tried to explain. She was trembling and afraid.

More workers piled into the tiny space.

After everyone had their say there was a lull.

She awaited her sentence.

'What shall we do with her?' The committee secretary asked.

'Arrest her,' they cried.

'What about using her?' he suggested. 'We could do with a cleaner for the toilets.'

There was a silence as the crowd considered the idea. 'Everyone complains about them,' he explained. 'She can perform social tasks to expunge her crimes. She can work as cleaner in exchange for living in our fine, clean basement.'

There was a loud burst of noise at this.

'What about the laundry?' they interjected,

'She can do it.'

'What about the kitchens?'

'She can get the food from the market.' someone added.

'We need her most,' each floor insisted, 'today,' 'now.'

*

Sofia expiated the 'theft' of wood by work as unpaid cleaner.

As criminal and outcast, she was given a list of chores to repay her social debt. She stood in the corner of the room as tasks, growing exponentially, were prioritised. The meeting went on for an hour.

Pregnant Sofia was desperate for the toilet. She asked to be excused, raising a noisy huzzah from her audience.

'See!' They jeered, 'use of our facilities. She must pay.'

'Add to the list!' joked a wag.

*

So Sofia, close to term, became cleaner for a commune. She lived in the basement on a pile of wood, and residents came down regularly to check if she had stolen any of their winter supplies. They accused her of petty crimes, and of theft from the house, and kept adding to the list as punishment.

*

The apartment block was a ghastly experiment in communism, compelling people to share basic facilities.

It did not work and it would never work well. The new facilities were already squalid when she arrived.

Each floor shared one kitchen, which no one cleaned, and one shower, which had a rota. Each apartment had a potty, and there was one toilet per floor.

The toilets were disgusting, and people called her at all hours, insisting that she unblock them, or remove drunken vomit.

Residents came downstairs constantly, picked over her tiny pile of bedding, and searched her belongings, accusing her of stealing pens, papers, newspapers, socks and anything which was lost.

She was permitted to keep some of the food which she purchased for each family. She lived off scraps.

Even so, lazy individuals happily dropped round to partake of food she had cooked.

'That smells good. It actually belongs to me,' they claimed, dipping their spoons in for tasty morsels, 'you have not worked for it. You are a beggar living off honest proletariat.'

When she had finished her daily tasks, she was parcelled out to one family per evening, to pick up children from the crèche and do the ironing while they went out.

Women came down to chat and ask for a little favour, in exchange for a kopek or two.

She often had a couple of sick children left in her keeping when parents went out. The nursery refused sick and contagious babies, so she might spend all day with a crying sickly baby, while also cleaning kitchens and toilets.

It was the hardest work she ever did, probably because she was heavily pregnant. She had little strength and was often forced to sit on the steep stairs because she felt dizzy. If she was found, they shooed her off.

'Lazy beggar!' they cursed her, and pushed her up to do their work.

The intimate living arrangements caused terrible arguments, and protagonists tried to pull her in all the time.

They hauled her upstairs.

'Sofia! Comrade! Tell them that the potatoes were boiling here five minutes ago. Tell them! You saw them didn't you? Thieves!'

Sofia could not say yes or no, and this made her enemies. The only way to gain favour was to lie, and expect payment for it. No one was rewarded for truth - that was *too* obvious. Making a lie sound like truth – that was kudos!

*

She spent hours alone in the draughty basement, too enfeebled to do much other than sleep.

Solitude allowed her time to think about the 'many hells' Yuri described.

This particular communal 'hell' had been created by the socialist builders of new society. It was designed to sweep away elitism, and replace it with science and equality.

The ideology of total egalitarianism was intended to fill every aspect of daily lives. At the same time the ideals of a perfect scientific existence meant their leaders acquired total power by controlling every aspect of the lives in their care. They directed the revolution from the abandoned palaces which once held exploiting aristocrats, while the nation struggled to find a means to survive.

Sofia listened to the arguments over every aspect of life in the commune, even over the use of the bathroom, and feared for the future.

*

She was trapped in the commune for four long weeks; paying back a half hour's sleep in the wood pile. She lived like a slave, and was treated as one. She did not escape because she was tired and pregnant, and she was, at least, safe.

The apartment dwellers were aware of her pregnancy though she made sure that no one knew how advanced. She could not rely on these hard people, toughened by the conflicts they faced daily. She feared that they might throw her into the street in labour.

It was her fifth child, and was born easily in spite of her state of emaciation and weakness. She had twinges for two days, and had to stop regularly to let them pass. The baby arrived almost as soon as she sat down to rest, as if she had been holding it in.

She threw the placenta into the bin, and lay exhausted, swaddling the baby in her dirty sheets.

It was a boy, and perfect. He scarcely cried and fed while she slept with him in her arms, and did not move an inch. He struggled occasionally, yet slept content. He was the calmest baby.

'Sergei,' she whispered. And put some saliva on his forehead, 'I christen you Sergei.'

*

She overslept and missed her chores.

That evening the workers returned from their labours, expecting pots washed and potatoes peeled - nothing.

The committee trooped downstairs to complain. They found Sofia with her child, lying like a kitten that had its litter.

'Oh! The beast has bred,' they sniggered.

Sofia was staggeringly weary after the birth; hormones were bringing her down. Tears leaked out of her eyes.

'I suppose we can let her off for one day,' the committee member conceded,

'She dirtied our wood supplies,' complained another, disgusted by traces of afterbirth on the floor.

'Another period of social reintegration is needed. We will arrange your timetable again.'

They muttered amongst themselves.

One of them added, 'we will send an extra blanket for the baby. Only you must pay for it in work.'

They left, complaining loudly about the state of the kitchens and how tired they were.

*

One of the committee remained.

Martha was something of a commune sexpot. She was a pretty woman, with a spine curvature which would worsen with age.

She was flirtatious, and had several cavaliers. She lived in the commune with her brother, who took care of her, as she could not do any heavy lifting. They were close, but her marriage prospects were low, and her brother would wed soon. Her future was bleak.

'Can I see the little one?' she asked.

Sofia assented.

She picked up the baby and stripped the sleeping boy without asking. She carefully inspected him, particularly his spine and legs.

She laid him naked on his blanket. His tiny arms waved around as he sought his mother in his sleep. A tiny dribble of milk leaked from the corner of his mouth. Sofia picked him up and fed him. She resented Martha's behaviour. She remained silent. She was a slave, and helpless.

'I cannot have a child of my own,' Martha admitted quietly. 'I want yours. I will pay.'

Sofia was silent, exhausted.

After a long silence, she whispered, 'I will think about it.'

'Make up your mind soon,' Martha warned, 'I want him while he does not know you. He is calm and quiet; I could not bear it if he wailed.'

She walked off, turned back and stated.

'He is mine. If you do not give him up, I will report you as a vagrant. Hand him over to me or he will end up in an orphanage.'

*

After Martha had gone Sofia dragged herself up. She fell into a bout of frantic activity, drawing on her last resources.

She had not rested properly after the birth, still she had to leave. She already had an escape plan. She wept as she gathered her belongings.

It was for the best, even though she had nowhere else to go. It was not feasible to keep a baby around such repulsive work. She wished she had one more day to rest.

She left at 2.00 am, as the proletariat slept.

She arrived at the station at 3.00am and crept around, looking for a train to jump into.

It was full of the same flitting shadows, and the patrol routes seemed to be unchanged.

She found a train heading west out of Moscow. She piled in, fed the baby, and slept.

There were tramps on the train, women, children and soldiers returning from the front.

They shared food and were endlessly kind to her.

She was immensely weak, and remembered being carried from one train to another in the night, clinging on to her baby.

Someone, probably a soldier, whispered, 'you were on the wrong train, Madame. *This* one is going to Lviv.'

15.

Cairo 1944

Katya married in Cairo, already seven months pregnant.

Bartosz insisted on a big party with free drinks.

Army staff were surprised that he married, and questioned that it was his child. Katya did not care. She had won her object and got out of the army. Her new life had begun.

Her husband had no intention of staying faithful. He had an Australian girlfriend and a Canadian boyfriend. He also visited the Cairo catamites. He was, after all, a superior man, to whom rules which bound others did not apply.

The marriage and child gave him a renewed freedom. It allowed him to claim he was a virile male and, for some odd reason, enhanced his desirability in the gay community.

Katya visited camp and overheard the gossip.

She passed by two English officers who didn't lower their voices much. They had won the war and were intensely arrogant about the Poles, who they regarded as rather milky and incapable of putting up a good fight for their own country, necessitating urgent baling out and taking on the cad Hitler.

Poles were also notorious for fighting dirty and killing wounded Germans, generally going a bit berserk in battle.

'There goes that bally Bartosz's chicklet. Very heavy isn't she?'

'I say, do you think it was actually *his*?' said the first, a twirling moustachioed fellow with a weak chin.

'Shh.'

'They don't understand a word anyway, old boy,' his friend hemmed, 'a bit thick don't you know?'

Katya walked by. She was above that kind of gossip yet listened intently.

'I wonder if she knows about Sally.'

There was a moment's hush as she walked past. Then they continued, in her full hearing. She was not expected to understand a word.

'What about the duke, don't you know? They are having quite a fling.'

They were referring to one of the gay officers, who was 'head over heels' over the flamboyant foreigner. The 'duke' was an officer in the army. His wife was at home in England and he was indulging in numerous flirtations with both sexes. Such crushes among British officers were fine so long as they were never consummated. Flirtations of that kind were accepted, particularly if the parties involved were married.

'Plain little thing, isn't she?' stated one of the officers, 'I heard he didn't want to marry her and tried to get out of it...'

Short of stopping she could hear no more.

*

Katya's ambitions had adapted to her new surroundings. Her life revolved around being respectable and bourgeois. However, she had a lot to learn.

A straying lascivious man was a completely novel peril. She grew desperately worried about being abandoned, which would lead to an immediate and fatal loss of status.

She attempted to control him using dangerous and subtle subterfuges. They had no effect. The closed society of the communist party was quite different to this open gossipy one. Vicious rumours that he liked weird sex only made him seem like a wild hedonist. Even the idea that he had a disease did little harm. He was bullet-proof in his self-confidence.

She bribed Bartosz with fine food and alcohol. Although he often appeared wildly drunk, he did not drink or eat that much. It made him ill, he explained, it affected his eyesight and balance for days afterwards.

She tailed her husband secretly and discovered that he was interested in pre-pubescent boys.

There was an illicit gay scene in the local market. Young Arab children cast flirtatious glances at men, seeking money in exchange for 'fun'.

Such behaviour would have meant execution in the repressive Soviets. She despised the West for allowing it to occur. At least if he stuck to children he was unlikely to leave her.

*

Oddly, Katya found Bartosz desirable and attractive, even though he largely ignored his new wife, or perhaps because of it.

She was not happy with her loss of power. The idea of motherhood alarmed her. She, who strode about the steppes like a queen, inspiring deadly fear, did not feel at all attracted by the idea of being at a baby's beck and call.

Pregnancy did not suit her. The heat and woman-unfriendly culture of Egypt made her depressed.

Pregnant women were isolated from army life. They lived outside the base, sat by the pool making fruit baskets and sewing buttons on shirts. They sat by the pool chatting with other females who dandled young infants. They were glowing and happy to talk about every detail of birth. Katya did not join in. The idea of maternity made her sick.

She was troubled, not by guilt, but by the fear that her crimes might be exposed. There was talk of holding the Germans to account for war crimes, and such an idea terrified her. Surely the Germans had only been involved in social engineering? They had a scientific case for their behaviour, just like the Soviets.

The idea of human rights did not appeal to her at all. She did not understand it. Humans could be manipulated by scientific principle, so long as they were of the highest. How could that be wrong? The Germans were being tried for the incorrect reasons. Surely they should be tried for attacking the Soviet experiment and pandering to the capitalists in charge?

*

She visited her sister. 'I don't want this child,' she moaned. 'I hate him. Take him from me. Adopt him.'

Anya considered her sister dispassionately.

Anya had always been jealous of her sister in the past, no longer. In the organised and wealthy pre-war days, Katya had been judged far more intelligent. There had been no hope of Anya getting a scholarship. She still remembered the harsh assessment of her Jewish grandmother, hard as flint, and tactless as only the rich can be.

Rebecca had looked her up and down then proclaimed, 'marry her fast, before she fades. She is a picture of her father, not a drop

378

of Braun.'

Anya no longer felt inferior to her sister. *She* had survived the labour of Kazakhstan without compromising her morals. As for Bartosz, he represented everything that the communists had described of the decadent aristocracy destroying the Ukraine. He was a typical bourgeois saboteur.

'Of course I can help with the baby. It will be good practice for me. Though it might not be a boy,' she advised.

This made Katya even more miserable.

'I don't want a girl. A girl has too much of a burdensome life.'

Tears welled up in her eyes.

'Women have no future in this world. Anya, please take the child, especially if it's a girl. You will, won't you? I don't want to be a single mother. I can't bear the thought of bringing up a child alone.'

Anya commiserated with her sister. Bartosz was a no-good wastrel, unlike her own fine mate.

She was extremely proud of her fine, clean-living husband, who had arrived from Russia on the same transport as hers.

Unlike Bartosz, Edek would always be faithful.

*

Anya had a future. She was leaving for England and had registered for work as a seamstress, one of the jobs permitted to refugees. Katya's prospects were in doubt, particularly if the issue of war crimes arose. She had already resolved to say that she knew nothing of her sister's activities. She could prove that she was entirely innocent, living as she had outside the elite compounds reserved for party members.

Moreover, her husband Edek would protect her. He was a fine-looking man and an excellent obedient soldier. He never questioned orders and had the neatest uniform on the base.

Edek was tall and handsome, with a fine mop of straight black hair and an open countenance. He rarely drank and spent a great deal of his time with the other refugees for his commune.

Unbeknownst to his superiors, he was also a sincere communist.

'Comrade Stalin wants us to be a leaven for the corruption of the west.' he stated to his wife as he chastely held her hand. 'We will show them how good communists live.'

Anya agreed. She was shocked by the depravity of Cairo. She was rarely invited to parties and when she went to dances, she mostly spent her time sitting and chatting with a few other girlfriends while everyone else got drunk and danced for hours. It was noisy and dull. She had never been asked out by any of the westernized Poles and the English servicemen utterly ignored her.

*

There was only one cloud on Anya's otherwise sunny horizon. She hid her fears from her sister and hugged them close.

She was not even close to pregnant.

She and had Edek had been married for two weeks. They not had full sex yet.

On this first night of supposed bliss the boy sat on their bed in Cairo. He twitched and talked about Comrade Stalin and hidden secrets.

'Comrade Stalin chose us,' he sucked in his breath and breathed deeply, 'to be the Komsomol[19]. We are the vanguard.' His bright eyes sparkled as he remembered the heady days.

He breathed in heavily once again - a most irritating habit.

'We are revolutionaries. We lead the people.' He turned over, and hugged his wife slowly and then let her go. 'We must lead the people again here. We are the chosen, you and I.'

He snorted and twitched his trousers. 'We may be asked to make the ultimate sacrifice at any time,' he looked deeply at her. 'We must wait for our call.'

Anya was not sure how marital sex went. She was sure it was not like this.

They went to sleep that night and every subsequent night, evading and denying the issue of sex and intimate contact.

She would have been happy to take the child, only she was not prepared to admit that her husband had no interest in her.

---

[19] Youth organisation controlled by the communist party of the Soviet Union

16.

Moscow 1945

Janek's ex-wife, Basia, was a hero's daughter. She had standing in the party as her father had risen to general.

As one of the generals at Stalingrad her father was feted as a hero. As nomenklatura[20], so long as his position was safe, he could do almost anything.

He had survived the 1942 army purges, and recognised the danger of staying in Moscow.

Every single party member, every single Russian, shouldered the blame for their near defeat. The triumph of victory could not belong to the heroes of Stalingrad. Stalin needed to prove it was his alone.

The general needed to get away from the internecine battles which Stalin utilised to remove all opposition. He abandoned Zhukov[21] to his fate by wangling a posting to the Ukraine, rebuilding the Soviet. It was considered a severe demotion, almost exile

The wily old man appeared suitably distressed by the appointment, while breathing a sigh of relief that he had ensure the safety of his only daughter, if not necessarily his own.

His daughter, as a fine example of the revolutionary proletariat, was to live among the people, acting as leaven for the revolution,

*

Basia had briefly enjoyed a life of privilege in Moscow, wearing Western clothes and perfume, and watching foreign movies.

She was unenthusiastic when introduced to her new role. Even she could see the gathering clouds of party purges and accepted that the Ukraine was wealthy and Westernised compared to Moscow.

Neither she, nor her second husband, was Ukrainian. All the same, this was a good place to make a new life. Of course, she regretted leaving the exciting parties and fun. She would be powerful

---

[20] These were the party faithful who held all the highest and most lucrative posts available irrespective of talent or ability

[21] General Zhukov led the Soviet army to victory and formulated the policy of pressing on to Berlin. However Stalin resented his popularity and sent him to exile in Odessa.

and privileged in her new role. She foresaw a life of snobbery and superiority.

Janek's old apartment would suit her and her new husband very well.

*

One bright spring day in 1945, she invaded Janek's home.

The loud knocks spooked baby Maryssa, who had retained trace memories of events which had wiped out her family not so long ago. She started howling pathetically.

Basia entered the apartment, having obtained the master key from the concierge. She was accompanied by soldiers, and her baggage was in a military truck outside.

'Hello, Janek,' she yelled, 'Asleep? You lazy old man!'

Janek was definitely in bed, as it was 6.00am. His heart thudded as he heard Basia's familiar tones.

She walked into the master bedroom, where the four-poster and its complex swags remained. She was astonished to see the rough-built peasant cot in an alcove of the massive room containing a hysterical baby soothed by another woman.

She riled up immediately, and, paying no attention to the baby, started hollering at her ex. 'So, you dirty old man! You had another woman all along?'

Janek's new wife stared blearily at the overdressed plump peasant woman. A stranger was using the coarsest language to describe her!

She stood up in flash, cursing her right back.

The two peasants, one with improbably dyed and frizzed hair in the American style, and one with traditional, long black plaits, screeched like fish wives. They were utterly incongruous in that magnificent boudoir as they hurled abuse in the lowest language of the streets.

Their two spouses observed the fracas, highly embarrassed.

Basia's husband was a fine soldier with grand ambitions. His uniform and was covered in decorations, and he sported a slightly ridiculous captain's hat which reminded Janek of a tin-pot Latin American dictator. Despite his height and strength, he already had a belly, betokening the overindulgence typical of higher party echelons. He stared at Janek with the intense arrogance of victorious military streaked with confusion at his wife's appalling behaviour.

After five minutes of yelling, the two women exhausted their repertoire of insults. There was relative silence.

Maryssa's sobs became musical and quiet. Janek picked up his daughter and walked her up and down, hushing her tears.

The henpecked men observed each other.

Janek spoke. 'Basia,' he introduced her, 'this is my wife Eva. Eva, this is my ex-wife. I told you about her.'

The hot tempered Eva noticed the bevy of soldiers accompanying the new occupants. They were already carrying large boxes upstairs and piling them outside.

Basia glared at her triumphantly; it was obvious who had won.

'I have brought *my* husband home to *my* apartment,' she announced. 'Boris,' she addressed her husband possessively. 'We are home.'

Several of Eva's choicer insults rankled in her bosom. She checked the ornate gold mirror which took up almost the entire wall of one alcove. *Did* she look a painted harlot?

She swivelled on her high heeled shoes, comparing herself to Betty Grable.

A good Komsomol graduate, she self-consciously pulled down her short skirt, which revealed plump hairy legs sheathed in silk stockings. This outfit, she reflected grimly, had been fine in Moscow. This was the provinces. They weren't ready for fashion.

She remarked on missing adornments and signs of poverty in threadbare furnishings.

'Well, this is a mess!' she commented. 'You don't know how to look after the place do you?'

Everything had been sold in the war except paintings, heavy ormolu furnishings and chandeliers. A few French ornaments remained, too heavy to carry.

The two women bristled at each other.

Basia imitated the arrogance of German officers very nicely.

Eva, vanquished, yet spirited, tapped her foot and looked a million daggers.

Basia was coldly angry at the new woman. She had expected Janek to stay faithful.

Her rival was prettier and slimmer too (although her nightdress made her look like a peasant, one of the poverty-stricken populace).

Basia glanced at herself in the mirror, and simpered. She gloried in the modern suit with padded shoulders and short tight skirt once more. Her hair was puffed up in front and she wore a feathered hat and American shoes. Perhaps the red lipstick, which she had worn for Janek, was a bad idea?

'This is *my* apartment,' she affirmed smugly, putting down the smart new handbag. 'You Polish must move. I am Ukrainian. I have the papers.'

Janek and Eva resigned themselves to their fate, in the presence of military force.

The soldiers, urged in by Basia, now carried crates of possessions into the rooms.

'Here, for this one,' ordered Basia, 'no, not here!' she pointed at another, 'this is the kitchen equipment!'

She lorded it over them, like proper nomenklatura.

*

Janek and Eva were given four days to leave, while Eva traipsed in and out of the department at all hours arranging furniture and ordering repairs and new works. Basia and her husband were staying at army headquarters while the renovations took place.

They were allowed clothes and personal papers, not even books, written in Polish, bound in fine leather, could be removed.

As they collected their belongings together, decorators started to paint the walls a bright powder blue. The fancy plaster work was being gilded, turning the fine apartment into of a vulgar Hollywood film set.

Janek was upset.

Eva snapped him out of it. They were lucky to be alive.

*

They visited the Raikom, where builders were busy removing pictures of Hitler and swastikas and replacing them with pictures of Stalin. The smell of paint and disinfectant hung over the place and queues of Poles went round the block.

He gave in his name, which was checked off on a list. Ushers hustled him to the front of the queue.

'Priority case!' they bawled.

He and Eva passed families who had clearly been waiting for days. His extradition had been expedited. His papers were complete.

He had work in a post office in Wroclaw, on the other side of the country at a lower rank. This was no longer a part of Poland. All Poles were to move to parts of what was once Germany in a massive population shift.

There was living space for him in a coveted newly constructed commune. He was assured that it was impossible for him to bring wife and child.

He casually dropped the name of the General, and the extra room allocation miraculously appeared.

He was lucky; Basia was focused on moving in and did not care enough to torment him anymore.

Their expulsion was a minor example of the new level of intimidation that the Soviets had adopted, whereby Soviet party members treated themselves as superior to any ethnic minority, an attitude which would result in bloodbaths in the years to come.

17.

Lviv 1946

Sofia arrived at the central station at 5.00 am in 1946.

It was not quite summer, and her heart leapt as she recognised her surroundings.

For the first time in what seemed like eternity, she knew where she was! Everything was familiar.

She walked past the alcove which had once contained the half bust of her husband. It now ensconced the head and shoulders of Stalin.

Lviv, as it was now called, was lit by the drab dawn of impending peace. Armies moved through. Hitler had been chased to his doom but the battle for territory and colonies was on. The Cold War[22] had begun.

The city was being re-organised, as Soviet leaders displaced whole populations to create an empire which was easy to govern.

She trudged through ruined streets hoisting her baby on her hip. Everything was recognisable, despite being shattered and broken. Perhaps her old apartment was standing, and Janek was living there?

The streets had been renamed and the language was Russian, which she could read. It felt slightly unfamiliar. At least she knew where she was. She made straight for her parent's apartment, which was in the centre of town in a highly luxurious block.

It was still standing.

Amazingly, the same old caretaker and concierge lived downstairs.

Mikhail recognised her despite her rags, and accepted her bonny baby in an unsurprised comprehension. The child was blond. There were many such.

'Is he there?' she asked eagerly.

'Maslow,' he noted dourly. 'The apartment is occupied by your

---

[22] The cold war (1947-1991) was a period when the threat of nuclear war between the soviets and their satellite states and NATO was real. Weapons of mass destruction got bigger, had longer range and more destructive capacity.

son's wife.'

'Did he survive?'

'Survived,' he affirmed, blank faced, 'not living upstairs.'

'Oh please, let me speak to his ex-wife. Maybe she will know where he is.'

He nodded and let her go.

*

Sofia struggled up the stairs.

The door had been repaired. She knocked, trembling and anxious. She wanted to see her old home. The baby sensed her anxiety and kicked and punched her vigorously although he was generally a quiet child.

The door opened a crack.

'Good morning madam,' she said politely, 'I am Madame Maslow.'

Basia cursed and slammed the door in her face.

Sofia waited outside, unsure what to do.

The door opened again. This time a tall Russian man accompanied her.

'Beggars are not tolerated here,' he stated firmly. 'I must ask you to leave.'

'I am only asking about my son,' she stammered, 'not begging.'

'Scrounger!' he cursed her as only Russian soldiers can.

She listened to the torrent of abuse patiently. His cursing meant that they were prepared to dialogue. Otherwise she would be kicked downstairs, or he could call security and have her arrested.

'I have come to ask about my son.'

Basia appeared behind her husband.

'Silence!' she shrieked. 'Scum.'

'I have returned from Stalingrad.'

'Criminal!' Basia howled at the top of her voice, 'Prison fodder! Saboteur!'

Doors opened. People stood outside with folded arms, to beat out a Polish class enemy. Coming to reclaim her apartment? She had just better try!

The hallway was filling with the occupants, the new upper class. The luxury apartments were now mostly occupied by Russian

387

army officers and their wives, living in new-found opulence among goods looted from retreating Germans. They had every modern gadget including televisions, which could not pick up broadcasts, and were piled into the rooms, gathering dust.

Basia looked at the curious faces and dragged her in. She did not want anyone to know her business. She was a respectable woman. She warned Sofia that her husband held a gun and an iron bar, just in case her ex-mother-in -law planned an act of rape or murder. She held on to the stalwart soldier swooningly.

'Thank goodness my darling is here to protect me from saboteurs.'

*

Basia's residence in Lviv had changed her. Her hair retained its improbable blond hue and she had kept the red lipstick. Her facial hair was very dark, her eyebrows inexpertly plucked, and the lipstick slightly misapplied. The overall effect was alarming.

She hugged her husband and turned to Sofia.

'What is it that you want?'

'I have just returned from Moscow,' Sofia explained, 'Janek Maslow, my son. Is he alive?'

Basia wrung her hands.

'That wrecker! Just like his mother! He was from a wicked Polish family of thieves who stole land and housing from the Ukrainian people. This has ended. We Ukrainians have reclaimed our land at last. Justice has been done!'

Sofia said nothing, guessing that Basia based her new nationality on marriage to Janek.

She looked around her apartment. It had been luxuriously refitted with items from the German occupation. Even so, the fake Rembrandt had survived in its old place.

'You are Polish,' her husband averred, guarding his wife from the class trickster who had come to undermine her ownership. 'You cannot stay here. All Poles must leave. This is the Soviet of the Ukrainian People.'

Sofia reassured him that she made no claims to their property.

A bluff soldier, he understood where his hysterical wife did not and took her aside and provided minimal information.

'If you go to the town hall, the police will tell you where Janek has moved. Get out now and leave quietly or we will have you arrested.'

As Sofia got up to leave, Basia addressed her husband in a loud whisper.

'She is carrying a bastard, and at her age. It is an immoral family. I was pushed into marriage far too young; they took advantage of me. I was just a youthful innocent. Luckily, I have *you* now,' she cooed.

She clung to her husband romantically; keen to show Sofia how wonderfully she had done in life.

Her husband was embarrassed.

'Go now,' he said.

A maid had materialised from nowhere. She was a Ukrainian girl, and looked at Sofia compassionately.

She escorted Sofia downstairs and closed the door on her.

18.

Lviv 1946

Sofia went to the market to find out what had been going on in Lviv in the last four years.

No Pole could stay in the Ukraine, yet to move they needed papers, and a passport with a specific address on it to leave. This was almost impossible to obtain since the shattered towns did not contain sufficient housing. To obtain housing the deportee needed a job, but the state owned everything and employed everyone. To obtain employment, the individual had to have fine proletarian credentials.

She discovered that she had to visit the Raikom to find out where her son had been relocated. She had the address of her old apartment on her papers, and showed them to the official at the door.

'Polish or Ukrainian?' the official demanded.

'Polish.'

She was searched for weapons and sent to the queue of Poles.

*

Sofia spent the whole day in the queue.

Life in Lviv had become a series of queues, which were abruptly dispersed for little or no reason other than that they should reform six feet away, causing waiting people maximum stress and disruption.

The individuals in the queue moved backwards and forwards like sheep, directed by officials who barked at them. The sheep watched the dog-like officials carefully, careful to ensure that they did nothing which would trap them in the limbo of homelessness. They were made aware of their nonentity status at every turn - even the sweepers in the building brushed their feet with dirty water; they were dirt before the broom.

Old ladies came past selling overpriced soup and pickled cucumbers to the marooned.

There were rules:

No talking to officials, no disruption, no eating once inside the building. A ticket was necessary for a toilet stop, and this cost money.

It was early summer; people lay in the old stable yard so as not to lose their place, slept there at night on the frigid paving stones. Some fainted in the heat of the day were sent to the back of the queue for the inconvenience they had caused. Some broke down and complained at abuse of authority. They were arrested, returning to the back of the queue with additional bruises to show that they had learnt their value to society.

It grew dark; Sofia remained there all night with other desperate individuals who needed somewhere to go. Sergei grew heavy and restless, and she sat on the ground to ease her back. She used her petticoats as nappies. It was fortunate he was a baby, as he spent most of his time sleeping.

*

On the third day, a grimy and unwashed Sofia reached the office, escorted by an armed usher.

It was the same town hall. A gigantic picture of Stalin hung at the centre of the room and people were gathered around the samovar talking in loud voices.

The staff were on another tea break, and complained loudly about the inconveniences customers had caused.

There were three desks in the room, only one of which was occupied. Another two officials were apparently working so hard that they were invisible. There was a notice on each desk.

'Comrades! Our staff have the right to be protected from abuse. Saboteurs will be treated as they deserve'

'So rude, these Poles!' she heard. 'Such pigs! One had the cheek to say I had not told him that he needed proof of address. Such matters are not my problem, comrade, I said, you need to be more proletarian. This is a communist country. I am not here to wipe your arse. He shut up, I can tell you.'

Sofia staggered before the desk, blanched with fatigue. It was not her place to seat herself before such fine bureaucracy.

'Papers.' was the peremptory demand.

She gave her passport and papers to the woman.

'Proof of address.'

The woman tapped her foot impatiently. Sofia handed over her address.

'I have not come about my apartment,' Sofia explained. 'I shall not be living here. I need a permit to join my son in Wroclaw. I need a copy of his address too. He has moved there already.'

'Why didn't you say so? It is the other desk over there.'

The desk was vacant and showed no sign of being occupied. Sofia stood before it quietly.

'Next!' screeched the woman.

Sofia jumped away.

The lady hollered to her friend in coarse Russian, assuming Sofia would not understand.

'Bitch for you, Olga. Bitch with brat.'

*

Sofia stood at the adjacent desk for 15 minutes.

A woman sat down at another empty desk, as she stood waiting and coping with her struggling baby.

A novice bureaucrat, she watched Sofia for the tiniest infraction, which would allow her to send the pesky petitioner right to the back of the queue, to wait for a further three days.

Finally Olga walked by.

'Still here Olga!' called the woman at the second desk, daring Sofia to call out.

Olga wandered around the office humming and shuffling papers.

After 15 minutes a woman sat down at the empty desk with her cup of tea, ignoring Sofia and her struggling child.

Sofia's back ached; her son was hungry and pushed at her shirt.

'Next desk for enquiries,' she muttered.

Sofia shuffled to the third desk where the young novice was sitting and cleaning her nails.

Sofia almost collapsed. She tripped. And fell over the chair.

'Clumsy!' laughed the young girl.

The girl got up and walked off to cause suffering elsewhere. Her job appeared to be searching for minor infractions.

'Sit down,' ordered Olga.

A surge of relief ran through Sofia's body. The baby fed himself.

Olga now did a little work on her own manicure.

After another five minutes, her grooming seemed to be complete.

She placed a form on the desk.

'Fill this out.'

Sofia filled it out.

The completed form stayed on the desk for a further half an hour.

Sofia, raging with thirst, dared not move.

Finally Olga took it, glanced over it.

'I cannot read this. Fill it out in capital letters.'

Sofia did so.

It rested on the desk for a further half hour.

People waited outside silently, so as not to disturb Olga and her fellows at work.

The workers had snacks, tea and chatted in rooms out of sight.

Loud laughter could be heard occasionally.

Sofia tried not to fall asleep or faint. Muffled coughs could be heard from the queue.

At the next table, a Polish mother wept to learn that her family of five were ineligible for housing or work. They had had been queuing for 5 days and needed to leave within the week.

'You are not a proper worker,' the woman explained patiently. 'No town wants people of the wrong class.'

'I can learn,' the man begged.

His wife piped up.

'I am a cook and cleaner,' she offered. 'I have worked in restaurants and factory kitchens.'

It was obvious that she had made this up on the spur of the moment. She was indubitably a housewife.

The official paused, and scanned her list of proletarian jobs.

'This is suitable employment,' she admitted. 'We accept such good proletarians. Under official regulations, you may take your family with you.'

She glanced at the man, 'perhaps your spouse can come too.'

The children cheered, quickly silenced by their father and mother.

'Let me see. We are building a new town in Katowice. You are eligible. Do you want to go?'

They agreed.

Forms were laid on the table for them to fill in. They obtained the propisa and housing eligibility papers.

The official left to talk to her friends while they were completed.

'Will this work never end?' She whined. Her friends commiserated.

They both got up to have tea.

Olga, who had spent several minutes on Sofia's query, chatting with her friends, now returned.

She handed over an official paper on which Janek's new address was scribbled.

Sofia murmured thank you.

The papers allowed her to move across Poland, an unheard of success for a single jobless woman.

Several in the queue watched her with jealous eyes.

The woman waved her away.

'Cursed Poles!' she complained to her friend in the back rooms. 'I work my fingers to the bone and they are not even grateful.'

She went back to her nails as Sofia walked away muttering thanks like a schoolgirl.

19.

Poland 1947

Sofia had no idea how to get to Wroclaw, and she had no money.

She was a destitute, yet still graceful, slender woman with a pretty young baby with fat rosy cheeks.

Like all survivors in that upheaval, she had become a consummate actress, able to transform herself from middle class woman to peasant hag, bent double with infirmity.

For the moment she walked along the roads as herself, happy to be home. Sergei gurgled happily and she wore her rags elegantly and with dignity. It was hard to see that her clothes were stiff with dirt and her shoes were falling apart. Although her skin was like parchment, it was clear and healthy, and she had stunningly blue eyes.

She tried begging on the streets of Lviv without success. People stopped and shouted at her.

'Comrade,' shouted a man in rags. 'Are you not ashamed to beg? What are you teaching your young babe? If you do not desist immediately I will call the police to take your child away.'

She hurried off.

During her next effort, a woman spat at her.

'Why are you pretending to have no money? A prostitute! Comrades, observe her German bastard. Comrades! She wants us to pay for her immorality. She dares to beg here.' The woman worked herself into a frenzy of hate. 'German floozy!'

Sofia fled, trying to remember where beggars congregated.

She went to the central market, sat down in a corner, and fed Sergei. She was faint with hunger and thirst.

A group of beggars surrounded her, looming aggressively.

'Get up, woman! Go away!' they shouted, 'you give us a bad name.'

*

Sofia staggered off, faint with hunger, certain that she would die soon. Black spots appeared before her eyes.

Out of the mist before her eyes, an ancient Polish tramp

appeared. He led her away from the threatening mendicants, who had picked up rotten tomatoes to throw at her.

'I will take her with me,' he stated.

They calmed down immediately. 'She's yours then,' they said.

Sofia stumbled into a corner and the stranger fed her bread and water until she revived.

He explained that the vagabonds meant no specific harm.

'They are not angry with you scrounging, just how you represent us. You cannot beg as you are,' he explained. 'Begging is a job like any other. You have to put in the work.'

He introduced himself formally, shaking hands. 'My name is Cesar.'

The line of supplicants no longer bothered her once she was off their pitch.

He pointed out a shriveled husk of a man, wearing the veriest rags. His leg was putrid and rotten and the smell emanating from him was awful.

'No one gives money to someone who they consider better off than them.

'That gentleman was a university professor with a chair in Polish history. He cannot work. Poles have a stamp on their passport. He cannot leave either, as a class enemy. No Polish city will take him and no Ukrainian will employ him. He is a marked man.'

The husk of a man croaked at passers-by.

'War wounded,' he sighed. 'I damaged my leg for the Ukraine. Help me young master. Help me young mistress.'

The chink of coins showed that he was successful.

'It is an art to get people to part with money. This is professor's only source of income. He is a gentleman. If he walked into the market properly dressed and asked for money, he would be kicked and spat at.'

*

There was a shift in the atmosphere of the market.

Look-outs had signalled that a patrol was on its way.

The market went into a frenzy of activity.

Women selling vegetables became extremely fat old ladies; meat was whisked into suitcases and bags.

The horrific beggar designated as the professor uncurled, grew taller and more human. His leg no longer lay at a weird angle and he strode off, closing a little tin of putrid rotten meat used for odour, and pocketing it. He was unrecognisable.

'I will introduce you to the professor. He rents one of the best sites, because he is good at his job. He gains sympathy for us. To gain a place among beggars, you must show commitment and aptitude as well as pay. A poor beggar lets us down,' he explained, 'no one wants to beg. We are not lazy and we are not rich. This is a job when no other work is available.'

He gauged her appearance. 'We help each other. I can get you a rig if you like. It is expensive. Don't worry, you soon recoup the outlay. We need to plan a story around the child.'

Sofia was touched by his kindness, and explained that she needed only sufficient funds to undertake the next leg of her journey. She was headed to Wroclaw (the Polish name for Breslau) to find her son, who had been expelled from Lviv (the Ukrainian name for Lvov).

Soldiers were by now patrolling the market square; there would be no business for several hours. The beggars now a lot smarter, congregated for a chat and a break from work. Jacek joined them as they strolled out of the square.

'This is Sofia,' he introduced her. 'She is seeking for her son in Wroclaw. She has nothing and no one.'

The men introduced themselves with the utmost politeness. 'Good evening Madame,' they shook hands, 'a fine day for a stroll.'

Most of them had originated from the professional classes and were reduced to destitution by circumstances. They cooperated according to a strict rule of conduct, ensuring no one used the same story.

Her tale was attended politely.

Her child was the son of a Russian soldier? They understood.

*

She was escorted to their den, a small flat in a semi derelict building. They paid rent and protection until the building was renovated.

The derelict flat was clean as possible in order to keep rats and mice at bay. Ex-military containers stored food which was cooked on a tiny spirit stove stolen from Germans. Stinking rags were doffed in a separate room. An oil drum held water from which the men drew tin cans of water to wash. Toilets were present, and, though they did not flush, they were kept clean by a rota.

'We have few women in the apartments,' explained the professor. 'You would be better off as a maid, or a professional person used to save a place in the queue. Women are trusted far more than men.'

He explained that looking middle class or prosperous was fatal - she needed to fit in among the new underclass.

'The women have an apartment here. They works as maids and shoppers, they wait in queues. It's reasonable money and relatively safe. They don't usually sleep here though, mostly they sleep on floor and in kitchens,' he raised his eyebrows significantly. 'It is safer, from the police.'

Sofia explained that she had already worked as a maid to a block of flats in Moscow, and described her tasks.

'Tsk tsk,' he disapproved, 'you should have been paid. They are probably picking up vagrants all the time to exploit them as unpaid slaves. People turn on each other to survive in these tough times.'

He sighed.

'The money here in Lviv is not good, but you should get something.'

Sofia ate and her body felt replenished. The food was stodgy and adequate. They sat on the floor, eating from a collection of crockery and cutlery which could only be described as clean. The politeness and manners of the group, dressed in the sorriest collection of clothing, and wearing the black smeared faces of beggars, was a sight to behold. Their dignity was all that they had left.

Standards *were* maintained.

She shared her story, and listened to those of her hosts. Everyone glossed over bad bits; the audience could fill in the blanks. They were impressed that she had been at Stalingrad, which had already been classed as a battle of heroic proportions fought by mythic heroes.

Sofia had made a sling for Sergei, who murmured quietly and dozed. He was the easiest child, so long as he was in his mother's arms. The minute she was any distance away, he woke up.

'You can sleep among the women. A few return here if they fail to find work.'

That night, Sofia slept among destitute women who had hung around the market offering to do domestic work for proletarian women.

They were mostly elderly, and several were sick. They accepted that she had no money to pay for the night's sleep without comment.

'Maybe tomorrow,' they prayed. 'Pay us tomorrow.'

Sofia did not get work the next day. The baby was a serious hindrance, and the women were unwilling to let her stay for free. They were decent women, yet could not afford to let her stay.

'Think about it,' they reproached her, 'we will not able to pay the police and they will evict us. Tomorrow you must pay.'

Fortunately, Cesar gave her some assistance. His wife and child had disappeared during the war. He was sure that they had found support and assistance, for was he not helping an abandoned woman?

He provided her with an outfit. She was to have a notice with her.

Family in Warsaw.
Please help me join them.'

She was dressed in foul rags and her baby was smeared with filth.

'Don't worry,' he assured her. 'It only looks bad. The worse it seems the better for you.'

Her face was a piteous mess when they finished, though they were not happy with her expression. She was coached for hours in a hangdog expression and querulous voice.

'The comrades need to feel you are worthless.' They assured her, 'They have to feel superior. Don't worry. It comes naturally after some practice. Just think about the sad things that have happened to you. It is expiation for the dead in your family,' his voice broke, 'a prayer for their survival.'

Sofia did amazingly well. She belonged to a pack, and was therefore safe.

If exposure threatened, the different market groups hung together well. They created innumerable diversions, and were rarely caught.

Everything in the underworld was surprisingly organised, and expensive. The gypsy boys, who signalled that a patrol was on its way, had to be paid. Authorities and gangsters charged heavily for protection.

Sofia counted her takings daily. After eight months she paid everyone off and had money left over for the move. She had to find a permanent residence for her child. She determined to leave the next day.

'Stay,' asked Cesar, 'we can use a woman on the begging team.'

She could not be convinced. She wanted to find her oldest son.

Part 6.

Secrets

Children do not grow up knowing the truth. They learn what their parents tell them.
They spend the rest of their life trying to work out the truth.
Generally, what they discover for themselves is not the truth either.
This is because no one really wants to know what happened.

1.

Brazil 1946

The Braun family spent a month in rented accommodation, sincerely celebrating the Sabbath every Friday. They revisited Jewish customs, creating massive shelters outside for Purim, and shut factories on the Day of Atonement.

Izaak wore a kippah and made a point of visiting the synagogue in the finest hired car, making his chauffeur sit outside in the boiling sun despite the rule against making work.

While they lived in Eastern Europe, the Brauns had despised the Hasidic Jews - a cult strongly reminiscent of the Amish of USA. They rejected Zionism, which promoted a return to Judaic roots in Israel. Now they sent a tithe of their profits to those who had predicted the persecution and saved lost children, while they had escaped.

He listened to the stories of other refugees crowded into cabins which should accommodate one of two persons.

New bonds were made. New myths arose among the survivors.

Jew could never rely on a non-Jew.

Forgiveness was out of the question. The holocaust bound them together, in a sacred mission to pay the world back for its persecution. They practiced their faith with a new fervour, and plotted revenge.

Up to this last traumatic year Izaak Braun had bonhomie for the rest of the world.

Now his world view narrowed and he developed hardness to non-Jews.

Always proud of his heritage, he became a proper, traditional Jew. He joined a growing number of refugees in Latin American countries in a tight clan. They were outsiders who stuck together.

He had no aspirations outside the narrow environs of his family and his tribe. They were not to be trusted.

He blamed himself over the disappearance of the German Brauns. None left in Eastern Europe were ever heard of again. David sent sporadic news from Marseilles for a further year, after which they too, vanished.

The news embittered them against the Catholicism surrounding them. Latin America was a sea of religious festivals saint's processions and carnivals. Their anger was compounded by the fact that Sophia's sons had survived, getting in to Britain easily, and utilising Braun money to pay their passage. The family discussed the Maslows and Sophia's apostasy. They resented her possession of the Lvov apartment. They speculated that Sophia had been outed as a Jew and sent to a concentration camp during the German occupation.

From now on Izaak was persuaded that he was hated and despised everywhere. If Argentinians were pensive, tired or depressed around him, he suspected that they were planning a pogrom against his race. Lounging men smoking cigarettes against the walls were potential Nazi sympathisers. If anyone cursed, it was a curse upon his origins.

*

They elected to settle in Brazil, where refugees had already established an expatriate community. Their money and jewels went a long way to make life comfortable. They left Argentina, travelling first class. The children admired the fascinating country around them and exclaimed on its beauty.

Rebecca insisted on keeping the windows and doors closed so that the heat was unbearable. She no longer looked for beauty but for danger. She was anxious about malaria.

Izaak was aware of the importance of money and power in his survival. He had been immensely rich, and had been able to move quickly when danger threatened.

His focus changed from making progress to making money. He was interested in generating wealth as never before, determined to regain what he had lost. He spent hours discussing finance and invested in U.S. war-bonds. His investments were immensely successful at a time when North American wealth grew disproportionally to that of the rest of the world.

He recovered his drive to succeed in the clothing industry, having the expertise to run a semi-industrialised business. He was full of ideas on how to apply it in American markets. Instead of caring about progress, he became as 'Jewish' as everyone expected. Why not? He would be treated as a 'Jew' anyway.

He opened a factory housing several hundred workers in Brazil.

He never boasted of his generosity and he made no attempt at industrial relations. The workers were paid the minimum wage, no holidays and fines for lateness and sickness, in order to drive costs down and maximise profits.

He planned to move United States of America once the war was over. In the meantime he fixed upon the production of North American clothing. He moved into making cheap jeans and tee shirts, checked shirts and leather cowboy belts.

He made his first million within a year, driving out competition with low prices and good quality wear. He always selected Jews in preference to more talented locals for management positions. Even on the shop floor, he would employ and old Jewish grandmother as seamstress in preference to an able bodied young girl.

'Her heart is in the right place. We must protect our people. There are only a few of us left.'

2.

Wroclaw 1946

In the new cold war against Capitalism, industrialisation had priority, so the housing crisis in Wroclaw was acute. Basic necessities were in short supply and industries expanded without quality controls of any kind. Factories had impossible production targets to meet, and lacked equipment to do so.

The government shop was always open, though normally empty of stock. When products arrived, a notice would appear in the window. Queues would form several hundred people long. No one even asked what was for sale.

One day this noticed stated:

'Big shoe delivery,' proclaimed the notice. *'Comrades, collect your shoes now.'*

The drama behind the shoe delivery was typical of the post war industrialisation, one of the first to teach workers just what to expect of the future utopian dream. Newspaper clippings in the window showed the managers packing off their first consignment of shoes for workers.

'Shoe industry built within one year!'
'Targets have been met!'

Cobblers were to be rendered unemployed as the factory created better shoes. This was the launch of a new shoe factory outside Wroclaw under the planned economy. A favoured worker, Eva collected her propiska[23] and joined the queue.

It was all true. The factory was constructed in the required timescale, and new machinery installed. Unfortunately, for the moment, pattern cutter machines only produced a left shoe in one size. Missing the launch date meant heads would topple in the search for the 'wreckers'. Therefore the factory duly produced thousands of left shoes in size 10. Success was reported to the Central party via Gosplan. Everyone survived. The only losers were the proletariat,

---

[23] Signed permit

who had thousands of left shoes, which were carefully stored.

However, the right shoe could turn up any day.

This was no unique event. Households collected half made and incomplete objects in the hope that they could be repaired: saucers without cups, forks without knives, etc. The revolution promised an expanded range of range of consumer goods while delivering extreme shortages of basic necessities.

It would take generations to work out that the new system of central planning clashed irredeemably with individualism and independence.

For now the Party was assured of its success in revolutionising and the Eastern Bloc. Officials viewed figures, and were assured that Soviet Proletariat could take on the world. Stalin was pleased; that was all that mattered.

*

Janek reinstated his party membership in Wroclaw, although it was grudgingly accepted. He had work with the Post Office, at a lowly rank. Eva was already pregnant. Janek's salary was very low, and only the fact that his accommodation was cheap allowed the family to survive.

For the moment, living conditions were primitive.

Most construction effort was diverted to industry, so massive crowds from the Ukraine swamped the available accommodation in Wroclaw, and more were arriving daily. The Party's future depended on producing industrial benefits. Officials devised space allocations for each person in the city and reduced it regularly. Once settled, people could not relocate without permission slips.

The party had created new blocks for the proletariat around the city. These did not meet demand. Instead of building new blocks, more floors were constructed on existing apartment blocks. Since water supplies did not reach beyond the fourth floor, those on the additional upper floors had to share the sanitary facilities and haul water upstairs daily.

Block committees did everything possible to prevent additional floors being added. Emergency meetings were held regularly. Overtired workers stayed up late, racking their brains for reasons why further construction was impossible. Excuses ranged from painting cracks in their walls to show structural instability, to filling up the block with extra people to show that the facilities were already overcrowded.

Janek's block had a slush fund to bribe the officials. It had already been raided twice to pay for essential repairs to the water supply, which was not properly installed. The monopoly on maintenance meant that workers in charge of repairing the blocks needed a bribe in order to prioritise the work; otherwise it might be a wait of anything up to 5 years.

After a struggle for 6 months with officials, the block committee succeeded in keeping their block to four floors. It was agreed to build a new block nearby. The municipal authorities were eying up the allotments attached to their block for an extension.

*

Life in the commune was series of battles for status and survival. Leaving food in the communal kitchen overnight was a temptation to thieves so residents kept food under their bed, against regulations. The kitchen was a mass of warring families.

Eva managed spectacularly well. No one ever bested her, even though she never seemed to resist the apartment bullies.

The communal kitchen on their floor was shared by five families. She kept a small stove in the bedroom and cooked breakfast on it to avoid the worst of the infighting. For evenings, the first watch in the queue to cook was coveted because everyone left a mess. The queue was arranged by seniority and Eva was happy to cede her turn.

'Comrade,' she offered on her first arrival. 'I will go last.'

She cooked delicious food, always a little too much, so those who followed her were able to use her gravy, her soups and her sauces.

'Comrade,' she told those who came in later, 'I have made too much. Perhaps you would care to share? It is a pity to waste good food.'

She soon achieved the coveted first place in the cooking rota.

Eva was a born organiser. She created rotas for every resource and made sure that a minimum standard of cleanliness was maintained. Other kitchens areas were plagued by cockroaches, foul smells and flies.

Eva created a bathroom rotation for her floor. It successfully identified those who left a mess. She made sure that they were noted and reprimanded - not by her.

It was not easy, and every single aspect of living was contested and awkward.

For example, it was difficult to find time to clean the hallway. It was a struggle to wash clothes in the communal laundry and find suitable hanging space.

Furthermore, the government was imposing more and more restrictions on the movement of people. Before long, life became hideously complex. A propiska was needed to change jobs, cities, houses and even for shopping at stores.

Eva got a job in the local gelatine factory boiling down beef bones to sell to the sweet factories of West Germany. She was able to start late because she was pregnant, and she bribed her supervisor with snacks and shopping services.

She organised a black market enterprise using stolen gelatine to make sweets at home, which she sold in the market. She had a productive allotment, and they ate of the produce sparingly, selling as much as possible.

'Home produce!' she sang in the market on the way home. 'Home, sweet home.' It could easily have been a song rather than a call for sales.

It was not long before the commune had to reduce space allocation. They expected to retain their three rooms because Eva was pregnant. Their living space was very comfortably arranged. They used some gold left from the Jelinskis to buy decent furniture and mattresses. The envious committee suggested that they share the living room. Marissa would have to sleep under the table of the living area and keep her clothes and toys in a box in the hallway. It would be awkward.

Every morning Janek woke up complaining. 'Where are we to find extra people? How can we cope?'

Food shortages were acute. The peasants farmed their personal allotments with skill. They sent grannies to market with spare produce and it was necessary to queue for the barest necessities. She obtained permission from work to visit the market daily, in order to bring back food from the black market.

'Comrade Supervisor, I have brought your orders of factory parts,' she announced, and added in a whisper. 'The potatoes were a good deal to day. I couldn't buy the tomatoes, they were overpriced and had black spots. Your change is in the bag.'

Even so, no matter how much money she made in the market, daily life required more time than she had available. The contradictions in modern communism made life impossible for proletarian women. Women like Eva were enslaved into compulsory paid toil.

Even so, men refused to take on child-care duties or housework. Children were necessary in order to get reasonable accommodation. Regrettably, state nurseries and work crèches were not necessarily good. Children came home with signs of ill-treatment and neglect.

A working woman cooked and cleaned; she queued and shopped, brought up fractious and neglected children. The granny was an essential adjunct to the working family. She provided essential extra space, and did shopping and housework. Those without a granny relied on abortion to keep themselves sane.

Eva had no granny. She worked hard, and stood in queues daily, despite being pregnant. She was exhausted and afraid for Maryssa, who would be obliged to live under the table of her tiny flat, and woken up when the lodger wanted food.

She lost her baby. The committee gave her 2 weeks to recuperate for her loss, when they would allocate her a new lodger, or perhaps a young married couple.

Eva was lying in bed, severely depressed, when Sofia knocked at the door of the apartment.

4.

Wroclaw 1947

Sofia arrived at her son's address two full years after war had ended. The German population of Breslau had left, just as the Poles departed Lvov. The place was overcrowded and full of the brutal square blocks that now blighted the once enchanting Eastern European city. It had not been razed to the ground like Warsaw and Stalingrad. It was regarded as a communist success. The population was almost entirely new and therefore under control.

Janek arrived from work, expecting Eva to have made his supper. There was no delicious smell as he entered his apartment. She was sitting opposite an old lady cradling a child. Marissa watched quietly from her mother's skirts. He checked again. It was his mother - sitting on his favourite chair. The walls swam around him for a good few seconds. He did not even hear Eva whispering and pinching him. Here was the result of his sins – a frail and feeble old lady watching him quietly.

She had a child!

'Tell her she can live with us.' Eva urged. 'It is the answer to our prayers.'

Janek did no housekeeping and absolutely no childcare of any kind. He did not understand the importance of a grandmother and did not want her to stay. She could rest for the night, of course, he could not turn his own mother on to the street, yet he did not want to face up to his own reprehensible conduct throughout the war.

In this city everyone had a new life. He was a war hero who stayed in Poland while his cowardly brothers had abandoned the country to its fate. His mother's presence obliged him to face facts: he had done nothing for anyone, and he had betrayed his mother, and his sisters.

Instead of facing facts, he blamed his mother entirely and was cold and withdrawn.

Sofia was so relieved to have reached the end of her son journey that she did not notice. She had forgiven and forgotten the circumstances of her arrest. She melted into the comfort and

410

happiness of having a roof over her head.

As soon as the initial greetings were over she asked if there was somewhere she could stay. Janek pointed to the makeshift bed under the kitchen table. The table was arranged to fold down. Underneath it there was a comfortable bed roll which could be unfurled. They unrolled it to show her the arrangement.

She immediately set about resting, just like any of the tramps and vagabonds that plagued the city. She was making up shelter for the night. First she stripped off her foul over-clothes and rags and folded them carefully. She placed them under the bedding. It was clearly habit.

*

Janek and Eva watched the fragile, debilitated vagabond make up her hide. She laid out rags hidden in her skirts. There were rags for washing, cleaning, and strips for nappies for the child. There was a pungent outdoors smell; she smelt strongly of the street. The child lay quietly and played with some items she had arranged for him: an interesting stone with a hole in it, a knobbly stick and some rattling objects on a string.

The baby watched his mother carefully, never letting her out if his sight. She stripped down to grey, but clean, petticoats, arranged her son so that he could feed himself, and fell sound asleep under the kitchen table in the space that they had been creating for their adopted daughter.

Before she had gone to sleep, she had carefully replaced the table and arranged her tiny environment so that it was possible to sit down. She lay in the minimum amount of space and slept motionlessly, like a dog or a cat. Sergei played in the confined area around her. He was able to crawl yet stayed in the space around his mother, carefully watching for threats. He played very quietly with toys she had laid out occasionally, gurgling like the contented child he was. After a while he was tired. He fed from her like a kitten and went to sleep beside her.

Janek watched his mother the vagrant with growing resentment, as Eva quickly laid plans.

'Look at the way she has moved in,' he grumbled. 'She wasn't even invited. It's our home, you know. It's just plain rude. I told you she was meddlesome. '

Eva had seen too many like Sofia to feel compassion. Her primary concern was to ensure that Maryssa's room was safe. She had already scheduled that Sofia would stay.

Janek remonstrated. 'No Eva,' he insisted, 'she will make our lives difficult. She is a meddlesome old crone. Let her find her own place.'

Janek could not dissuade her. 'She stays,' she insisted, 'or I leave. I cannot manage here alone. And I prefer a meddlesome member of the family to a complete interloper who will steal our flat.'

Janek was a weak individual and depended on Eva for everything. He was overpowered. He sulked for days before he got used to having his nemesis around. The sight of her caused his heart to flutter at the ignominy of his past actions. He was determined to get rid of her. He was shocked at the state of Sofia's clothes and her son's rags. He weakly resolved to replace them, then didn't get around to it. She might have to leave.

A vicious rumour-monger, he was brilliant at undermining enemies.

Women are spiteful, yet only a man could take up truth and distort it by sheer malice. He spent hours convincing Eva that Sofia hated her. He persuaded her that Sergei carried nameless diseases which would infect future children.

*

'Mama has been to prison, haven't you?' he reported. 'You are a criminal. It says so on your passport. What have you been doing all these years? Why don't you tell us?'

Sofia said nothing. She was determined to forget the past and start again.

'Is there some dark secret?'

He considered denouncing her, but conscience would not let him do it twice. It was too dangerous.

Sofia did not deny his stinging criticisms and never refuted his allegations. As a beggar and vagrant carrying a child with her for over a year, she was in a terrible physical and mental state. The boy was a large burden for someone who had to spend hours standing and working in order to feed him. She was a shadow, while her child was bonny and plump.

412

Sofia cried when alone, although she remained grateful that her pilgrimage was over. Her son was safe. The commune accepted her presence. She had the correct papers and they could do nothing.

Eva grew spiteful and unkind, and Sergei became fractious, keeping the family awake at night and screaming if anyone other than Sofia picked him up. Maryssa grew jealous, as Eva gave her little contact. It took time for everyone to settle down.

Sofia's value was obvious from the start. From her first day at the flat, she went to the market to get supplies and to queue. In the evening, she boiled potatoes and prepared a soup from the bone that was left over from their last meal. From then on, Eva provided her a list of tasks daily, which she completed.

It was no less than she had been doing for the last year. She had expected to work.

*

Sofia kept the whole floor sparkling clean, so clean, in fact, that residents from other floors sometimes crept up to use the shower. The Maslow's condition improved. In point of fact they deserved a little extra space as a result of two extra heads in the household. The committee grumbled, but allocated them part of the corridor.

As it was at one end of the house, Jan built a partition and blocked off a private space. The resulting large cupboard housed his mother. It had no windows. There was room for a bed.

Sofia slept among boxes, left shoes, the iron and booms. She was pathetically grateful for being placed out of the way.

Eva had time to devote to work and her wily plots led to promotion to party representative at the gelatine factory. Her stipend rose to more than Janek's and the family grew quite prosperous. Janek wangled the installation of a tap in the cupboard - a massive luxury.

Some higher ranked party members had built tiny kitchens of their own, and he made a hundred different plans for the tiny cupboard his mother inhabited.

Eva silenced him. She had more practical objectives; expanding her black market business. Sofia was taught the production of gelatinous sweets and was allocated a small part of the profits. The business prospered. They expanded into cakes; with home-made

413

soup and supper for workers on their way home. Sofia worked and drudged over the long hours they were out, while tending a pair of young children.

Janek grudgingly accepted his mother's usefulness. He remained surly to her.

Sofia did not care. She had experienced worse and her paramount concern was Sergei - he needed to grow up in safety. She lived in the cupboard until her son was two years old, when the child obtained the space under the table as his very own. Sofia ministered to the children, including Eva's new baby, who arrived within the year now that life was easier. The children fought like siblings.

*

Sofia felt content. She defined her boundaries by helping others. She chatted to god endlessly, and thanked him for the survival of her children.

She was stunned at learning about the concentration camps. She felt guilty at surviving the holocaust of Jews in Lviv and Wroclaw and missed the Brauns. She decided that they were dead and prayed for them in the quiet of the night and when Sergei and Eva played quietly during the long days.

She reproached herself for Janek's betrayal, observing his dislike with a sinking heart.

She prayed daily for those she had met on her pilgrimage using a rosary, made from string and strips of tin. It had been made for her by Ivan in Moscow Station depot.

Eva was broadminded and generous, but Janek encouraged her to resent the newcomers.

Sofia worked to become worthy of her place in workers' housing on behalf of Sergei. Her sacrificing attitude increased the meanness of her oppressors. Janek grew more and more like his father daily.

Eva had converted to Communism and often nagged her mother-in-law for her religion.

'Why have you betrayed your people?' She moaned. 'You are a class traitor.'

Nonetheless, the traitor was expected to prepare the next day's market supplies all day, cook them a hot meal, wait on them and wash up afterwards, while they congratulated themselves on the fruits of their honest labour. Over time, Janek forgave himself for the betrayal of his family, and became smug and complacent. He never ceased to censure his mother.

'This is the life,' Janek stretched out and yawned, 'we are the proletariat and deserve to relax.' He glanced at his mother disdainfully. 'We, who work all day, deserve our rest.'

5.

Afghanistan 1948

Dania settled in Afghanistan on the North West frontier, a barren and mountainous region of little value, although it produced excellent opium. The Uzbeks welcomed their brothers as refugees from oppression and the tribes made many bonds by marriage.

He had listened to Lucia's advice on how to deal with communist soldiers and his newly acquired strategic skills meant he became leader of his clan.

He gained the reputation of defender of freedom, a hero who had rescued many of his fellow tribesmen in a dangerous trek across deserts and mountains.

At village meetings he was asked to recount tales of his exploits in Kazakhstan. The local youth listened reverentially.

They always enjoyed the story of Lucia, the love of his life, had sacrificed herself, dying in order to save him from the evil Andrei.

*

Over the years, Dania's clan rose to dominance in the region.

His version of freedom was couched in strongly religious and Sharia Law.

He deployed his troop in local tribal vendettas and gained land and large flocks.

He never forgot his vendetta against the Russians. He filled the caves of vengeance with the names of those he remembered, and a few he invented. He swore eternal vengeance on Russia and all of her people.

Every single member of tribe and family were inculcated with implacable hatred for Soviets. All boys were trained in military pursuits from an early age. They supported their father in all things, and the family grew in status and respect.

It was a strictly defined version of liberty which required complete subjugation of females and obedience to religious law.

According to his morality, women were weak and sinful, easily seduced by even the sight of a man. The female sex was incompetent, and, like the flocks of sheep the men tended, they had to be incarcerated in order to be free. They were a religious danger to men other than their husband and could not be allowed to roam. They wore the full Afghani burqa and stumbled around on the stony ground when the tribes moved to new pastures.

He ordered young girls to be married to old men so as to be freed of their innate lasciviousness. He arranged the marriage of his 8-year-old daughter to a 47-year-old council member in order to repay debts incurred on his arrival in the country.

As part of the religious council, Dania participated in trials of women who were suspected of adultery and unchaste behaviour. He was enthusiastic in demanding the ultimate penalty, and gained a high reputation for courage and integrity in such matters. He rose to a village leader and eventually headed a tribe formed of refugees from the Communist terror.

*

He built up a high reputation for justice among the locals. Tribal councils which he headed were often in favour of rape as a method to settle disputes.

In one famous case, which was touted as a sign of his wisdom and integrity, he had prevented a 10 year old girl from being kidnapped and gang raped in a dispute over property. Instead, he had taken her home and kept with him as a concubine for a week before returning her deflowered to his enemy.

The girl had mortified her family, and she was tried and stoned for her crimes. Her death ended a long-standing feud and her name was expunged from her family's history thereby assuring peace. Dania's reputation for mercy and justice was greatly enhanced by this action.

Over the years, Dania became an excellent entrepreneur. He traded opium with the outside world, producing fine hashish laced with opium, stamped to prove its provenance and quality. His warrior sons joined other Russian exiles to supervise the production and sales of drugs through Pakistan and India. His knowledge of the mountain passes was unsurpassed and his sons were implacable to rivals. He regarded the rest of the world as his enemy and made a prodigious fortune from drug-running.

His strict adherence to Sharia, together with fast growing wealth, ensured his selection as tribal leader. He became immensely influential.

*

Dania counted Lucia as his first wife. He never forgot his exasperation at her disobedience and lack of courtesy. Her legacy to him was an obsessive hatred of outsiders and their women.

His remaining wives were in their teens. His third wife (if Lucia was counted as a bride) was a twelve year old Pathan girl, pale and almost blond. He beat her if she looked up at him.

She was not allowed out of his compound, not even to meet her relatives.

She first fell pregnant at 13 and later bore him another four, three boys and two girls in quick succession until he got bored of her. Her bitterness at his other wives assuaged his pride although he 'gave' her a further four children over the years.

He had 20 children in all, a reasonable, by no means outstanding number for the region.

He divorced once.

The young girl was barren. At 14, when they had lived together for 2 years, she still had no children.

The provincial council agreed that she had bewitched him into marriage. She was burnt to death to cleanse the village of evil.

He attempted to return the witch's dowry; her family would not accept it. They rejected their daughter.

He beat his wives, who had no recourse - obedience was a matter of dogma. In his eyes, women learnt their value from confinement, and unquestioning deference to husband, brothers and father. Any resistance to his wishes brought disgrace on the wife's family.

His wives were expected to obey him and his sons once any boy-children reached the age of seven.

6.

London 1948

The refugees from Eastern Europe clung together.

All that mattered to them was re-establishing their previous status. They inhabited poor working-class districts of London, yet retained old fashioned ways, polished shoes, and a tendency to bow or click their heels in salute to passers-by.

The locals thought them overdressed and giving themselves 'airs'. They jeered as the men bowed and clicked their heels and laughed at the women's fancy hats and fur coats. Children gave Nazi salutes as they walked by.

As a result the community withdrew into itself and pretended that the world had not changed.

They moved into cavernous Victorian mansions and filled them with fine antique relics of their past, valueless in the post war era.

*

When the refugees from camps in Iran and the Lebanon streamed into England Katya feared that her crimes would be exposed.

However, most of them concentrated to survival in this grey new world. No one was interested in reporting atrocities. The fear of deportation was very real. They had seen what had happened to the Cossacks and were terrified that the same would happen to them if they caused any trouble at all.

The past haunted them. Some turned to drugs, and there were mammoth jars of Dexedrine on the shelves in many old fashioned kitchens. These were American battle drugs left over from the Normandy beach offensives.

Large numbers used these drugs to die by their own hand (it was called 'stomach cancer' and surprisingly common).

The remainder constructed a background using strictly limited facts.

Over time it was clear that increasing numbers of parents had joined the resistance and acted in improbably heroic ways.

Many of the refugees had dreadful injuries and permanent

damage to their organs. They were torn by nightmares of the desolation wrought by extremist views. They had lost homes, possessions and cultural heritage, as well as their cherished faith. They usually knew who the torturers and fifth columnist were and simply avoided them.

*

Meanwhile, Katya was obsessed by the reports of international war crimes and felt sure that she was in danger of prosecution. She need not have worried, before long it was clear that the West was interested in uncovering *German* war crimes, and ignoring events in the Soviet Union.

She was pleased to note that the double speak of Soviet party propaganda was repeated as truth by local socialist activists. They silenced anyone who questioned the truth of a Soviet nirvana as right wing propagandists.

The Polish refugees, who had experienced Soviet hospitality in the gulags, kept absolutely silent on their experiences in Russia. Their fear of reporting what had actually happened allowed Katya to bludgeon her guilt into submission.

She grew to hate Poland and Polish people and longed to be accepted as a British national. She refused to entertain the idea of ever returning to Poland, even as most of her peers cherished such hopes.

*

The Poles settled in enclaves where they could create their own social groups.

The Maslows shared the house in Clapham, where many Poles lived. It was full of fine Victorian housing which was considered ugly by the British and was therefore cheap.

Casimir paid for the huge house with his discharge money. He Katya, Anya were three family units. They lived on three separate floors. They and their children, Bartosz's grandmother and a great aunt barely made a dent in the massive echoing rooms.

*

Bartosz had settled down, and Katya used every possible wile to keep him under control. It helped that he was incompetent and unemployable.

The Poles were permitted to take on a limited number of jobs, one of which was a draughtsman.

At Bartosz's first job he had come home to declare he was to be made director of the small engineering company.

The first time it happened Katya was overjoyed.

She cooked him a great dinner and the three families settled down to celebrate this success over vodka and blinis smothered in fake caviar.

It wasn't true of course.

He had been fired for incompetence.

It became more and more obvious that Bartosz could not operate in a society where he was of low status. He collected unemployment benefit and point-blank refused work as a cleaner or a waiter. He had been brought up to believe that poverty was a disease and that those who served others were the lowest of the low.

At that time it was not necessary to take these jobs so he got away with being a layabout. He lived off Katya's meagre wages and rented out rooms.

He was increasingly disgusted by his wife and now frequented the pre-pubescent rent boys who hung around locally, servicing middle class men on their way home from work.

Katya had no peace, fearing imminent arrest for war crimes and endlessly turned her defence over in her mind. Eventually she became more confident in her lies.

She decided that Elena personified her guilt. She had been through a severe bout of post-natal depression with Ela and believed she was a bourgeois revisionist for some reason. She did not deserve to eat.

She never picked up the child, who rocked quietly in the corner unless picked up by someone else.

The family were concerned.

Katya needed help.

7.

Wroclaw 1949

Janek used his connections to obtain his brother's address. He wrote asking for parcels, having heard that second hand fur coats were far cheaper in England than Poland. This was true; the rich were moving out of London and pruning their wardrobes. Fashionable furs were to be had for pennies. However, postage and tax was prohibitive.

Janek informed them that Sofia had miraculously appeared when the war was over. She had walked from Siberia to Wroclaw, and they had a tiny brother.

Janek complained vociferously about having to keep his mother.

> *Dear Casimir,*
>
> *It is wonderful to hear that you have done so well. Mother is living with us and we are bearing the brunt of supporting her. She is old and frail. She is taking up valuable space.*
>
> *'Why do I have to look after her?' He griped. 'There are three of you, four, if we include Anya, who has her own house. We live in a tiny flat and don't even have a kitchen to call our own. At least take her for 6 months and see if she can help you. She works pretty hard though she is seriously in the way here. Give us a break. '*
>
> *p.s. Please send stamps. I can use them here. I can sell them to collectors. American stamps are particularly valuable.*

Sofia was pressurised by Janek and Eva. Janek had contacts among the committee managing the block. He was persuaded that they would not mind the absence of his mother. He could build his own kitchen at last – a great status symbol.

'It is not for long,' he urged, 'Sergei will be fine. He has accepted us at last, and he is such a quiet child.'

Sofia adored Sergei. She resisted as long as she could.

'It is selfish not to see your other children. They want to see you so much.'

Sofia immediately felt guilty. She knew that she did not love her other children as much as she loved Sergei. He was a beautiful child, and the two shared an inseparable bond.

*

She obtained a propiska easily; even though borders were tightening as the Cold War bit deeper.

'Let the West have her!' said the party official managing exit visas. 'She is unemployed and valueless to the state.' She received a letter inviting her to England, and money for the fare from Casimir. Sergei would have to stay.

Bartosz had returned for a brief period and Katya was pregnant again. Her pregnancy worried the extended family living in the draughty Victorian mansion. They were disturbed by the neglect of baby Elena. The child was a nuisance, rocking on her bed quietly, and showing all the signs of serious neglect.

They agreed that Sofia could usefully help with the new baby. A large space was carved out for her in the cavernous house. The mansion had been divided into three flats. The family rattled around the massive, draughty rooms. Close friends of Bartosz occasionally came to stay, camped and lisped with him for a couple of months, and departed when the relationship was over.

Sofia explained to Sergei that she would be back within six months, and prayed with him for a long time.

The boy nodded at her seriously, until she left him at the train station. She waved goodbye for as long as she could and felt her heart would break when he disappeared from view.

The child became hysterical when she left.

He cried and howled for 12 hours and paced the room for two weeks like a trapped tiger. He ripped at his hair and face, and subsequently forgot his mother. He quietened down and made friends with Maryssa.

The two became inseparable.

*

As soon as she had left, Janek sent to another letter to his siblings.

Casimir,

Mama is finding it hard to cope here. She needs more space. She will not ask you but she would be so happy to live in England. We have adopted Sergei and all will be well if you keep her. She has a visa for 6 months. I

423

am sure we can extend it indefinitely. It will cost you of course, since you are rich.

Think about it seriously. You will have someone to cook for you and do the shopping. She can nurse your children too. She is no trouble. It is just we need the space.

Regards,
Janek.

8.

London 1949

Katya and her brother prospered. They had not suffered like those newly returned who clung on to the pre-war past in the Polish clubs. They integrated.

Within four years Katya was earning good money as an accountant in an organisation where she fixed discrepancies in complex spread sheets. She supported her husband, though she remained uneasy.

*

There were several children living in the house and they played together, looked after by any adult who was not engaged in sewing or other employment.

They grew up in the debris of the extremism that had blasted through Europe like a tsunami and were relatively free of controls.

There was no doubt of the sincerity of their parent's tales. However, the interleaving of myths and propaganda made them contradictory and difficult to follow. Each child heard different versions of the same events. They fought to defend their parent's views, having no understanding of what they meant in a shadow of conflict. Meanwhile, their parents constructed new beliefs and rewrote their life stories endlessly repeating them to the children with minor changes.

'I was never in Lvov,' they would hector some passing child, who neither knew nor cared, 'How could I have known what was going on there?'

Indeed.

*

Katya had formulated a defence of her actions in Kazakhstan. She concluded that god did not care about what she had done. He had disdained the heaps of dead and permitted her to act as she did.

She was still in touch with the massive spy network in London. She knew all the locations of the secret bunkers in London and the plans that had been made in the event of nuclear war. There was a militia living in London who were to eliminate the rulers and ensure that they did not reach the bunkers. However, she was not one of them.

Meanwhile, the purges were in full swing in Soviet Russia and she attended secret meetings where she agreed that some individuals had to be punished for their counter-revolutionary spirit. They had caused all the suffering during the war.

Katya had no status among the spy network, she was completely expendable. She was terrified of discovery.

Over the next few years, she externalised her responsibility for the tortures and interrogations which she had willingly performed. Her daughter, Elena, became the personification of all that had been wrong with Russia.

The girl nearly died of starvation several times. Katya placed a wet towel over the girl's face regularly and put her under a running tap.

'Wicked creature,' she whispered. 'you will not report me. Understand?'

She sealed the two-year-old in tiny cardboard boxes, rolled the over and over and kicked them, banged them with broom handles and yelled at the child.

'You will never give me up. I'll kill you first.'

The little girl spent hours locked in cellars and cupboards, not daring to move.

However, as the family grew more aware of Katya's 'neurasthenia' they took action and fed her.

*

Elena spent her early years in darkness and in shade, under the massive mahogany table, under heavy Victorian chairs, sheltering from her ferocious parent.

Katya's harangued her child, convinced that the girl had somehow judged, watched, and witnessed her past actions. She regularly leapt at her daughter slapping her hard.

'Stop staring! What is it you are staring at? What do you see?'

'Nothing,' replied the wide-eyed girl. She didn't see anything.

'You think you can judge me child? I'll get you before you get me,' she whispered to the sleeping girl.

*

Katya became convinced that Elena was the incarnation of the shaman's revenge. She was certain that the child meant her harm and would discover her sins to the world.

She had to go.

She formulated a plan to smother her with a pillow.

'After all, how hard can it be? I have sent so many to their death. It was so simple.'

She slipped a drop of vodka in her child's milk. Late at night, she crept in, covered her daughter's face with a pillow and held it there.

Instead of expiring quietly, the girl struggled and bawled. The two dropped struggling to the floor, and, as Elena shrieked in the throes of nightmare, her mother fled.

The next morning Bartosz found his daughter lying on the floor. She had been sick everywhere. She was bleeding from her nose and her face was badly bruised.

Katya insisted that she had fallen out of bed.

*

Bartosz, the utterly self-interested became suspicious. Although he beat the girl and accused her of being evil and satanic, even he became aware of the dangers the child faced. If she died the authorities would take an interest.

When Katya locked her daughter in the drawer of one of the huge Victorian cupboards he would rouse the entire house to search for her.

They couldn't let the girl to die, in case the police investigated the family and deported them.

Even Casimir expostulated at the child's treatment.

Katya was adamant in defence of her actions.

'Hard as diamond, cold as ice! See? She has no compassion. She judges me all the time.'

She piled on misinformation and rumour.

Visitors heard of the child's sulks and her spite.

'She looks so sweet,' was her favourite refrain, 'under that pretty face is a malicious heart.'

She pushed Elena away.

'Don't touch me. You don't need love. You have stolen enough from the people. You have everything already.'

'How dare you eye me like that? How dare you have those cold judgmental eyes? You have no understanding and no kindness. Do not touch me. Why can't you just die?'

She was still in touch with the massive spy network in London and occasionally attended their political sessions.

The purges were in full swing in that country and she fully accepted the idea that some individuals needed to be cleansed and punished for their anti-revolutionary spirit.

She was worried by the curses of the Shaman which said that the souls of the dead would follow her to her grave. She dreamt that Elena was one of those vengeful creatures. She wasn't guilty now, she would be.

*

When Casimir received Janek's letter it seemed like a perfect solution to the problems with Elena. The child was showing signs of neglect and they were afraid that the health visitors would notice her constant rocking and silence.

Everyone was worried by Katya.

She was pregnant again.

What would happen?

The arrival of Sofia would solve all of their problems.

*

It took several months to arrange for Sofia to come to England. Travel from behind the iron curtain was strictly limited and any visitor had to spend a great deal of money on propisy. It was all paid for by Casimir, who had risen to managerial position in his company.

*

Sofia arrived in England on a wet cool day. Casimir collected her from the station. She was amazed at the wealth of the war-torn country.

The National Health Service provided the children with free milk and orange juice and baby formula was free. The family had taken to using it in multiple recipes, and although everyone lived on bread and butter for part of the week, they had enough to eat.

Sofia arrived. She was neatly dressed in an outfit she would wear until she died; a grey woollen waistcoat, a long black skirt and a pale grey shirt. She wore nun-like lace up shoes and walked with a slight stoop. She never lost the hint of tramp and beggar.

She bore a few Polish craft goods from Janek and a long list of things he needed from the West.

Her children had gathered to welcome her home. They had obtained Polish vodka, caviar and sour cabbage. There were slices of garlic sausage on rye bread. It was mostly peasant fare;

Sofia had no idea how hard it was to come by such things in England. This was a feast.

She wept tears of joy as she greeted each of her babies and thanked the lord that they had survived. She examined their faces, holding them in both hands joyfully to see the traces of their former selves in the mature adults.

Casimir was fat and balding. He had been a handsome young man, he already looked middle-aged. He was a serious and intelligent, already successful.

'Welcome home mama!' he hugged her enthusiastically. 'I have lost all my hair,' he admitted jovially, 'look! I have acquired a wife.' He introduced his pretty aristocratic wife, who had married for money and advantage, as she had been taught to do.

Anya was just the same. She was lively and energetic and had not ceased to sneer at her mother.

'You are just the same mama,' she claimed, 'only older.'

There was sarcastic and aggressive ring to her voice. Anya was growing bitter at her inability to have a child. Edek was refusing to visit the doctor, and growing increasingly tormented at the idea of physical contact.

Sofia turned to Katya, who had, up to now, successfully cloaked her past. She had a tiny circle of friends who were also from the NKVD, and never went anywhere that unknown Poles might turn up. She was almost a recluse, and nurtured and protected her past like a baby.

It was different with Sofia, who had never found the art of pretence. She was no fool, and immediately realised precisely what her daughter had done.

She trembled slightly, avoiding her daughter's eyes. She stared at her daughter with both pity and despair.

*

At that horrific moment, cold vengeance gripped Katya's heart. Her mother must be eliminated.

Anya also watched Sofia coldly. There was a triangle of ice in the packed room as Casimir shouted jovially and excited the young children into frenzy.

Katya hid her face. Anya watched balefully. She had no compunction in letting her sister carry the burden of the past and apprehended that she had been found out. She watched discreetly for what her mother would do next.

Nothing happened.

Sofia, who had built her life around love and forgiveness, did not see what she could do with the truth. She had no idea exactly what her daughter had done; only what she had been. She had no evidence other than the feel of those in Magadan whom she had served and prayed for. She tried to acquit her daughter. However, the ghosts of the dead hovered around her screaming that it was not okay.

Sofia avoided contact with her daughter. She helped her as much as possible. She worked hard, cleaned and cooked nonstop.

She kept away as much as possible spending a lot of time with little Elena.

*

Most of the Polish community were fascinated by the Nuremberg trials, where German leaders were tried for war crimes under international law.

Katya felt angry. She was sorry for the camp commandants, who had in her opinion just been doing their job and obeying orders. She lived in raw terror of exposure. She had nightmares where innocents like her were exposed and executed; they were abandoned by their families living out their last hours in solitude.

She vented her rage on Sofia. She knew that her mother would out her as a war criminal and did everything possible to undermine her credibility. She told Bartosz her mother was Jewish in order to evade suspicion and to isolate her mother further. He had powerful Nazi sympathies and refused to sit in the same room as his mother-in-law.

'Can't you get rid of her?' he asked his wife. 'She is a Jew.'

He was certain that he could recognise the innate evil and ugliness in the Jewish physiognomy.

Like the Nazi hunters, he appeared to have a very clear idea what a Jew looked like - even though Eastern European Jews were identical to Poles and Ukrainians. They were mostly unrecognisable – even to each other.

The first part of the plan was working.

Katya talked to Casimir.

'I don't need mama,' Katya complained, 'she is horribly in the way and Bartosz hates her. She eats like a horse, and she can't work on anything other than cleaning. I am bleeding money keeping her here.'

Casimir insisted that his mother stayed until Katya's second daughter was born, just in case there were problems like there had been with Elena.

*

Sofia was very unhappy. She could see her daughter's hatred and malice but could do nothing about it. She spent increasing amounts of time in church. Her obsessive cleaning ensured minimal interaction with her daughter whom she found entirely repulsive.

Whenever possible she spent time with Elena.

Elena, to her mind, looked just like her beloved Sergei. There was less than a year between them and they had the same haunted eyes. She lavished affection on the girl and the child grew happy and contented.

It made Katya jealous.

*

When her second daughter was born Katya did not let Sofia so much as hold her second child. She bonded with her second daughter possessively and crooned and talked to her all the time.

She saw her second daughter as a good proletarian - Jasia was deserving of all the good things in life.

The cold war had found purchase in that Clapham household. Elena was the evil capitalist stealing resources from the true proletariat. Elena could have nothing.

*

After 6 months, Sofia begged to return to Poland.

431

Casimir wrote to his brother.

Janek,

Mama is coming back to you. She was not happy here. She misses her life back in Poland and does not know any English. She couldn't find any decent work.

Katya heard her crying in the night. She tried looking after Katya's baby, unfortunately, our sister found her intrusive and annoying. She prays all the time which is a little vexing. Perhaps she misses Sergei.

It was delightful to have her over and we are sending you some furs and some coffee.

Best wishes from the family.

*

Sofia took the train home. She had a little money, and, living by her Buddhist principles she had paid off Katya for her hospitality, by working as a cleaner. She spent her remaining earnings on gifts for Sergei and Janek and paid heavy duties on the furs that Eva had requested. She had saved a little money too. That would pay for Sergei to have extra coaching in gymnastics.

9.

Wroclaw 1950

There was no welcome on her return home to Wroclaw. The door opened on the tiny flat. They let her in.

'Hello mama,' said Janek.

He took the parcels and cases from her hands and opened them. He tossed her clothes to one side and carefully checked the remaining contents.

He unpacked her gifts, turning each over critically.

'They have everything Sofia; can you explain why they have been so mean?'

There were cans of instant coffee, bars of chocolate, and a lot of second hand children's clothes. There were sparkly second hand party dresses and pair after pair of fine wool socks.

'Is it true that you get free cigarettes in England? Do they contain drugs to keep the workers narcotised?' asked Eva. 'Did you bring any?'

Sofia tried to explain that this was not the case. She was not believed.

Janek too was dissatisfied.

'Where is the English money Sofia? I heard that you worked. Did you bring any back? We can use foreign money in the government shops.'

Sofia handed over £100.

'Why so little? You were working, weren't you?'

'I had to pay rent. And I bought you all these clothes. You asked for them. Remember?'

Eva was counting the money.

'I was hoping to pay for extra lesson for Sergei.'

'You have been living here rent free for years! You have been doing nothing, living the high life. You paid Katya. This is ours.'

They were furious that Sofia had spent most of her earnings, and accused her of hoarding it.

Sofia ignored them after a while.

'Where can I put my clothes?' she asked.

There was no space for her anywhere.

'We weren't expecting you back,' said Eva apologetically.

Her room had been converted into a kitchen.

'So where is Sergei sleeping?'

'He lives under the table, like before.'

'Where is he?'

Sergei was under the table, rejecting his parent. He held Maryssa, and stared at his mother like a wild animal, retreating under the table with Maryssa when she spoke to him.

'I do not have a mummy,' he stated. He hugged Maryssa, 'she is my friend. I have a friend.'

He turned to Maryssa, gripping her by the hand, 'You have a mummy.'

He turned to Sofia.

'She sometimes shares.'

He held on to the teddy bear she had given him, and inspected it carefully. He held his new truck and the Mechano set under his arm. Maryssa had a doll.

He turned to Maryssa and embraced her.

'I will share my toys. She lets me play with her toys,' he informed his aching mother. 'If I don't ever snatch at them.'

He waved his teddy bear at his friend.

'I have some of my own.'

He crawled further under his table.

His bedding was there, and he could tug out his duvet and sleep on the floor in the corner of the room if he was tired. He made his little bed now and lay in it. He sucked his thumb and watched the intruder suspiciously from the corner of his eyes. His gripped his toys as if expecting them to be snatched away any moment. Sofia was conversing with Janek. Out of the blue, little Sergei interrupted the conversation.

'I don't like you,' he addressed his mother. 'Go away.'

He tucked his head under the covers and hid.

*

It was obvious that Jan and Eva had not expected her back.

They were chagrined at the child's behaviour.

'We didn't think you were coming back, mama,' claimed Jan. 'We have already converted the old room.'

Sergei made sounds of distress, from deep under the covers.

'Sergei has been very happy,' averred Eva, 'today is the first day he has been like this. He calls me mama.'

A little voice shouted from the covers.

'No, I do not. You won't let me.'

*

Sofia slept on the kitchen floor on the first night.

Sergei slept under the table alone, unwilling to share his den with anyone.

After a week, Sofia moved under the table again. Her son gradually accepted her.

She never knew if he remembered her.

He never trusted her again.

They slept under that table for a further two years until Eva's second child was born. Then the Maslow's were awarded another room, carved from some poor neighbour who had unfortunately lost a child.

Sergei and Maryssa shared a room for a while. Then he moved onto a sofa bed in the sitting area. His clothes lived in boxes in the kitchen.

Sofia slept under the table for a while, and then moved onto the floor in the girls' room.

Her youngest son grew up highly independent. He doted on Maryssa, who was almost eighteen months older and a lot smaller.

He was large, athletic and handsome. Jan secretly called him the peasant boy.

10.

The Maslows London 1950

Katya clung to her younger daughter, Jasia. She was the perfect proletarian and would stand up for her in the afterlife - if it existed. After all, if she could persuade *one person* of her innocence she believed she would be safe from the curse which pervaded her dreams.

Casimir was satisfied that all was well with the family. Bartosz was rarely home and he was paying Katya an allowance.

The rest of the family did their best to ignore Katya's deranged beliefs about her first child. It was true that her obsessions were damaging, yet they believed that she was just one of multiple survivors suffering mental as well as physical trauma.

Everyone was struggling to make sense of the broken dreams of Europe, refurbishing discredited myths. The gods driving society forward were dead or severely wounded. Social tensions had created faith in the justice of the war.

The absolute devastation of so much of Eastern Europe made them questions its wisdom. Without replacement philosophies, confusion reigned. Where was the philosophy behind freedom when most people lived in grey poverty, denying the rights of anyone outside their tiny world?

Katya, who had participated in the deliberate starvation of groups of Kazakhs, became obsessed with food. The dead haunted her dreams, and she thought they were stuck to the door of the house in the freezing weather.

She washed the door obsessively, morning and night.

'It has to be clean,' she insisted. 'Who knows who has been touching it?'

She tried to convince herself that the dead had deserved to starve. It was right to starve bad people. They did not deserve to eat.

That was why Jasia deserved to eat; not Elena.

'You shouldn't be eating. You don't merit it.'

And so the gulags lived on in the abuse of the next generation, spurred by the denial that such places had ever existed.

Elena made do with scraps she found in the other households.

*

Of all the Poles in that Clapham household, Bartosz had not suffered any crisis of faith. His confidence in the pre-war myths of aristocratic superiority was absolute. He moved easily into a lazy predatory existence, caring for absolutely no one other than himself.

As he became unemployable, the difference between his stories and the real world made him seem totally unbalanced. He retreated into fantasy. He took on Lucia's heritage and claimed to be the son of Princess Maria Orloska. It gave him the status at the social gatherings of Polish refugees he now attended assiduously.

He chatted up the demented old crones and touched up their children. He talked of salons and grand parties, bowed and scraped and gave everyone the feeling of the good old days.

He seemed like a charming duffer, but was an evil man.

He did not murder steal or kill, and was too indolent to do things which incurred risk.

Instead he preyed on the weak, mainly women and children. He despoiled young prepubescent children for preference, and liked to humiliate them so long as there was little danger of being caught.

He insisted that his helpless targets had asked for his perversions. According to him, his victims were essentially evil, possessed by Satan, and fully deserving of punishment. He thought of himself as a combination of god and Satan, and above both. His behaviour made him feel omnipotent. He remembered the superiority of the Nazis and imitated it.

'I am of the superior race,' he declared. 'We can rule over the unimportant and they must bear it.'

Her husband's descent into self-delusion worked like a dream for Katya. He fed the desire for manipulation and his nastiness made her feel better. She manipulated him, and fed him her daughter.

'Just like a boy don't you think?' She suggested. 'And she adores you. Can you see the way her eyes follow you around? Such a pity she is not a boy.'

*

To Katya, the child *was* possessed.

After Sofia's visit she had acquired new energy for survival and

437

frequently made an anguishing wailing sound when Bartosz visited.

One night, when Bartosz crept into the room at 2.00 am, she escaped his grip and ran to her mother. She shook her sleeping parent violently.

'Mama,' she cried, 'please don't let him hurt me. I hate it. Why is daddy doing this to me?'

There was silence.

Bartosz met Katya's eyes.

There is a dark side to power. It is hidden behind the sparkles and comforts of wealth. It is that fact that the riches have to be dragged form somewhere and from someone. For Bartosz it was to be taken from children. He touched them up obsessively claiming they had led him on and were possessed by the devil.

They looked at each other, complicit.

Katya turned to her daughter. 'Dearest,' she warned quietly, 'you must bear it. It happens.it would be far, far worse for you if this was Russia. '

'Help me!' the child begged. 'Mummy, make him stop this, it is wrong, it hurts. He is a bad man.'

'No, he is not,' replied Katya, 'go back to your room. Daddy will join you there.'

Their daughter howled and shouted.

The house was silent.

Her sister slept in a locked room to which her mother held the key.

Casimir and his wife stayed out of Katya's family matters. It was nothing to do with them. If they heard, they said nothing.

As the absorbed the full extent of her mother's betrayal, her body went rigid with hysteria, fear and despair. She was carried to her bedroom stiff as a board.

*

The traumatised, child fell ill.

Her colds and shivers developed into tuberculosis. The doctors warned the families to isolate the child.

Elena was sent to a nursing home to recover or die.

Katya was ecstatic. Her guilt would wither and expire with her child.

*

The child flourished away from her parents and returned home stronger than ever.

However, the doctors had been concerned that the girl was so thin. She also had a few broken ribs.

From now on she would be carefully monitored by professionals outside the family. Her parents left her alone. She would survive.

11.

Canada 1950

It was only when Lucia arrived in Canada as a war bride carrying a young child, that the practical difficulties of their union were revealed. Fortunately by that time, they had an intimate bond and were able to argue through the possible solutions in a cogent manner.

She and the child were treated as foreign imports. She was checked for infestations, disease, mental illness and political correctness. Her child was checked for every kind of genetic defect. Caleb was questioned as to his motives for bringing home a foreign bride, although with his background it was considered excusable.

Caleb bore it well, having experienced such intrusive questioning from school onwards.

*

Caleb worked as a logger in summer and a trapper in winter, not for long.

He took led the household, though he rarely, if ever, disagreed with his wife. He discussed every decision with her and thought about her advice. As the man of the house his word was final, he secretly admired her skill and innate leadership. She was his cook, his cleaner and his support in life, just as woman should be.

Lucia had listened to her mother's advice for years without considering it. Now she applied the principles of managing a large estate.

'Look after the land. It nurtures us,' Maria had said. 'It supports us. If we neglect the land, it will cast us off and pay us back in sickness and despair.'

Post-war British Columbia was booming. Lucia recognised the inordinately low price of land around Vancouver, and advised her husband acquire an estate at least twice as large as the one in Poland.

He was proud of her. She *was* one of the cold-hearted ice women he had known in his competition days. They attracted money.

It was not just that she was a good and shrewd investor. She felt for the land and enjoyed riding and tracking and all the things which he revered.

She repeated her mother's rather trite sayings endlessly and seemed to believe she had been a notable wise woman. He did not mind – she was perfect for him.

When mineral wealth was discovered on their land they ensured that it was mined responsibly and without massive damage. Caleb was desperately proud of her business skill.

Caleb and Lucia forged roots to the earth based on forgiveness for past wrongs. They inhabited a world where getting up in the morning was a pleasure, and it was possible to delight in their surroundings. Ultimately, they got on because they were reconciled to their lot and forgave those who had harmed them.

They healed.

Lucia's son was soon joined by a brother and sister who looked like their father. They raised their children in security and happiness.

*

Caleb's oldest boy was blond and Russian looking at a time when few looked like him. He was very unlike his brothers and Caleb and Lucia debated endlessly whether to tell him his true parentage or not.

It would never have worked well - either way.

The boy knew he was different and he resented it. He became very aggressive with the slightly disturbed air of a spoilt puppy.

Caleb did all he could to make the boy feel wanted and happy. He too, was from an interracial marriage and understood the trials his step son went through.

*

Finally, when he was 11 years old, Lucia told him that he was the son of a Russian officer. It was not true, yet she could not bring herself to tell him the truth.

Misu was very unhappy. It was the height of the cold war and all things Russian had a very negative image. He hid himself in his Indian heritage and worked hard to gain authentic Indian roots.

Caleb made a big effort to accept his step son.

He was not often home. When he arrived, all attention centred around him, as the man of the house. Whereas during the day the boy was the centre of attention.

The situation worsened with the two often at loggerheads.

Finally Lucia suggested that he was sent to a private school which would teach him some discipline.

He was sent to an exclusive private school in Toronto. It was full of foreigners on long term contracts to exploit the arctic wastes.

The boy flourished among the embassy children who had few roots.

He was a clever, serious child and his Indian heritage did him no harm among the foreign girls. Good-looking, highly musical, and arrogant, like his cousins in Russia, he was soon one of the stars of his class. His parents were very proud of him.

12.

Wroclaw 1955

Sofia was immensely proud of her youngest son, and for once she had reason.

He was a sensitive and very pleasing child, like a cherub.

He was not much like the other children in the Maslow household, who favoured Jan Maslow; or like the tiny Eva, who was dark with the slanted blue eyes of the Ukrainians.

He adored his niece Maryssa, who was three years older. They were one year apart at school and the girl was studious and withdrawn. Despite this, the two remained very close.

*

The tiny flat in Wroclaw was overcrowded, and living conditions were harsh.

Poland was poor. The communist regime clung onto the idea of world domination and supported unrest for financial and political gain. None of the satellite states it had acquired gained anything from their adherence to Soviet policies. All investment went into heavy industry.

Profits from industry were being fed into arming nuclear warheads in the Cold War. The population lived with the barest comports.

There was little building for the workers, and space was strictly controlled. It was not possible to own many personal items as the space allocations for individuals in cities were tiny. The flats were dark and dank, and food was sufficient, but dull. Because space was so tight, every item of furniture had two to three functions and going to bed was a complex logistics operation.

Bullying was endemic in those overcrowded domestic conditions.

*

Jan found life with his mother annoying and she was quickly established as the victim and whipping post. She was an embodiment of disgrace.

Every day she went to church walking many miles to the few churches which were allowed to exist. She prayed for the war crimes she had witnessed and so that her daughter would repent of her crimes. She prayed outside when the churches were closed and always wore black, like a true peasant.

Janek hated it - all this turning over of the past, all this necessity for forgiveness.

Surely it was over and forgotten?

This was a brave new world! Yet his mother clung on to its dreadful origins.

All the same a granny was essential to his household. No one else could queue for food and basic necessities. The allotment had to be weeded and watered; the house cleaned. She practically ran the house.

Still, he blamed her for his choking memories; and when no fault could be found with her labour, her boy was considered responsible for all arguments among the five young children. He was left out of many treats, though his mother made sure that he ate.

*

A great deal of Janek's frustration fell on Sergei, who was often involved in fights with his siblings. At such times, Sofia insisted that only she could discipline the boy, even preparing to leave if she did not gain her point.

She punished him by explaining that his behaviour was her fault; she had not explained the moral code properly and he had failed to understand. He was innately good, and if he did not have the correct information, how could he be blamed for acting badly?

In the first few years of his new life the boy often fought with his siblings over his favourite toy, his lucky stone, one with a hole in it. He had kept since he was a baby. No one was to touch it.

Maryssa became obsessed with it, and when she took it one day, he threatened to kill her. She ran crying to her mother, who pronounced him to be a psychopath and murderer.

This worried Sofia, who remembered his father. Eva pressed the point home.

'He is a killer, a psychopath, like his father,' she insisted triumphantly.

Sofia did not reply. Sergei's reputation as a deranged individual was confirmed.

*

The loving child sensed his mother was truly upset. He turned to his mother for guidance.

'Is it wrong to kill someone mummy?'

He twisted his little fingers around, and squinted at her anxiously.

'Why is it good to kill Germans? Are they bad people?'

He had heard that many Germans had been killed in the war, and that killing them was just.

Sofia hugged the tiny child and tried to speak the complete truth.

'You should never kill people,' she explained to 'unless you think it is absolutely the right thing to do. You should not kill unless you personally think it is right.' Sofia reviewed her life, and added. 'Of course, it is always wrong, although there might one day be a situation when it has to be done. It is a sin, of course. Sometimes there is no choice.'

She confused that young impressionable head.

'So I can kill Maryssa? She took my stone and I told her I would kill her. It is ok?'

'No, that is not a sufficient cause. It would have to be something very bad.'

Sergei was excited.

'Like Uncle Jan, when he makes you cry? Can I kill him?'

He seemed unduly elated at the prospect.

'Not that either,' she hedged. Tears filled her eyes, 'killing is a crime and the state will execute you after a trial.'

Sergei knuckled his eyes.

'I don't want to die. I won't kill Maryssa only tell her to give back my stone. Auntie Eva took it. I hate her!'

It was a tiny flat. Everyone was listening, probably even the next door neighbours.

'Of course, if you did kill someone, even if it were for the perfect reason,' she added, 'you would face punishment for killing, by god and man. Your actions have to be counterbalanced somehow, perhaps by going to purgatory or maybe going to prison. So if such a situation arose, then you need to weigh that carefully. Do you understand?'

Sergei hugged his mother, seeking reassurance.

445

'Did you kill someone mummy?'

Sofia did not reply, and hugged her son. Tears filled her eyes. She could not explain what had happened. As a result, he grew up with the impression that his mother was a murderer, and that he was in some way tainted by her actions.

*

Sofia was perfect victim material.

She had the highest opinion of her children and had faith that they were superior to her. She genuinely believed that they were perfect beings and delighted in their meanest achievements.

She was proud of Janek, and insisted that he held an eminent position, when in fact; he was little more than a postman, and a censor of mail.

The result was the opposite of what she intended. The child was convinced that she had done something very wrong and deserved to be punished.

Sofia felt bad about herself. Instead of investigating her lack of self-worth, she tried to pay off her imagined sins by praising her children and giving the all she had. She failed to make them feel good. They felt highly entitled while at the same time they could not live up to her standards and felt criticised and humiliated. They knew how far they were far from her praises. They loathed her obeisance, and despised her remorse, while accepting that they were better than her.

13.

Miami 1955

Izaak was on a mission to become a multimillionaire. As soon as he settled down he revived his ideal to become an innovator in the clothing manufacture, while relinquishing all socialist ideals of a happy contented proletariat.

He never showed scars of his vile experience at the hands of anti-Semitic mobsters. He had utterly changed his view of the world. He no longer saw common people as ignorant and misguided.

They were potential enemies and killers.

He supported all Nazi hunting initiatives with vast sums of money and funded rebuilding of synagogues in the young state of Israel. His wife often went on holiday to Eilat and he occasionally joined her. He learnt to speak Hebrew outside the synagogue and was deeply proud of the nascent state of Israel.

Rebecca had become quite fundamentalist. She had hardened her heart to all things not Jewish and collected Chagall assiduously. She rarely spoke to non-Jews and was deeply suspicious of any friendly overtures from goys, particularly as they often resulted in requests for money and support for various charities.

Sofia had learnt of her parents' survival. Janek had managed to seek them out. He was still trying to gain financial from his family.

His grandparents were extremely wealthy and powerful and he was wary of approaching them. Instead he enlisted Sofia's assistance.

Sofia was delighted. Her prayers had been answered. She lit many candles in the tiny corner of the local church building. The place had been swept clean of all religious artefacts. Nevertheless the socialist meeting hall was persistently utilised by a small group of worshippers. They said masses alongside a defrocked priest who worked as a grocer during the week.

She wrote to her parents:

I am so glad that you are well! I thank the lord that you survived. As you can see I also managed to live through this dreadful war.

I have a young son, Sergei. I am living with Janek, who remembers you kindly and would love to hear from you.

You affectionate daughter,
Sofia

Izaak was amazed to hear from Sofia. He was already a bitter man. He decided that she had survived on the basis of rejecting her Jewish faith and was disgusted by her reference to a Christian god. Rebecca advised him to reject it on principle and he agreed.

'She disowned us in order to survive. She is a traitor to our people.'

He never replied. He had truly hardened his heart to anyone not of the faith, even those of his own family.

*

It was time to employ a realistic capitalist business ethic and give up namby-pamby socialism. He established many clothing factories in Brazil and saw himself as a cut-throat businessman changing an old fashioned and primitive country. He carried the hell of past persecutions to his workplace. He strove to anticipate disaster by avenging himself on the poverty-stricken who had little idea of Judaism.

He became the oppressor they thought he was.

'You may well hate me,' he charged them. 'I will make sure you suffer for your hatred first.'

His employees were poorly treated.

He did not mind employing women and children. Any complaints led to instant dismissal. No tale of hardship worked on this hard-hearted man, and there were no holidays of any kind, unless required by law.

'I am treating them as they would treat me in the same position,' he proclaimed to his intimidated managers. 'In fact, I am treating them somewhat better. I do not insult them and I stick to my contracts scrupulously. They have their agreements and they know what they are getting into.'

At the first hint of political instability in the country, he shifted his entire operation. He moved his factories around often. As soon as he heard of better profits to be obtained in, say, another Latin American country, he would up his whole factory and move there, firing the existing workers with little or no notice.

'Business is driven by market forces,' he explained to his children. 'We must bow to the market. Our investors would not be happy unless we pay the top dividend. We owe it to them.'

*

By the mid 1950's the slightly paranoid family suspected Brazilians of plotting future pogroms and revolutions, and moved to America. Their warm-hearted and highly-paid nannies followed them because the children had grown dependent on their affection. Money was no object and they moved the entire Brazilian family to Miami and build servant's quarters for them all.

They built an elegant mansion in Miami flanked by their own stretch of private beach. It had a private road and a dock which berthed an ocean going yacht. It was always stocked with everything the family might need to flee in case of disaster.

It was a tough time for the inhabitants of that stretch of coast. Miami was at the centre of many conspiracies and plots of the Cold War.

Each sizable estate had its own bomb shelter, regularly cleaned and kept in readiness with aired and clean sheets and turned down linen. Armed bodyguards patrolled the beaches and were instructed to shoot on sight.

There was a large army base nearby. The residents discussed the impending nuclear conflict and made plans to survive. Most of them were pro McCarthy and 'nuking the Russians'.

Izaak was already an old man who he did not willingly relinquish control. His sons worked for him while he directed operations.

Before he left for the States he had moved most clothing manufacture to Asia where labour was cheap.

'This is how capitalism works,' he told his investors. 'We always get the best quality at the lowest price. This is why we are the market leaders.'

The Latin Americans offered him better rates. Surely they knew that his departure would devastate the economy?

He was adamant about moving his factories to wherever prices were lowest. His staff had little influence on him. He easily extinguished all opposition and had a brilliant understanding of the market which he used to swingeing effect. His shares were market gold.

As his business grew, presidents of tin-pot dictatorships began to fight to obtain lucrative contracts with his company. He shored up their parlous economies, as long as prices stayed low and no longer.

*

Izaak remained the head of the family. He was strict but fair with his fatherless grandchildren. He reverted to his inflexible attitudes to women.

His attitudes to rebellion had hardened. Sofia had disappointed him and betrayed her family. His workshops were full of female workers, which made them easier to exploit.

Meanwhile, Rebecca became even more distant from her mothering role - and far more neurotic. She celebrated every festival and dietary rule, which meant the children were aghast at the idea of unclean food creeping in to their home. They saw the new state of Israel as god's gift for the holocaust, biblical Zion.

The children didn't realise that their grandmother had post-traumatic stress disorder, and had flashbacks when she remembered the names of Jews she had once known. She obsessively followed the Nazi hunters and suspected all Brazilian Germans of Nazi sympathies. She had been devastated as details of the concentration camps were revealed and discovered the fate of her sons and their families. She kept a diary in which these names were stored. Private detectives were sent out to find out if her remembered acquaintances had survived. If they were short of money, or their descendants were, she would pay large sums for their education and offer them funds to immigrate to Israel. In point of fact, her donations were responsible, among others, for Maryssa's subsequent escape from Poland, along with countless others on whom she lavished the profits of Izaak's empire.

She maintained Izaak's ideal of the frigid, non-emotional woman and reinforced it by political inflexibility on all matters Jewish. As a result, she found it hard to be affectionate to her grandchildren and they were mostly brought up by nannies and servants.

They were raised in a highly insular society which regarded the warmth and vibrancy of Brazil and Latin America as highly suspicious. Their grandmother's horror stories frightened the

450

orphans and they suffered severe nightmares. They were taught that most people were secret Nazis. They were terrified that god was watching in case they forgot to obey the Sabbath, in which case they would be roasted in ovens

'Grandma,' they worried, 'Consuela wears a cross. Is she planning to kill us in our sleep and steal our money?'

Instead of reassuring her charges, Rebecca took their idea seriously.

'Maybe she is,' she replied seriously. 'I will have her watched.'

Consuela stayed, because the children were totally dependent on her. She had to give up wearing her cross.

The highly trained and loving nanny was supervised by a succession of young Jewish girls who came from Israel to work as au pairs. They were vapid and political and determined to go out at every opportunity, even with Brazilian boys, which shocked their employer. All the same they were considered more trustworthy than kind Consuela.

14.

London 1955

Elena was a bright child. She looked very like Sofia. She learnt to read at an early age and was able to count almost as soon as she could walk. She read English before she spoke it.

She was aware that something was wrong with the world and resolved to discover it. There were seven children living in the house. They were not permitted play with the English children, not even the next door neighbours.

Elena was very isolated. Her mother took care to make her feel that she was not like other children and that she was the guilty party if anything went wrong. Her father's invasions of privacy made her feel that she had done something wrong and deserved to be kept away from all fun activities. She was anxious to discover how the world worked in order to expiate her wrongdoing. An intensely observant child, she had an excellent memory for long forgotten conversations, often tripping up complete strangers when they contradicted themselves.

It was not long before she guessed that there were untold secrets in her extended family.

She delved for the truth indefatigably.

Casimir often talked of his courage in fighting for the Battle of Britain and his desperate fight to save Warsaw. It was typical of the little myths that the Poles had developed to explain their behaviour.

Elena remembered every word.

'Uncle, you said that the Polish army fought in Warsaw. And they all died. You were in the army, and then in France at almost the same time. How did you get away? Weren't you there?'

Casimir fought back by getting huffy and angry.

'You think you're so clever. You're just a little know-it-all.'

*

Mama's confidante, Svarovska was an active agent and a civil servant. She loved to whisper of missions in central London where she worked.

One day she was telling Casimir of her dreadful experiences in

452

the gulags.

Elena picked up discrepancies in her story.

'If everyone in the gulag died,' she enquired 'how come you are here? How did you get out?'

'You see?' pleaded Katya. 'She is such an annoying brat.' The two retreated to whisper away from her.

*

In 1955 Casimir moved out to a new home in a street nearby and gave the house to Katya.

By now she knew that Bartosz would never hold down a job. She did not mind this too much. She hated being a housewife and it gave her the opportunity to work full time. She was an excellent mathematician and soon obtained finished her training as an accountant. However, she worked long hours and often did not get home from work until 7.30 in the evening.

Her girls often stayed out as late as possible after school. There was no reason to go home to an empty unheated house which might contain an abusive father.

The streets were not that safe, although safer than home. The inhabitants were mainly cockneys moved out from the East End during the Blitz. They had a strong community spirit and organised trips from the local corner shop to the seaside twice a year and also hop picking in August.

On two Bank holidays in the year, children piled into two coaches, excitedly singing at the top of their voices:

10 – (or 9?) green bottles

She'll be coming down the mountain

One man went to mow

A long way to Tipperary'

They were not longer bullied by the local boys. In the past they had been accused of being responsible for the bombing of their city. When they went on trips to the seaside, there was usually a spitting truce from the boys at the back.

After several raucous hours on the coach, they spilled out to a frozen sea full of jelly fish.

453

There was sticky rock, kiss chases, stinking seaweed. Those without swimming gear splashed into the sea in underpants and vests and everyone returned wringing wet.

Foreigners and other outsiders hung around and ate chips, watching the shouting and screaming fun.

It was very exciting, though mama decided it was 'common' and they were never to behave like that, nor to ever say 'cor'bli'me' or 'bloody 'ell', swearing of the most severe kind which would lead straight to hell.

She had high hopes of getting her children places among the British aristocracy and sent them to a private school as her contacts had told her that this was essential if her children were ever to gain work as Soviet spies.

It was an excellent plan, in theory. However, post-war Clapham was not the place to commence a successful foray into the British aristocracy.

*

Clapham was poor. People struggled to make ends meet. Everyone had to work to support the family. Children started work at fourteen and worked on Saturdays while at schools. Their mothers worked as charladies and their fathers worked in the docks, as coal merchants and in the many factories dotting the area.

The streets were always full of children whose parents worked long hours. They played on the common and wandered around the streets, hanging around the corners and playing five stones or tossing pennies,

The girls were dimly aware of dangers of the common. Perverts lurked in the wooded areas. The men usually avoided well-dressed and clean kids, in case there was a protective parent around. There were plenty of blighted children without risking trouble, but they singled out foreigners.

The safest place to play after school was a charming park square on the way home. The park adjoined the local library, which was a bequest of the rich philanthropist who had left his home to the nation. It was housed in an Italianate villa with wonderful grounds including a long lake with fountains in the Palladian style.

The playground was supervised by a stout cockney creature who chatted to favourites and despised foreigners. If a snotty bully felt obliged to chase the girls, there would be at least one strike before a quiet reprimand slowed him down. In any case, it was relatively free of gangs of loutish children, who singled out foreigners.

The playground was a health and safety nightmare, hosting dramatic falls to the sharp stony tarmac a long way below towering play-equipment. Seriously grazed knees and elbows could go to a hut for disinfectant and plaster, and return to contend with bone-crunching apparatus such as the Umbrella - a set of iron seats swinging dangerously round a cast-iron pole. The top of the climbable device risked an unsurvivable fall to concrete below. The danger was all part of the fun.

*

The library was a safe-haven, particularly in winter when it was cold and wet. The librarians saw what was going on in the playground and knew when ruffians and perverts were about.

One of them regularly ventured out to hustle the 'good' children into the library.

She sat the vulnerable children in front of picture books. It was a bit boring/ Still, Elena was happy there. She read through all the decent children's books and, after some discussion, the librarians allowed her to withdraw books from the adult library.

Most evenings she sat alone in the library with the books and her sister played outside reading book after book.

*

The senior librarian singled Elena out, and regularly handed her some ridiculously academic book, mostly in Greek or Latin.

'There!' she would coo,' Read this. You will like it.' (Virgil!) 'Here's an exciting bit.'

The head librarian adored extreme violence, clashing steel, burnt flesh, sacrifices of fat for the gods, and homosexual love (mama got quite cross about that).

Elena dutifully extracted the general gist so as to be sufficiently knowledgeable. Not much understanding was needed, as the librarian would get excited and take over. The old lady was delighted to recount the classics. Later, Elena learned that she was a highly educated classical scholar from Oxbridge who was enjoying lonely

455

emancipation.

The stories were a bit grim.

Heroes faced awful deaths and were dragged round and round for days on the back of a chariot. There were long dawns during which gods argued and pontificated. There was lots of oratory, and page after page of similes likening city walls to totally dissimilar mountain ranges.

*

It was not long before other intellectually stifled librarians guided her reading. She dutifully read their leather-bound tomes though she only partly understood what was written therein. She read Freud and Descartes, she read Marcus Aurelius and the history of Ancient Egypt. She studied the history of the English people as written by the honourable Bede. Snippets of those tomes made it through to her childish brain.

Whenever possible she headed for the older books in the prodigious ornate bookcases.

She was particularly fascinated by the richly-bound and heavily-illustrated archaeology and the travel books. They were clearly part of a Victorian collection and part of the endowment from the wealthy benefactor.

They resided in marvellous carved bookcases and were limited editions of Victorian expeditions now lost. When the library was knocked down in the 70's these old books were thrown into a skip or burnt together with the rare wood inlaid carved bookcases, parquets and mahogany doors. The library was crafted from rare tropical trees cut from paradise.

They burnt well.

*

The benefactor's personal collection included missionary guides for Africa and Victorian archaeology books in embossed leather bindings and printed with wonderful dramatic pictures.

They petrified Elena, discussing nightmare diseases her parents assured her could not possibly exist (she subsequently discovered that they did).

Missionaries seemed to chiefly fear the worms, which could get through every orifice, even though skin and hairy areas, climbing over trousers, down collars and up sleeves not carefully fastened. They had the habit of popping out at night like nightmare aliens.

There were also tales of horrific sacrificial rites, lost souls, spirits, manifestations of the smoke and mirrors kind, and demons and witchcraft. All of these were matters which any good missionary had to prepare for.

She sat alone in the most deserted part of the library, away from the unemployed newspaper readers and old men dozing in the sitting area, imbibing hideous, ghoulish stuff which was absolutely unsuitable for an eight year old child.

There were petrifying illustrations showing a hero missionary pointing his finger at a cowering witch-doctor, or leaning on his cane and lecturing some African child, wearing a hard hat and puttees to keep out the worms, collar and cuffs carefully buttoned.

It was pure Horror, and gave the girl an appetite for research among old books which she never lost.

*

The child was lonely, though she did not miss what she had never had. Her sister's bullying (egged on by mama) was not as unendurable as what she witnessed in the streets. The English children often had harder problems to deal with. She was self-sufficient, if emotionally scarred and damaged.

There were compensations. The area epitomised the final decay of the Victorian empire. There were walks, books, deserted Victorian mansions, the wonderful decaying park, an open common, and lakes with broken intricate fountains, gothic rock formations, and abandoned knowledge of all kinds.

And she wasn't a missionary!

She drank up information like a starving orphan and digested it at leisure. The real world made no sense. Knowledge out of books helped her understand, and she hoped to find the way out of hell.

She spent her youth in the library studying, seeking the difference between truth and lies, learning logic and philosophy, and decoding riddles about the past.

15.

Rye 1956

When Elena was about 12 years old, Katya fell pregnant.

The family couldn't afford another child. Abortion was difficult, illegal and expensive, performed at home by an illegal medic who specialised in such matters.

The abortion would be a messy business. It was a complex logistics exercise to be undertaken over Easter vacation.

The children had to be away for at least a week, preferably two. Jasia was to stay with Anya. Anya refused to take Elena, having heard of her difficult nature.

Elena was sent, together with her older cousin Agata, to Rye.

The pair were to stay with a childless couple who supplemented their income by running a bedsit.

Easter was low season and the owners were happy to take the girls for a very low rate.

Apart from staying in Anya's house in Acton, Elena had never been on a real holiday, staying in a guesthouse like real English people. She was looking forward to it.

*

The girls were met at the station and driven to the Guest house on the outskirts of Rye.

The guest house was deliciously comfortable compared to the icy houses with echoing, cold rooms the girls inhabited in London. It was their first sight of fitted carpets, and hot radiators in the bathroom. They had fluffy towels, and cooked breakfast with cutlery in order. There were cornflakes and choice of food. The table was laid (like Christmas really), and it was warm at night. The girls had taken gloves and socks to wear in bed, unneeded. The entire house was neat.

Rye was deserted; the weather wet and inclement. It was not like Weston Super Mare, Clacton or Brighton. In fact, the girls' high fashion clothes (millions of petticoats and almost patent shoes) drew disapproving stares from the residents. After all, this was a high class resort.

There were no boys in town and they were totally bored, having lived life on the edge (i.e. avoiding spitters, perverts, flashers and catcalls). They strolled the tended gardens and streets of Rye. No jeering louts, and no shouting that they were toffs and cowards for losing the war, no kickings for being bloody foreigners - bliss.

*

The owners of the guest house, Piotr and Magda, were different to anyone Elena had met before.

They were working class Poles ever (few of the poor had escaped) and it was difficult to understand their Polish. The two of them were being paid magnificent reparations by Germany so that they did not need to work. They ran the guest house as an interest, to meet people.

They were both blond - natural, pure blond and blue eyed; handsome and very healthy in an Aryan way. Magda's long hair was plaited and her cheeks were naturally rosy.

They were in late twenties, though they appeared younger. They were always home, although Piotr worked with horses at a local stud farm for fun. They were kind and affectionate to each other, and particularly interested in Elena, having heard that she was clever and intellectual.

Piotr was unusual for a Pole.

For a start he did not fancy himself as attractive (he was) and his wife was equally modest about her stunning looks. He was an intelligent guy, with the type of body-builder physique. Magda was the female equivalent.

They owned a horse - untold wealth for a Pole. They kept animals, a pet sheep and chickens in the fields around, which they owned.

They both rode.

She felt safe-ish with them though their friendliness was suspicious.

*

It rained, so there was nothing to do.

Elena had Plato with her - a present from the librarian. It was supposed to change her life.

She found it dull, but it was a point of pride with Bartosz that she read it. Bartosz had boasted of his daughter's intelligence to Piotr.

'She can read Greek,' he claimed.

She couldn't.

The librarian had tried to explain the idea of Platonic love. Elena hadn't a clue what it was. She did not understand why adults seemed to find it funny that she read Plato and said things like:

'Oh Plato. Platonic Love.'

It was a mystery and no-one wanted to enlighten her on the subject.

She had read several romances in the adult library and still had little idea what love was, let alone platonic love.

Her mother claimed to love Jasia. But Elena sensed that their relationship hinged on some secret.

Katya had stated more than once that Jasia would never betray her.

*

Piotr had been enormously impressed by Bartosz's boasts about his daughter and proudly directed her to his enormous Comic Collection.

Elena had read *Superman*, graphic novels, *Eagle, Victor, Bunty* and *Girls friend*. Piotr's collection was quite different. It was all Science Fiction, *Stranger than Truth* and stuff like that.

There were no pictures, just short stories, with perhaps a small illustration of a space ship under the heading.

The covers were lurid, typically showing a woman, underwear showing, cowering before a flying saucer.

He was keen for her to read them.

'You are a reader' he stated, 'read these.'

*

They were disturbing in the same way as the Victorian travel and archaeology books in the library.

They were different though; printed on cheap paper, already falling apart, poorly written, short words, and full of pseudo-science.

All the same, it was frightening stuff.

Elena didn't make much of a dent on his collection.

She skimmed a lot that was not worth reading, and cut to a disturbing core.

Just like the librarian, he wanted to discuss what had been read.

'What do think of flying saucers?' he seemed to genuinely want an opinion and Elena felt seriously flattered. He seemed to care!

'Are they true? Do they exist?' Were they possible?

'Of course not,' she replied.

(After all, the worms that lay eggs in the scalp and climb out through the soles of feet were invented horrors.)

She was disturbed by his intense stare, the way he cared for her opinions.

Her knowledge of science fiction was based on *Dan Dare* and *Superman*.

Of course that was made-up.

He was uneducated; even she sensed that, yet so sincere. His wife was equally earnest. She related stuff about the war which Elena had only picked up in drunken ramblings and spitting insults.

*

One day Elena asked if they wanted children. This was immensely cheeky and would have got an hour's talk from her supercilious aristocratic aunt about manners.

'Definitely not,' Magda said (she had answered!).

'Why not?' she asked, even more brazenly.

'Because of what happened at the concentration camp,' she replied,' they messed me up over and over again.'

Then she looked at Elena in a way that made her feel not a child.

'I have had many operations here,' she pointed to her womb. 'I do not know if any child I had would be normal.'

This was creepy, after reading stuff about super babies and alien spawn.

In the curious manner of a naive 11 year old she asked for details.

Magda answered directly once again.

'It is too horrible for you to know.'

*

The next morning at breakfast Magda was upset.

'You asked me about my children, and I have had several,' she confessed tearfully. 'I do not think you should know what happened unless you want to. It is up to you.' She hugged the young girl 'Whatever you decide, it is wrong to read that crap,' pointing to the comics. 'Piotr wants you to know what truly happened.'

Of course Elena wanted to know more. She had grown up with so many secrets and lies. And this lady, a grown up, was promising to tell her the truth for one.

Who wouldn't want to know?

Poor child. She was too unsophisticated for the game they were playing.

They seemed to be having an argument.

'She has to make a choice.'

'She is so young.'

'She will listen.'

'And she wants to know the truth.'

'She is still a child.'

Piotr flattered Elena. She would be a professor, a judge, or someone very important. The girl drank it up.

Agata was supposed to be looking after Elena, and guessed that some dark secret was to be revealed.

'Don't listen,' she advised, plonked in front of the TV screen.

'Surely we should know the truth?'.

'Up to you.' She said. 'Nothing to do with me.'

She sat by as these highly-disturbed adults discussed whether a tiny child should learn the dark secrets of war.

*

The next day they started their story, with contrite glances at each other, clasping hands like children who have broken a window.

Once started, confessions proceeded at a relentless pace. They never contradicted each other, as if they were in court.

They trusted each other and had probably gone over every word many times over.

'First you need to know that we come from a concentration camp', they admitted.

'Oh,' Elena stated knowledgably. 'You were starved. You are Jews?'

Jews everywhere had fought to make their story heard.

'No,' they said. 'We were not starved, far from it. We were

experimented on. We were part of an experimental programme.'

Elena had not heard anything of experiments.

'We presented our evidence at Nuremberg. It was thousands of pages. There were hundreds of us. Yet it has never been published, nor even recorded or stored.'

They glanced at each other for support.

'You should know what happened. You *have* to read it.'

They glowed with happiness at the thought someone would read it.

'You must choose. You do not have to. Maybe you can help us when you become a professor.'

They were so naive, so sincere and so keen. They were desperate too, adults reaching out to a withdrawn geek - for help.

*

Elena had been protected by librarians and teachers (until private school, where she learnt a new meaning of bullying).

She even had her copy of Plato with the original version printed on each page in case she should want to cast a glance at the Greek.

She was a child, with no knowledge of the real world outside books. These two seemed so forlorn.

She went.

*

The spare bedroom contained no bed, only a desk, a chair and rows and rows of bound depositions, marked for Nuremberg court, with blue grey bindings. They were bound in blue grey covers and already had a musty feel. Each of the books was about 100 pages long and many of them contained long witness accounts which had been poorly translated into English.

They were carefully typed. There were about a hundred booklets, each relating to different locations and experimentation processes.

The experiment files - X files for short, the stuff of nightmares and also comics and films to come - X men, Dark Angel, X files. It was a cruel joke that the victims would have to hear again and again.

The room was painted hospital blue, the desk a Van Gogh painting, utilitarian.

She was to sit at the desk and read. No books were to leave the room.

Piotr would sit with her if she liked.

'No thanks.'

He sat outside like a warder, guarding his books.

*

The top shelves contained rows of depositions. The bottom shelf contained a row of published works on the concentration camps, mostly paperbacks with sensational illustrated covers.

He had a lowbrow tasted in literature and considered Elena a genius.

'Ok', he ordered, 'Start reading. You are fast, read it all.'

She couldn't.

The stuff took time for a young child to absorb.

She started with the published stuff, to get an overview.

The figures, the numbers, and photos of starved and tortured souls - that was quite bad.

Then there were the individual stories from guards and group leaders of the camp houses. They survived by making a pact with the devil. Only the monster had been defeated and they were left with their crimes.

They confessed their brutality; their attempts to exterminate the useless and lame, the application of industrial practices and machines to process humans.

It was human-farming, using abattoirs for killing as efficiently and cheaply as possible and making good use of the by-products. It was hard to take in.

*

One day of this and the child was pale and ill.

That was not the end. Magda and Piotr became implacable. They could tell that Elena had read and understood by her pale and drooping stance and her unwillingness to read more.

The next day they willed her to go back, cuddled each other for comfort, begging sympathy for their ordeal.

Immediately after breakfast, Piotr urged the child upstairs.

'Time to read the truth. We need to inform people, explain how it happened. Here it is. Start with the simple stuff.'

He knew where to put his hands on every single story. He had the whole set of information organised logically, and she was to learn about it in order.

No doubt he had a strategy.

He wanted her to speak for the victims dotted over the planet with their forgotten depositions.

They had spoken at Nuremberg.

The world did not want to hear it. At the same time the scientists wanted to continue.

*

They got up every day with their traumas and their scars and they wanted someone to tell the world about the secrets which had been covered up at Nuremberg.

'Don't forget,' they adjured. 'Don't forget us. Don't let it happen again.'

Even the tawdry little paperbacks on the concentration camps gave her nightmares. She was agitated and didn't want to hear any more.

*

Next day the weather was not so bad. 'Please let us go out,' she pleaded.

The girls went out, dressed in their best London clothes and drawing the attention of dirty old men. Agata was happy to search for (pretty rare) boys in Rye, help Magda cook and discuss lady matters and didn't want to hear a word about war secrets.

'War secrets? Haven't we heard enough of those? My mama talks about nothing else other than the suffering at the gulags. Please just shut up.'

Rye was exotic and warm compared to London, and it was pretty. Elena yearned for the quiet calm of the local library. She was homesick.

They sat by the quay, looking into cafes and walking the cobbled streets in search of the slot machines and chip shops. They investigated everything, even finding a stick of rock to take home.

It was a feeble and skinny middle-class version of the fat sticky rock they knew so well.

*

The next day rained again. She went back, urged to be careful with what she read. The nightmares she heard about seared her soul, ensuring that nothing ever seemed that bad again.

Hell was on earth - that was certain.

The depositions were precise, factual, emotionless and uncomplaining, torn from memories striving to prevent what had happened from reoccurring, and ultimately, ignored.

Piotr sat with her this time, silent and unmoving. He did not stir, and sat on a hard chair that he had carefully carried in together with a newspaper which he slowly perused, like a man who does not read well.

His stance was watchful.

'Do not try to pretend you are reading', it said. 'I will know.'

She could not pretend she was reading.

Magda dropped in with tea and biscuits. She watched, from a distance, to see how the child took the information.

Elena felt cowed and delinquent for not wanting to read.

The situation felt wrong, abusive.

It *was* wrong.

'It's not fair,' she rested tired eyes.

They quelled rebellion with the flame of obsession.

'Who else will listen?' their eyes said. 'We have collected it all together until you to help us publish. Tell the world. No one cares about what happened. It has to be told or it will never end.'

She went on reading.

The rain did not stop for days.

'We are so lucky to have them,' they insisted. 'You are a lucky girl. You have the direct line to the truth.'

Such damaged people did not understand that the agreement of a child was fruitless. It was a story, held on to by mad men, waiting until it was safe enough for the telling.

'And by the way,' Magda whispered 'The fact we have them is a secret.'

*

A lot of the material they held has since become common knowledge, although not the full range of experiments, nor the full extent of the horror.

Much of the data had been removed by the victors and the abuse of people and animals continued in secret laboratories.

Piotr and Magda wanted it to be known.
The victims were crying out to be heard.

*

At the time, the country was in the grip of cold war. These two held on to political dynamite in a spare bedroom in Rye. Here *was* the stuff of conspiracies and hidden histories, scribbled by mad men on the walls of their conscience and suppressed by scientists in the Western and Eastern blocs

16.

The Nuremberg Files

The first group of depositions described experimental research on the best and most efficient ways to run the concentration camps.

Each camp was an experiment assessing the intention was economically utilise the flood of humanity blocking up space in Europe. The intended aim was to eradicate the camp population, while at the same to time proving to the victims that it was right to die.

Victims had to die willingly for the good of mankind and to purify the world, like lambs in the slaughterhouse, who peacefully and quietly queue for execution.

*

Upon arrival at the camps, victims were sorted into subjects of different kinds, for genetic experiments, breeding experiments, prostitution, warrior programmes, investigations into the paranormal, behavioural testing, record keeping etc.

The only way to evade death was to become a guard or an administrator of some kind. It was also possible to work with the experimenters themselves or to improve the system in some way.

The ultimate aim of this meta- experiment was to make the inferior peoples extirpate themselves. Thus it was aimed to make the camps 90% run by inmates.

Many of the experiments in the camps were managed by inmate professors and medical practitioners.

Very few 'pure blood' commanders were involved in the day to day running of the experiments, although there was fierce competition for designing them and for the credits of success.

The overreaching aim was to employ a core of elite German guards, doctors and mathematicians, supported by a body of prisoners who undertook violence and oppression of their fellow inmates in exchange for food, cigarettes and uniforms.

Instead of rising up and using their massive superiority of numbers against this tiny minority of controllers, the inmate guards jealously implemented their privileges and power.

This was part of an experiment. Ratios and relative numbers and figures were carefully monitored as part of the experiment.

Camps were designed using logistics, mathematical modelling and operational research.

Each camp house applied different mathematical models and rules.

These were pitilessly administered and the effects on inmates were recorded and observed.

Each inmate had a number and type for the purposes of mathematical modelling. Where research was based on behavioural programming the serial numbers were re-used, given the suffix a, b, c etc.

Only one set of those records had been carefully secreted in that little Rye house.

Details on the administration of other camps had been taken away and stored in archives.

It was clear that a high percentage of torture and oppression had been micro managed by selected inmates, and carefully observed by statisticians.

The camps were neither peaceful nor cooperative - rather a mass of individuals struggling to survive.

Families were deliberately separated and social and religious groups mixed up in a way that fractured all normal bonds.

The results were carefully observed and recorded.

It worked.

Piotr sat up when she finished the last page of this section. He knew every word of the written depositions.

'I am certain,' he said, 'that even now, these figures are being decoded and analysed and used in detention camps.'

*

The depositions were framed scientifically.

Once man had created hell, any experiment was permissible.

Many of the tests seemed totally futile.

Then again maybe the successful ones had already moved into everyday life.

The research projects listed in the booklets encompassed every single question that a power-hungry male mind could devise.

Each one applied for funding and resources using scientific standards and based on suitable human material.

Waste and profligacy were high.

'Did you read the comics?' asked Piotr with his mad stare. 'They are continuing the experiments and claiming it is extra-terrestrials. It is all a cover up.'

He was haunted by Roswell.

'Venusians!' he almost frothed, 'They are ape children, our children!' he averred 'They were sent up to the stratosphere to freeze to death. They cut their vocal chords to prevent them screaming during the testing. Read it here. Read it.'

Who wanted to know?

'Look,' he pronounced. 'See this Venusian writing. It is German. German!'

It was indeed German.

*

The list of experiments was carefully ordered.

Piotr ensured that Elena read every single one of his bound copies.

They had been carefully typed, and were marked with official stamps.

She had no idea how he had acquired them, except that he and Magda had been witnesses at the closed trials.

The first set of experiments involved tried cryogenic freezing.

They froze victims for different lengths of time and tried various revival techniques.

One hour, 1 month, 6 months, a year.

They froze brains, and tried to cut down on brain injuries with different methods.

If they needed different types of brain injuries to run in parallel - where to find them if not in the camps?

Compare brain injuries? Just injure inmates.

They froze embryos torn from pregnant mothers, spliced embryos with animals of every kind to see what would happen.

They attempted in vitro fertilisation taking eggs from girls like Magda and freezing them.

*

470

The next book described transplants of all kinds, legs, arms, livers, kidneys, and hearts.

It was easy to find experimental material and there was a glut of humans needing to be used up.

They took healthy limbs and attached them to those whose limbs they had cut or blown off.

They experimented on spinal injuries.

They cut away different amounts of liver to check for regeneration.

*

The depositions described how young teenagers like Piotr and Magda had been taken up in street sweeps and moved to experimental camps.

They were fed and housed, waiting to learn what would be removed and whether they would survive the injuries inflicted for surgeons to practice on.

With this amount of human material available, it was possible to check on levels of anaesthesia. It was easy to compare types of healing and levels of pain tolerance.

Subjects were compared in wards made up specifically for the purpose. They were held in hospitals attached to camps which had been subsequently obliterated by the victors.

The allies had swept up the experiments and their results. The details were now being used to continue testing in secret laboratories all over the world.

Victims had pig's hearts implanted, animal limbs attached. Cyber-limbs attached after removing healthy limbs. Bones coated in steel and steel joints and limbs. They were cut in half and spliced into machines, their agonies recorded and observed.

Those chosen for surgery waited in the holding camps, claimed Piotr. They had to tend the tortured victims of experiments already under way.

They knew that they were doomed.

Magda had nursed limbless and otherwise tortured patients who had been healthy the day before. She had nursed those with steel hands screwed to once perfect hands, those with steel bones and joints replacing their once healthy bodies.

They had both witnessed the suffering of those with new transplanted eyes and those with skin burnt to different levels to try out various salves and cures. Wounds inflicted and left to heal themselves for control purposes.

The women were made pregnant and their foetuses operated on or removed for experimental purposes. Full-term babies were removed at birth, never to be seen again.

*

Other experiments tested human endurance.

The effects of sleep deprivation, running until joints collapsed were observed with clinical precision.

They investigated brain washing and psychic experiments, the effects of fear and induced psychosis and mind control.

Inmates were compelled to fight with different drugs in their veins, to kill and to exhibit animal behaviour, to test sexual capacity and endurance.

Researchers opened up brains in the same way that anti-vivisectionists show in pictures of cat experiments.

They were tested for telepathy with electrodes deep in their brains, then killed off as useless.

Skulls were opened and the brains were subjected to electric shocks, they dropped chemicals into the open brain. They inserted needles and tubes, removed clusters of nerves and stimulated others. In these experiments the vocal chords needed to be cut.

Screaming distracted the researchers.

*

Further books listed investigations into the possibilities of germ warfare.

Diseases were collected and introduced, wounds deliberately caused and infected.

Perhaps it laid the foundation of later surgical miracles.

'Surely this is enough for me to know? Is that what happened to you?'

Intense stare.

'Of course not.'

'Ok. So can I leave now? Can I go home?' the child was trembling and unfit for more.

472

'Don't you want to know the rest?'

'No,' she felt trapped and scared. 'Is there more?'

She needed her heartless mummy.

*

Magda's pity, which had been wiped away by working in labs, resurfaced.

The next day they went to Hastings, in their posh car, with heating and working wind up windows.

There was an icy spring breeze.

Elena confided in her cousin, who covered her ears.

'Shut it!' She warned. 'You know I hate all that bookish stuff. You are just so weird. You have no common sense!'

What about concentration camps then? Did she not know about those?

'Well, you know,' Agata admitted in a smug little voice. 'Our families were war heroes.'

(The number of heroes and dissenters among the refugees!)

'Mummy and daddy escaped after many trials, just like the movies. They helped thousands and saved Poland.'

Elena tried to explain.

Agata covered her ears.

'I'm not listening. Get back to your books. I don't believe a word you say. You have no common sense.'

Agata was uninterested in the stories.

'*My* family saved the world from evil. So *we* have nothing to worry about. Anyway, you always did make things up. Why don't you just go and be a professor?'

She spat this out like it was a prostitute.

*

The next day the reading took another turn, to the super warrior programme.

There were two main strands to this research.

The officer class - the super race - were to be drawn from gifted Aryan children with extraordinary intelligence at birth, or children of high ranking officers.

The medical experiments involving cyber 'mech' suits, cyber limbs etc., were for them.

473

They were also to be trained in mind control land psychic methods of coercion.

There were records of stupid helmets for telepathic transfer and control using brain enhancement helmets drawn pretty accurately in comics.

Secondly, there were super warrior troops.

These were designed to be obedient and powerful grunts who would cow opposition to Aryan dominance over the whole world.

These men had to be possessed of animal strength for combat on the front line, brutal killers totally loyal to their masters (in brain helmets!) and without a care for their personal survival, only that of their masters.

Nest there were the intelligent and cunning killers and spies, designed specifically to run campaigns and conduct the war while their masters relaxed on holiday in the mountains.

*

It was clear why Hitler managed his campaigns the way he did.

The troop classes were bred for specific campaigns, fighting types and terrains.

The experiments attempted to create what were called transgenics or mutants by splicing both eggs and foetuses with wolves, apes, dolphins, birds etc.

They also implanted humans with ape parts, forced females to have sex with animals to see if they could 'naturally' produce offspring, or attempted to bring foetuses to term 'in vitro'.

They derived battle drugs from animals and human glands and experimented with hallucinogens. It was not clear if these had worked because parts of these depositions had been redacted and large sections were blacked out. She could not understand if it had worked.

*

There were children, born by Caesarean section. Magda and other women nursed them and fed them.

Most of them looked weird and had operations from birth.

The women provided eggs for experimental purposes and the men sperm.

The babies lived in clinical conditions and were constantly

474

measured weighed and checked for any disease. The sick and mental were despatched for extermination.

According to the depositions, ape children were used in painful and dangerous experiments to test their tolerances.

They were taken to high altitudes, experienced extreme heat, cold high speeds, poisons and used to pilot the 'flying saucers'.

So there really were such craft? It seemed that there were several experimental antimagnetic craft. They made most human pilots sick because to the effects of very high magnetic fields on the brain. They were trying to breed a transgenic immune to this type of magnetism.

*

The testimonies stated that humano-ape transgenics thrived, though they lacked the bloodlust required of shock troops. However, they remained useful as pilots of experimental craft and for dirty conditions, working with poisons chemicals and radiation.

How many had survived the war?

This too had been redacted.

Other types, which had not yet been evolved, were still at the experimental stage. They were to be used in more warlike situations and there was hope for troops with canine and wolf in the mix.

*

Then there was genetic work, which seemed hopeless and fruitless, causing suffering to both human and animal, with the removal of eggs and implantation of foetuses, operations in the womb etc.

The work with embryos was popular with doctors as it often led to spectacular and interesting deformities.

It generated interest among high-ranking visitors.

All types of operations on foetuses in the uterus were explored. Work in vitro was attempted although unsuccessful in producing live births.

Life had been created, but did not survive.

*

Magda watched as the girl read.

'I am sure that work in these areas is continuing. I have heard of secret sites using mental patients and condemned criminals, as well as abductees, for material.'

'When Germany fell, the victors saw what was in the labs', stated Piotr, 'they were extremely shocked yet did not close them. We stayed where we were until professors and doctors came to observe, under heavy guard. The professors took all of the results, the papers and the publications. They drove away like looters. They herded up the researchers and took them away and they fought over the transgenics like animals. They let us go after questioning, even though we wanted to give witness to what had been done.'

'When I read these comics, I can see that they make a mockery of our suffering. They are continuing the work unabated. Others are experiencing what we went through.'

'You must make this right. They won't listen to us.'

*

They showed Elena the pictures of supposed aliens, and the drawings of the Venusians at Roswell.

'Magda pointed to a dead humano ape child.

It was a boy, but its sexual organs had been removed and it had clearly had an operation on its vocal chords too.

'That could be my son,' wept Magda. 'They made us breast feed them and operated on the poor creatures endlessly.'

Perhaps it was true.

If it really worked them the research was just too promising and too heartless.

Men who worshipped at the altar of science had the opportunity to beat women at birthing.

It was the scientific dream where man sacrificed the living in order to create a world under perfect control.

*

Piotr was bitter.

Researchers had worked hard to make their work acceptable to the public by disseminating myths of extra-terrestrials and super-warriors in comics.

They were doing whatever it took to ensure the origins of the work were forgotten and the crimes of the past washed away.

The original German professors, war criminals to a man, became the gentle and caring fathers of the mutants, venerated in fiction, not the torturers and white supremacists of historic fact.

476

The origins of the mutants were hidden in the mists of lies. The experimental camps even figured as schools for the gifted!

*

It was obvious that the last sets of experiments were nonsensical and even whimsical.

These were psychic experiments to investigate telepathy, magic and the paranormal.

Researchers were testing books of magic and attempting to raise the dead.

There were even experiments to build Frankenstein to Mary Shelley's design and investigate the legends of vampires and Zombies.

Mothers were taken from babies to see if they had a telepathic link or recognised each other.

It was horrifying. The investigations into the paranormal seemed to have been created on a whim, to use up all of that useless humanity and sloshing around the camps waiting to die. An alternative to being gassed and made into leather coats, lampshades and sofas.

It seemed endless. There were experiments to test random ideas: on poisons, chemical pollution, diseases which were known to kill and maim, sexual deviancy and behavioural conditioning, lobotomies and amputation, electrocution, asphyxia, drowning, frostbite, sensory deprivation, solitary confinement, child abuse of all kinds, crushing, exhaustion, diets, organ removal and transplantation, prosthetics, cyborgs, antimagnetic energy and flight, altitude sickness and oxygen deprivation, rocket men. The results of that research had since been picked over by the victors and built on by tyrannies everywhere.

*

Piotr and Magda, the almost illiterate and handsome peasants, wanted to discuss what she had read.

They were sure mixing animal and human DNA had not ended. The human porpoises and talking apes, they insisted, should have equal rights to mankind, medical care and schooling.

The idea came from war, oppression and tyranny of man over woman and beast, all this research should be public and transparent.

477

They believed that there were X men and mutants living hopeless lives in laboratories with no rights although they were brothers and sisters. Their lives were subject to the whim of men in white coats who had no mercy and no love.

'It hasn't stopped.'

The experiments entailed the torture of sentient beings.

'Listen to us,' said Magda. 'Help us to be heard. There are still operations on new-borns without anaesthetic, live embryos spliced, mothers dragged from their babies and told that they had been sterilised after their eggs were harvested.'

Piotr showed her another lurid comic about alien abductions.

'You can tell,' he said. 'These abductions are endemic in all countries involved in research.'

Magda whispered that the experiments satisfied the womb envy which plagued science and medicine. They could no longer be condoned.

The pair were distraught.

'Our lives have been ruined, but we have to save the others. What about these others? You have to save them.'

The psychopathic perpetrators remained unpunished to forge ahead in their work, living and working in suburbia in secret laboratories protected by Cold War legalities.

They could do nothing. Any 'communist' and 'subversive' protesters could be imprisoned under official secrets acts with undisclosed powers.

War criminals were the founding and unsung fathers of surgery. The original healthy victims, and the mental patients and prisoners who subsequently followed them to the world of medical research, were leading medical advances.

No one cared one jot about them.

*

'These records had been used to found new branches of medicine,' Piotr said bitterly.

The pitiless pioneers ensured doctors had a good idea of what was possible and had documented knowledge of the mechanics.

Instead of being punished, they were employed in secret labs.

And experiments continued; on mental patients and prisoners, army volunteers and bomb victims in forgotten places.

Animals and apes of human sizes would become extinct to help drive the research forward.

*

This information was very hard on Elena.

She lost her appetite and became afraid to leave the house.

Even so, Piotr and Magda did not give up. They kept telling the poor child more.

The pair did not describe precisely what they did, but she realised that they would be called mutants.

They were genetic experiments, super warriors.

*

She felt sorry for them.

They had shared copies of their unheard depositions with others. Each of them was dedicated to telling an uncaring audience that the work started in Germany was continuing in secret labs all over the world.

They were hoping to prevent it.

They didn't stand a chance.

*

Magda admitted she had given birth to several 'deformed' children. She mentioned half chimpanzee E.T. types that were beloved of US movies.

These were a successful part of the breeding programme as transgenics were biddable and quiet, strong and not particularly aggressive.

They had both verbal and telepathic skills. It was recommended that they be castrated and their vocal chords should be cut so as not to 'distress' the researchers and obstruct them from forming bonds with subjects.

These transgenics were 'pink' like the Venusians of Roswell.

They may have been like mules. She suspected that 'greys' were the product of African-American and chimpanzee, US born.

It was possible.

*

Both of them claimed that successful transgenics had been grasped by the various victors at the close of the war.

Their offspring lived in experimental labs hidden all over the world. Whole laboratories had been removed and rebuilt in places like Area 51, Porton Down and Siberia.

17.

Clapham 1956

Elena slept for most of remaining visit. She was exhausted and traumatised.

Piotr and Magda let her sleep late and invited her out to see their animals. She avoided them as much as possible, in case they asked her to see anything else.

They sat whispering in the corner and offered her the finest food, which she ate and then sat alone in their garden, playing with the chickens.

Anuta watched TV endlessly and occasionally dragged her cousin to Rye where they sat on the bleak sea front watching seagulls and eating chips.

At the end of two weeks, she rushed into her mother's arms.

'Mama! Mama! I am so glad to see you. I am so glad to be home'.

Elena was delighted to see Jasia.

She no longer worried that the house was cold and the bare floorboards insufficiently were covered by torn linoleum. She did not mind being deprived of food at times when her mother was tortured by nightmares. She needed help and debriefing, even now imagining child wolf soldiers waiting behind the curtains.

She told her mother everything seeking reassurance and commiseration. After all, her mother had nightmares about events in the war too. Maybe she knew about these things and had something to say.

*

Alarmingly, it had the opposite effect to the one she expected.

Katya went absolutely crazy.

She accused Elena of persecuting her, plotting to get her into prison.

'Never speak about all of this as we would all end up in prison. Even you.'

She warned it would be entirely her fault.

'We have already had visits from the doctor who wants to make sure you are eating properly. And now he is going to say I have to be deported. It's all your fault.'

She smacked her daughter and warned her never to speak of this to anyone.

'That pair! Criminals. Wreckers.' She reverted into Russian curses and foul language. 'This was a secret! Who do they think they are! I've a good mind to report them.'

It was not just Katya who was concerned.

Everyone in that Clapham household was riven with fear that they would be somehow associated with the war crimes. They were afraid of being deported like the Cossacks.

There were furious whispers around the kitchen sink among adults, with the child as *persona non grata* for bringing these secrets up.

The pair living in Rye had reached out for help. Unluckily for them, Elena was the daughter of a war criminal in hiding. A child could not root out war crimes and she had no idea if the depositions were genuine or true.

Where had they obtained them? They had claimed to be part of a hidden group of concentration camp survivors. The books in the farmhouse had been painstakingly collected with a view to publication at some later date.

Judging by what she heard, the Polish community were planning to shut them down.

After all, if the final pieces of evidence were destroyed, who would know?

*

Her mother silenced her, and the family, desperate to succeed in the brave new world of England, succeeded in burying the past.

The girl recovered, and forgot most of what she had been told.

She never mentioned it to anyone and it slipped into nightmares and dreams.

Nonetheless, she never forgot those depositions.

The details drove her forward in every tragedy she faced. Nothing could ever be as bad as the things she had read there.

'Get a grip,' she would say, whatever happened could not be that bad.

*

As an adult it was clear to her why judges at Nuremberg had not wanted to publish such horrors to a world slowly recovering from a vicious struggle. They found it hard to accept that it was so easy to demolish intrinsic personality, unshakable morality and humanity. The records showed that few were genuinely prepared to die rather than compromise their goodness and their removal had the same effect as the killing of leaders did to herds. It created a bovine and tractable herd.

The research work of the Nazis had exposed the mechanics of oppression and showed how the mind automatically created an alternative reality where good was redefined as anything which needed to be done in order to survive. In other words, man had created his own hell. God definitely did not need to build one.

It was no accident that after the 'hot' war of 1939-1945 there was a further period of 30 years of 'cold' war.

The victors carefully absorbed the information stored in the camps and the testimonies of the camp survivors.

No one wanted to know too much about what had happened. It was a long time before it was possible to admit these things at all.

In the meantime, the moral vacuum allowed psychopaths to generate weapons of mass destruction, ever larger nuclear bombs, germs to send into the atmosphere with the intention of killing millions, gasses to kill and maim and super warrior programmes.

All these nightmare scenarios were openly stated to be tools for peace and defence.

18.

Moscow 1957

Anatoly's meteoric rise through the party ranks had a lot to do with the fact that he had done nothing and achieved less. He kept a baleful eye on Lucia using the spy network.

He learnt that he had a son.

It rankled that the boy seemed happy and satisfied without his real father. Only the Cold War made it impossible for him to do any harm.

At the end of the war Anatoly moved to Moscow.

He had successfully managed the giant collectives and had survived the purges.

His experiences with Lucia were studied enthusiastically by the trainers of the espionage corps. Anatoly was careful when telling the story. He tried to give his interrogators what they wanted. T

The narrative became intensely distorted as he included events to fit their expectations. As he dined out on tales of Lucia's exploits it could be said that his exaggerated tales lent a hand in the training of the sex spies of the 1960's.

*

Miraculously he survived every twist and turn of party policy, somehow gaining the reputation of a martyr at the hands of a spy.

He married a fetching Russian girl who had a tiny part in the spate of propagandist movies about the defence of Stalingrad.

She starred in the movie about a girl who had followed her swain into battle and shot a sniper.

It was immensely popular and considered as an agitprop coup. Anatoly fell for her mostly because she bore a striking similarity to Lucia.

He was not cruel to her, rather slavishly besotted and snivelling. She despised him and he rather enjoyed it. He had gone from sadist to masochist as his fortunes waxed and waned.

*

Anatoly had two further children, but was not certain that they were his. He had not daring to divorce his wife when she was openly unfaithful with senior party members.

His second son looked nothing like him, but he never mentioned it. No one in the party every rocked the boat.

Anatoly's eldest boy, Dmitry, was clever and able. As the son of a film starlet and from a good socialist background, he was eligible for every extra offered by the splendid education system.

He was least affected by the growing rift between his parents, who did not divorce until he was 10 years old.

The younger boys, Vladimir and Gregory, were too small when the arguments started and were consequently hampered in their studies.

*

With the rise of nepotism in the party, Anatoly was able to ensure that his three boys went to schools selected for future leaders.

Graduates from these schools would move into positions of power all over the Eastern Bloc. They automatically took high posts in satellite states, usually working for Cominform or high-level posts in Soviet-style secret police systems in the Bloc countries.

Sometimes they worked in television or other propaganda areas.

The best graduates were offered posts in foreign espionage.

*

Espionage College was the Eton of Moscow, where the graduates learnt to watch American TV and to live typical American lives in order to fit in perfectly.

They lived in the lap of luxury, having access to all Western goods. They were taught that the economic advantages of the West were transient and they were confident of technical success, reassured by successes in the Space Race and keeping parity in the nuclear frenzy. They learnt the best of the dialectic and were committed to the state.

A selected few, among them Dmitry, were taught American history and learnt to speak English with a flawless accent.

They were to be sent abroad to obtain influential jobs using nameless contacts and communist sympathisers. Or embassy work in Western countries, where they managed complex contacts and information dissemination with press journalists in Soviet pay. Tasks involved espionage, intelligence gathering and spreading

485

disinformation.

In general Russian espionage was successful.

The decolonisation of the British and American Empire had allowed Russia to spread the word of revolution in Africa and Latin America.

Marxist philosophy had successfully outperformed capitalism in over half of the globe.

The young recruits for the new Cold War were assured that history was on their side; the days of Western supremacy were numbered. The West could not win, because exploitation and war-mongering were inherent in capitalism.

It was evil. It was rotten and corrupt. It would fall.

*

Dmitry was quietly confident that he would play a significant part in the future of world peace through his work.

He was tall and handsome and rather similar to his half-brother Misha in America.

Right up to graduation, he was fully reliant on a single version of events, promoted by strictly controlled media, and had not developed critical faculties.

An enthusiastic supporter of the party and popular in school, he was destined for higher things and the pride of his bully father.

He was confident in Russian technical superiority, persuaded that shortages were temporary and that consumer goods would shortly be abundant.

He did not perceive the Berlin wall as confining people, rather a method of preventing class enemies from stealing Soviet education and skills, which belonged to the state.

These traitors were selling their souls, which belonged to the state, to the highest bidder. They were hustlers deserving to be punished for their attempt to steal Soviet knowledge.

He was perfectly confident of Russian military superiority and American cowardice in the face of their superior nuclear arms.

Many of his friends were cosmonauts.

19.

Wroclaw 1960

Sergei was a talented child. He was graceful, tall and strong, a demigod among the stunted youth in that house. Sofia fed him well; he had special privileges at school and was collected twice a week for extra gymnastics and dance class. He had several girlfriends and strings of admirers.

He looked nothing like his siblings and must have taken after his father, although Sofia remembered very little about that encounter so long ago.

He became increasingly aggrieved that his mother had accepted her status as a drudge. She had adopted the posture of a beggar woman while travelling across Poland and had now assumed the stance permanently. It had the advantage of making Janek less hostile to her youngest son.

Her beggarly posture protected Sergei from persecution, although her defeated air made him feel like a bad person, for reasons which he could not understand.

Despite his success outside the family, within the family, his status was as low as his mother's. Attempts to defend her were obviously signs of malicious violence and she rarely succeeded in protecting him.

He had little opportunity to help, because the roles of family members were ingrained and there was no space to grow.

*

Mealtimes were scenes of strife. He was expected to help her with the cooking and housework, and rarely did.

If he came home and she was rushing a great deal, and he had nothing to do, he would help her a little, and then claim the credit.

She praised him to the skies.

One day, when she could not finish the chores, she asked him for help.

'I'm extremely tired mummy,' he complained.

A long day at school and a heavy gymnastic workout was a heavy burden for him.

The kitchen was in a mess and she was exhausted. She commiserated and understood. He had his own life. She had no part in it.

'Go and lie down darling,' she reassured him. 'I will manage.'

*

The food was late in arriving, and the onions were burnt, imparting an unpleasant flavour to the meatballs in gravy.

Jan and Eva and the children complained vociferously.

'This is inedible. It is crap. You have ruined good meat.'

'You are trying to poison us.'

'We work all day and you cannot even prepare an evening meal. I bet you sat around all day lazing about.'

'Praying,' sniffed Maryssa. A loud guffaw arose from the children. Everyone had little digs to add.

'Hanging around with that useless priest again.'

'What do they get up to?'

Loud sniggers greeted every comment and Sofia tried to shrug them off.

'There was a long queue in the market,' she excused herself. 'The shoes you wanted required me to wait from 6.00am to noon.'

She rustled off to fetch them.

'Here they are.'

Eva picked them over carefully and bustled to put them into store. 'Didn't they have them in my size? You should have checked.'

'I did,' replied Sofia. 'I honestly did. This was the nearest size I could get.'

A pause. 'They might fit Sergei.'

'Well, you weren't there early enough, because I heard that they had them. It is pure laziness.'

'Gossiping with the no-good housewives all day I expect. I see the old ladies sitting in cafes while honest people are toiling.'

Sofia knew how much she worked. She accepted the judgement and was puzzling how to do more when Sergei kicked over his chair.

'She is working flat out can't you see? You are spiteful and mean to a helpless old lady. She is your mother, for god's sake!'

He turned on Janek.

'You are a traitor to your own mother!'

Janek cringed with the memory of his multiple betrayals. His conscience was deeply calloused by the life he had led. He had recovered instantly.

'Don't stand up for her; you're as bad as she is.'

Sergei was taller than Janek, who was already tall. He stood up to the weak man.

'If you don't like the food,' quipped Sergei. 'Why don't you cook it for once?'

'I bet she has been running after you,' Jan replied. 'It is your behaviour which interferes with managing things. She lives here for nothing and we can expect a little help.'

'A little? She does absolutely everything. You are the laziest creep in the area she's an old lady...'

'How dare you!' shouted Janek, 'you live here for nothing. I support you out of the goodness of my heart. You should be helping your mother. In fact I expect you to do so from now on.'

*

Sergei loved his mother, even though she was bullied by everyone. He rejected her pacifism. He resented the fact that she gave away everything which was precious to her. He frequently hollered at her and got into terrible tantrums, for which she would apologise.

He was picky over food. If he left food he did not like Sofia ate it up.

'I was saving it for later.' he fumed, 'now I have nothing to eat.'

'I did not know that the food was to be eaten; I threw it on the compost.'

He was sulky and thoughtless; although he usually repented some days later and bought her a gift.

Nevertheless, he grew up a rebellious teenager, disobedient to Janek and surly to Eva. He was insulted by constant adverse comparisons with Maryssa, whose talents were more in keeping with the family ethos. She was top of her class and had a reputation for being best at maths in the school.

She was considered infinitely superior to Sergei even though he was already a noted ballet hopeful.

*

At 15, he began to lie lied about where he had been.

He had been an extremely sensitive and loving child with the best intentions, but now he became hostile and threatening. He had learnt denial from her and used it when needed. He lied to her whenever he could and shouted her down if she questioned him.

Sometimes he returned with a bruised eye or cut lip she worried about his wounds and wept over his torn clothes.

'Perhaps you were attacked.' She prevaricated. 'All the same I do not think that violence is ever the answer.'

'It *is* the answer, mummy. It truly is. You *never* stand up for yourself! Where has it got you?'

*

By the age of 16, he had lost his virginity to his young groupie girlfriend, who exhorted him to drink and smoke. He often got involved in fights.

Sofia acted out her disappointment by weeping quietly and getting depressed.

'Sergei,' she suggested, 'you may be a bit of a thug. I can see it in what you wear. This turned up collar, it is meant to intimidate, and you stare at people so aggressively. Did I teach you to do that? Was it something I did?'

Sergei shrugged off her attempts. He despised her pacifism. She did not notice. She was already blaming herself.

'I have placed my children in this purgatory,' she brooded. 'I have caused them to fail. I have not led them as I should. I am a poor example, too proud and angry.'

She apologised for hectoring her son.

*

He escaped by staying overnight at a girlfriend's house.

'Personally,' she told him, when he finally returned home. 'I ask you to think about your actions carefully. I may have misunderstood you and this may be the right thing to do. Maybe I am stupid and I don't understand things.'

'Yes,' he whispered to Sofia. 'You are stupid mummy. You really are. You never stand up for yourself and don't support me at all.'

Aloud he said something entirely non-committal and sauntered off, revelling in Eva's baffled animosity.

'Why do you not beat that ugly oaf?' she screeched. 'I have never met anyone who deserved it more.'

Sergei made faces at her behind Sofia's back. He hated his half-brother and his wife, and he had a low opinion of Sofia. She could contradict herself three times in one breath, and always ended up apologising.

He wanted to leave school and work, but Sofia begged him to stay. She wanted Sergei's son to have a chance at life. To her he was the personification of all that had happened in the darkest days of the conflict. Her son was the one thing she could influence for the good.

If the truth be told, she loved her last child more than any other and she believed him to be the expiation of her guilt at surviving when so many others had not.

*

The school had proposed he enrol at the school of the arts.

Arts were alien to Maslow family tradition which had always concentrated on the sciences.

His teachers pushed him to train for gymnastics and ballet.

Sofia tried to provide gentle guidance and advice, while leaving him free to make decisions.

'Darling,' she offered, 'it is up to you. You must do what you think is right.'

Jan did not see any value in such a career. He wanted him to get a job and to help his mother.

'Janek,' begged Sofia, 'he has talent. He has to practice the piano and he has rehearsals for his performances. None of the children help, I do not expect it.'

'Nonsense, he is strong and healthy, he has plenty of time to hand around the streets. Let him help you.'

'What's with dancing anyway,' he scoffed. 'It's not even a proper proletarian job.'

Sergei stood up and started to swagger.

'You really want to know? I bet I'll earn more than an under assistant post master. Postman more like.'

Sofia tried to shut her son up.

'I am fine,' she insisted. 'I look after myself.'

491

Sergei huffed around and clattered the plates.

After the meal was over, she turned to Sergei.

'I am doing it for you. Keep studying and do well. Be a good person.'

*

Sergei did not feel good.

He was blamed for all that was wrong in the overcrowded household. When he fought for her rights, she admonished him.

'Sergei, my dearest, we must not argue with our fate.' she was mindful of her karma and assumed that they was living in purgatory. 'It is best to do as we are asked. You should remember that I love you. Love is so important.'

She recalled the lost children on the trains in Moscow and Stalingrad.

'So many children like you have died in the most awful circumstances. The lord our god is protects you. We have been through many trials together, only you do not remember.' She sighed heavily. 'You are the most fortunate child.'

As he became larger and more athletic, his mother gave him her profits from the sweet kitchens, which he grasped at needily. Yet he loathed her for making him feel selfish.

Despite being a talented musician and brilliant ballet dancer, he was marooned in a sea of resentment. He inhabited a thuggish world, and could have been a sociopath. Fortunately, Sofia's sweetness combined with the raw strength and survival instinct of his father. Art gave him an outlet for his feelings and when he expressed his emotions in dance he was stunningly beautiful.

Education and training were subsidised by the state. Both music and ballet tuition were free, although only the talented were expected stay in classes. Sergei had talent. He radiated stardom.

*

Janek was annoyed by his step-brother's fine qualities. As space allocations grew larger, he pulled a few strings based on his contacts in the party to seek out scholarships which would take Sergei out of their orbit. Eva used her party connections to obtain a coveted audition with the Bolshoi Ballet. The school were enthusiastic and funded the journey.

Sergei was accepted from hundreds of candidates, provided he retrieved his Ukrainian nationality.

He agreed.

As he left home to fulfil his destiny, his mother recited multiple rosaries for his future success and wept heavy-hearted tears at his delighted acceptance.

*

From then on, the family followed his career from news. His biography described a fatherless boy, cared for by the state from birth.

According to his biographers, Sergei the star owed a heavy debt to socialism, which had provided the resources for him to reach the top of his profession on the basis of talent alone.

The young man went along with the myth though he did not forget his mother. She was invited to Moscow to see her son perform the lead in Swan Lake, travelling luxuriously in a carriage reserved for party members.

*

She spent her whole time staring out of the window and trying to find the places she had passed over 16 years ago.

The area had changed out of all recognition. She was dreadfully impressed by the station. She was far more impressed by it than by the grandeurs of the Kremlin.

'Moscow central station has not changed,' she kept telling him excitedly. 'I was here with you as a baby. Perhaps you remember?'

He son hugged her. She was so tiny and shrunken! She grasped his hands.

He was a success. She was a failure and did not want to humiliate him.

'You were born here, Sergei,' she kept repeating. 'This is your home.'

She attended the performance of his first night. He was rapturously applauded. She met the cast.

*

The visit was not a perfect success. Sergei wanted her to have a good time; she wanted *him* to have a good time. Relations were a little strained.

493

'Do you like this?' He asked.

'Yes, do you?' she replied.

'Mama, it is for *you*,' he stressed.

'I am only happy if *you* are happy.'

*

Sofia had scoured her mind and body of all personal desires. In doing so, she had forgotten who she was. Her only goal was to atone for her sins so that she could reincarnate in her next life in a place of peace and not in one the hells of war.

Her son took her to the sights. She met his girlfriends and chatted politely to the staff. She felt awkward.

He resented that she was not ecstatic at his success. But she *was* proud of him. He did not know how proud she was of his success. To her, he was the essence of the suffering in Stalingrad. He represented courage and survival.

It was just that she was ashamed of her poverty and uselessness among the wealth and splendour of the theatre. The dancers wore Western clothes and played Western music, they were beautiful and healthy. She was a poor old crone and an embarrassment.

At the end of the visit Sergei invited his mother to come back to Moscow.

She offered Janek and Eva go instead. The matter was dropped.

*

As the iron curtain fell over the soviet empire, defection became an issue. Articles in Pravda explained that emigration restrictions were justified. Those leaving should pay 'education tax', since the people had the right to recoup its investment in the populace; therefore, illegal defection to the 'West' was treason.

The Maslows heard that ballet dancers were beginning to defect, or at least, demand to perform guest tours with other ballet companies.

It seemed a remote possibility, until they heard that Sergei Bogdanovich had defected during a tour in the USA, along with several other ballet dancers.

He was nineteen, and on his first tour.

20.

Petrograd 1955

Sergei had been determined to leave for the West. He had no ties with Russia. He knew that there would be reprisals for his family if he left, he didn't care. Sofia's circumstances could get no worse. Perhaps his fame would even improve her position.

Indeed, his mother was secretly delighted; she knew that it was a better place for her son.

*

Even though Sergei's biography had called him 'fatherless', his defection had repercussions.

In London, Katya had been living her grey old life. Psychosis overtook her occasionally and she spat it out at her daughter but in general she enjoyed her life tallying complex audits managing tax evasion for large corporations.

She maintained her innocence by creating a domestic universe in which Elena was culpable for all her sins. She daily regretted the absence of real force which had ensured success and notoriety in the past. And she resented the fact that doctors constantly asked Elena if she was happy at home and eating well.

Elena did not fear her. She merely smiled when her mother was at her most threatening and often said things to deliberately enrage her parent. She had been reading about Russia and had realised that her mother had to be a party member. How else could she have obtained medical care for her typhoid?

'So you were a party member? What was your role? Who was this Andrei Aunty Anya talks about a lot? Was she you boyfriend.'

Katya tried to threaten her daughter. She gave her the stare which had destroyed many a tortured victim in Kazakhstan.

It did not work in London.

Elena only laughed.

'Mama, you're not a party member anymore. You can't do anything to me.'

*

When a controller contacted her about Sergei, Katya sprang to life as if she had been a wilted plant in need of water. She had been a sleeper for nearly eighteen ears; and sank into gloom over the fact that they had no need of her.

In truth, she was a low-life with no influence, working for a company which had been infiltrated already. Moreover, the KGB was inundated with candidates from within the British nation. MI5 was riddled with agents. What need for a piece of scum like her?

She was briefly activated but had heard nothing of Sergei. After this interlude there was once again silence Freon her controllers. She heard no more and relapsed into greyness.

By now, she had fully forgiven herself. She now had vivid dreams of her interrogation successes. Her Partkom boyfriend had gained shining beauty in her recollections and she constantly relived their tragic parting.

She dreamed of collapse and disaster in England and her resuscitation as an agent.

*

In Wroclaw, the Maslows faced more serious repercussions.

The secret police knew that Sergei had not contacted anyone in London. There was little that they could do in England anyway.

Behind the iron curtain the family were marked out as potential traitors. Secret police questioned Sofia. She had been followed when she visited her son in Moscow. Their conversations were carefully transcribed and on file.

Janek was furious, and Eva talked of evicting her treacherous mother in law.

'We have nurtured a viper,' she cursed. 'You were always a nasty hypocrite. I bet you told him to leave. You are a class traitor. I should have you denounced.'

Sofia wept and assured that she knew nothing.

Things got seriously nasty and bullying.

Janek was triumphant. He had won. It was time to remove his annoying parent at last. They had little need of Sofia, who was growing weak and would shortly be in need of care. This was a perfect opportunity to get rid of their potential burden.

*

The family sat around the table sharing their evening meal.

Janek moved in for a killing blow.

'We need more space as the children grew older,' he began. 'Sofia is taking up a lot of space. She can find somewhere else to live where they can use her. She is unnecessary.'

For the first time Maryssa sprang to her grandmother's defence.

The girl had already fought to defend Sergei many times over. She loved her parents, but the last weeks had tried her sorely. She looked at Sofia's crushed figure and realised that she loved Sergei and his mother too. She was furious with Eva for threatening to denounce Sergei's mother.

'He is famous, mama. You never even liked him. I think you are jealous. I bet you wish he was your son. I don't think we would hear anything bad about him then.'

Eva spat out that Maryssa was not her daughter. She was adopted.

It was the end.

21.

Wroclaw 1955

Maryssa learnt her history and was overcome by sorrow.

All of the suppressed grief of the tiny child came out in tantrums at her adopted mother. The family heaved with emotion and disruption. Maryssa spilled out her years of resentment and loneliness at being brought up by a working mother who had multiple interests and little time.

She had only Sofia to cling to. She had been neglected. Her step parents had never loved or cared for her.

Eva was shattered. Even Janek was affected. They truly had made every possible sacrifice for their adopted child.

Maryssa rejected them. In all that sickening revelation the girl clung on to her roots. The fact that she was Jewish was a raft to connect to her parents.

She denied the fact that Sofia and Eva were Jewish too. Only her parents were truly Jewish. They were martyrs, who had given their lives for their faith.

She despised her adopted family for denying religion and her roots. Not even Sofia was free from her criticism.

'Granny, you have a kind heart, though you are still a traitor. You abandoned everyone, your father and mother and even your own son.'

Sofia did not deny it.

As for Jan and Eva – they were entirely to blame for the extermination of her family.

'You let then die!' she screamed. 'You let them go to Auschwitz without a fight.'

The Maslow's had no defence. It was impossible to explain how it was, what is had been like. In any case, Janek felt guilty and could not explain his actions. He had not exactly formulated a plan to save the Jelinskis and regretted taking the family in.

Harrowingly, he remembered how he had dreamt of getting his hands on their gold, without ever actually doing anything about it. He shuddered with remorse at remembering how glad they had been of the extra money and how they relished their new life without stress. He knew himself to be innocent of their blood.

It was far worse for Eva. Unknowingly, Maryssa had tapped into a seam of guilt which Eva had long hidden away.

*

Eva had abandoned her family during the holodomor[24]. She was only eleven when she ran away, and, although she could in fact have done nothing for them, she felt intensely culpable. She remembered the famine, and her all-conquering desire to set off alone without her fundamentalist father in his ridiculous side-locks.

Maryssa had learnt history at the hands of the socialist regime and there was no compromise.

'You could have helped them and didn't,' Maryssa stated harshly.

Eva did not defend herself in regards to the Jelinskis, because the accusation was true at a deeper and more grisly level.

Everyone, even the Jelinskis, knew their fate and they succumbed to their doom.

'It is people like you, who do nothing at all, that allowed the holocaust to happen,' asserted Maryssa.

Her words sparked open the unfinished business raised in the war.

The pair *had* done their best for the Jelinskis.

They did not attempt to defend themselves because they had not acted heroically, and in any case, they both had a lot of cowardly sell-outs to hide.

*

Eva wept for her mother and father and the little children, already dying when she left.

Janek sighed and held his head in his hands. He had betrayed his family for 30 pieces of silver. He had denounced all of his friends, and anyone else for that matter, just to save his skin.

Eva was shattered; she had given her soul to the party.

Her original creed and belief in communism was a distant

---

24 The Holodomor was a man-made famine created by Soviet policies in the Ukraine in 1933. It is also known as the Ukrainian Genocide.

memory. As a *partiyna*[25], she attended party meetings weekly, and learnt the word of the faithful like all religious learn the word of god by rote.

She suspected that she was justly punished, and would not communicate with her favourite step-daughter any more, and just sighed and wept quietly.

She was no communist after all.

The family went through a particularly rough patch. The walls of the house were thin and Miriam, (her new name), had loud blazing rows about true communism and god.

Eva was heartbroken at the hard-hearted child she had nurtured and adored.

Maryssa blanked her.

Eva was not her mother.

The loving step-parent was excised. Just like that.

'Mother! No! Murderer!' she shouted during one heated occasion.

*

The words were branded into Eva's heart.

She had given up everything for the child.

The fur coats from England had been turned into a coat and muffs for Maryssa and the children, while their mother wore a peasant sheepskin.

Eva could not feel the ends of her little fingers on account of working and queuing in that hard winter when the Jelinskis had gone. She had nurtured Maryssa as atonement, and she was forsworn.

She was denounced!

*

Marissa became Miriam the convert. She joined a group of Jewish fundamentalists hoping to emigrate.

She ostentatiously observed the Sabbath at their home every Friday and set a small zone in the tiny kitchen which was to be entirely kosher and pork free. She turned her nose up at their food, and grew horribly thin on her sparse diet.

Innumerable approvals were required before the application

---

[25] Member of the communist party

could be made to the passport office.

There were police checks, employer references and statements from the state housing commission - with no time limit set for action.

For two long years, her application was denied, without appeal, on a variety of ridiculous grounds, such as national security.

Apparently there was a danger that she would release state secrets!

Janek and Eva made peace with Miriam. They supported their daughter and tried to do what they could to help.

Nothing worked.

However, the Israeli state, and even the USA, intervened on behalf of Jews who had relatives in the new state.

Maryssa researched her family, and discovered an auntie in Israel.

She avowed that she had no family in Wroclaw, and, since she had never been formally adopted, this was true.

Jan and Eva were required to make a number of formal admissions about Miriam's origins.

They were reprimanded for their actions and faced a bit of party harassment for failing to be honest. It was not too bad. They had to confess at a specially arranged session when several comrades harangued them on behalf of proper party spirit and right action.

They had to write a confession and received an official reprimand from regional leaders.

Perversely, there was also a great deal of secret admiration for their deeds. It definitively improved their status and reputation.

*

After two years, their daughter joined her blood family in Israel. Her aunt welcomed her at a huge party, where dancing went on far into the night.

She lived on a Kibbutz, where she experienced the Jewish version of the socialist dream.

She learnt English, with a heavy Jewish accent, and Hebrew.

The singing, dancing and communal life was wonderful at first. Ultimately, it was not enough. The socialist dream was not hers, and she could belong to it.

*

501

Miriam missed her Polish family and regretted deserting them. She missed Poland; she missed Eva, her siblings and home.

All letters sent to Wroclaw were marked 'return to sender' and she assumed that they did not want to speak to her again. It was a heavy blow and left her bereft.

The fact was that the family never received them; they did not even reach Janek's little post office.

Miriam was lonely and despondent.

She went to England and visited her family in Clapham.

They were not welcoming, and inhabited cavernous empty rooms which seemed lonely to a girl who had spent her life in a tiny flat.

She contacted various Polish organisations in the UK. Most of them seemed to be cloak and dagger stuff. She suspected them to be fronts for spies and all manner of weird behaviour. They organised trips into the country to investigate what she speculated were nuclear installations. At least one of them was an agent.

*

To Miriam, the Poles who had left during the war were astonishing. Her cousins had no idea at all what life was like behind the iron Curtain. They imagined a different world where Poland was full of castles and balls. They lived in untold plenty and called it poverty. They wasted food and ate badly, never cooking or meeting over dinner, and sitting over tea.

It was too solitary for her. She worked in London as a nanny and saved up large sums.

She did not give up in her search for her roots and easily located Sergei.

He was so famous that she could trace his every performance.

She contacted him and he replied speedily and joyfully.

He too, missed his family. He was keen to hear what had happened to Sofia when he left. He invited her to the US to see him perform in a new ballet.

22.

London 1959

Elena maintained her interest in study. She chose Russian History for her university subject, hoping to unravel the truth about her family.

Katya observed her academic prowess with growing resentment although she did not say anything about her choice of subject.

Elena took her A-levels early and went to university at 16. She specialised in Soviet history.

When she graduated she chose an MA project studying Kazakhstan in the Second World War.

*

The subject was recondite and there was not too much information available in Western archives.

Even from superficial study, she quickly guessed that her mother had been an NKVD officer.

She returned from university for the summer vacation in some excitement.

'Mother, have you heard of the starvation of the Kazakhs?'

'Yes dear,' admitted her inscrutable parent. 'It happened a long time ago, before I was there.'

'What about the deportations? Were you there? And the relocation of the centre of government to Tashkent, you must have been right in the heart of it all.'

'I did not see any of it, my sweetest,' replied her mother in a honeyed voice. 'We lived in a quiet out-of-the-way village.'

Elena was used to her mother's impassive and cool ability to tell lies. She was fascinated by the subject. It seemed to answer so many questions which had troubled her.

She decided to approach her directly. After all, surely not all Russian officials were involved in war crimes. Her mother might easily have been a Partkom secretary. She would have a first-hand view of some of the most exciting and important events in Russian history.

'Were you a party official in charge of the deportations?' she asked her directly. 'You are always telling us about Andrei. Who was he? It sounds like he was quite high up in the Partkom.'

'He interrogated and tortured me,' stated her mother impassively. 'He did not believe in god. He was an atheist, and an intelligent man.'

Ah, so she was involved with the decision makers. Elena had listened to the tales of many tortured individuals and she was sure that her mother had not been one of them.

'Mama, you knew him awfully well. He cannot just have been a random interrogator. You knew exactly what he thought; you know everything about him.'

Her mother's expression did not change. Her stance became threatening.

Elena observed her, trying to work out if she had been an innocent bystander in the events which shook Russia and led to so many deaths. Her mother certainly looked cold, hard and intimidating.

This expression had always worked interrogation.

As usual, it had no effect on Elena. She had been reading a lot of detailed accounts of the war and wanted to find out exactly what had happened.

'Did you work with him?'

'How could I? He was an interrogator, trained in German methods.'

Elena looked at her mother. At some subconscious level she remembered her mother's cruel behaviour, her guilt and fear of discovery.

'It makes a wicked kind of sense then. Did you get involved in the torture of innocent people?'

She had read every scrap of available information to get at this essential question.

She needed to know.

Mother and daughter confronted each other. This was what Katya had always feared. She had prepared for it over many years.

She narrowed her eyes at her daughter in a way which had struck fear in those who were under the control of armed soldiers.

It could never work in a drawing room.

'Of course not! What are you suggesting?' she asked silkily.

504

Elena knew she was right. She had been studying this subject for a long time in an effort to get to the truth. It explained such a lot: her mother's reclusive behaviour in the face of Polish gatherings, her hatred of the Polish history societies, which tried to establish tenure over confiscated lands and the way certain Poles looked at her mother, as if she was a worm or some slimy thing. .

'Mama, you must have been an interrogator. Look at the evidence. How did you even survive? How did you get out? How could you have received treatment for typhoid when so many died of it untreated? Millions of Poles died of disease and you attended a top hospital. It does not make sense.'

Katya applied her most ghastly expression.

Grown men had wet themselves at this basilisk stare. It wasn't the same, those grown men had also been staring death by torture in the face. They had seen others die; they had observed the tortures of Andrei.

Elena knew that there were many trained spies among the refugees, sent to the allied countries with the specific intention of providing information for their Soviet handlers.

'Are you an operative, mama? Are you a sleeper?'

Katya addressed her daughter with frigid ferocity.

'How dare you! Snake! Betrayer of our family!'

Oh, she had prepared for this! She had a plan for just such an eventuality. She had not spent all those years in England worrying about discovery without formulation many escaped plans. She was activating one of them right now.

'Bitch! You have insulted me and obliterated my trust,' she screamed. 'You are a witch! Get out! I do not want to see you again.'

Jasia came into the room to see her mother weeping dry tears.

Katya grasped at her daughter with a piteous expression.

'Beloved child, come here. See what your treacherous sister has done! She has insulted me, darling, and all of us. She is jealous of your beauty and success and hates all that is good and true.'

Jasia fell on her sister.

She scratched her face and kicked her mercilessly in the shins.

'Mummy was a war hero!' She wept. 'You are damaging the family with your jealousy of me.'

Katya and Jasia dragged the unresisting Elena to the door of the house and threw her out.

'Never return here,' threatened Katya. 'I do not want to see you again. You have betrayed your family and I believe you to be insane. If you come here I will call the police and I will tell them that you have robbed me.'

'Can I pick up my stuff?' begged Elena.

This was nothing like she had expected. She had, for some reason expected her mother to weep and repent of her crimes. She had expected reconciliation and forgiveness.

'Get out. You have nothing here. I never want to see you again.'

Elena stumbled out of the house.

A few curtains twitched. The neighbours had heard the screaming and wanted to know what it was about.

Elena shouted into the street, knowing that she would be heard by everyone nearby.

'You whore! I never want to see you again!'

'You are throwing me out. At least let me get my stuff.'

Oh, it was the perfect street theatre.

Was Elena pregnant?

If so, then her mother had every right to throw her out

Jasia shouted through the window.

'Get out, you tart.'

The neighbours turned to each other, pregnant then.

The last words Elena heard from her parent were,

'I am innocent.'

*

Katya gloried in this success. She was free of nightmares for months.

In this time she decided to create herself a new life and new universe, where she could live with her younger daughter and Bartosz.

She bound her younger daughter with lies, ensuring that she had a prop for her old age and a witness to her innocence.

It was fortunate, because Bartosz was left a lot of money by a distance relative who trusted that he was Maria's long lost son.

He left Katya immediately and married a woman thirty years

younger than him with a young son.

Katya tried to get him declared insane and used every while she could to destroy him, without avail.

Luckily when Bartosz left her, she had her younger daughter to rely on.

*

Elena had a grant. She got a summer job and returned to college digs.

The whole thing had confirmed her suspicions. She was still utterly traumatised. She had been shamed in front of the street. And her family believed the allegations.

She tried to apologise, to no avail. Her mother had taken a stand. She would not hear of a rapprochement.

The scandal tore through the extended family, whose bods had in any case been loosened by the economic freedoms afforded to women. Nevertheless, the gossip bonds were still intact.

Some weeks later, one of her cousins asked her directly if she was involved in prostitution and racketeering. She asked in the hushed and shocked voice of one who already knew the answer. There was little point for Elena to ague.

It wasn't an easy thing to deny.

The truth was that the ancient creaking Polish society, which had been built on past social status, had no place for Elena. Her father refused to speak to her and put down the phone if she rang the house. The scandal had given him a starring role as a grieving father.

Her sister rang her every now and then to scream insults at her and then slam the phone down before she could reply.

Perhaps she was evil?

She had been brought up in an atmosphere of lies and half-truths. It was hard to understand the difference between right and wrong. Her absolute impartiality in moral conundrums was precisely what made her an excellent researcher, but it was not a recipe for everyday life.

She no idea of what was right and what was wrong.

She survived by moving her life onto the academic world, far removed from the real world. She became an expert in Russian affairs.

Part 7.

Harvest

The future is not solely decided by politicians and leaders.

They depend on the good will of their subjects.

Their choices are backed by the majority. They are mapped out by believers and driven forward by faith.

The only other way is to use extreme force. Even then, who will apply that force?

1.

Berlin 1964

Communism had won in Eastern Europe. It was winning in key locations all over the world. Over half of the world map was under its aegis.

The ideology held the moral high ground. It was a fine credo and should have worked.

It didn't.

The fact was that Russian society was just as hierarchical and despotic as the despised Western regimes.

There were key differences of course. Instead of being driven by the urge to gain capital, the leaders sought power and control over others. In some ways this made the state more clearly a hierarchy.

All the same the ideology was powerful. Despite central control of all ideas and motivations, there was a strong undercurrent i-of internationalism among the party idealists. This was because its underlying faith was based on world revolution. It meant that the ideal world would only occur when the entire world was communist. Any imperfections in Soviet society could be explained away by the fact that world revolution had not yet taken place.

The ideology was at its most obvious among the spies working with Western regions. These Soviet spies were in close contact with European and American Socialists. They saw themselves as high-minded individuals determined to proselytise the west.

They needed to prove that Communism was a superior way of life. However, in order for world revolution to take place they had to show the value of the Soviet way.

*

Dmitry had been to the finest spy school. He was fluent in English and wore western clothing, liked western music and blended in with any American youth.

Upon graduation he had a choice. He could stay in Moscow and brave the internecine struggles for power there, or go on assignment and get involved in real revolution. It was heady grass roots stuff.

Such an option was not open to all the school boys, on the lucky few with intelligence and aptitude.

He jumped at the chance.

*

Dmitry's his first assignment in West Berlin was a severe shock. The commodious apartments and luxury lifestyle of the ordinary people in that country made him heartily depressed.

He basked in luxury and walked around luxury stores without needing special credentials to buy goods. He met young Germans and they chatted freely about any subject without the slightest fear of reprisals. They seemed to have an excellent grasp of history and access to information and records which could only be dreamt of behind the iron curtain. It was a little confusing and although he enjoyed himself immensely, he needed a long period of debriefing after a two week stay. He had to be assured that the wealth of the West Berliners was ephemeral and based on massive exploitation of the colonies.

'What about the shops?' he asked, 'they are full of the most luxurious goods. These are only available to the highest party echelons over here. How can our great Soviet ever match such opulence?'

His handlers showed him pictures of alcoholics and mental hospital patients, slums and industrial wastelands in European countries. They displayed the plight of Mexican immigrants and Afro-Americans in USA.

'You are not allowed to see the poverty of the working classes,' he was informed. 'Those poor wretches would be happy to eat the scraps on our floors.'

Dmitry asked to be able to meet these poor workers. Surely he could help them to rise against their oppressors. Were they not ripe for revolution?

'We have operatives on this task,' he was told. 'We have trained you for infiltration to the plutocrats in USA, where you will politicise their youth.'

*

Dmitry was slowly acclimatised to his future role. It seemed that several of the operatives had been brainwashed by American culture in the first weeks and it was judged important to accustom them to the conditions in their target area before undertaking real work.

He was introduced to Western life in Mexico, where he met existing operatives holidaying in Acapulco. His hair grew long and he wore the comfortable jeans and tee shirts of American youth.

Acapulco was full of child prostitutes and the poverty of the local Indians was everything he had anticipated.

He realised that Berlin was a massive propaganda exercise and was shocked and amazed that this amount of money was available to evil western capitalists.

'They could use the money to feed these poor people here,' he told his new friends, who clucked non-committedly at his statements. His handler chuckled at his new protégée, still wet behind the ears!

*

Dmitry spent 3 weeks at a fine hotel, swimming and discussing life in the United States with a ravishing female operative. They never spoke Russian, and walked about the city in the evenings, stared at by fat old Canadians. They were both attractive, and someone even asked for their autograph, assuming his girlfriend, Ivanka, (aka Joanna), was a Hollywood starlet. She was involved in sex espionage and related him salacious stories of what some of the top American senators got up to in bed.

It was laughable.

He enjoyed his stay. He did not meet his controllers and communicated by phone, using complex codes.

He was to start by being given a few soft assignments. Ivanka was to be his handler in the first instance, and then he would be assigned more difficult jobs.

2.

London 1965

Elena was by now a successful academic. She held an excellent post in a redbrick university and wrote many papers and books on Russian history.

However, she felt rootless. She had been cut off from her family. Every effort to contact them was shunned and decried.

Katya was triumphant. She had successfully expelled her child, the personification of her guilt. She had been successful in expelling the shaman's curse!

No one would ever know what she had done. Elena was her guilt. She could never return. She was entirely free of responsibility for her past actions, on the surface of things at least.

*

Katya used disinformation to blacken her daughter's When Bartosz demurred she threatened to out his philandering among local children. She warned him not to speak to his daughter.

She bruited stories of all kinds:

Elena had attacked her younger sister; she had stolen money; she was a drug addict and a prostitute; she was insane and had spent long periods in mental hospital.

Elena heard some of these rumours and was devastated.

*

Katya had limited success in actively destroying her daughter's life. It might have worked even ten years earlier. Unfortunately, the old hierarchical order was cracking up.

Everything in London was changing. The city had suddenly become the centre of the fashion world and was full of hipsters.

Elena, who completed her studies at a London University, became caught up in this new world. She stepped into a new life, without need for family or connections. Everything was changing and almost anything was possible.

She registered for a PhD. She obtained a job lecturing part-time as well as working as a research assistant.

She moved into a tiny flat with two other lady academics. They ran a small alternative newspaper, which promoted sexual freedom.

'It's cool to be gay,' declared one of their headlines.

The paper was denounced as pornographic.

After a spectacular court case in which the government failed to prove pornography, the paper was taken over by more radical groups.

The whole circus of defending the action and the takeover of their minor publication was considered a great success.

Elena was free.

3.

Miami 1965

Izaak was now a very old man. His fledgling dynasty was fraught with conflict and divisions. He worried incessantly about leaving his empire to a worthy successor. He was not sure of either of his grandsons. One brother talked of war and revenge; the other just drank and disappeared for long stretches of time.

Izaak's eldest grandson, Jacob, took a gentle path. It was as if he had remembered his grandfather's original efforts to improve the world. There were dreadful arguments over his womanising, and drinking.

He was hardworking and dedicated, and worked hard as the figurehead of the business, although he lacked Izaak's skill and vision. He allowed his grandparent to walk all over him and rarely made significant business decisions.

Jacob adored the Latino way of life, and, from the age of 16 onwards, kept a succession of sultry mistresses. He drank heavily, and Izaak had to extricate him from multiple personal entanglements with gorgeous Latin women.

Their youngest, Malachi, took dual Israeli and American nationality. Rebecca still dreamed of revenge for the loss of their loved one and he took on the burden. He spent long stretches of time in Israel and worked on secret Israeli military missions. He came home talking tactics and war. He claimed that the Jews would shortly retaliate and wreak vengeance on those who had persecuted them. He was working on obtaining nuclear secrets for Israel, and went on long expeditions shooting alligators in the everglades. With his shaven head and aggressive stance, he represented the stalking rage of the remaining Jews.

Their middle child and their only granddaughter, Beth, wanted to save herself and her people. Nevertheless, she feared that launching nukes would end in the destruction of the United States and Soviet Russia. A feeling of fear, combined with helplessness, overshadowed her youth. She had lost her father. Fellow Jews recounted the dire fates of relatives and friends and lived in a climate of fear.

She was a pretty girl, with dark hair a bright blue eyes, an accomplished singer and a brilliant tennis player.

As a dominant male and owner of a Fortune 500 company, Izaak was out of touch with the focus of history, and did not observe how women's roles were changing. He had planned his granddaughter's future in detail. He was looking for a suitable candidate for her hand, hoping his son in law would help him run the organisation.

The plan was that she was to work in the office all summer and then go to France with Rebecca, where she would be introduced to European culture as well as several hopeful young men.

*

During one of the major rows with Jacob Izaak groaned out loud.

'Who is to run this empire of mine? Who understands this business? No one!'

'I'll do it,' offered the intelligent and sensitive Ruth, 'I can help you, grandpa.'

'The little darling,' he replied, tousling her black curls, 'it's not for girls. It's a man's work.'

Her task was to obey, and to be a perfect wife and mother.

Even so, he ensured that she was highly educated, which was not a good strategy to employ if trapping a woman into soulless matrimony.

It would fail him again.

All through Beth's childhood, the world had remained on the brink of total war. The general view was that Soviet invasion and a global war were imminent. Nuclear war was inevitable.

Her family held long discussions on different plans for reaching their shelter in the event of a 4 minute warning of nuclear strike. The shelter had complex outer and inner doors and ventilation systems to keep radiation out. They were protected by traps to prevent intruders reaching them in the event of a direct strike.

The family discussed different ways to exclude the servants, and occasionally practiced going down there to stay the night.

It was dark and dank, and Beth hated it - she could not imagine living there for 2 years.

The wealthy inhabitants of Miami lurched from crisis to crisis, fearing invasion by sea, nuclear holocaust, and an Anti-Semitic uprising.

The nuclear stand-off over Cuba[26] had been a matter of crucial importance and the assassination of Kennedy[27] drove most of the rich people to rush into their shelters for several weeks.

It was a particularly frightening situation as death was inevitable, either silent and instantaneous, or slow and painful, by radiation poisoning. It was a civilian war and civilians were helpless.

There was no way to prevent it and they had to exclude everyone in order to ensure their own survival.

*

Beth grew up in a cloistered rich enclave and attended small private schools where almost everyone shared the same background. Her grandparents could not protect her from everything. She watched television and knew that there was another world out there.

She wanted to explore it.

She fought hard to leave home in order to study at university. Perhaps her studies would find a way to create a peaceful and responsible clothing industry? Or maybe she could find a way to unify Christian and Judaic paths?

The very word Christian drove her grandmother to hysterics, so she soon gave up that idea.

She was interested in clothes design. Maybe she could become an American fashion designer?

Her grandmother was pleased with the idea.

'I'll help you my darling,' she said. 'I have always fancied something in that line.'

Her grandfather was accepting of the idea that Beth should study fashion.

Still, he was extremely hostile to the idea that his granddaughter should study far from home.

Beth had almost resolved to run away from home when at the

---

[26] After a botched invasion of Cuba in 1961 there was a crisis over missile sites in Cuba. USA and USSR were on the brink of launching deadly missiles, but USSSR blinked first.
[27] The President was assassinated, presumed to blame for the disasters over Cuba by various powerful groups.

last minute her grandmother stepped in.

She sensed the deep rebellion in her granddaughter.

'Izaak,' she reminded him, 'remember Sofia? She needs some time away from us, or she will rebel.'

Izaak was won over.

*

They agreed on Boston.

Rebecca insisted that she had to stay with a good Jewish sorority, and visit some distant cousins every Friday to make sure that the Sabbath was correctly observed.

Beth lived in comfort and luxury in a female sorority house and brooded on her future as the pawn of a massive enterprise.

As an intelligent and thoughtful person she was increasingly frustrated by university.

Education of the 1960's was geared to the elite males, and therefore to direction and decision-making. Each course, even financial management and accounting, which she was studying as part of her degree, discussed the moral issues and implications facing those with the power to make choices by male managers.

The university was designed to create leaders. As a woman, she was never going to lead.

Beth had no choice as to her future. Grandfather had written to her three months before graduation.

She was to go to Europe for a month with her grandmother to choose clothes. He sent her a credit card.

'Spend as much as you like' he wrote.

Then he had selected her for a secretarial post at his company.

'It's a responsible post,' he declared, secretary to the top manager in our US operations,' he wrote. 'You'll be in charge of the whole typing pool, and several under-secretaries. It's a great opportunity.'

Then of course she'd want to get married and settle down. She *might* meet someone at work. There were a few upcoming young men he'd like her to meet.

She could play all the tennis she liked. It was an open office. She could get involved in the design of new sportswear at some point if she was still interested.

Beth was not thrilled to hear of the future Izaak had planned for

517

her - not at all. She had been studying with the future captains of industry and she knew that she was at least as clever as the shining stars in her classes.

She listened to her future and fumed. She was determined to live her own life.

She did not comprehend a marriage state where she was to be a pure virginal chattel. At university she had met with goys for the first time and was bewildered by the freedom of life outside her home.

The girls were allowed out with boys. They could wear whatever they liked! They wore their hair long and straightened and stayed out late whenever they wanted.

The Jewish sorority girls attended many boozy parties and dressed in skimpy outfits which would have shocked Rebecca to her core. Beth went out to parties, got very drunk and lost her virginity to a footballer, Jamie. She was sufficiently pretty and charming to subsequently become friends with the team.

She adored and admired Jamie, her bovine jock, and secretly - well not so secretly - chose him as her own mate. She was going to open her own clothing company in New York and design party dresses and casual clothes for the modern woman.

Jamie disdained her stalking puppy-love and laughed about her to his mates. In fact he found her awfully attractive, even though she was Jewish. He returned to her room at nights for hot passionate sex.

Good times.

*

Jamie was heavily influenced by hippy culture, and he was also fully aware that his girlfriend was an heiress to a multimillion dollar empire.

The university was heaving with grass and dope smoking parties. People danced on the grass and lay in the sun. The football team grew their hair long and evaded the draft. They smoked pot in her room and traced the colours made by music on their posters of Jimi Hendrix and Marilyn Munroe.

He talked of freedom and doing something real with his life.

He was no poverty-stricken youth but heir to his father's extensive car sales business (nothing like the squillions of the

Brauns).

He wasn't that interested in her fortune. He had a much smaller one, yet he did not fancy what sounded like a stifling kind of life in Florida. He was revolted by his own future as head of this discreditable line of work. He wanted to drop out.

They listened to the Doors, Grateful Dead and Janis Joplin.

The students were stirring.

Many considered civil rights to be important. Beth was horrified to hear of the segregation in the Southern states and guiltily thought of the way Rebecca talked about their staff.

None of the rich kids supported the war in Vietnam. They did not want to be called up.

The university campus had frequent demonstrations where the rich elite carried banners

'Make love not war!'

4.

1966 Revolution

Things changed quite suddenly.

Soviet High Command was in turmoil. Apparently, there was a massive protest against the Vietnam War in San Francisco – exactly like the protests in Red Square in 1918.

The revolution was on at last!

The spy networks went wild and deep cover operatives such as Dmitry and Joanna were activated for immediate duty.

*

This was a top priority call. All available operatives were headed to San Francisco in order to recruit new spies among the deserters and rich drop-outs.

*

The intelligence analysts had reason to be jubilant.

The neighbourhood was already the centre of the rock-and-roll lifestyle. The place had been slowly filling up with deserters and drop outs throughout 1966. By 1967 College and high-school students were arriving in large numbers.

San Francisco's government leaders panicked, and alarmist articles in local papers spread to the national press.

This had opposite to the required effect and thousands of hippies joined the scene daily. The coolest, who were regarded as leaders by the stoned out masses, formed the Council of the Summer of Love.

'For the times they are a-changing'

Soviet intelligence read the signs.

Revolution had come to the USA at last!

All that work by the internationalists had finally paid off. The Soviets had need patience. Stalin, that bounder and cad, could not wait.

Observe, said the political analyst. Here was a group of the young, the rich and the famous, heading to a major city to refute the authority of the draft.

There were even community anarchists, providing free food, and free theatre. There were free concerts with electricity drawn from the lamp posts, and people were living in tents and vans, smoking pot and talking of the love revolution.

Surely this was the start of communism?

Operatives were needed in large number. It was time to direct these misguided capitalists into the political implications of equality.

The analysts in Moscow carefully read the slogans.

'Women's Rights, we are all equal and all free'

Was that not indicative of revolution?

Did the students not have identical slogans in 1918?

The draft dodgers squatting in the park burning imperialist draft cards were the equivalent of the May demonstrators of 1917.

Oh, if only Lenin were alive to see it!

This counter culture had exploded into a revolt against an oppressive regime.

*

The analysts were right.

The council of Love had just declared a human be-in which would change the world with transcendental consciousness.

'We are expanding human consciousness,' the hippy press reported.

It was no Bolshevik Soviet, although they had their own underground newspapers, music and art.

The run-down houses in the Haight-Asbury district had mostly been converted into communes and there were free concerts and happenings in the park.

'All human beings have equal rights; we are one kind, Human Kind'

Intelligence identified that this presaged revolution at last – provided it was engineered into proper channels.

The press reported 'A Gathering of the Tribes'.

Analysts agreed these were prototype revolutionary caucuses. The Berkeley radicals were increasingly militant about the American government's Vietnam War and several were in the pay of Russian operatives.

Even *they* reported that socialism had arrived in the USA.

The intellectuals were sending in details of a massive following among the people, mostly consisting of Haight-Ashbury hippies, who supported peaceful protest, love pageants and love-ins. The police were dumbfounded and the authorities powerless to act.

We can change the world
Rearrange the world
It's dying - if you believe in justice
It's dying - if you believe in freedom
Dying - let a man live his own life
Dying — rules and regulations
Who needs them?
Open up the door.[28] '

Soviet sleepers and active operatives converged on San Francisco. They were instructed to manage the revolution and ensure that it happened in the correct Leninist order.

---

[28] Chicago Song by Graham Nash

5.

The summer of Love

The Boston university Campus was about to break up for the summer.

The young men who were graduating that year had received draft papers.

They didn't want to die in the impending Nuclear Holocaust and did not believe in the communist threat, they watched the deaths of soldiers in Vietnam on TV, and rejected further struggle. They were terrified by the draft.

'Hell no, we won't go'

Rich hippies in colleges all over America were abrogating their capitalist responsibilities.

They no longer wanted to lead the world into war and exploitation. They discussed equality for black people and poor people.

There must be some kind of way outta here
Said the joker to the thief
There's too much confusion
I can't get no relief[29]

Jamie, Ruth's gorgeous boyfriend, hectored Miriam.
'Don't be a bread-head, dude.'
He had no intention of joining his father over the summer. He was heading for San Francisco.
'Your dad is so into bread. Like, he's seriously rich, man. You don't need to get more. What's it for anyway? Your dad's like an exploiter. So is mine. Let them do their thing. We have to, like, love everyone. Let's share the love. Peace, not war. The world is going to be destroyed if we don't make love.'

*

The entire generation rich privileged youth were giving away the baton of power. They were shocked by the destruction wrought by

---

[29] All Along the Watchtower song by Jimi Hendrix

the parents gave up the struggle.

'We need to be, man, we need to live and love. Life is for loving.'

Years later their management roles would be taken up by a new generation of up and coming bread-heads from the poorer middle classes, who had a hunger for success and happily took on the abandoned roles.

For the moment the rich kids saw a world of freedom and happiness opening up. Everything was going to be all right. They did not need to work; they did not need to fight.

Jamie and his friends were off to Frisco for the summer.

'Everyone jump upon the Peace Train
Come on now, Peace Train
Get your bags together,
Go bring your good friends, too
Cause it's getting nearer,
It soon will be with you [30]

Beth was entranced at the idea. She was tired of the nights in the nuclear shelter and the talk of revenge for war crimes. She was fed up with hearing that there were commie spies waiting to kill them and steal their money, or that Cuba was about to invade.

'How many years can a people exist
Before they're allowed to be free?' [31]

She elected to run away like had Sofia before her. She brought her faithful friend, Sarah, a dizzy young girl who was very immature.

Sarah's family had lived in America since the 1900's and she had a lot more freedom. She provided Beth with the courage to run away with grandpa's credit cards.

She had read the scaremongering articles about hippies in San Francisco. Those dropouts were entirely right! Suddenly her life made sense.

'Turn on. Tune in. Drop out.'

---

[30] Peace Train Song by Cat Stevens
[31] Blowing in the Wind Song by Bob Dylan

*

She and Jamie flew to San Francisco and moved into an expensive hotel where they slept and smoked dope during the day.

On their first night in that carnival atmosphere, they headed out to the streets and joined the milling throng, eating vegetarian food pressed on them by tripping anarchists.

'Eat this, man,' insisted the diggers, 'it is pure good food. Not meat, no death.'

> *Imagine no possessions*
> *I wonder if you can*
> *No need for greed or hunger*
> *A brotherhood of man* [32]

It was the first time the two girls had eaten non-kosher food - it was delicious, larded with acid and grass.

They got lost, gave up searching for Jamie and his mates, and spent the night lying on the ground in the park, looking at the stars in the sky and listening to a happening, with free rock playing in their ears like an epiphany. Everything made sense.

> *'Acting funny but I don't know why*
> *Excuse me while I kiss the sky* [33]

*

Back in Miami, Izaak and Rebecca waited for their daughter. The plane tickets for Paris had been purchased, and her bags were already packed.

Rebecca was to help her granddaughter to buy designer clothes in Paris. Once her wardrobe was sorted, they intended to join the rich socialites who hung around San Tropez.

They waited, and learnt, with sinking hearts, that their granddaughter had joined the losers and misfits congregating on Haight-Asbury.

She was ruining her own life and deserting the cause Izaak had dedicated his life to.

---

[32] Imagine song by John Lennon
[33] Purple Haze song by Jimi Hendrix

*

The elderly Izaak had not given up the reins of power and he was not going to let her go as he had done with Sofia.

This time he intended to use duress.

He hired a detective to bring her home, and the police were informed of her kidnap.

Unfortunately Izaak was not alone. The scale of the problem was unmanageable. A whole generation of plutocrats had dropped out.

An entire generation of dazzling, wealthy youth had abandoned war and declared a summer of peace.

If they were to die tomorrow then they would have a love-in today.

6.

San Francisco 1966

Lucia's son, Misha, knew his origins. He was blonder than his siblings. He was a worried child. His mother had told him that his father was Russian and that she had been married in Russia.

She spoke with a Russian sounding accent too!

He was disturbed from the first that he was connected to an evil empire.

Misha was blond, with blue eyes and high cheek bones. He had a markedly Eastern European look which it was possible to pass off as part native. Nevertheless his friends commented on his unusual appearance.

He felt isolated and apprehensive at the fact that some of the children called his mother a commie spy and often got into fights at school. He was keen to deny his Eastern roots and chose to follow in the footsteps of his step-father. As soon as he was twelve years old he became a fully-fledged member of Caleb's tribe.

*

Misha hung around with the despised Indians during the vacations. He was clever and a deep thinker. He felt the injustices of their life keenly and was annoyed and humiliated by the institutional racism which *they* faced.

He was aware that his life was easy, and *he* did not face the same discrimination. It was because his family were so wealthy.

Early on, he made the decision to take up the law. He determined to take up the cause of Indian rights. As it was, his adopted people rarely successfully took on the Canadian government. They were constantly ripped off by lawyers who promised them their rights, and never delivered.

The whole family were highly active.

Lucia was interested in building up the land and rode around each speck of their extensive estate on horseback. She planted trees and nurtured the herds of wild deer. She was keen to create a business which would give the land a purpose.

She formed a plan to smoke salmon and sell it to the restaurants many miles away, sending it to Ontario and Montreal by plane.

The family owned a small copper mine which made large profits. They were far more proud of the modest amount of money from the agricultural business which employed Indians.

Lucia was keen to diversify, selling salmon caviar and venison, which were popular in Montreal.

Caleb ran the business and the pair of them both agreed to plough every profit possible into the land and the children's education.

The inhabited a capacious log cabin in a huge compound overlooking the sea. The curios and Egyptian artefacts lived in crates in an outhouse. They had not been opened.

'The land is the key to our comfort,' his mother claimed. 'If we do not link to the land we have nothing.'

*

Misha came from a wealthy, protected background, and was thoroughly shocked to learn of the race riots in USA.

The African American cause added to his resentment of the Canadian government, which treated the Indian councils as ignorant savages. His parents were keen for him to have a profession, and were gratified when he determined to work as a lawyer, to improve quality of life for his people by taking on the unfair laws.

Like all the Canadian hippies, he was horrified by the concept of a nuclear war over issues so far from his home.

Canada was in no way connected to the Cold War. All the same, most of its population centres were likely to be decimated by radioactive fallout anyway. Nuclear apocalypse was a logical possibility based on warmongering sabre rattling on both sides. Montreal filled with warning towers providing a 4 minute warning of death. There were useless drills in case of attack.

'Eighteen today, dead tomorrow'

Death was not a problem to the young. It was survival in the fallout of nuclear war which they feared.

The youth of Canada were riveted by stories of the nuclear winter (in a country where winter was already lethal), and the post-apocalyptic future.

Survivors would have to live through a nuclear winter, watching the land expire by an invisible poison.

The chosen, who had access to shelters and would survive underground, kept their location secret. The rest, who would be left over ground, determined to attack the shelters, and an apocalyptic game was played out, between the rich owners, who hid their shelters and placed defences around them, with those who survived above ground determined to thrash healthy survivors.

*

Misha had completed his legal studies and already well into his internship when the hippy movement arrived in Montreal University.

Suddenly, Indian beads and fringes, long hair and feathers had become cool. He returned to university for his final year and found that his Indian heritage inspired awe. The students were fascinated by all things Indian and he was deferred to as a master of cool.

Misha joined protests about war, and discussed resistance to inequality. He listened to Bob Dylan and attended his concerts.

'How many roads must a man walk down
Before you call him a man?'[34]

He grew his hair and dressed in coloured shirts. He wore beads.

A year older than most hippies, he was immensely popular. His talk of Indian tribal practices and his exotic looks were a seductive mix.

Girls threw themselves at him and he had to avoid travelling in lifts alone with a woman, even his lecturers. He became cruelly dismissive and not a little vain.

*

It was not until he started work at a top law firm that he was fully swept up into the hippy movement. The law firm took on large numbers of cases from young American men, hiding in Canada and evading the draft. Lots of people had actually left the country to get out of fighting, hiding in Canada. They wanted to be pronounced insane or incompetent, and the law firm took up their cause.

---

[34] Blowing in the Wind song by Bob Dylan

These rich young men, evading the draft in various ways, often took Misha out for meals. They smoked grass and introduced him to psychedelic music.

The words of bands like the Grateful Dead and Jefferson Airplane were treated as religiously profound.

The hallucinogenic properties of grass combined with the music. It was as if the voice of the musicians in San Francisco had heard his confusion and distress and found a solution.

'We are all one people. Humanity is one.'

Misha related to the stoned-out sounds, having ingested multiple psychic compounds during Indian ceremonies. He absorbed the new improvised styles and learnt the electric guitar in order to create a Western Indian fusion sound.

Stop hey what's that sound?
Everybody look what's going round
What a field day for the heat
A thousand people in the Street[35]

He was keen to help his tribe.

The haunting words of the music drew him to San Francisco.

His legal career could wait.

He took a year's sabbatical in order to hear the Jefferson Airplane and Grateful Dead play at Golden Gate Park, where he heard that they had established regular happenings in conjunction with Ken Kesey.

*

He left for the happening, heading for the place where people's minds were opened to love and peace.

He hitched to San Francisco and stayed at girl's houses. The journey was an experience in itself as he was fed and bedded by others on the road across America.

An ever-growing troop of hippies intended to add their voices to the anti-war protestors.

Everyone was on a voyage of self-discovery using drugs and sex

---

[35] For what it's Worth song by Buffalo Springfield

to find the spirit within.

Are you going to San Francisco?
Be sure to wear some flowers in your hair.[36]

Misha and his tribal friends built a tepee at the Golden Gate Park using money from a crowd of wealthy women living on parental credit. It was properly constructed around a hearth and painted with slogans and flower designs in bright colours.

He was quickly joined by several authentic Indians from the Arizona area as well as many who claimed to have Indian blood. They drummed and chanted and danced and made love.

Misha, with long blond hair in plaits decked in eagle feathers, smoked a pipe of peace, convinced that they had changed the perception of Indian peoples forever. So many journalists took his picture that he considered charging.

He met Janis Joplin, Quicksilver Messenger Service, Mothers of Invention and Jefferson Airplane. He was part of the Council of Love.

*

Despite the apparent freedom of the 'Be In', there was a hierarchy of cool. There were leaders, mostly those who rolled fat joints, while the less cool listened for their deep pronouncements.

Young deserters and a few limbless veterans of the Vietnam War inhabited camplets around his giant tepee. They strummed guitars and sang old Bob Dylan ballads. Banners printed outside their sleeping area proclaimed:

Draft Beer, not boys
Make love, not war

Some of the intellectuals on summer vacation had pow-wows nearby. They slept in hotel rooms paid for out of the conference money. Their students guarded their space at night, so it didn't matter. The nuclear disarmament crowd often came by to discuss the iniquities of war and genocide.

It really was all happening here all around him.

---

[36] San Francisco song by Scott McKenzie

7.

San Francisco 1967

Miriam flew to America alone and arrived in San Francisco late at night, checking into a cheap and rather run-down hotel near the Golden Gate Park. She had high hopes of meeting with Sergei.

There were very pretty painted terraced houses all around which seemed to have colourfully dressed students sitting on every step and leaning out of every window.

The Park was milling with hippies living in vans. The city was buzzing. There was a love-in at the Golden Gate Park[37].

She had arrived during the Summer of Love.

*

San Francisco was heaving. The area could not accommodate this rapid influx of people.

At her hotel, she was shocked to hear noisy music filling the corridors. Hippies were packed 12 to a room. Young people were sitting in the corridors.

As she arrived at her door bearing a suitcase, they welcomed her to the city.

'Where are you going?'

She took out a card and read the address.

'The Fillmore. Can I get a cab?'

Several voices pipe up.

'Hi man! Are you splitting for the Fillmore? I'll bum along because it's happening there.'

She stepped over a sleeping couple. They were embracing closely and the girl had her legs wrapped around the young man.

Miriam turned away. It was obscene.

Someone grabbed her by the hand.

'Hang Loose. Are you crashing here?' she nodded.

'Peace-out,' he professed. 'Feel the love.'

He followed her into her room.

---

37   Park in Sand Francisco where approximately 100,000 young people converged in 1967 for the Summer of Love

'This is a nice pad, cleaner than the park.'

Young people were drawn from all over USA by the hope of a new Utopia away from the very real perils of a Nuclear War.

The smell of dope was intoxicating

'Man, we are so crowded in here!'

'No.'

'Aw man? Can some of the guys here sleep in your pad? It would be far out. Have a toke and mellow out after your journey.'

All Poles smoked.

Miriam took a puff and mellowed out.

She had never taken drugs before, and returned to her room with a group of new friends.

They played guitar, sang and talked nonsense which she could not understand. She fell into a heavy jet-lagged sleep, lying in the arms of a complete unknown.

*

She awoke to a heap of people lying everywhere. She did not quite remember how several of them came to be in her bed.

Other folk were sat on the floor of her room. Apparently they had not slept. They were immensely affable and told her that they were on their way to the Human Be in.

Some girl had opened her suitcase and was trying on her clothes.

'Weird threads,' she stated, trying on different dresses and picking through her underwear.

Maryssa was indignant. She dragged back her clothes and possessions and re-packed her suitcase.

The young woman, who was wearing a long skirt which was probably from a theatrical costumier, had creased her fashionable cotton dress made in the latest American style by a Palestinian tailor.

'Heavy,' complained the girl, as Miriam dragged her clothes away, tutting violently.

'Uptight,' agreed the others. 'I dig what you're saying. Sister needs to tune in.'

Miriam felt like crying, she had planned to wear it for her first meeting with Sergei. She *was* very uptight, and stomped downstairs and asked management to remove some squatters who had broken into her hotel room at night.

She handed them her suitcase for safekeeping.

'I will return this evening and I expect to have a clean, fresh room, empty of squatters!' she yelled. She had a blinding headache as she headed off to meet Sergei.

'Yeah man, sure thing,' they agreed, 'chill, dude.'

As soon as she had gone, the desk attendant threw her suitcase onto the pile of rucksacks in the back room.

'That is one uptight lady,' he told no one in particular and lit up tiny joint packed with grass.

*

Miriam was lost. She had a map to the theatre - the area was highly confusing, like nowhere she had seen before.

There were actors playing on the streets and women baring their breasts with flowers in their hair. People kept offering her what she now realised were drugs.

She recalled all the propaganda she had read in school as a child.

It was true!

And her cousins in Clapham had laughed at her too!

They were deluded.

She was very shocked at this openly corrupt behaviour and refused many friendly offers.

Sometimes tall, good-looking young men in bare feet stopped her when she declined.

They asked her why not.

'It's cool man, you should try it. It will open your mind. Peace and love. You need to be, like, aware of the peace flowing from the music. Look at the sky man, it is so divine. The peace is coming from all of us.'

The sky was dark and foreboding - warlike.

An African American man with huge hair came up to her and tried to hug her.

She flinched away.

'Lady, you gotta just be. This is a human be-in.'

'Don't be uncool dude,' he stared at the sky, which boded rain later in the evening, 'we are going to disarm nuclear warheads and turn them into flowers.'

She had the greatest difficulty in extricating herself.

*

She was held up again and again and as a last resort accepted a flower for her hair from a wasted young woman, who was walking through the streets saying, 'flowers for all the heavy people out there.' She had picked some of the flowers from the park and insisted on plaiting some in Maryssa's hair.

She held Maryssa's hand in a gentle clasp.

'Where are you from?' she asked.

'Israel,' she replied.

'That is so cool!'

She shouted to her friends. .

'Hey man,' she gathered up some of the wasted young students walking through the streets. 'This chick's from Israel.'

'Welcome,' they hugged her and said 'shalom.'

They passed her joints and she smoked a little, trying to fit in and feeling increasingly frustrated.

A crowd was gathering.

She snuck away as people started hugging and kissing each other.

She had an appointment and she would be late.

She hurried along the road, consulting her nonsensical tourist street map at each corner.

A guitarist strummed by some railings. He had a small audience who were passing around joints.

'How does it feel?
To be without a home
To be a complete unknown
Like a rolling stone[38]*

As she paused to stare, someone slipped her a blue paper with a butterfly on it.

He folded her fingers around it and encouraged her, 'take it man, turn on, tune in and drop out.'

She was suspicious, tasted it to see if it were a sweet, sucked on it, then spat it into an overflowing bin.

She guessed it to be a paper sweet, or even a sweet paper.

---

[38] Like a Rolling Stone song by Bob Dylan

These people were foolish!

Nearing the Park, she could hear the thump of loud rock music.

*

For someone who had been brought up in the grey conformity of true freedom it seemed like chaotic and frenzied inferno.

Her headache remained, only now she saw wonderful colours emanating from outlandish foreign music.

She suddenly worked it out, she was being brainwashed!

She could see the blood flowing through her hands.

She heard her heart beating gently and streams of energy poured out of her fingers.

Everything had an aura of colours, colours she could touch, push, and hear.

She hung on to her sanity and reached the theatre at last, not daring to ask the bizarrely dressed individuals who roamed the streets in case they pulled her into another brainwashing ritual. She was afraid that she had been given some kind of deadly poison, and the minute she reached her destination at the stage door, she burst into tears.

'I have come to see Sergei Bogdanovich,' she blurted, 'please let me in, there is madness outside.'

*

The door security smiled at her.

The tall burly black man was smoking a joint and chatting to a hippy, who was dressed as a jester.

Down the road a gaggle of young people were leaning against a fire hydrant and giggling. She was certain that the KGB was waiting for her.

The men noticed the flower in her hair.

'Sure dude,' he agreed. 'Sergei's here. Go right on in. Stay cool. It's all good.'

She ran in.

'Sergei!' she squealed in the quiet and air conditioned cool of backstage.

'Sergei, help me. This place is hell! There is revolution!'

She discerned him in the relative quiet and ark of the backstage and fell into his arms.

536

Sergei had changed.

He was taller, a lot stronger and leaner with long blond hair.

He was wearing the hippy garb of everyone outside and was barefoot. He was talking to a group of stage hands about future performances.

He looked round; he was tanned and his hair was dyed almost white blond.

He had amazing white teeth, which Maryssa realised were new.

That very moment, in her stoned out state, she fell for him. She was his forever.

*

Sergei immediately recognised his dumpy little cousin Maryssa and hugged her to him.

Her heart was beating and she fluttered about in a panic.

'They are indoctrinating me. It is a revolution of mad people,' she wept.

Sergei laughed gently.

She was the same old Maryssa.

He felt a wave of warmth for the old days. She was pretty and fresh without the night time pallid skin of the theatre, much larger than any ballerina. Her eyes were wild, and inebriated.

Was she tripping?

'What are you on my sweet cousin?' he stroked her dark brown hair. The flower was askew and she appeared demented.

'Nothing,' she panicked. 'I have not been drugged. I have been careful. This is an evil empire. Come let us go to my hotel where we can be safe.'

Then she remembered.

'No, it is full of mad people. They slept in my bed with me. It is gangsterism.'

He took her gently by the hand.

'Come with me,' he suggested. 'I will take you to meet our Indian friend. He will tell you about freedom. He talks to us all. I go to see him every day.'

Maryssa was thoroughly stoned.

She veered from love to despair at every step. She had

preposterous thoughts in multiple colours.

Sergei was far taller than her, stronger and better-looking. He had a halo around him and was floating on air like a seraph.

As she visualised it, a pair of rainbow wings materialised behind him.

'Maybe we could marry or at least have sex,' she blurted out, rubbing her eyes to shut out a vision of him naked.

Her out-of-control mind veered off in all directions.

She shattered her own dream.

'I am too ugly,' she moaned. 'You would never marry a goblin.'

She was outside her body and saw a goblin walking beside the seraph. The pavement beneath her was transparent and she could see the stars underneath it.

The universe was under her feet.

*'She says she loves you
And you know that can't be bad[39]'*

Sergei was used to female admiration and generally took up any offers of sex. However, he was a little alarmed to see the tell-tale signs of obsessive fan-like devotion in her eyes.

'She is totally stoned,' he decided, 'and having a bad trip. I hope this doesn't get too heavy.'

She kept stroking his arm in a suggestive way, smiling at him sexily and then pulling away and muttering to herself like someone possessed.

'She can't come back to my place, and I can't take her to any straight place like a Pizza parlour,' he concluded.

He turned in the direction of the park were the love and peace would cam her.

'You're tripping' he explained. 'Where did you get the acid? You shouldn't just take it. Not now, anyway. Not until you know your way around.'

He had become a shining creature, and the sky was full of popping sounds interspersed with transcendental music.

Ecstatic tears poured down her face.

---

[39] She Loves you song by Beatles

'I am he as you are he as you are me
See how they run like pigs from a gun and we are all together
I'm crying[40]

She pointed to a multi-coloured house in the district.

Hippies were sitting on the steps and chanting.

She ran towards them, took them by the hand and kissed each of them on both cheeks; they were charmed, and kissed her back.

She ran to him and kissed him too, on the lips and provocatively. Sergei guessed she was well into her trip.

'I am taking you to meet Misha,' he asserted.

She nodded beatifically.

He added, 'isn't it a coincidence? I asked him if he knew Russian and he claimed his mother was a Polish countess. He is a good man and pretty cool. He will ensure you are ok.'

He took her unresisting hand, keeping his distance.

'Sergei. I love you. We are not cousins,' she blurted out.

She was too stoned to know what she had intended to say and words fluttered from her inner heart.

'We are not even related. I am adopted. I am a Jew. My parents died. We could get married if we wanted.'

In her hallucinating mind, she was wearing an enticing white wedding dress. They were floating in the sky.

She searched for her mother, but her mother had gone.

She burst into howls of grief.

Longing for her family surrounded her in a sheet of many colours. She felt totally alone and shivered uncontrollably.

'I lived in Israel on a kibbutz. It was lonely.'

She forgot everything in her intense desire for a loving mother. She saw a woman saying goodbye with her eyes. Eva was holding her tight.

'Mama,' she screamed, 'where are you?'

She switched madly in her mind. Now she was a young girl holding baby Sergei.

He was rocking and whining, grieving for his mother. She held

---

[40] I am a Walrus song by Beatles

him again, only he had grown colossal.

'I missed you so much.'

She pressed her body to his.

She could smell the heat and sweat of his body- it was full of multiple shapes and sounds. It was masculine and divine.

> *'For somewhere in my mind there is a painting box*
> *I have every colour there it's true'*[41]

Sergei watched her wave her hands at invisible images on another dimension.

She was weeping, snivelling wetly and wiping her smeared lipstick on his white tee-shirt.

It was embarrassing.

She needed to be taken to somewhere safe.

*

He tried to settle her down with different groups in the park. It did not work. She was blabbering in Polish and Hebrew.

People were waving her away.

'She's on a bummer,' they expostulated, 'don't bring us down dude.'

'Let's hide under the table?' she whispered in a loud stage Polish. 'Can we go there now? Come with me. Please. Come with me. We will escape the KGB and get married.'

A couple sitting on the stairs of a brightly painted house stared at her balefully.

She pointed at them.

'They are watching us. People are following me. It is the darkness. We must run away.'

'You are having a bad trip,' he reassured her.

He needed to get her off the streets. If he was not careful they would drag her off and lock her in a room where she could howl until she came down.

'I will take you to the tent of peace. You will soon chill out.'

> *Just lately when I look inside my painting box*
> *I seem to pick the colours of you*

---

[41] Painting Box song by Incredible String Band

8.

Height Ashbury 1967

Dmitry headed for the central area.

It was to be the focus of Russian infiltration, since it had been judged by intelligence to be the equivalent of the Square in Petrograd.

He sat at the edge of several dope smoking circles and worked his way in until he faced Misha.

It was the first time Dmitry had smoked pot, and he mellowed out immediately.

He sat quietly and listened.

His status in the cool hierarchy was low and he did not feel able to speak.

*

Everything seemed to take on a new meaning and he became deliciously confused. He wanted to be like Misha!

He chilled into the dream and listened to the music and chanting, when a young boy held his hand and asked him if he was gay.

'Gay?'

The boy's hand slid to Dmitri's thigh. He drew closer.

'Yes gay,' he whispered.

Dmitri came to.

He was deadly afraid, and suspected a plot.

He looked around the group with fear and loathing. They were CIA, every one of them. They were only pretending to be nice. They were going to corrupt him, drag him into a compromising situation and then interrogate him, drag him off! There had to be a photographer nearby, with one of those spy cameras, hidden in a necklace or something.

He got up as subtly as possible (in order not to arouse any secret police) stumbled out of the tent. He crashed into people and tripped over in his haste to reach his safe house.

It was a tiny almost derelict clapperboard building surrounded by hippy looking operatives who kept undesirables out. People kept knocking on the door and asking if they could crash there. It was driving the militarily trained operative crazy.

Dmitri did not get an answer to his frantic knocking until he remembered the code.

The door opened.

'I have been drugged,' he reported, 'they are on to me.'

They pulled him in.

*

He was debriefed.

Doctors checked him as he reported every word he had heard. Mostly it was a load of freaky buzz words.

'Far out.'

'Peace.'

'Love.'

*

The operatives calmed him down. They said that there was a large gay scene in San Francisco and it was likely that the boy really was gay.

Perhaps he thought that Dmitri was gay too?

Dmitry was disgusted.

'I'm not gay,' he insisted. 'Neither was he. They surrounded me, they were trying to compromise me.'

He did not feel that the boy was homosexual as they described, although he could not feel positive about anything in that maelstrom. He was feeling utterly paranoid. He could hear the blood drumming in his ears and felt his heart beating in his chest. He could hear the blood flowing through his ears and even suspected the doctor of being a double agent.

'You are feeling a slight paranoia. It is the drugs, CIA drugs. They can have this effect.'

He tried to understand what was happening. The doctor explained that the CIA was giving away drugs to prevent the revolution.

It made sense from afar.

However, although the Head Office in Russia was certain that this was the Revolution, no one at ground zero felt too sure what was going on outside. They were on the phone the whole time asking for advice.

542

'How can we deal with the music?' they asked. 'It is controlling the masses. Have we any counter music? We sang the Internationale, some people joined in. they said it was far out.'

There was jabbering on the other line.

'Yes, we did that.'

Jabber.

'Yes, we have a red flag. Of course, we do. People like them. They embroider them. They wear them.'

Frantic jabber.

'Yes, we wave it around. Sometimes they wave it around, mostly to music.'

Jabber, jabber.

'Yes, we did that too. But they did not rise up.'

Another operative was gabbling on the phone in Russian.

'I explained about Lenin. They agreed. They said he was a man of peace with his heart in the right place.'

Jabber jabber.

'I don't know why. What do I do now? I need more instructions.'

The revolution, which from a distance had sounded entirely correct, seemed to be out of control.

And bizarrely, it was also somehow lacking in violence.

The doctors checked Dmitri's bloods.

'You have been given a CIA narcotic.'

He was ordered to take speed to counteract the effects of the soporific and meditative drug.

'The hashish here is laced with opium,' the spy handlers explained. 'It is a ploy by the Americans to quieten the populace and prevent them rebelling. They mix in the crowds and give the narcotics away. Avoid it at all costs.'

*

He was sent upstairs to get new orders. His normal handler was nowhere to be seen. The house appeared to be in turmoil.

Everyone was barking conflicting orders. Several were on the phones to places abroad and in America and relaying what was going on.

'Yes, they are wearing Che Guevara tee shirts. Yes, they love Castro. What now?'

Confusion reigned. The Russian handlers were giving out speed to those going into the fray in order to combat the anti-revolutionary drugs being given out by the American military.

They re-dressed Dmitri in velvet loons and a tie-died tee shirt. He was warned that American operatives were everywhere.

They could be recognised because they were wearing feathers, velvet and flowers in their hair.

The safe house was stocked with arms, ready for a violent overthrow of the regime.

He was directed to give them out at the first opportunity; send revolutionaries to the safe house. He was given tiny cards to give out.

'Only do not give out cards to the crazy ones. We have the greatest difficulties with them. They keep coming here and asking for things. The women are the worst.'

Another operative, a large man in military fatigues, updated him on strategy.

'The situation is fluid.'

'Head Office is sure this is it.'

'It may yet turn to proper revolution.'

'We have to be ready. The mayor is being followed, and several officials have our snipers on them. It is only a matter of time.'

For the moment, people were not taking the free weaponry which operatives handed to them. Disastrously, no one on the streets wanted guns or violence.

In fact, operatives carrying them had been overwhelmed, disarmed, drugged and 'sexualised'.

The situation was tense. Those who masterminded the revolution were not sure if the Americans were on to them and got increasingly het up.

The house was stocked with combat drugs, but Vietnam veterans were already well-provided with purple hearts.

Nevertheless, operatives were making sure that extensive supplies were widely available to counteract the soporific effects of opium for the masses. It was a battle to win the upper hand. It seemed obvious to the operatives that the hashish and acid were being distributed by CIA agents. The people taking the battle drugs simply danced themselves into a frenzy and collapsed.

*

Dmitry was ordered out on the streets again. He was given his own stash of combat drugs to counteract the effects of hashish and instructed to make it freely available.

He duly took speed and returned to the outermost circle in the tepee.

He sat quietly, then became twitchy and talked about sweets and food endlessly.

'You're speeding man. Chill. Take some of this.'

Dmitry tried to refuse; then an appealing young creature placed some on her tongue and kissed him.

He could not deny her.

'That's right sister,' someone said, 'he needs acid to calm him down.'

The effect was instantaneous and overpowering.

He fell back on the ground tripping.

The tepee had grown to gigantic proportions and the sky was filled with the hiss and crackle of the stars singing.

He giggled as a star came to earth and stroked him on the tummy.

It was Gina, a young heiress to a shopping mall owner who had disappeared a couple of weeks ago. Her parents had called the police to no avail. .

'Hello.'

Dmitri lay on the ground tripping wildly.

'Wanna come home with me?'

Gina was relishing the sexual freedom of the pill. She took him home for sex.

*

Afterwards, they lay in a room full of Indian prints which swirled around his head madly. A poster of Jimi Hendrix played music at him and talked in Russian.

He blabbered back in Russian, hallucinating wildly.

She formed the opinion that he was German. He was equally clear she was East German. He spoke to her in German. She replied in English.

They understood each other during the trip. Sex was brilliant and better than anything he had ever experienced.

When he came down in her room, he had no idea how he got there.

'Brilliant trip. Good acid,' she told him. 'We went to Venus together. I think we were speaking in tongues.'

Dmitry remembered it clearly.

What was going on?

He no longer cared.

He waited for her to roll a joint.

'I will check in later,' he said. 'They need me art headquarters. They can wait.'

'Yeah man, check in later. Let's check in later. Let's check in together.'

Everything in the peace camp made sense. Peace would save the world.

'I have to meet some friends,' he explained, and paused.

'We're starting the Revolution.'

Everyone agreed. The revolution? Of course, it was happening - it was all around.

'Check in later',' she said.

She kissed him fervently.

'The love revolution. It's happening.'

'Yeah, later. It can wait. It's happening.'

A man walking by agreed. He hugged them both.

'Yeah, the happening is all around us.'

He stayed there for another day eating fried onions and boiled lentils which tasted like manna.

*

The next day he returned to make his rendezvous with revolution at the peace camp.

There he found that the operatives on speed were resolutely blocked out of the circle as young students tried to bring them down and chill them out.

A tight group of military-looking young men, they remained at the edge of peace, talking endlessly and without meaning and generally annoying people with warlike talk.

Beautiful girls, who liked the look of their bodies, sat by them, stroking their toned physiques suggestively.

'Make love, not war,' they said.

'Chill.'

'This *is* revolution man, chill... Peace out.'

Some of the young spies had already fallen away from their purpose, just like him.

*

He strolled past the operatives. He could see how uptight they were. He almost approached them to explain.

'This *is* the revolution! Lenin had it all wrong.'

He could see the effects of the love and peace vibes radiating around the world and ending war.

It was mesmerising.

*

He had mellowed out, and was able to get into the inner circle at last.

The crowds of seated tripping and smoking individuals parted like the Red Sea in the face of his intense cool.

He met the Indian at last.

Misha handed him peyote.

Everyone knew that the Indian was the son of a Russian princess. He had been adopted by an Indian tribe and was the essence of hip.

Russian! Dmitry thought he understood the revolution at last.

It had emanated from the Soviets and found its maturity here at the centre of the energy flows all over the planet.

This *was* the Revolution. It was a revolution of peace; it was a revolution of the mind, of vibes.

Far out! He looked at Misha, so very Eastern European looking.

*

He *had* to be an agent – deep cover.

'Operative?' asked Dmitry, 'I am here to bring *peace* to the world. It is time for *change*.'

These were code words, chosen for their innocuous sound by the handlers in the safe house. (Intelligence clearly had no idea of what was going on in real life.)

'Sure man,' acceded Misha, not understanding a word of the world of espionage. 'We are all operatives for peace around here.'

'Sshh,' interrupted Dmitry.

He imagined Misha as Lenin, a peace Lenin.

No one else could know this.

'Why not? Stay cool. You are right. This is our new operative world. Like, we're all changing history here now.'

A murmur went out to the circles of acolytes.

'We are operatives for peace!' was the new word.

Dmitry fell back and joined those sitting in the tent as the gentler, freakier, buzz of peyote kicked in. He was silenced. It was happening everywhere.

People were changing in front of his eyes. It was revolution at last.

'You won't fool children of the revolution!
No way yeah [42]

---

[42] Children of the Revolution Song by Tyrannosaurus Rex

9.

Love-in 1967

The hippy movement hit the universities early on. By 1967 most young English academics had already travelled to India during the long summer vacations and dabbled in drugs.

That year, they turned to San Francisco for the summer vacation. The happening was going to be the cool place to be.

Elena and her three flatmates had resolved on the peace route to human salvation. The ladies, who had been to top Public schools, were at the leading edge of change and had been heavily influenced by the hippy movement from the first.

The three of them saved up money in order to spend all holidays away. They travelled as part of a large gang from a Women's Lib collective in Ladbroke Grove. They were wearing the latest outfits from Portobello Road and were sure that they would fit in and find friends easily.

*

They were accepted the moment they arrived. It was a thrilling experience. So many people who thought and felt alike! The vibe was overwhelming. Pure joy, threaded here and there with bad trips and comedowns.

Elena's friends soon joined a heavy women's lib group. They had taken over several houses and spent hours smoking dope and talking sexual politics.

Elena was not so involved in aggressive feminism. She didn't really believe in much.

It was weird how English people weren't interested in anything outside England. She tried time and time again to explain that people were dying in dreadful conflicts in Latin America as a result of the US and Russia backing opposite sides in internal country conflicts. The cold War was being fought out among third world countries which were ill equipped to manage modern life, let alone modern warfare. The two sides were arming people and fighting had escalated with the advent of deadly weaponry.

English people simply ignored the tragedy of arming simple

peasants and discussed grand ideals as if anything other than English lives did not matter.

She gave up listening to the high-minded discussions which did not take into account the realities of poverty and child abuse. She wandered off to explore the different groups that had settled the park.

*

Elena was tall, and attractive. She was dressed in the latest cool available in Ladbroke Grove. As a result it was easy to join in. People were kind and welcoming.

She spent a few days with the peaceniks burning their draft papers and on the run. It was interesting to see how differently the young men saw the conflict when they were directly involved. She tried to talk about the injustices elsewhere in the world.

Eventually she gave up. These were the privileged. They were not interested in the underdog.

She moved on to relative quiet of the folksy vegetarians who dressed in beautiful mediaeval clothing and rich velvets.

She fitted in perfectly. It was a beautiful world, calm, with fine music and beautiful clothes the tents were particularly fine, draped in velvet with joss stick burning outside. Women were cooking rabbits they had caught somewhere, or was it rats? Anyway, they smelt fine.

The women offered her food and listened to a folk singer playing Bob Dylan tunes. Magical.

The men were discussing returning to a simpler way of life.

'We could take up smithing.'

'And run sheep.'

'Spin wool and make our own clothes.'

'Do you have any idea how scratchy wool is?' said Elena. 'And smithing is hard and dangerous work. I've been to India and seen how it's done. The men who did it looked like they had been poisoned by coal smoke.'

The men looked at her shocked.

'Dude, we'd do ethical smithing!'

The women drew her away. Women did not speak in this world. They cooked and did the chores. They did not speak before their men.

She moved away.

*

She witched between other groups over the next few days, none of which fitted her view of the new world. It was strange to see the camp splitting into gentle factions based on the new world which the hippies were building here. This was peace. This was the love revolutions. They were building a better world, without war or conflict.

She sat with the soldiers who had burnt their draft cards. They were defiant, and acted like any deserters. They were living life on the edge. They took loads of drugs and danced naked around the camp fires.

*

On the second day she sat with young girls who sat silent and admiring around half naked college boys with stunning physiques. The men spouted platitudes while the girls looked on adoringly.

No one quite fitted her mood.

*

On the third night she slept under the stars, smoked pot and listened to music.

She joined the gay groups, who talked earnestly of prejudice and fighting straights.

She moved among the heroin addicts who insisted it was uncool not to try at least one shot of the potent and dangerous drug.

There was no one she could talk to and she began to feel lonely and isolated

*

On the fourth day, she had almost decided to return to the women's libbers. She had originally deemed them unduly political, but they seemed like an oasis of sanity now.

Then she saw the huge tepee lighting up the sky...

*

Elena came crashing into the tent. She was uptight and definitely not cool. She simply stepped over the cool protocols.

Fascinating, yes, or she would have been downed by the bad vibe from the acolytes waiting outside the tent.

551

Only her graceful step and cool Moroccan clothing (from London) allowed her into the inner sanctum.

Misha was disturbed.

He frowned. He was trying to engineer an atmosphere of perfect peace in an imitation of his Native rituals. She had broken his carefully crafted concentration.

And she was female. Females were supposed to sit at in the outer ring taking the last toke of any joints being handed around. And quiet, they were meant to stay quiet and submissive.

He tried to overpower her, although overwhelmed by an instant bond of attraction. She was foreign looking and her black hair and blue eyes were a startling mix. She had strength, grace and exuded intelligence.

His posse of women united to expel the potential threat.

'Hey man,' pronounced his first woman. 'There is no space.'

Misha silenced her.

He beckoned her over as she sought for a place to sit down and found none. He laid on the magnetic charm which seduced most women.

'Yeah,' he fixed Elena with his most ravishing stare. 'Let's step outside.'

He got up, to the consternation of his harem.

The tepee had been an oasis of calm. Now, warm visions collided with reality. The atmosphere grew cold and chilly for a moment. Their centre of attention was leaving.

Misha turned to his Navaho mates.

'I am leaving for a walk. We are going to meet the others. Back soon.'

His friends knew that it was a woman. They took the pipes and charcoal and moved it before them, preparing more grass and peyote.

Everyone mellowed out. The buzz returned. Apart from a slight, silent disturbance among Misha's women, the change of leadership had gone almost unnoticed in the drift of stoned trippiness.

*

As they walked through the crowds they assessed each other carefully.

Elena was nearly six feet tall, but she felt dwarfed, for the first time in ages. The man was gorgeous, dressed in the beads and clothes of an Indian brave.

'What do you want?' he looked deep into her eyes. He looked her over. She was magnificent - a fitting mate.

'Peace,' she replied.

She looked so exotic with her black hair and blue eyes.

'Are you Indian?' he asked.

'Yes,' she lied. 'I am part Indian.'

She wanted him to like her and was already basking in his interest and fascination. Her normally cool head had been subsumed as her body screamed for sex.

'Let me show you our camp,' he offered.

They were floating off on a river of sensual dream.

Misha's first woman rushed out to join them. She was not going to allow anyone else in to the posse.

'Yes, *we* can show you everything,' she gabbled, holding tightly on to Misha's hand. 'We can show her together.'

They fell to earth.

She was not going to leave, that was clear. The trio walked around and introduced Elena to the different camps. Misha was the essence of tall dignity, Elena his haughty equivalent.

Finally, he walked Elena to his personal sleeping area and closed the flap, locking his woman out.

She sat down patiently, listening for every sound, bathed in a haze of awareness. Misha opened the flap.

'Hey man,' he stated.

'Hey,' replied his woman.

'Hey.'

She inched away, backing on all fours, like a wolf guarding a carcase.

'See ya, then.'

She stood up and walked off, then squatted down, keeping guard from a distance.

She rolled joints as a bribe, and carefully stashed them in her Indian mirrored bag.

Misha closed the flap and started to strip.

His body was golden fine.

Elena jumped in alarm; her emotions crashed around like a foundered ship on the reefs. He turned, half-dressed, and tugged at her dress.

Tears filled her eyes.

'What's the matter?' he asked.

She broke down.

'I am no slut looking for sex,' she wept. 'I did not come for this.'

'Free love' he replied.

When that did not work he sat back and re-assessed her.

'What do you want then?'

'I came to learn.'

'About?'

She looked at him, 'Love,' she swallowed, 'and peace. There is none... anywhere. We must stop war.'

He regrouped, and continued to undress her, slowly.

'This is love,' he reassured her, 'and Peace.'

'No,' she replied. 'It is not equality.' He reminded of father. 'And you are a predator.'

He was startled by the accusation.

He lived on a permanent high of sex and drugs, buoyed up by the adulation of the crowds passing through his scene. He was jolted by the truth and opened to her for the first time. He hadn't actually noticed her before. He didn't really notice the women he coupled with. Yet this one seemed real and close to his soul. It was perplexing.

'I am not just another body. And I am not a thing, or an animal. I don't want to give up my soul like your women, hanging around for a kind word.'

So she had been influenced by the Women's libbers. She believed in equality. She taught hundreds of students a year. She wanted to be considered as a person.

He saw her with his peyote fuelled vision.

She was divine; her energy was gold and silver, although she was hidden and flawed. It made her fluoresce with shades of light and dark. It was weird and deep.

He observed as she started to get dressed with shaking hands.

Despite her desire, she refused to accept subservience. She had been working for liberation. It was not to be found here, at the heart of the revolution. This was just a travesty. He *was* a predator.

Their meeting had become a clash of ideals and a melding of spirits at the same time.

She knew that she *would* fall for him, and probably had already. But if she gave up herself, then life would feel worse than ever. He stared at her jerky movements as she fumbled with the ties of the tent opening.

A final jibe.

'Peace here is for men, it seems,' she remonstrated with suppressed indignation. 'I came to the wrong revolution.'

He grabbed her by the hand.

'No.'

She was uptight, and still he deemed her worth pursuing. He dropped his marauding instincts; she had reached him.

'I genuinely like you.'

'Truly?' she trembled like a child.

She was one of the many vulnerable, abused children who had headed for Haight.

He revised his previous opinion of her and knew that he needed her as much as any woman.

'Yeah, absolutely.' His eyes had lost their cold fire. 'You know that is, like, what we both want.'

It was a jumping, irrational moment. The drugs heightened every nerve, making it coloured and multileveled, star-driven. Their palms were eyes, wide open. They exchanged souls.

When the truth is found to be lies
And all the truth within you dies
Don't you want somebody to love
Don't you need somebody to love[43]

*

They stayed in the tent talking and smoking, and having sex, to the bafflement of the guardian women, who increased in numbers

---

[43] White Rabbit song by Jefferson Airplane

555

as the time lengthened.

The posse set up camp outside, cooking vegetarian delicacies, smoking dope and playing music outside. There was a little 'happening' and followers found excuses to collect, leave stuff, sit inside for long periods, and bring messages from friends and news.

They were driven away by relentless Misha.

Elena did not even notice.

*

She heard the story of his life, as woman should. He came first in all things. When she had listened to his life story, he asked her where she came from.

Her blood ran cold. She could not tell him.

No way.

'England,' she extemporised freely. 'My mother had me out of wedlock. The American soldier was Indian. I never knew him.'

She was digging herself in deep, depending on the fact that her mother had thrown her out and it would never be confirmed. She wanted him to admire her and to think she was cool.

She hated herself for feeling so strongly.

'She was Russian.'

Her story caught his interest and she mixed in parts of her real life.

Bartosz became her step-father.

She could not stop lying. Her hormones were talking.

Misha was hooked.

'Stay with us,' he asked. 'This is a community. I can get you a space.'

Love was an alien concept to Elena. She already distrusted the man lying naked beside her. His ardent interest alarmed her.

She fended him off with her academic career.

'I'm here for a month, and then my visa runs out. I am going back to my college.'

He had a far cooler aim - to free the whole world of oppressed peoples by becoming a lawyer.

It scared her. She felt swamped by his personality and crushed by his aims. Her instinct was to deny romance, and live without people.

She had to protect her soul from happiness.

To love and lose would break through her delicately constructed sanity. Every safety protocol howled against involvement.

Wouldn't you love somebody to love?
You better find somebody to love.

It was hopeless.

Despite the deepest misgivings, Elena joined his tribe, determined to leave when term started.

For two short months, she noticed only him, evading vicious status battles among his harem, who needn't have feared. She was bound to personal freedom.

Whenever he was too intense or possessive, she walked out.

Tears are running down your breast
And your friends, baby, they treat you like a guest

When she joined other groups and found other men for casual sex, he hunted her out and drew her back to the fold.

They would fight, then order would be restored.

They argued about the relationship in the quiet of the night, like husband and wife.

She automatically took the seat of importance, shocked the tribe by speaking (women did not speak), holding opinions (still less hold opinions) and interrupting him if she disagreed with something (no one else, male or female, did that).

And when the new academic term started she left, just as suddenly as she arrived, leaving a great hunk of her dreams there in the park.

Misha returned to college shortly after and their summer of love fizzled to a close.

When the garden flowers are dead
And your mind is so full of Red
Don't you want somebody to love?

10.

Peace

Sergei and Miriam approached the tepee on the same day as Misha returned with a subdued Elena in tow.

As a famous person, he sat in the inner circle, cradling his cousin and toking on any joints passing by. He normally evaded possessive women hungry for marriage and tried not to feel trapped by Miriam.

He was not particularly beguiled by the plump pretty girl. He was used to finely-toned and fit ballerinas and, furthermore, she was a most un-peaceful person.

She was fine so long as he held her. Any time he let her out of his arms, she jumped about like a crazed rabbit. He told himself that this was because she craved for her family in Wroclaw and commiserated. He didn't let her go. The truth was that for some reason he did not want to release her. In fact, she had struck a nerve about home. He recollected the tiny, ugly flat, and felt surprisingly heartbroken.

'Home,' he inhaled it and breathed it out.

He savoured the sounds of the Polish she spoke. She reeked of home.

He was relieved that they were not related. He tested the prospect of sex.

It was – ok.

She was droning on about the importance of faith and the holocaust and the injustices of life. He did not listen. Every now and then, she would start talking in Polish.

'I love you.' She kissed his hands, speaking Polish. 'Remember Sofia's bigos?[44] I miss garlic sausage. It's pork! Sofia's food!'

The smell of cooking onions wafted in from outside. It felt so nostalgic.

'Sofia was always kind to me. She cried loads when you had gone, 'It is because am so happy for him. He will be famous.' She was right.'

---

44 A traditional Eastern European dish made with pork and sauerkraut

Sergei remembered the sad old lady that was his mother. He saw her and heard her voice.

'I hope you are a good boy.' The vision said. 'I love you very much and I am glad you are doing well.' The vision was bound in chains.

Tears filled his eyes.

He tried to hide them, so as not to bring everyone down.

'I need to help her,' he decided. He wished he could write. She had given him everything.

Sergei yearned to discover everything that had happened when he left. He tried to extract every fragment of information about his home.

Instead of feeding his cravings, Miriam was off on a tangent.

'If you marry me,' she whispered, 'we could both become Jewish. My new, proper, family would welcome you with open arms.'

He pined for details of what had been happening after he left. Maybe if they had sex she would shut up a bit and tell him what he wanted.

'Let's go back to my place.'

They got up and left.

*

As they traipsed through the humming crowds, Sergei settled that it was nice to be with his flipped out ex-cousin. She stirred up his memories. And although he did not know it, her behaviour was reminiscent of Sofia's dragging him on the trek through the wastelands in search of home.

He felt deeply comfortable and very protective.

She walked alongside him happily, and then abruptly she was off again, grabbing his hand like an anchor, floating and bobbing among the crowds.

She spun into happenings, dancing in a stoned-out way which was acutely disconcerting to the trained and graceful dancer.

She listened to the Mamas and Papas in floods of tears, and flapped around ecstatically to the Moody Blues.

Nights in white Satin, Never reaching the end

She decked herself in flowers and tried to undress.

'We are free!' she yelled into the crowd.

Several young men moved closer, willing her to get naked, and join other young women writhing on the ground, making love where they were.

Sergei grabbed hold of her.

What was she on?

She smelt of the earth; of roadsides, train trucks and fields. It was a trampy sort of smell - unique to those who sleep outside.

'Clothes are a kind of skin. They protect you.'

She was jittery, frail - so suggestible! He grabbed her hand tightly.

'What's that?' she asked timidly.

She had reverted to alarm in a flash.

She looked up at the sky.

*

The dogs of war circled above, brightly lit, radiant, with the destruction of cities gripped carefully in their jaws.

She wasn't the only one looking.

People were pointing at the sky excitedly.

That is how it was - tripping. Everyone on acid saw the same things, and the vision skittered among the intoxicated like a medieval sighting of cherubim trumpeting the apocalypse.

She nuzzled him and he could smell her skin, full of hormones and ready to breed. Mesmerising.

'Ok,' she scrutinised the multitude around her for KGB.

She dragged him off to a quieter piece of ground and clumsily attempted to remove his trousers – no seductress.

'We can live in one skin.' she insisted. 'Let us join together.'

She rubbed herself against him suggestively, clumsily feeling him out carefully with her hands.

'For goodness sake!' She had no shame!

Her antics amused him.

She gave up just as suddenly and flitted off to run around the

---

45 Night in White Satin song by Moody Blues

park.

He sniggered; even though he was unwilling to abandon her. It was funny.

Sometimes she stared at pieces of rubbish, rolled up silver paper and drink cans for minutes at a time. She kept pointing up at the sky at the four horsemen, or the dogs of war or whatever it was.

He let her wander around.

'From uptight Polish bitch to demented hippy in a day,' he thought with a wide grin.

'Sergei, look at this,' she muttered, her bottom in the air like a dog sniffing a bone. 'It's amazingly cool.'

She was picking up the language, rolling around, getting filthy, and acquiring the grey sheen of the true hippy.

Indisputably, he decided, she was merging into the happening. She leapt into Yiddish, Hebrew, German, French, English and Polish by turns. She constantly talked of sex, then refused to go to his place.

Why don't we just do it in the road?

Twice they met groups of kibbutzniks who were ready to take her in.

They chattered wildly in Hebrew and she sat with them quietly.

He teased her out of their clutches carefully. She was *his*. He just couldn't let her go.

*

They worked their way through the crowds, back to the inner sanctum of the tepee.

He walked in slowly, resplendent as a supernatural being.

Ballet training had made it possible for him to exude emotion and presence. His arrival, quiet and slow, caused a stir among the inmates of the tepee as he and Miriam settled into the crowded space.

He stepped among the seated on his toes, disturbing no one, as his girl tripped over and trod on anyone in her way and left a trail of destruction.

The tent was full of people as usual.

In the miraculous paths of karma, the group within were now intimately interconnected. Perhaps the sun and the moon had willed then to meet here, or it was a plot by the earth itself.

They had, apparently, all met by chance.

> *'You can tear a plane in the falling rain*
> *But you won't fool the children of the revolution*

Some of the smaller fish were vibed out and left.'

Misha barely moved, acknowledging his friend's arrival with the merest twitch of an eyebrow.

'Peace.'

Sergei held Miriam in his arms and she sat quietly, listening to the good vibrations of the universe. A distant chant from the Veterans and deserters camp permeated the tent making it somehow more peaceful.

> *'One, two, three, four! We don't want your fucking war!'*[46]

Beth was already in the tent.

She had met one of her lecturers.

He was agreeably surprised to see the young multi-millionairess and had taken his decorative young student to the peace tent, intending to seduce her. He considered her worthy of him: exquisite, rich, clean and innocent, and potentially marriageable.

Unfortunately for him, drugs made Beth intensely aware.

She could see him with her tripped out eyes. His face took on a Lugosi[47] colouring of black and white. His silvering hair, normally so distinguished, looked scary as hell. As he spoke, he licked his lips like a vampire.

'Let's do it,' he said.

He approached to kiss her and she resisted his lengthening fangs.

'Wanna leave?'

She point blank refused to leave with the predator.

He did not mind, he could pick up another cute young girl instead.

*

---

[46]   One of the cries of the Anti-war protesters who were pro nuclear disarmament

[47]   Bela Lugosi played Dracula in the classic 1930's movie

As he departed, his place was taken by the seriously tripped-out Dmitry.

'Wow man,' He landed on the moon. 'It's mind-blowing here.'

She took his hand, noticing the tiniest trace of an accent as the drugs loosened his control over his second tongue.

'Don't I know you?' she broke into Yiddish-accented Russian.

'Don't talk,' he adjured, remembering the far out trip of yesterday, 'we are on the moon now. We have landed. We have come to start the revolution.'

She noticed his moles and his clear brown skin.

He stared at the slant-eyed, distinctively Ukrainian girl.

'Are you one...' he started.

She touched his lips.

'We are one,' she agreed.

They stared into each other's eyes, breathed each other in and locked together in eternity.

Under the influence of peyote, it seemed as if they had known each other for hundreds of years. Their separate worlds were left far behind and splintered into tiny pieces.

'This is true peace,' said Beth. 'All people are one.'

*

The prospect of war retreating.

'This is peace,' affirmed Misha. 'The war must end.'

Outside the tent and all over the sky the dogs of war gathered and howled at them.

'Enemies!' they growled. 'You are enemies. Kill those who killed us. Vengeance! Where are your dead and unmourned? Avenge them or die!'

The symbols on the tent shone back at the sky.

'We shall not kill;' they chilled back, 'this war must end.'

*

A whole generation, children of rulers and upper classes lay under the sky and refused to fight.

Purple haze, all in my brain
Lately things they don't seem the same
Actin' funny, but I don't know why

563

'This must end,' they decided. 'We do not want apocalypse.'
The moment passed.

*

At the centre, Misha sat with Elena.

She looked like the young Sofia, though her expression was very different. She had more strength of mind, undermined by neurosis. She trembled lightly at the feel of happiness and love, like a greyhound about to run a race.

She was tranquil for once. She had encountered affection, and revelled in the presence of her mate. She basked in his tiny movements towards her - he gently stroked her back and brushed away the long hair which was falling into her face.

*

The four horsemen, who had been riding the firmament in search of annihilation, settled above the tent of peace.

The full pack was present.

A decision would be made this day.

Dmitry was seated in the inner circle, enraptured by Beth.

He had fed her speed and they had also ingested peyote. They were gabbling madly, entranced by each other as they chattered in several languages.

'Where are you headed?' he asked her.

'Anywhere,' she replied, 'I have to get away from here or they will find me.'

Beth turned to him and whispered,

'I am looking for America. I want to be free.'

'Me too! I have to escape or they will get me.'

They looked into each other's eyes. Yes, they would liberate each other.

'I will join you?'

She gazed at him dotingly, and he feverishly tried to think of where they could hide.

'Surfing in Malibu?'

'Cool,' she replied. 'Let's go on the road.'

---

[48] Purple Haze song by Jimi Hendrix

*

It was the highest romance. Bluebirds flew round them and they saw a golden sky, like a Disney movie. It was a trip, breaking loose. They cuddled in the warmth of their romance, and whispered ever more improbable plans for a future together.

Wolves in electric sheep-clothing, circled closer, growling in death metal tones. Rock music clashed around the tent.

Above the three couples, the words painted on the tent glowed in the evening sun.

Love and peace'
Make love not war'

They were going on a trip.

On a rocket to the fourth dimension,
Total self-awareness is the intention'[49]

Sang from the circles of hippy camps as evening dark settled in. Around this particular camp, the balsam of peace wafted across towards the tainted red stained sunset.

My eyes are open to all colours bright'

'This is where we are meant to be. This is our time,' whispered Miriam, as she snuggled into Sergei's arms.

The protagonists of future conflict had met.

The hawks hovered above, gleefully anticipating doom. Black smudged clouds scudded across the orange sunset glow, breathing animosity in zephyr whispers.

'Let us destroy communism forever!' screeched the riders on the storm.

The sky burnt blood red in the setting sun.

'Look what that evil empire has done. We can wipe them out in one fell blow!' bayed their wolf pack.

'Make love not war,' was the reply.

Nearby, deserters and veterans burnt the American flag - token of state. No one was going to fight.

---

[49] Lyrics from Hair Musical by Sasha Allen

Lit sparks from campfires rose to join the Milky Way.

'Peace brothers.'

Night fell blue and smoky. Instead of watching a post-apocalyptic dawn rise, the warriors smoked a peace pipe. The threat of nuclear war receded.

'You won't fool the children of the Revolution
No you won't fool the children of the Revolution
No no no'

Postscript

Beth and Dmitri were on the run for a year before they were caught.

Dmitri was shipped back to Russia for re-education. Like several other operatives he was due for a spell of incarceration. His father saved him.

Dmitri never really believed in the Soviet regime after this. He was convinced that they had mismanaged a true revolution. He had been there. It was real. It was happening. And they had blown it.

He left Russia during Glasnost[50].

He currently lives with his boyfriend in North London.

He is still an agent.

*

Beth was captured by bounty hunters and taken home. She was skinny, highly stoned, and babbling about world unity and peace. She was also six months pregnant. She was sent to America's top psychiatrists. She broke down several times and married several times too.

None of her husbands matched up to Dmitri.

She is a famous clothes designer. She uses only ethical materials and employs local, well-paid seamstresses. Her daughter was brought up by nannies and is currently a top model.

*

Elena too, found that she was pregnant on her return to England. She decided to keep the baby.

She did not trust Misha. She did not tell him of the pregnancy and she did not answer his calls. She became a professor and never married, although she had several long-term lovers.

Her son is a writer.

*

Misha became a top lawyer defending drug cases and deserters. He had many girlfriends and finally settled with beautiful young woman from his step-father's tribe.

He is a highly respected activist for Native Canadian and

---

[50] Part of the reconstruction of the Soviet Union and end of Cold War Period in 1986

American right. He has several children.

Elena follows his twitter feed.

*

Miriam and Sergei married. They have an open relationship.

Sergei spends a lot of time on tour and has had several roles in Hollywood movies.

One of his children is a composer and another is a budding film starlet.

*

Sofia died peacefully at a great age.

A collection of newspaper cuttings about Sergei were found under her bed.

Sergei attended her funeral and paid for her headstone.

It says

Sofia Bogdanovich

*

Eva became a catholic activist. She was heavily involved in the Solidarity movement to liberate Poland from Russian dominance.

Janek spent a lot of time on his vegetable patch.

Their children are involved in local politics in Wroclaw municipality.

*

Katya lost everything in the divorce. She moved into a council flat and became extremely paranoid. She was sure that the descendents of her victims were going to kill her. When she had a stroke, her beloved daughter Jasia gave her an overdose of sleeping pills.

Jasia lives in he purchased council flat, which is in the heart of central London and worth millions.

Jasia has a head of extremely short shaved hair and is known to all the local Mayfair drinking haunts. She likes to tell people about her illustrious father Bartosz, a Russian prince.

Her son is a local artist.

*

Dania became one of the Taliban leaders who fought and defeated Russia in the 1970's. His children are still fighting American contractors in Afghanistan.

*

Anatoly and his children became oil magnates after the fall of Russia. They are still in government, all of them. They are widely suspected of being involved in gangsterism. They are.

*

Izaak died at the head of a respected sports clothing company. Jacob succeeded him. The company is involved in sports clothing and is run on more ethical lines than before. Jacob tries hard to change things, but is usually overborne by shareholders.

*

Rebecca's art collection went to the Guggenheim at her death.

Epilogue.

The years of peace after the fall of the Berlin wall provided few outlets for budding interrogators, torturers and dictators. They have not disappeared. They just no longer rise to power.

The disappearance of imminent nuclear threat has changed the nature of war.
The battle for freedom has become a battle for women, children and minorities.

The technological revolution has changed the dialectic. Society's top earners must have excellent communication and team skill s.
The economic empowerment of those of a gentler, feminine persuasion has weakened the paternal hierarchy.
Women can escape abuse. Children can get access to resources. The divorce rate has risen.

The paternalist and male-centric technologies and hierarchies have not given up the right to oppress.
They utilise religion and politics to prevent change.

They will fight.
They can do nothing without widespread support.
The psychopaths are there, waiting for conflicts spill over into open warfare.

As always with the spin of history, it is up to us.

Tereska Karran

Ba Hons, PGCE, MA, PgDip, PgDip, MSc, PhD

Tereska is an author and artist.
She has two websites
https://ArtbyTereskaKarran.com
https://StreetPublishing.co.uk.
She has written several books:

Science Fiction:

The Terraform Trilogy (which consists of four books)
Analysis of a Natural Terraform (A.N.T.)
Defenders
Origins
Redemption

Chronicles of the Dark Ages
The Toltechs
Shaders

Historical Fiction:

The Spoils of War
Shadow of the Zenana

Academic Non-Fiction:

An Architecture for Artificial Intelligence
Monetary Value in Virtual Transactions

Art and Poetry:

The Book of Hours

Facebook
Art by Tereska Karran
Writing by Tereska Karran

Twitter:
@ArtbyTereskaKarran
@WritingbyTereskaKarran